Shadowrealm

Tales of the Supernatural

L. A. Hudson

Published by Shadowrealmebooks.com

Copyright © 2009 by L. A. Hudson
Second Edition, February 2009

Library of Congress Control Number: 2008909228

ISBN 978-0615250236

Published in the United States of America

Dedication

To my family without whose love and support this book would not have been possible. With special thanks to Bonnie & George Hudson, my parents, my sister Deborah Denise Gormley and my good friend Marv.

.

Table of Contents

The Ritual

Her body had been dead for some time, her face ashen with eyes already sinking under closed lids as she lay in darkness upon a cold stone altar.

Gabriel slowly lowered the stiff limb, whose hand he held gently back down to its side and directed his senses upward to sweep out over the expanse of land surrounding the property. The image of familiar landscape came into his mind's eye, with recently fallen snow blanketing everything in a cottony shroud. Even higher, his mind could see out over the forest that lined the west side of the property separating Woodhills House from Woodhills Lodge.

On the path in the distance they approached from the lodge, hand in hand. It always began that way, with the woman so sad her pain seemed etched across her face. Her companion's expression was loving and compassionate. He was obviously being attentive to her feelings and needs.

It seemed the cycle was to begin again and so soon. The duration's between them were becoming sickeningly short and he began to wonder when it would end?

Gale had been tossing and turning in bed for the better part of two hours, envious of Kevin's ability to drop like a rock at any time it seemed.

She kept waking up and that was odd. She never had a problem sleeping before meeting him, but why should Kevin bother her? He was the most wonderfully perfect man she'd ever met.

Gale never believed the old saying of love at first sight. It always seemed truer that love was the result of time, understanding, patience and most of all trust. That was the oddest thing about their relationship. The whole situation was so totally alien to her emotional laws.

As she watched Kevin quietly sleeping beside her Gale realized she didn't even know him. Yet there was something there, some magnetism that overwhelmingly compelled her to be near him.

During the days when they took quiet winter strolls hand in hand she never had reason to question the relationship, he was just that wonderful. It was only during the nights like that one when Gale's own doubts would assail her, denying her sleep and forcing her to question her sanity in their relationship. Her vacation had ended days earlier, the Friday of her arrival at Woodhills House and she hadn't even bothered calling her job.

With a sick feeling Gale wondered if her termination notice hadn't already been sent by now. She was giving up everything, for a complete stranger.

Again Gale asked herself what the hell she was still doing there. She'd met Kevin only a week earlier, a chance accident. She had been sitting on a bench in front of the fire. Behind her, the lobby of the ski lodge had been alive with activity. She sat alone watching the crackling embers of the flames and warming her chilled face and hands. The argument she had with Stan, her boyfriend, was still playing in her ears. Gale realized it really was a stupid, trivial fight and her fault. To think, she suggested ending their trip early. She behaved childishly, believing he'd been paying far too much attention and spending way too much time with a certain snow bunny ski instructor. When she suggested the trip she planned to be the ski bunny, but soon grew tired of watching the two of them having all the fun. She didn't like being the third wheel, but it was his vacation too and he was just a beginner, after all.

"Stan, I'm going into town to do some sightseeing, maybe some window shopping." She told him hoping he'd get a clue and decide to join her.

"Fine, fine," he said distractedly, giving her a royal brush off.

They'd been standing at the top of the hill and Stan's eyes never strayed as he watched *her*, a smile on his lips as she gracefully glided down the hillside. Gale remembered how hot her face had been. She stomped off silently to leave him standing there, certain he never really heard her.

When she returned, dusk had settled over the slopes behind her and she found them sitting cozily in a shadowed corner of the lodge. Gale had taken only a few steps towards them when something forced her to halt. There was something to his gestures, a certain familiarity she knew without thinking. Instantly she recognized the maneuvers, right down to his facial expression. She knew his next action would be to reach out and caress the woman's face before kissing her. It was the same series of gestures he always used with her.

She'd never felt so heartbroken. She turned away. Tears rolled freely down her face as she made her way through the lobby and corridors of the lodge on her way back to her room.

'To hell with him,' Gale decided as she tried to forget the fact that she loved him and found herself in front of the elevator crying. The world had turned cold, gray and untrusting. The elevator doors slid silently open and again her eyes locked upon that now familiar face and smile. She'd ran into Kevin, yet again.

The first time was the morning of their arrival. Stan had tripped over Kevin's baggage at the front desk and everyone around them started laughing except for Kevin. He had been so gallant, apologizing profusely and Stan gave him a quick brush off in his embarrassment. Gale was aware even then how intently Kevin stared at her.

Next was in the restaurant of the lodge the following morning. Stan was in bed sleeping late so she'd been eating alone. Kevin came over and asked to sit with her. 'Well we are in a crowded restaurant.' Gale told herself.

"Of course," she'd said finally.

"My name is Kevin Verney." He extended his hand to shake hers.

"Gale Rieson."

"I hope your husband won't mind." He said giving her a knowing glance and Gale immediately noticed how his eyes seemed to sparkle.

"Oh we're not married, just good friends." She said looking

away embarrassed. The last part had been a lie. Their relationship held so much more and she didn't know why she'd made light of that fact. Stan was profoundly more than just a friend and though they'd never set a date it was always understood that they would spend their lives together. Marriage was just something she kept putting off more than Stan had. She'd been afraid of changing things, of loosing her independence.

"Actually," Gale said bridging the momentary silence, "it's strange I'm the one down here so early. Stan is usually the early riser and I'm the late sleeper, but ever since arriving here things have seemed surreal."

"It's the fresh mountain air." Kevin had said flashing a brilliant smile. "It affects people differently."

It started that way. She ran into him twice more during the week that she vacationed at Woodhills Lodge. Kevin's family bought the hotel years earlier where he lived just outside town.

After that breakfast, doors always seemed to open just before she placed her hand upon the knob and she would raise her eyes to find him standing on the other side. Why did it seem he was always there smiling, so warm and friendly?

Kevin's smile vanished quickly upon seeing her expression and he asked her what was wrong.

She felt like a fool stepping inside the elevator. The doors had closed behind her as silently as they'd opened sealing the two of them within its small and intimate confines, and she knew she would tell him all, a total stranger.

Still crying, Gale revealed how her heart had been torn apart completely by the man she loved. Kevin reached past her to press a button on the elevator panel and it gently halted. He then opened his arms to encircle her within them. It was as if they'd known each other all their lives.

They stood there talking for some time, in the quiet of their own private world. She couldn't remember what it was she found comforting, but when she exited Gale found the sky was again blue and the world still full of rich beautiful colors.

That was five days ago. She left the lodge with Kevin without saying so much as a word to Stan. Kevin had taken her to his home.

It was rustic looking and beautiful in its masculine charm, sitting amidst a densely wooded forest of pine trees that surrounded and isolated it from the lodge and its tourists. She'd never seen such a massive wooden structure. It had to be well over a hundred years old.

As Gale mounted its steps, she was swept by a wave of apprehension and stopped frozen upon the door's threshold. Kevin took her hand, giving her a warm reassuring smile and she allowed him to easily guide her within.

It was filled with oddities from times past. The place seemed to be a throwback to the days when the area must have been teaming with bison and antelope because their mounted heads gazed down from every angle with eyes long past seeing. Perhaps that was what gave her that eerie feeling about the place. As for Kevin, she knew her feelings were just those of the wonders of a relationship fresh and new. Like all relationships it would soon settle into the ordinary and mundane but so far each day had been a new and wondrous experience.

Gale smiled as she turned on her side to again gaze at Kevin's sleeping form. She allowed her fingers to brush through his hair and observed his peaceful countenance. She allowed her eyes to sweep along his strong brow and watched the slight flutter of his long lashes before settling her focus upon the curve of his beautiful lips. She always thought Stan handsome, but now he paled against the Adonis sleeping nearly silently at her side. For a moment Gale wondered how such a catch could still be unattached. She fought against thoughts that sprang to mind of secret girlfriends he might have in strange towns too numerous to mention, maybe wives.

'No,' she told herself, her luck in love had to get better.

Occasionally garbled words escaped his perfectly formed lips. Meaningless gibberish he'd repeat over and over. Gale smiled thinking to herself that she'd have to remember to tell him of that in the morning.

The clock on the nightstand read 2:00 in the morning and Gale wondered what was wrong with her. She couldn't remember ever having such an extreme bout of insomnia. Restlessly she allowed her eyes to roam about his darkened bedroom. Like the house it was expansive and filled with oversized period furniture, cast in silhouette. Moonlight from three large windows on the west wall filled the room giving it a gray misty quality. In the farthest corner, deep wells of shadow seemed to concentrate into eerie forms. Gale looked away, forcing her attention elsewhere when a minor movement there caught her attention. It was near to the floor and Gale lifted her head off the pillow, straining to see it. It was grayish in color whatever it was. She could just barely make it out from the surrounding darkness.

'Great,' Gale thought, 'rats.' She hated rats, now any chance she had of sleep that night was irreparably lost.

It remained stationary for some time, and her eyes never left it as she prayed it wouldn't approach any closer to the bed. She thought briefly about waking Kevin but decided that would be childish. Several minutes later in the quiet stillness of the room it still hadn't moved. Beginning to think it some trick of light Gale began to relax. 'Imagine being afraid of something as foolish as mice.' She thought to herself, her muscles beginning to unwind.

Gale continued watching it as her eyelids began to droop. With a heavy sigh they'd nearly closed before Gale again saw movement from the corner and once again was on alert.

Twin grayish forms advanced towards her side of the bed, hopping in a strange alternating fashion, first one than another. There were two of them. Their size grew with their approach and Gale's eyes widened as they got close enough for her to clearly see. They were shoes. The closer they got the brighter they became and their luminous quality began to spread upward. Before her eyes ankles appeared, then pant legs. Gale began to scream.

In an instant the room was filled with light from the lamp on the nightstand near to Kevin.

"Gale, what's wrong?"

His voice was strong and protective as she felt his arms

encircling her shoulders. She cried against him for several seconds unable to answer.

As he gently stroked Gale's hair, he continued to whisper in her ear that it had only been a bad dream.

Gale pulled away from him to look into his eyes. "I was awake and it was there," she pointed to the area of the floor where she'd seen it. "It was there!" She struggled to say more but couldn't.

"It's all right." Kevin said soothingly as he pushed back her hair from her face and tried to calm her, tenderly asking her to start over and tell him everything. After several minutes she was breathing deeply, her cries having nearly subsided. She told him what had happened, and Kevin considered for a moment.

"I've lived here for many years," he said softly, "and you must believe me when I tell you that there is nothing here that can harm you. Gale, you've been under a tremendous strain lately, and I know you've had trouble sleeping. You told me that yourself only yesterday. You know what I think happened?"

He waited for Gale to respond and when she did it was with a sad childish pout. "What?"

"They say when you're deprived of sleep for some time you begin to hallucinate. I think that even though your eyes were open you were actually dreaming, but Gale it *was* a dream. I'm sure you won't have anymore of these wake-nightmares, or whatever they call them." Kevin then smiled at her. "You were just doing the lazy man's version of a sleep walker who never gets out of bed." Kevin laughed gently and hugged her tightly. "Now I promise to keep all the bad boogie men away." He whispered amused into her ear.

There was something about the quality of his voice that seemed to pacify, and calmness washed over her. Gale tried to move and glance in the direction where she'd seen the apparition, but his grasp upon her was too firm to allow that freedom. Though somewhat immobile she felt safe within Kevin's arms. It was only a few minutes before Gale was asleep against his chest.

Kevin reached up and switched off the light while still holding her sleeping body firmly against his own, casting the room again into darkness. Just before the light vanished it seemed to concentrate into the figure of a young man dressed in antiquated fashion. He cast an angry scowl toward the specter that merely averted his eyes downward before disappearing. Snuggling close to his new love, Kevin allowed his arms to completely encircle her. He took a deep breath and smiled before closing his eyes to sleep. In a short while he would introduce her to Gabriel properly.

In a dark world Kevin turned to find Gabriel standing there. As the light around them both began to increase, he could see that they stood within the expanse of an enormous cavern that he knew all to well. Well enough to recognize that the space was slightly altered somehow, and immediately Kevin recognized he was dreaming.

It's not fair.

"Since when were you ever concerned about fair? You routinely walked all over people with your riches and your arrogant attitude. All while you lived. Don't think I haven't done my research on you."

You're right I behaved badly, and I did a lot of things that I'm not proud of. Now I pay the price for my actions. I make no excuses. What would be the point? My time came and went, and I'm beyond changing anything of who I was or what I did, but you still have that chance.

In my defense though the situation was different then, as was the world, but we are not talking about me are we?

"That's my point exactly!" Kevin shouted angrily pointing an accusing finger. "This is the business of the living isn't it? That leaves you out! You have no say in what goes on any longer. That being the case," Kevin continued, "maybe you should keep your damn opinions to yourself. Besides, fair is relative isn't it? I mean is it fair for me to be deprived of what you take for granted."

You are only angry because you know I'm right.

"The only thing I know is that you're getting on my nerves. Sometimes I wonder why I even bother. What I should do is board this place up like the tomb it is. That way your essence will have completely disintegrated long before anyone else ever steps foot inside here again."

At that Kevin turned away hoping to leave the scene and the conversation, but Gabriel it seemed was far from finished.

Then why don't you. I never asked for any of this!

"Why do you insist on feeling sorry for yourself? Things happen for a reason. You died and yet here you are. Don't you know what that means? Sure, you're a little less physical than before. Yet it's as if you didn't die at all, but why you? Don't forget that it's because of these experiments that we understand how you're sometimes made more tangible. Gabriel you have the power to influence the physical, the minds and the emotions of the living. Don't you understand the power that can give us? Now I know this experiment has had some costs…"

Costs!

"…and I'm sorry about that. It seems there's one fundamental truth in this universe, you can't get something for nothing. Towards that end, sacrifices have to be made. Gabriel, why not everyone? I want to know why. If my consciousness can survive death, then I want that too. Don't you see? It's got to be infinitely better than the alternative."

You don't know that.

"And you don't know it isn't. The bottom line is I will continue to do things my way until I'm completely satisfied I understand this thing. I won't stop, not until I can consistently repeat it. Not before. Now I'll say this only once more, if you appear to her again before I'm ready for you to there'll be trouble. You may be dead, but I can still make things uncomfortable for you, and I know you're not too far gone to see that!"

I won't let you continue using me like this!

"Fine, then go somewhere else."

You know I can't.
"Then I guess it's settled."

Gale came into the living room the following morning to find Kevin scowling angrily as he looked out the large bay window. Outside a crystal blue sky shone over the towering trees and beautiful snowcapped mountains framed there. A sight that was clearly lost upon Kevin.

"What are you doing?"

Kevin's expression melted into an easy smile. "Not a thing, just thinking."

"Well, it must be appalling thoughts from your expression just now." She said hoping he'd confide his problems, but there was only silence as he again turned to the window. Abruptly, he returned his attention to her as if in afterthought.

"You seem refreshed. I'm surprised after last night." There was malicious amusement in his eyes that mocked her. It was a side to him Gale had never seen before, reminding her she really didn't know him.

"I feel so foolish." She said genuinely embarrassed. "I'm sorry I woke you like that, but I could swear I saw something."

"Not to worry," he said grasping her hand in his and kissing it gently, "I suppose this can appear a creepy old house if you're not used to it." It was only then that he'd noticed the purse that was thrown across her shoulder. "Going somewhere?" He added.

Gale watched his eyes grow shades colder, becoming unreadable.

"It's been so much like paradise here," she said slowly moving away from him until he was forced to release her hand, "one can almost forget the real world."

"What are you saying?" Kevin said softly, eyeing her intently. All the while the smile never left his lips. Yet Gale felt something threatening in the cold stare he leveled upon her.

"The real world is all around you, even here believe it or not."

16

"I know that silly." Gale forced a stiff laugh. "Despite last night I woke pretty early this morning. While you were asleep I walked back to the lodge and called my job. I was certain I'd been fired by now. You know I was supposed to be back last Monday. I'd planned to leave a message for my boss. Fortunately, she came in early to do some work and I caught her. Anyway, she was really sympathetic, and she said I could consider this my remaining week's vacation."

When Kevin hadn't reflected Gale's level of interest she added, "I'm due back on Monday."

Kevin expelled a long breath. "I see."

Though he hadn't moved physically Gale nevertheless felt a growing distance between them.

"I thought we had something together." He said disappointed. "This is a surprise for me."

"I feel the same way, but Kevin I have to work."

"Why?"

"What do you mean why?" Gale gave him an incredulous look. "For all the basic reasons I guess. Food, shelter, what do you mean why?" She said suddenly angry.

"Don't you have all of that here?"

"Yes, but..."

"Then you don't care for me?"

"I do..."

"Then there's no reason to leave. Gale I love you."

Before Gale could react she found Kevin had bridged the distance between them and both her hands were again within his. Yet somehow it felt different now, this time she felt trapped.

"I've known this from the first moment I set eyes on you at the lodge," he continued, "but you were otherwise...entangled. That day in the elevator crystallized everything for me. It made me realize destiny brought us together." He smiled broadly then. "And obviously wouldn't take no for an answer, and neither will I. What else can you call it, the way we kept running into each other? I know you feel the same way I do Gale, otherwise you wouldn't be here.

Gale, you only have to tell me your needs and I'll see to them, I promise."

All she could manage was a smile as his eyes searched hers. She was aware of the tremendous charm he now attempted to lavish upon her, but it seemed to fall in tatters all around.

"Kevin," Gale said through clenched teeth, "that's not why I'm here. I don't need anyone to provide for me." She pulled her hands free.

As she sat watching Kevin over the lunch he prepared especially for her Gale smiled across at him, all the while wondering what it was she'd seen in him. Sometime during that morning the rose colored glasses dropped from her eyes, perhaps to shatter to dust. Sure Kevin still seemed handsome but only mildly so. Certainly not the Adonis she imagined over the past few days, and even if he was such a trait had never affected her so profoundly before. Perhaps it had just been a rebound thing.

Before Gale realized it she sighed and it hadn't escaped Kevin's attention, he'd been watching her intently off and on since their conversation that morning.

Kevin talked incessantly, trying to bridge her growing silences. She would only nod or occasionally agree with his comments as they continued to eat their meal. The charm of her surroundings, as with Kevin's own allure, was evaporating to mist leaving her with only a depressed feeling.

He'd been telling her something about the history of the property, old Indian reservation … massacre … sacred grounds.

"Lunch was wonderful." Gale said standing abruptly forcing him to stop in mid-sentence. At his curious expression she added apologetically, "I think I need to walk off the calories, perhaps a stroll through the woods."

"That sounds like a wonderful idea. I'll join you." Kevin said smiling pleasantly and also rising.

"Thanks, but I need to be by myself for a while. Do you mind?"

"Yes," his voice reflected bruised feelings but then Kevin added softly, "but I understand. Have a nice time."

"Thanks." Gale reached out grasping his hand and pulled away when he attempted to kiss her.

He stood rooted to the spot as she made her way to the front door. All the while she was aware of his eyes upon her. Only after she closed the door and could feel and breathe in the frigid air did Gale feel free enough to let out her breath. She immediately felt herself relax. At the same time her mind kept asking at what point her paradise became a prison.

"Gabriel!"

Kevin continued to shout the name several times more before he stopped. His eyes flashed with anger as his mind raced through alternatives for getting even.

"Don't play games with me Gabriel. You're only making things worse. I swear you're making things worse." But the entire house remained silent.

He forced himself to calm down, taking deep breaths before continuing in a quieter tone.

"Gabriel haven't we already gone over all this? Listen, I know you don't like this situation. I get no enjoyment out of it either, but it must be done. Gabriel you benefit from this as well, have you forgotten that? So will she if she's lucky. We're scientist you and I, and this is our laboratory. Gabriel, if I were doing something that wasn't possible than I could see your point of view, but it *is* possible. Doesn't Janet prove that? We just need a consistent track record, that's all. If I can duplicate that success our efforts will be justified. Why can't you see that? It will be a monumental step for all of mankind."

When the area around him remained silent Kevin's instincts continued to tell him he was not alone.

"I know you're here somewhere. Damn it Gabriel, answer me!"

The sky above Gale was gray, cloudy and sending down a fine shower of snow that danced within whirling winds. It had started just after she returned from the lodge earlier that morning. In the hours since, it had dumped more snow than she anticipated. At nearly up to her knee high boots, it made Gale's strides tiring and twenty minutes later the chill of her face, hands and feet forced her to stop and reevaluate her plans.

She was deep within the forest. Taking the same path she'd taken only that morning. At least she thought so, but her inability to see through the vales of falling snow had Gale badly disoriented. Worse, she was nearly frozen. Those facts alone were sufficient to compel her to return to the house, but her mounting irritation with Kevin overrode that instinct. She was in no mood to return to a house that was quickly becoming a prison. Gale determined she would continue forward a while longer.

The problem was Gale couldn't say with certainty Kevin had changed. As she considered it, Gale realized it was obvious he hadn't. He was still as caring and attentive as always. Only now it seemed contrived.

'Maybe it's my perception of him that changed.' Gale told herself as she continued through her arctic surroundings. 'Was I really that far off the mark? Or am I slowly becoming deranged? Well in either case, putting distance between me, Kevin and this whole ordeal won't hurt.'

Gale shook her head, forcing herself to forget the last few days and the events that led her to Woodhills House. Instead she focused on the environment, looking for familiar landmarks that would lead her through her snowy surroundings back to the Lodge. Within the legion of trees now surrounded her, Gale felt like little more than a mouse forced to navigate a gigantic winter maze. She continued reminding herself that each of her frozen steps brought her that much closer to reality and her world of normalcy.

Looking behind her, Gale saw the path of her boots in the snow. Beyond a few feet's distance they were completely erased. She was quickly passing the point of no return but was confident if she continued her straight path eventually she'd find her way out of the forest. Maybe end up back at the lodge, if she survived that long. However, Gale realized there was little point going back to the Lodge beyond catching a ride into town. She inquired about a room that morning and found it booked throughout the following weekend. But the thought of a room in town, however shabby, was preferable to the alternative at her back. Something told her there was little chance of Kevin taking her there. Also, the fact that all her suitcases and other belongings were back at the house was of little consequence.

Gale thought briefly about calling Stan, who must have returned home by now. Instinctively she knew he would return for her. That way she wouldn't have to face Kevin and Woodhills House ever again. He could keep whatever she left there, but that was an absurd thought. Why was she running from Kevin? He'd given her no real cause. On the other hand Stan was the reason she'd ended up there in the first place. He cheated on her with that bunny, of that she was sure. So while Kevin was a bit possessive he wasn't crazy.

With resolve Gale determined to return eventually to face Kevin and tell him of her plans to return home. She wouldn't run from two men in less than two weeks.

"Good day Madam."

Gale twirled around, startled to find a stranger less than arms length from her back and her startled gesture nearly caused her to stumble backwards.

He was a slender mustached man with long side burns and collar length honey-blond hair. He bowed deeply from the waist and when he again righted himself he leveled sharp hazel eyes upon her.

"My apologies dear Lady," the man said smiling sadly as he gave another slight bow, "it was not my intention to frighten you. My name is Gabriel Hallenger." He added in an accent that was deeply southern. "I observed you traversing from a distance. This is foul weather Madam and anyone out in it must have a fairly dire reason. I thought you might require assistance."

"Thank you, but I'm fine. I was just strolling." At his curious expression she added, "For the air."

"Well there does appear to be plenty of it." He said with that same sad smile. "You're from Woodhills House are you not?" He asked.

"Yes, I've been visiting. Do you know Kevin then?"

"We've met."

"He's such a kind man." Gale said attempting small talk and suddenly regretting her impulse to venture out alone. As she spoke her eyes scanned her surroundings for signs of other wayward travelers. That she had no real hope of finding, when in the distance she caught sight of a red ski jacket coming quickly towards them. As she turned her head fully towards the figure she recognized Kevin's voice calling to her.

"As they say," Hallenger added at her back, "appearances can sometimes be deceiving, and it would be a grave mistake for you to return to Woodhills House Madam."

At that Gale returned her attention to the man who was now nowhere to be seen.

In silence she walked back towards Woodhills House with Kevin at her side. She refused to bring up the man she saw in the woods. In truth, Gale was certain he'd now think her some kind of nut. First her nightmare of the night before, now disappearing strangers in solitary forests; besides, she told herself, he would chalk it up to fatigue, worry or some other rational explanation. Neither of which she could rule out. She just wasn't up to the ridicule. If it was her mind, why was it continually telling her to leave Woodhills House?

She had been huddled on the sofa with arms folded around her knees deep in thought when Kevin came in and sat in a chair opposite her.

"You've been quiet all afternoon."

"I was just relaxing." Gale said lying, trying to mask her growing apprehension for remaining there. She promised herself she would tell Kevin as soon as possible she was leaving, but her nerves had given out on her. Once again Gale courted the possibility of sneaking out in the dead of night.

"I never did ask about your walk, did you enjoy yourself?"

"Oh yes, it was exhilarating, I don't think I'll ever get used to all this fresh air."

"You stood there for so long, I thought perhaps you were lost."

There was a searching quality in his eyes, and Gale realized she was again under careful scrutiny.

"I was fine," she lied, "just taking in the surroundings. I wanted to remember as much as possible of the beauty of this place for when I get back to my life."

"I thought this was your life?"

For some reason Gale found that statement angered her, as if her world now revolved around him.

"As a matter of fact it isn't. I have a life back in Chicago you know! With a job, friends, relatives and everything else that accompanies a life, and thank you for reminding me of that." She said rising from the chair in anger to leave the room noticing he'd simply sat there coldly staring at her, a strange expression upon his face.

"Family," he said smiling again as she reached the doorway. His face reflected disbelief. "Tell me about your *family*?"

Gale turned on her heals, clearly shocked. After her tirade Kevin had chosen that one word to focus upon. The one word that had been a lie, and somehow he'd known it. How did he know?

His question had been asked warm enough. His smile had been pleasant, but everything in his mannerisms now rung with insincerity for Gale further angering her.

"I'm tired," Gale said waiving her hand in dismissal, "if you'll excuse me I think I'll turn in." With that she left the room and went up stairs.

Kevin hadn't followed her up and Gale had been grateful for that. She needed time to think and to sort out her life. Inside the bedroom that they shared, she strolled over towards the window in time to see dusk settling upon the land silhouetting the forest in the distance. Things had seemed so perfect before arriving at Woodhills Lodge. Her life had been perfect, and she'd been with the man she knew she loved. Now everything lay in ruins. It all started unraveling right after Stan tripped over those bags. That was when she had met Kevin, and as she stood there considering Gale realized immediately afterwards they'd run into Stan's ski bunny. She'd said something about seeing them on the slops and offering them a good deal on private lessons, but she really meant Stan.

Perhaps Madam, he's been as much a victim in this circus as you.

Gale spun round to find she was alone within the room, her mind again playing tricks upon her. It had been the voice of the southerner, the one she'd seen in the woods but who apparently had existed only in her mind. That is, if his lack of tracks were any indication. In any event she wouldn't start talking to herself and answering nonexistent voices. Gale told herself that once she left Woodhills at least she still had her job. Her biggest problem would be facing Stan in the small apartment they shared? Now it seemed she also had to worry about being crazed.

It's truly remarkable the number of opportunities that one receives in life, don't you think?

Gale's eyes continuously scanned the room to find it empty and at the same time she was aware that physically she heard nothing and yet within her mind the voice continued.

Opportunities that can save you time, money, even life sometimes. Take your own situation as an example. Here you have received numerous warning as to danger, some verbal others instinctual. Yet you've refused to listen or act upon them. Perhaps, Madam, I can provide you with something you will act upon.

"What the hell does that mean?" Gale whispered, embarrassed she spoke at all and for an instant visualized walking down crowded grocery isles talking to nonexistent people as every sane person stared.

It means Madam, that maybe you should take a stroll down to the basement. You might find much of interest down there.

"Just leave me alone!" She shouted into the empty room.

"I'm sorry. I didn't mean to intrude."

Gale whirled round embarrassed to find Kevin standing in the doorway with a tray and two cups upon it.

"I just thought you might like some hot cocoa."

"Kevin, I'm the one who should be sorry. I guess I'm just a little on edge. So much has happened so quickly. I'm really sorry. So that's for me?" Gale smiled towards the tray.

"Here you go." Kevin handed her the cup and watched her as she took several sips. "I'll give you some time to unwind. I think I'll drink mine downstairs, I've built a fire that's warming the room nicely. If you feel up to it come down later."

"All right, perhaps I will. Thanks."

Kevin smiled briefly and left the room.

Distracted, Gale set the cup of liquid upon the side table and was still listening to his retreating footsteps when the cup went crashing to the ground.

"What the hell?" The dark brown liquid was quickly spreading across the small rug beside the bed, on the side concealed from the bedroom door. Gale made a disgusted noise as she gazed down at the mess.

"I'm having nothing but bad luck, why is all this happening to me?"

Because you allow it dear Lady, and as you near the end of your existence, which will be soon, remember I have tried in earnest to help you.

Go down into the basement!

After that the room had gone completely silent. Gale had lain there across the bed, awake for nearly an hour before she heard the bedroom door creak open. She knew Kevin was probably checking on her to be sure she was all right and tried to feign sleep hoping to avoid conversation. She could feel his eyes upon her from the doorway, and after a few moments he left closing the door silently behind him.

When the sound of his footsteps faded, Gale swung her bare feet off the bed and down onto a soggy rug and cursed. She walked over to the window and looked out into the night. The world seemed intensely black far from city lights, darker and colder than she could have imagined. It was difficult to visualize that snowy world in the summer, when nature would awaken.

Gale returned to bed forcing herself to try for sleep. She hoped to take her mind off the voice she heard and her growing desire to follow its advice. She'd lain there for nearly an hour, miles from her goal and preparing to take Kevin up on his offer of watching the fire. It was better than staring at the four walls.

She opened the door and walked down the darkened hall approaching the foyer. As she neared the steps, Gale heard the sound of voices. One was unmistakably Kevin's. The other was that of a woman and a voice she'd heard before.

"Relax, I told you she's asleep."

"This is risky. After this Charlie we must stop, it's just not working."

"I've kind of gotten used to Kevin." He said sounding playful but then Gale heard his voice turn serious. "What are you talking about? Of course it is, honey just trust me. This is going to work." There was a slight silence before he added with amusement, "So how's your new lover working out."

"Damn you!" The woman sounded angry. "How can you stand there and say such things without feeling anything? Don't you care at all for me? That you could stand there and just accept my doing such a thing!"

"Darling it's for the project. I just focus on that. It doesn't mean that I don't love you, or that you don't love me." Kevin said soothingly.

It was the bunny from the lodge and she was downstairs with Kevin. It seemed that they knew each other well. Gale felt her knees weakening and reached out for the wall in support as she sank back further out of sight.

"Then you've slept with her," the woman's voice dripped icy rage, "you slept with her!"

"Just as you did with Stanley what's-his-name. We knew it might come to that and we agreed upon it. Remember?"

"I never slept with him!" She'd shot back angrily then added hesitantly. "I didn't have to. He had no real interest in me, not like that. He only had eyes for his Gale. We only kissed once, and it took nearly ever ounce of will I had to compel him to do so, but I made sure she saw it."

Perhaps it had been the heaviness of her heart that had caused Gale's knees to buckle at that instant. She felt herself sliding down the wall into a pool of bitterness, guilt and self-loathing. She'd made such a spectacle of herself for a man who it seemed had staged everything, but why? The image of Stan crystallized in her mind as a flood of tears escaped. As if her tears controlled both the twisting and distorting of her visual world along with her heart. In her ignorance and distrust Gale realized she alone had been the one to cheat and betray, the only man she had ever loved or had ever loved her.

"Well," Kevin said coldly, "she's lost to him now? I've made certain of that."

"How?"

"The usual way, small amounts of it in everything our dear Gale has been eating or drinking since her arrival. You know it's really convenient knowing how to cook and a final heaping portion in the hot cocoa I gave her tonight. I made sure she began to drink it before we left and I checked on her only a few minutes ago, she's sound asleep. Tonight we finish this unpleasantness and who knows maybe tomorrow we'll have something to celebrate."

"I hope so. I no longer have the stomach for keeping this up. Charlie maybe Gabriel's right, perhaps it won't be that bad."

"Don't go weak on me now! You know how much I love you. I'm doing all this for us."

Gale realized she'd heard enough. She had to get out of that house at all costs.

"So, what's that status on our prince charming?" Charlie, the man she'd known as her wonderful and loving Kevin asked in an amused voice which rooted her once more to the spot. "Is he gone?"

"No. He loves her, maybe as much as I love you. I would never have believed another love could be as great. The police have been telling him that they suspect foul play. I tried to get him to return home but he said he would never leave, not as long as she's missing.   That call of hers back to her office only strengthened his resolve. Now he's been given reason to hope."

Gale heard the woman sigh heavily.

"Charlie, sending her back to him is the right thing to do. How can we in good conscious destroy two people who love each other so?"

"Oh I'll send her back to him all right."   He said laughing briefly. "We will do what we must to survive and to stay together my love. Besides, he can't possibly feel as deeply for her as I for you."

"Then I suggest you prepare what you'll tell him tomorrow." She said coldly. "He's knocked on nearly every door in town already looking for her. I delayed his coming here today, but I'm sure he'll be here tomorrow."

"If so, I'll deal with him," he said easily, "just as we have with the others. There's room enough for both our love birds down there I guess. Though I confess, I haven't buried my last love yet."

There was a moment's silence before he added hastily, "Darling, wait, I'm sorry, you know what I mean. You know you're my only real love."

Gale tiptoed back towards the bedroom, she had to get her strategy together, or at the very least find some type of weapon she could use if she had to. She'd just closed the door and turned to find the southerner seated upon the bed.

"Who the hell are you?" She whispered alarmed.

"Your only ally, I'm surprised you don't already recognize me as such by now."

"If that were true you'd have told me outright this afternoon about that... that... bastard."   Gale whispered venomously and nearly in tears.

"May I call you Abigail?"

Gale looked at him momentarily crazed before responding angrily.

"No!" She said hotly, "My names Gale."

Gabriel nodded continuing, "Dear Lady, you must keep your

wits about you. It's far too late for hysterics. You heard Emily just now. Tomorrow your love will surely arrive, and just as surely Charles will kill him."

"I won't let that happen. I'm leaving. All I have to do is get to the lodge or to town for help."

"I was pleasantly surprised you made it back to the lodge this morning. It's unfortunate you didn't have foresight to remain there. You were quite lucky my dear but I think you'll find it a bit more challenging by night. Impossible in fact without even the moon to guide you and I think you'll find the temperature has dropped dangerously."

"What other choice do I have?" Gale responded louder than she'd meant to. She turned alarmed and strained to listen until she felt confident no one over heard her.

"Rely upon me Gale," Gabriel told her softly, "I swear upon my honor I will allow no harm to befall either you or your gentleman."

"And I should trust you, with both our lives?"

"Gale, this house has played host to many women and each time I've tried in my limited capacity to assist them. Each time I've laid my plan before them in the hopes that together we can stop this slaughter of innocents once and for all. As you've probably guessed, each time they've chosen flight or various other inappropriate and unsuccessful plans. The basement is a graveyard of failed plans. If you insist upon traversing the woods, in darkness, in sub-zero temperatures unaided, I can do nothing to stop you. Mark my words in a very short while Charles will be looking for you, and it will only take him a short while to catch you. Then everything for you and your gentleman will be finished."

"Well what's your plan?"

As part of Gale's mind listened intently to the southerner the other part mentally chastised her for allowing her instincts to over rule her judgment yet again. It had been those fouled-up instincts that had landed her in her predicament. Yet those same instincts now told her she could trust this man. The fact that he really didn't exist had been pushed entirely from her mind, but as he finished she'd begun to doubt her sanity again.

"I can't believe I wasted time listening to you. You're insane!"

"I assure you Gale, I am not."

"You're right. I'm the crazy one. You expect me to stake my life on your pagan ritual?"

"It is not *my* ritual. It belonged to the Indian tribe that once inhabited this area, and when done correctly Gale I assure you, it does work."

"Yet Kevin," Gale winced, correcting herself, "Charlie, hasn't had much success."

"Limited success would be more accurate." Gabriel corrected.

"Give me a break." She whined.

"I beg your pardon?"

Gale waved her hand impatiently dismissing the statement.

"If you promise me you won't panic, everything will be fine. I just need to know you will do as I ask. Agree now and I can and will protect you. We will be able to end this monster's activities tonight, once and for all." When she didn't answer he added, "He's coming, give me your answer!"

Gale turned her head towards the door also hearing the footsteps.

"I promise." She blurted out hastily, "What do I do?"

"Are you familiar with the game of playing possum?"

Gale lay upon the bed curled up into a small ball as the door creaked opened. He was there, her executioner.

Every fiber of Gale's being told her to leap from the bed, to protect her self or to run. Yet she could easily imagine the other victims as they'd done just that and with fatal consequences. But how could she just lay there and allow herself to be murdered? As she lay there feigning unconsciousness Gale wondered which death was worse, fighting back or passively allowing it to happen. The latter was definitely the more cowardly of the two and not the way she'd choose to go.

Being carried down the steps, Gale fought the impulse to correct the uncomfortable bend of her neck and to resist the impulse to correct the swaying of her arm, which dangled brushing his side.

It seemed as if they had gone down hundreds of steps and still they continued to descend. Until she could hear his footsteps echoing in what sounded like a large room. The basement Gale thought. There she was lain upon something cold and raised from the floor judging from the angle she'd been lowered. Then there were sounds of flames igniting, and Gale felt a wave of panic. What if the ritual involved burning her alive? The impulse to open her eyes was nearly uncontrollable but she had to believe in Gabriel's plan. From what he'd told her, others had been in her same predicament, panicked and tried to run and ultimately had been killed. No, there was just no other way.

Soon Gale heard chants and the voice had been Kevin's or Charlie's. The words where undecipherable but she recognized certain phrases as sounds Kevin had spoken in his sleep. They seemed to go on forever. Then there were the sounds of heavy footfalls, rhythmic in nature. As if in dance and Gale wondered where Hallenger was. She continued to remind herself of the plan, the order of the ceremony, and that Hallenger wouldn't interfere unless...

The dancing stopped and Kevin's voice had begun to shout loud verbal passages and again the sounds of spontaneous bursts of flames. Several more times the sequence played out of prayer of some kind, then flames.

As Gale lay there immobile, still feigning unconsciousness the air around her seemed to change and grow cold. She heard sounds, faint at first. Then drums beating in time to the words being spoken. Its pitch grew, as if approaching from somewhere distant. She startled at the touch of cold hands as they ran the length of her body. What was happening?

Unable to resist any longer Gale's eyes flung open, in time to see wispy figures encircling her. They were dressed in Indian garb and danced around her in time with invisible drums. As she lifted her head, Gale found herself lying upon an altar of stone. She looked across at Kevin and found him immersed in his chanting, oblivious to her.

Despite her ignorance of exactly what was going on Gale understood that the ritual was nearing its conclusion, and what the consequences of that fact meant for her. At that point Kevin let out a loud joyous screech opening his eyes to gaze upon her with a cold smile. When he realized she stared back, his smile vanished.

He shook his head slowly. "You shouldn't be awake," with the realization his eyes flared opened wide with shocked disbelief that slowly melted into horror, "you shouldn't be alive." All the while the specters began to enclose him. "NO!" Kevin screamed as he bolted towards steps that were carved into a stone wall, mounting them several at a time. As he ran the specters followed, weapons raised in pursuit. Kevin only got half way up the stairs when they overtook him. Though the instruments of violence had not been real, the marks they made left permanent and fatal impressions.

Kevin's scream echoed throughout the vast cavern as Gale had lain there, still upon the altar, too shocked to move. It was several seconds before the echo of the last scream fell silent. With it the specters had vanished leaving Kevin's body huddled midway up the steps. Perhaps it had been the pull of gravity that sent him tumbling abruptly down the steps. To fall in a bloody mass at its base, his eyes open wide in horror.

A cold hand touched her shoulder and Gale screamed.

"Calm yourself Gale, it's only me."

Gabriel Hallenger stood behind her and next to him was the snow bunny from the lodge.

"You!" Gale nearly spit at the woman as she tried to leap from the altar to charge at her, but Gabriel stopped her.

"It's time for proper introductions." Gabriel's voice and mannerism were soft and untroubled, as if nothing out of the ordinary had occurred. "Gale Rierson, this is my sister Emily Hallenger."

"Your sister," Gale was momentarily dumbfounded, "I don't understand." She swung her legs off the altar to stand but they refused her support, and Gale felt Gabriel's cold touch preventing her fall. "Why kill me?"

"Because I loved him, I could deny him nothing. Not even

when what he wanted was so heinous.

"Love doesn't excuse your actions!" The instant she'd said it Gale immediately felt her face flush hot as she thought about her own part in the sequence of events of the last few days.

"I know my dear, can you ever forgive me?" She spoke in a tone that mirrored her brother's in southern inflections, something Gale had never noticed at the Lodge. Yet now it seemed so obvious but she seemed sincere in her question.

"No," Gale shot back, "of course not! What did you hope to gain? For that matter, what the hell just happened?"

"It is a very long story," Gabriel began, "and believe it or not Charles truthfully told you some of it.

Two hundred years ago this area use to be inhabited by a Native American tribe whose name I never really could pronounce. By the time I came through here there were no more than a hand full of them left. I don't really know what diminished their number, I suppose they succumb to a series of harsh winters in preceding years. This house was built upon their sacred land."

"You mean burial grounds?"

"Gale what do you take me for? No, I would never build upon a graveyard. As best as I could determine, it was simply a place were they believed their gods walked. Their actual burial grounds were somewhere north of here, I believe. I spied upon one or two of their ceremonies, and it certainly did seem something was alive within this place. I determined to leave the area, despite wanting it sorely you understand? But then my dear Emily became gravely ill. We had no doctors with us, and in my grief I turned to the Indians for help from their spirits. They refused telling me we were not one of them, non-believers and such. I had no doubt that members of my group had done much to offend them, criticizing their beliefs and way of life. I'd certainly heard much from them as they tried to dissuade me from taking Emily to them, but her condition gradually worsened. I had to try all avenues to save her, my only sibling. I begged, pleaded, still they refused. She was already so very near death, and I believed they had it within their power to save her. I suppose grief snapped my sanity.

One thing led to another, and their chief was killed. Before long we'd battled. It didn't end until my men had killed those that remained. We divided their lands and I performed their ceremony, over Emily's very nearly dead body. You see I have a gift for remembering such things, even spoken words I don't understand. To this day I cannot rightfully tell you what the chant is requesting, but it certainly elicits a response. Yet it didn't seem to work and Emily died. In retrospect I suppose it did work. The problem was I didn't know what I was asking for." At that Gabriel smiled.

"Why did they turn on Kev... Charlie?" Gale turned to look towards Kevin's body whose head had turned mysteriously in their direction as if watching them. The expression within his eyes appeared vacant and the look of horror had vanished completely. She was nearly overcome with fear when Emily's cold hand grasped her forearm firmly.

"You no longer have to fear him dear," Emily said gazing sadly in his direction, "he... we, cannot harm you now."

To Gale's mind, Emily seemed on the verge of tears. She released Gale's arm and raised a handkerchief to her eyes momentarily. When she spoke again, her voice sounded stronger.

"But I believe you were about to ask about the potion." She said smiling weakly at Gale before letting her gaze drop to the dirt floor.

"Oh yes, the potion," Gabriel said quickly as he gently took the arm his sister had only just relinquished navigating Gale a few feet distant from her, "the victim must drink the sacred potion over a period of five days."

"But I didn't, at least I don't think so?"

"Charles placed it in your meals and I switched the plates. Each time he attempted to fill your delicate system with the liquid, he was himself ingesting it, and it seemed the spirits were also aware of this fact."

"I still don't understand. What did he hope to accomplish by killing me?" It had been the question burning within her since she'd stood listening to the two of them in the upstairs corridor. It seemed many had died before her. What was it all for?

"Why did you leave your sweetheart to run to the arms of my own?" Emily asked from behind her, causing Gale to swing around angrily. Yet Emily's expression of sadness as she watched her lover's corpse grow cold and gray had been too profound for Gale to lash out at the specter. "I'll tell you why, you did it for love. It's quite powerful isn't it? You can do tremendous things for love, and not all of it for good. You loved your Stanley. That love sent you straight into the arms of another when your heart perceived betrayal, but that wasn't entirely your fault. I forced the strain between you two."

"Tell me about it?" Gale replied hotly, but if Emily heard she gave no notice.

"I fell in love with Charlie when he inherited this place a few years ago and I believed him when he said he loved me."

"It seemed we'd been here for an eternity," Gabriel added solemnly, "unseen, unfelt until Charles bought the property two years ago and stumbled across my journals. At the time it seemed that fate had brought him here to rescue us. A student of Native American cultures who was able to decipher at least some of the entries, which I'd copied from native art I found.

Charles performed a purely random selection of one of the rituals, which he called Dance of Power. He was attempting to amuse one of his lady friends with a ritual he said was to feed the spirit. Well it certainly fed us. Unfortunately, it was at her expense. She died but it made us stronger, and we were able to interact with the physical world again. Afterwards we could be seen, heard and felt, and when we wished it we could influence the emotions of the living. That was when Charles became aware of us. His interest in my diary of course grew. However, the most important ritual, the one that placed us within this place, that was the one dearest to Charles' heart. It was also the one that needed practice due to certain omissions."

"You see my dear," Emily smiled wickedly at her brother, "dear Gabriel omitted key points within those pages." She grabbed her brother's arm encircling it within her own, "Omissions he never confided to anyone, not even me. I used to think you were just being cruel." Emily dropped her head onto her brother's shoulder saddened. "I'm sorry."

Gabriel brought his hand up to her chin to lift it and smiled reassuringly at her. After a moment she released him to continue.

"Poor Charlie had been testing the waters ever since. Trying to complete the ritual and find the meaning to it all, particularly the survival of the mind and soul after the death of the body. Yet I'm sure it was more a protection for himself than for me or mankind.

The closest he ever came to success was a single accidental time, with his Janet person, but that particular spirit faded over the course of a few days. She was his one and only success and so he continued until meeting you. Afterwards," Emily added sadly, "we were strong enough to be seen, felt and more importantly, leave this accursed prison. We were as strong as when we were alive. Better I suppose because now we could influence others, up to a point. That was why you were able to see me within Woodhills Lodge. I had form, of sorts and I could physically feel what you felt, for a short while. But it was all at the expense of others you understand. They paid the ultimate price to give us a gift that was only temporary at best.

I used my influence on your Stanley and then upon yourself to force the events that separated the two of you. It brought you to this place and into the arms of my Charlie with amorous eyes.

As for me, well, dear Gabriel kept trying to convince me that what Charlie and I were doing was wrong. I suppose the allure of life, of feeling, and of again influencing the world indefinitely was just too great. Also, I really did love Charlie. The Dance of Power and the ritual that caused us to be here are so similar I can't help but feel that he was close to achieving his ends."

"I don't believe the ritual was ever meant to return life to the dead." Gabriel said abruptly. "I believe it was only meant as a tool to seek advice from their ancestors. Obtain information to guide and protect the living and to allow the departed to comfort the bereaved. Charles was greedy and took it several steps too far."

"My love for Charles blinded me. I convinced myself our love was worth anything, even the lives of innocents. Of course now I realize he'd never been honest with me or himself for that matter as to his true motives. Oh maybe he loved me, as much as he's capable of loving anyone, but when he killed it was entirely for self-preservation. However that's something I cannot blame him for, can I?

Once the foundation was in place and you'd been turned away from Stanley, it was easy enough to convince your mind that Charles was the right man for you. In essence, to force you to see Charles as I did, but it's not a thing that can be kept up for long. Not when your heart belongs to another."

"We've led such solitary existences here within the boarders of Woodhills House." Gabriel said sadly, "I don't know how we exist, only that we do. I loved this place all my life. Once I found it I never wanted to be anywhere else, but after two-hundred years, it's become a prison." Gabriel looked away uncomfortably. "In truth, I've always believed we were anchored here in punishment."

"We can't say that for sure," Emily corrected, attempting to comfort her brother, "we've been too afraid to leave."

"What will you do now?" Gale asked looking from brother to sister. "You can't stay here forever."

"You're very kind to care," Emily said, "especially after what we've put you through but do not be concerned, we both died a very long time ago."

With it now over, Gale could feel herself beginning to fall apart. Once again her knees began to weaken beneath her, and cold hands reached out to steady her, pulling her again to her feet. As she looked at those hands, Emily on the one side and Gabriel the other, supporting her, Gale noticed they now seemed more translucent than before.

"I just want to get out of this place, to go home." She said lightheaded.

"You are in a cavern well below the foundation of the house." Gabriel pointed to where Kevin still lay in a huddled bloody mass. "Just take those stairs up, and you'll easily find your way back to your room. Tomorrow you can leave this place and return to your life."

"Are you kidding? I'm not spending another night in this place."

"What sense would that make to survive this horrific ordeal only to die out in the elements tonight? You'll never find your way to the Lodge in the darkness. You'll leave tomorrow." He added with finality.

When Gale had made no motion to move Gabriel turned to his sister.

"Emily, please help the dear lady back upstairs, while we still can."

"Yes, of course." Again she placed her cold hand upon Gale's forearm.

Oddly, to Gale's mind Emily's hand now felt more like a cold draft than a physical touch as the specter gently led her towards the steps. She'd averted her eyes, walking nearly blindly in the hope that she wouldn't have to see Kevin's body at its base. Gale continued to do so as she mounted them until she'd reached a third the way up, then fear again forced her eyes to pay attention. She'd become afraid that she might fall from the un-railed steps onto the corpse at its base. It wasn't until she passed the threshold back into the structure above that Gale relaxed.

Back in the bedroom she'd once shared intimately with a murderer Gale found sleeping the remainder of the night impossible, as she'd expected. With the first rays of dawn she quickly packed and raced down the step towards the front door.

She swung it open nearly fainting to find someone standing on the other side. It was Stan.

For a moment they'd simply stared at each other before she'd flung her arms around him, eyes tear filled. Gale had been too overcome with emotion for words. He'd held her tightly and she sensed he was also too moved to speak.

"I've been so worried." He said finally.

"Me too," Gale said lifting her tear stained face from his chest, "I just want to go home!"

From the second floor bedroom, Charlie could see out

over the forest that separated Woodhills House from the Lodge on the other side. While he could no longer tell with certainty, it seemed the weather was more temperate then only the day before. That reminded him that the snow, as with the season, would soon abate giving way to spring.

From beneath came the sounds of a door slamming and they exited the house. He'd watched bitterly as the lovers, Gale and Stan, made their way slowly down the path to disappear, hand in hand into the forest.

At a touch on his shoulder Charles turned but had been disappointed to find only Emily standing there.

"Oh, it's you." He said angrily returning his gaze to the window. "How could you let this happen? You were supposed to be watching him and all the while he was killing me."

"How could I know that? Even a ghost can't be in two places at once. You were the one who sent me on that fools errand to entertain her boyfriend."

Emily turned away from him hurt, but Charlie hadn't noticed and didn't care. She was only of limited use to him now.

"At least we still have the book." He turned again to face her, his expression softening. "It wasn't your fault darling, it was mine."

Charlie came forward to grasp her hands within his own kissing them gently.

"We underestimated Gabriel my love, but you can get someone up here to recite the ritual that can give me, us… strength greater than his, before your own wanes." He said caressing her hands within his own. "You will help me won't you?"

"Of course," Emily said pulling away.

As she moved towards the door, Charlie had once again returned his attention to the window, his expression immediately hardening.

Emily exited the room closing the door softly behind her

knowing he no longer had strength to affect objects or to be physically seen by the living.

Downstairs Gabriel stood before the last embers of the fire and smiled as she approached.

"I don't believe Gale was aware of his presence within the bedroom." She'd said mildly. "He seemed irritated by that."

"Well, wait until he's had more time under his belt." Gabriel replied dryly then added with amusement. "The fire's nearly gone out my dear, shall I feed it?"

"Let me."

Emily walked over to retrieve an old leather bound book from the mantle and tossed it into the fireplace. It fell onto the fires in an open position and they both watched as the flames danced across its pages, each one instantly igniting. In nearly no time, the two-hundred-year-old volume was gone.

Gabriel walked over to his sister extending his hand to take her arm.

"We've been cooped up here for far to long my dear. Let us take a stroll to the boundaries of this property and see what awaits."

For a few seconds, Emily had looked upwards uncertain but then seemed to come to a resolution as she placed her hand upon that of her brother.

"Yes, lets."

With that they'd both walked out into the early morning sun. Neither turned nor remarked as they listened to the silent screams from the dwelling at their back.

The Attic

Doesn't she ever quit? It's been nonstop ... almost an hour now!

Andre reached out in the darkened compartment of his '73 Impala to turn on the radio. As with the dozens of times before, all he received for his effort was loud annoying static. After a second or two he switched it off again.

"Andre," Angela whined, "why do you keep doing that? It's hard enough getting good reception in the city on that old AM thing." He could see her hands sailing about in the darkness for emphasis. "It would take a miracle out here in the middle of no where. Personally, I wish you'd just quit messing with the damn thing. You know how temperamental 'baby' is. You want her to stop on us, out here, in the middle of nowhere? I don't know why you don't just junk this ugly damn thing and get something nice, something with air conditioning. God knows it's not worth a dime in trade-in."

"We're riding aren't we?" Andre snapped back hotly. "It's not temperamental and I'm not getting rid of it, not as long as it gets me where I need to go!"

"Fine, fine, but I'm not the one getting mad at the damn radio."

With that Angela laughed. For what Andre couldn't tell. She certainly didn't have a clue why he was really angry, and he hadn't found her joke about being stranded in the middle of nowhere that funny. The silence that followed seemed deep and resounding despite the sound of the car's engine, and the wind that whipped through the open windows and around the cabin as they drove eastward. Angela was clearly angry and silent for the moment. Andre found himself hoping it would last, at least a few more minutes.

She'd been talking nearly nonstop for the better part of the last hour, about everything, her home life and family, friends at school and her new job and responsibilities. Andre had been silent the entire time. She seemed to revel in the sound of her own voice and opinions, but Andre realized it wasn't completely her fault. It had been some time since they'd pickup anything on the radio. He knew Angela was simply trying to bridge the silences that kept springing up, wall like between them. He was comfortable enough around her to feel they didn't always have to talk, she wasn't. It was like everyday was the first day of their relationship for her. Maybe that was the initial attraction for him. Yet he did wish she'd give it a rest at least for a while. His head was beginning to pound. Andre wasn't sure whether it was the circumstances prompting his trip or a growing annoyance to the sound of Angela's voice. During the seven hours they'd been on the road he'd continued to ask himself what it was that he'd seen in her. Sure Angela was a graceful beauty; tall, slender, and pretty, with a dark chocolate complexion he always found so appealing. Yet external beauty had never been the dominant force for him. Plenty of the girls he found himself dating had more intellectual pluses than physical. Angela Freemont had been the exception. Now as he drove Andre realized when their trip and his business was over, they would go their separate ways.

Angela had started talking again, and mentally Andre tuned her out. He brought his gaze upwards from the desolate road to the right corner of his wind shield were a crescent moon hung in the night sky to pierce his cars interior.

As the car left the outskirts of yet another small town, the last of the streetlights parading past them created a strobe effect within the cars interior. In Andre's mind there seemed a beat made by each that passed. As if drums were heralding the decreasing distance between him and destiny. That thought caused a cold dread to build within Andre's soul, a sick feeling each decreasing mile pulled him closer towards a mysterious dark fate. His parents laughed when he mentioned something similar days earlier but that had been before they received the news of his Aunt Irene's death.

"It's bad enough being in a hick town. Why did she have to live on the outskirts?"

Andre could feel Angela's eyes upon him and knew this time

she awaited a response.

"I'll admit the town of Carlton is small, it's only about seven hundred or so people. But she doesn't live on the outskirts, she lives in the town."

To which Angela only yawned.

"Now we've still got another seventy miles or so to go." Andre continued. "Look Angie, I know you're tired, it's been a long trip, but we're almost there. Why don't you try and get some sleep."

For a few seconds there was blessed silence within the car before Angela picked up one of her previous conversations, something about her girlfriend's boyfriend problems.

It had been thirty minutes since they'd seen the last car upon the nearly deserted stretch of highway that they'd traveled. At the same time Andre became aware of his actions, Angela voiced it.

"Andre, I don't think your Aunt's in a hurry to see us, and I sure as hell ain't in a hurry to meet her, since she's dead and all. You know? So why the hell are you racing all a sudden?"

Andre glanced across towards Angela and could feel her annoyance in the darkness.

"Sorry." He lifted his foot off the accelerator and allowing the car to coast until the speedometer fell to seventy-five. It stayed there only a few minutes before Andre's foot turned lead upon the gas pedal again.

"Andre!"

Andre broke saying nothing but was aware of the slight tremor of his right knee. It had only been by firmly depressing his foot that he'd been able to stop its shaking. He realized he'd have to find a less dangerous way to quiet those nervous impulses.

Oddly Angela fell into silence. Afraid of renewing her incessant chatter, it was several minutes before Andre dared turn in her direction, but curiosity eventually forced it. His sideways glance revealed she was finally asleep. He hadn't meant to, but a sigh escaped his lips. It seemed part of his problem was solved, at least for a short while.

Andre hadn't bothered waking her when they entered Carlton's town limits, '…population five hundred.' He smiled.

43

"Wow, it's even smaller than I remember." He said softly, immediately regretting it as he glanced again at Angela who was still sleeping peacefully.

He passed neatly kept houses, each spaced by acres of land and realized it wasn't the shoulder to shoulder beehive living to which he was accustomed. Already Andre missed the skyline back drop as he drove down one small street and then another, feeling for a second time as if he were being irresistibly drawn. His eyes finally fell upon a small silhouette to his left in the distance and on impulse he broke sharply throwing them forward and waking Angela.

"Where are we? Have we arrived?"

He'd been anxiously racing there nearly the entire way. Now with his destination in sight, Andre found himself coasting down the dark deserted street.

"There." He said in response nodding towards their objective and Angela's eyes followed.

"That's it?"

Before them the silhouette of the hundred fifty year old Victorian from his memories loomed into view, now ominous in its feel. Ten years later Andre Sanders had returned to his childhood home.

In his absence the shrubs surrounding the property had become giant sentinels isolating the house from its neighbors. Turning into the semicircular driveway Andre glanced up at them briefly as he passed and was left with a sense of dread.

As he approached Andre couldn't help noticing the colder, far more sinister darkness that seemed to concentrate about the place, which the cars headlights cut through scalpel like only to be reclaimed hungrily in their wake. He pulled up before the front door and they both stared out the cars driver side window in silence. Andre briefly considered the possibility of accomplishing his task without leaving the security of his vehicular talisman but recognized that to be a foolish thought. "Well let's get this over." He said switching off the ignition and lights but sat there for several seconds before finally exiting with a sigh.

The atmosphere of the place held an oppressive vacuum-like quality. Andre found himself suddenly exhaling; unconsciously he'd been holding his breath. He hadn't been aware of the sounds accompanying the night until he noted the absence of them, as if something were draining the life from the area leaving only dead silence. He suspected Angela also sensed an unnatural strangeness to the place as he watched her silently exit the car to join him. They both stared up at the deserted dwelling. It was still large and mysterious, just as in his memories. Yet there was something else now, something he couldn't define but perhaps it was just his Aunt's death that made it now seem monstrous.

"There sure is a lot of garbage up here." With a careless gesture, Angela let the book she'd been holding drop from her hand, it fell to the attic floor with a thud that echoed eerily across the dark attic. She glanced across smiling at her boyfriend and was disappointed to receive only a bland stony expression in response. Without a word Andre simply resumed his search through a box of oddities, which he'd been squatting over for the past several minutes. Outside a gorgeous summer day awaited and Angela longed to be free of that depressing old place in favor of exploring the town.

"She musta been one nutty old lady." Angela continued almost to herself, more to fill the oppressive silence than for any anticipated response, and she'd received none. This time when Andre glanced her way she'd seen clear signs of something. What was it irritation, disappointment perhaps? Andre only shook his head slightly before again returning to his search. Angela bit her bottom lip forcing herself to turn away before she said something she'd regret.

'Girl just get through this.' She thought. 'When all this is over he'll be back to normal, but it's like he's a different person. Since entering this brooding old place last night his mood seems to mirror it. Maybe he's reliving old memories of his Aunt. But even if that's true it doesn't give him the right to treat me like a child. And what the hell is he looking for anyway!'

In irritation Angela allowed her foot to kick a box near to her foot and the bottles it contained seemed to almost cry out as they vibrated against one another.

"Angela be careful!" Andre shouted, his eyes reflecting anger but the scowl immediately melted into embarrassment.

"I'm sorry." He straightened up holding his back in support and a pained gasp escaped his lips. "Look, you've been up here for almost an hour. What say we get outta here and see about getting something to eat."

Andre brought his right hand up to stroke the top of his head with its short brown bristly hair. It was a distracted gesture, a habit of his whenever he struggled to remember something.

"You know it's been almost ten years since I've been back to this place, but I'm sure I can find some restaurants around here."

For a few seconds Angela tried to hold onto her anger but her stomach forced her ego's surrender. It was nearly noon and the single cup of coffee she'd had for breakfast had run its course. It had been the only safe bet in the kitchen that wasn't in the process of evolving.

"Fine," she said finally, her anger still more than apparent. "I need a break from this place." She glared at him for a few seconds as she struggled to regain her lost patience. When she spoke again it was in a kinder softer tone. "I think you need one to. It's almost one, how long have you been up here?"

Andre smiled sheepishly turning towards the stairway. "Not long." He said over his shoulder as he continued towards the stairs.

Angela laughed as she managed to catch his forearm forcing him again towards her and wrapped her arms about his waist. "Exactly how long is 'not long?'"

He let out a mock groan realizing she wasn't going to let go of the question. "Okay, since about ten, maybe ten-thirty."

"Liar," she laughed. "I heard you rummaging up here from the bedroom before eight this morning."

"That's what I said." Andre pulled away. His expression was one of amusement but he avoided her gaze.

"You mean since last night! Andre are you trying to tell me you've been up in this cold, dusty, musty old place since last night? You must have come up here right after I went to sleep! What the hells so important that it deserves all that!"

"I needed some time to think and remember. Besides we'd only just gotten in and I knew you were tired. I was just too stressed to sleep so I came up here."

"So you've been up here ever since? Andre, you're going off the deep end. You know that don't you? There's nothing up here 'cept boxes upon boxes of garbage." Her tone was harsh yet kinder than she actually felt.

"You don't understand." He said turning his back on her.

There it was again, that look of disappointment that suddenly fired her anger again.

"Understand what! That you're going loony on me?"

"No, what it means to loose someone you care about."

Angela made a disgusted sound before biting down painfully on her bottom lip. She would let her thoughts go unsaid, for the moment at least. She moved past him on route to the stairs, perhaps after she refueled she thought.

"It's not garbage." Andre replied softly to her retreating form.

Angela turned to find him gazing across the attic, to the lifetime's worth of mementos collected by his ninety-eight year old spinster Aunt.

"You're talking about my Aunt Irene's life, and mine." He added, "You know my whole childhood is remembered here." He added sadly.

"Hey I'm sorry, it's just that..." Angela paused searching for delicate words.

"What's wrong?"

"Wrong?" Angie said sarcastically, "Hey nothing! I love spending my holidays indoors, especially beautiful Friday afternoon's. I particularly like killing time in cold dusty attics. God this place must have an insulation factor of a zillion." She glanced at the naked crossbeams noticing there was no insulation at all. "It's eighty degrees outside. I would think we'd be baking like potatoes up here. Why is this dammed place so cold?"

For a moment there was silence and she'd remembered her first impressions of Andre, her boyfriend of six-months now. The first time she'd seem him, a handsome slender man with a bright complexion and short cropped light brown bristly hair. She'd actually had enough nerve to ask him on their first date '...what he went by.' It had taken him a few seconds to realize she'd meant race. He'd smiled embarrassed but had not been offended. It seemed he was always smiling, so eager to try to please her, always willing to devote his time and money to her interests. Yet since their arrival at his newly acquired home, Angela had found Andre Sanders a Mister Hyde, sullen and moody. Not the way she'd behave had some Aunt she hadn't seen in ten years suddenly die, leaving money and a beautiful old Victorian home to her. It was like winning the lottery, but not for Andre. It was getting difficult to know what would set him off. As best as she could tell, they were surrounded by junk, worthless bazaar items collected by a lonely, possibly crazy old woman over a period of nearly a century.

'Why the act,' she thought to herself, 'it's me after all. If you cared at all you'd have been back to see her in ten years!'

"I remember some of this stuff." Andre said breaking Angela free from her thoughts. He'd returned to the large box he'd spent so long fawning over and picked up a small statue to examine. "Like this, Irene picked this up in South America." He placed it gently back into the box with a gesture of extreme reverence before straightening up again. "Over there, see that other statue on the shelf? It's from Africa."

Angela stifled a yarn as she simultaneously wrapped her arms around her stomach to silence it as well.

"There are several items from there around here somewhere." Andre continued. "These are all relics from my childhood. A lot of this stuff even predates Aunt Irene." The smile that spread across Andre's face was a sad one. "When I was a kid we'd spend hour's together going through this stuff. She'd tell me everything there was to know about each of her artifacts."

"Artifacts," Angela laughed harshly, "you make this shi... stuff sound like museum pieces."

"Some of them should be. I told you they're old." Andre continued to smile clearly lost in his past and continued speaking, almost to himself. "Irene was fond of traveling, meeting people and finding common ground. She was looking for her roots long before the novel, and an accomplished world traveler at a time when it wasn't common for a black single woman to be traveling on her own. She was always proud of the way she could fit in almost anywhere. Anywhere there were people of African descent that is."

"She must have had a lot of interesting stories." Angela said glancing down at her watch and wondering how she was going to snap him out of his reverie.

"It was all interesting, but I always knew she was holding a lot back. I could see it in her eyes whenever she was retelling her adventures. They'd gloss over kind of and then the story would abruptly end. I always had the feeling I was getting the kiddy version of the story.

As for Mom, well she never really saw eye to eye with her sister, and Dad couldn't stand her. I believe its because she was so independent. All he'd ever say was that he didn't like her putting a lot of heathenistic ideas into my head. You see Irene spent a lot of time researching ancient religious beliefs and practices.

Well, I always thought she was the greatest. She was the only adult who really had all the time in the world for me, after she'd settled down that is. She must have thought in retirement she'd have our family to be near to, but Mom and Dad had other ideas. So we moved out to California, and did I cry. I was almost eleven when we moved away. It just seemed so dammed unfair. She was more like a Grandmother than an Aunt to me. I swore I'd write her everyday. You know the promises that kids make and she said she'd come and visit. I did write daily, for that first week. Then I found friends and got into a routine within my new life. She came to visit a few times but as I said she and Dad never really got along. The last time I saw her was ten years ago. Well," Andre's smile faded completely, "you know the rest. Two weeks ago I got a letter from her attorney telling me she'd passed away and she'd left everything to me."

Angela spread her arms to encompass the room.

"Wow... everything! You must have felt like you won the lottery. I mean this is really a cool house. With this much property it's gotta be worth a good three or four hundred thousand at least." Angela looked up and across at Andre and her expression changed. She seemed almost giddy with delight, as if something tremendous had only just occurred to her. "But then there's the furnishings, my god, she never threw anything away did she? I'm no expert but my uncle is, and from hanging around him so much I'd swear you've got some really valuable pieces downstairs. What was I thinking?" She slapped her forehead with the palm of her hand. "We've gotta get him up to this place to see the stuff before you do anything." She said nearly breathless. "I swear other people have all the luck."

She grabbed Andre's elbow playfully but his expression sobered her immediately. It was clear he was seeing her in a new light.

"Well," he said sadly, "let's go." He moved past her and had almost disappeared down the stairway before her angry voice halted him.

"Listen, I've tried to be patient with you but enough's enough. What the hell is your problem?"

"Angie, I loved that old lady. You just don't understand. This stuff is meaningless compared to losing her. We had so much in common. She was really the only person I was ever been able to talk comfortably with and about anything."

"Oh really," Angela placed her hands upon her hips to highlight her indignation and was satisfied when he quickly closed the distance between them to hug her tightly.

"You're the best, you know that." He said softly before releasing her. "But Aunt Irene was one of a kind. She always seemed so wise and tried to give me so much, not material things, spiritual things. She tried to impart wisdom." He said laughing, "Talk about your archaic terms."

Andre looked down towards his feet and it became clear to Angela he really was hurting. She'd thought it only a respectful pretense till that point.

"It must have hurt her that I just seemed to forget about her." Andre's voice rippled faintly as he turned away, "I regret that. I should of come back to visit, I'd always meant to."

Though he had his back to her now, Angela could almost see the glassy quality that must have reflected in his eyes.

"She must have known you cared." She said soothingly as she struggled for her next words realizing how sadly unprepared she was whenever it came to giving emotional support. It was the one thing she could never bluff her way through, the one thing that never came easy. "Otherwise, she'd of left this stuff to some charity." At that he whined slightly almost under his breath, but in the quiet of that attic everything seemed unnaturally amplified. She forced herself to laugh as she continued talking, refusing to allow them to again fall into one of those uncomfortable silences, that always felt like an argument in itself, one with no winners. Worse, it felt like defeat, a feeling she hated. "The rest of the house is a treasure, but you've got to admit there's a lot of weird shit up in this attic. Okay maybe its not garbage."

"You only believe that because you don't know what you're looking at."

Somewhere along the line Andre's mood had changed. The self-recrimination and pain of only moments before now seemed to have melted into a kind of acceptance.

"Are you a religious person?" Andre asked abruptly.

For some reason Angela found the question startling and was silent.

"I mean, if you were in a church and saw crucifixes laying about everywhere, and statues of saints, would you consider them junk?"

"No, of course I wouldn't! Andre we've been together almost half a year. How could you ask me that? I go to church every

Sunday, you know that!"

"I didn't think you would." He said soothingly. "Don't you see? That's my point. It's the same here. Angie, you're surrounded by religious artifacts from dozens maybe hundreds of different tribes and cultures from all over the world. Your problem is you're too used to slapping a value on things, and if it has none it isn't important and doesn't matter. You can't see things for what they really are. But it's not always that way in other parts of the world and people worship as many different things as the mind can imagine and they're not all good."

"Is that the way you see this place, like some kind of shrine?"

"Okay, it's true that there are differences between your traditional church and this place. That much is obvious but Angie, the only difference that matters is that in ordinary churches you normally expect to find only good, normally, but in the world there isn't just good is there? It's composed of opposing forces. There's the good that nurtures, protects and if you're sensitive enough, advises. There are also those that mislead and attempt to destroy, evil. Both have to be respected and in this place it's the same."

"Andre that's crazy, they're not the same thing. No one should respect evil and I don't care what you say this place is far from being a church!"

"Good and evil are a package deal, Angie. You can't have one without the other. Respect them both enough to understand and recognize them, cause there'll be plenty of times when the line between the two will be pretty damn faint. That way you'll always know your path.

You're right that this isn't your traditional church. That much I've already admitted. But just because you don't see the glossy pews, expensive stained glass and gilded statues doesn't mean these items don't hold religious significance. You're allowing your eyes, no your prejudices, to blind you."

"Sounds like you're making your Aunt out to be some kind of Satan worshiper to me."

"No I'm not!" Andre shouted hotly and then took a deep breath before continuing. "You're making this harder than it has to be.

You know how you've always heard about the constant battle that exists between good and evil? Irene believed in it to the severity that you just don't see anymore. During her travels she became good friends with many different kinds of people and a trustee for the objects you see around you. Sometimes it was because the old ways of the tribes she visited were changing to the point were the dying elders no longer felt comfortable entrusting it to their 'modernized' children. Sometimes it was because the village had all but died out. I'm sure there were other reasons as well, but the end result was that Irene vowed to protect these sacred and yes, sometimes corrupt forces. Both hold religious significance for their faithful, tremendous power for those who believe and occasionally even for those who don't!"

"Oh please! You don't really believe that garbage do you?" She waited for an answer but none came. "The only thing I see for sure is that it's a good thing your family moved when they did. That nutty old lady was driving you nuts my friend!" Angie laughed harshly this time oblivious to his feelings. She could tell immediately that she'd pushed his anger farther than ever before, but as usual he held it in reserve. Only a slight twitching of Andre's jaw muscles and the glare in his eyes gave it away. Angela turned her back on him to walk towards a wooden crate in the rear of the attic. What had he expected?

Angela continued rummaging about as she tried to figure the best way to get him back on track towards lunch until she found something that amused her. She walked over and picked it up. It was an oddly shaped little thing, barely visible in a dark corner and placed upon old blackened rags. She looked across at Andre who now stood leaning heavily against the stairway banister, his arms folded across his chest, still clearly angry. Angela wondered briefly why he hadn't just left her up there.

"Like this," she picked up the odd little object that clearly appeared nothing more than old trash and glanced across at Andre amused, "so this is a religious object?" She mocked, but realized instantly he was refusing to meet her gaze. There was only that dreaded and depressing silence. "Looks like a dried up squash to me," she shook it gently, "that somebody used for some kinda container or something, and she left it laying on sooty, oily rags. Yeah, she was a great caretaker for the faithful. With all her money you'd think she'd upgraded it to plastic, maybe a wooden box or something." Angela laughed into the surrounding silence but her amusement wasn't shared. "What do you think is in it?" She asked finally shaking it hard and could feel something lightweight stirring inside. She glanced across at its new owner who instead seemed lost in thought. "Maybe it's booze." She said finally and her hollow laugh echoed about them as she pulled at its stopper."

Andre's eyes had been staring unseeingly at the row of shelves before him that was also covered with oddities but looked across at her distractedly.

"What?" He asked, returning his attention towards Angela, his eyes falling upon her hands and her actions. "Angie, don't do that?" He straightened up attempting to cross the distance separating them but not before she'd pried the top off clipping her nail in the process.

"Shit!" Angie brought her finger with its chipped nail up to her face to examine it closely. "I just got a thirty dollar manicure too. This has got to be the trip to hell." She tossed the odd little container back down into its crate and twisted her face into a grimace. "Awe, what the hell is that smell? Somebody found a way to bottle body gas." She laughed but Andre's expression sobered her. He was watching the fumes as it escaped the container and she noticed that it encircled her. She waved her arms impatiently attempting to disperse the stench before giving up and moving towards him. As the distance between them decreased, Andre's alarm became more pronounced.

"Oh come on, I don't smell that bad. Do I?"

She smiled at him, but his eyes were rooted behind her upon the container and amber colored fumes that escaped from it. As she turned towards it she noticed that it seemed to drift in irregular movements towards the stairwell to the second floor and after a few seconds it had disappeared completely.

"Shit." He said stomping his feet. "Shit, shit, SHIT!" He clenched is fist in anger shaking them furiously at her.

"Okay, what did I do now?" She asked irritated.

"That's why she wanted me to have this place." He shouted kicking the box at his feet hard and immediately seemed frightened by his action.

"Yeah, yeah, I know religious shrine and all." Angela rolled her eyes in impatience. She'd had enough of his mood swings, angry silences and deranged beliefs. What was supposed to be a fun filled trip alone for just the two of them had turned sour. It started off bad and got worse the moment they stepped over the threshold of that shadowy old Victorian nightmare. At first the exploration thing had been exciting, poking about the place, but they'd moved well past that during the last hour or so. Now Angela found herself bored with the whole thing.

'He's always so levelheaded.' She mused. 'Is this what happens when he's under pressure? He's completely lost it, mentally morphing between Jekyll and Hyde. I can deal with one or the other, but not both.'

Angela smiled realizing she was fighting an impulse to toss the surrounding shit right out the front attic window artifacts or not, but Andre was the sentimental type. That had always been one of his endearing charms but at that particular moment it was also a weakness. She was certain that was what fueled his depression, and in his present mood his actions might be unpredictable.

Distracted Angela wiped her hands onto her new knit sweater and a dust streak stood out upon the light beige fabric like ink on a page. She made a disgusted sound.

"Angie, there were things that she'd told me, things she expected me to do and not to do when she died. Things she never told another living soul. She'd prepared me for this day over a decade ago. Back then Aunt Irene and I, well, we seemed connected somehow. Shit! Why couldn't I have seen that from the start?"

"What the hell are you talking about?"

"Don't get me wrong," he said ignoring her, "as I said there were things she kept from me, but I think she told me enough to keep me safe. She always said her diaries would explain the rest."

Andre exhaled loudly bringing both hands up to the sides of his head, as if he were attempting to keep it from exploding. "Just stay calm." He told himself before again looking towards Angela.

"None of this is your fault Angie, it's mine. I should have remembered. In fact its all my fault! I should never have brought you here. I clearly remember her telling me not to *ever* open the marked bottles."

"Marked bottles? Hell, don't look at me! I haven't touched or even seen any marked bottles."

"Oh yeah," Andre pointed his finger at her, waving it irritably, "go back over there and turn that damn thing over." But Angela remained rooted staring at him in disbelief. "Go!"

The threatening undertone of his voice urged Angela's tentative steps, causing her to turn and watch her back as she went and the lunatic behind her.

"Well!" Andre asked impatiently and came to stand at her side, "are there words on it?" He waited for a response and Angela could feel his glaring eyes upon her. "Read it, out loud." He whispered coldly.

Angela looked down at the bottle swallowing hard her own anger but upon closer examination of the container had instead burst into spontaneous laughter.

"Evil Contents," she looked at Andre as she continued to laugh, "it says *Evil Contents*!" She continued laughing until the severity of Andre's expression quieted her. "Awe Andre, hon you don't actually believe any of this? It's just the delusions of a crazy old woman. Either that or some kind of joke with the punch line called on account of death."

"She never thought so. Aunt Irene believed there was a lot up here that could harm." He fell silent. For several moments a look of misery and disappointment reflected upon his face.

"You just don't get it do you?" He said finally. "You have no idea what you've done."

As Andre continued to stare past her his eyes glazed over.

Angela suspected whatever misery he was feeling was more self directed than at her.

"She was the guardian and entrusted the responsibility to me when she died. I failed her."

A light suddenly came on in Andre's eyes and he snapped into action.

"I have to find her journals. She'll have everything in them I need to put this thing right again. Instructions, on how to communicate, drive them out, or recapture them!"

When his eyes locked again upon Angela's face he clearly saw fear reflected there and added. "That's what she did Angela, it's what interested her, religion and beliefs of African descended cultures. In her travels Aunt Irene saw a lot of things, things that really scared her. She watched secret ceremonies, rituals that aren't even remembered anymore, and definitely not done for the tourist community."

"Andre you're really scaring me, and how good could she have been? Clearly she wasn't objective enough to know all that's just a lot of..."

In the quiet of the house the sound of the attic door slamming at the base of the steps caused both startle, momentarily freezing Angela words in her throat.

"What's that?" Angela whispered, instinctively moving towards him.

"Start looking for the diaries." Andre whispered.

"Andre stop it, we've got company down there." She whispered. "We have to get to a phone and call the police. They know the old lady's dead. They probably think the place is empty. They're here to rob you." Realizing he wasn't listening Angela punched his shoulder with her fist.

"Andre I said get a grip, they could kill us!"

"It could be worse than that Angie, much worse!" He yelled turning to search shelves and boxes, no longer concerned with the level of noise he made.

"Will you be quiet they'll hear you!"

"Who the hell cares? They already know where're up here.

You let them out, remember?"

"Andre ghouls don't frighten me. Only the physical and that's what we've got down there. Please don't loose it on me now. I need you."

Andre continued searching ignoring her, engrossed in his obsession to find the journal. Crashing sounds from downstairs caused both to look at each other simultaneously.

"Don't just stand there like an ass," Andre said sharply, "help me!" This time the look on his face clearly told of his fear.

"Later, I'm outta here!" Angela said with resolve moving quietly towards the stairs leading to the second floor.

"I'm not leaving this attic, not without the journal." He told her flatly but Angela was unaffected by his words.

"Angela it would be suicide to face them without it. We'd never be able to defeat them and we're safer together."

"Right," Angela's voice dripped with sarcasm, "even if we were married I wouldn't abide by that 'till death do you part' shit."

She'd taken her first step down the attic steps when the door at the bottom began to creak slowly open rooting her in place. Angela glanced back over her shoulder at Andre who was now throwing items about insanely. She returned her gaze towards the stairway about to make a break for the door only to find the amber colored energy she'd let loose only minutes earlier, heading back up towards her. She eased back up the step.

"Andre…" Angela turned running back towards Andre who grabbed her tightly as it rapidly followed to encircle them.

For Angela every hair on her body stood on end as the mist encircled them. Objects began to fly about as they continued to hold each other tightly. Some objects crashed towards the attic floor to reveal similar entities that escaped to mingle upwards and join its larger host. Others levitated around them remaining unbroken. Those that were freed, moved in an irregular lumpy fashion and at times seemed to form face-like images within its mist.

Andre shook Angela hard, forcing her attention again upon him.

"Look around for the journal!" He shouted amidst the shattering noise.

Angela gazed at him in disbelief. When the impact of his words fully hit her she wrenched herself free to run for the stairs. As she did so, the entities divided. Half following her down the stairwell, those remaining hovered about Andre, rotating about him in an ever decreasing circle.

Andre realized he was trapped just as from somewhere below came a long frightening scream.

The entities were nearly upon Andre, attacking from all sides when his eyes were forced shut. From some distant horizon he could hear the whisper of a soundless yet familiar voice echoing within his mind.

Child, remember what I taught you. You know what to do. I trust you to do what's right. Don't give them a means to enter and hold on to you. Remember, no fear and no anger.

It was Irene's voice and he could feel her influence upon him keeping his eyes closed, but at the same time he also knew that was the extent of the influence she would use upon him. It was up to him to remain calm, concentrate and listen to her words. With her silent voice she'd echoed conversations he remembered from over a decade earlier and realized that he had to keep his emotions under control. When he opened them again it was to the realization that the energy now appeared less concentrated then before and was moving away.

You have your own power, use that against them. It's the only way to block their entrance into you. If you're angry or afraid, it's a clear channel for them to ride right into you. They'll rap themselves around your soul until they strangle it. Andre you must keep your mind and energies focused, on their insignificance and lack of power over you.

Andre realized they were looking elsewhere for an easier victim and headed back downstairs to vanish as quickly as steam.

Everything around him fell silent, and Irene was gone. For a second he stood there in indecision realizing he was helpless to fight against the entities without further instruction from Irene's diaries, but his heart pushed him into action and towards the unknown, where he knew Angela was helpless.

Andre moved down the stairwell cautiously until he reached the second floor. He paused in the quiet of the upstairs hallway before moving towards the first of the five bedrooms on that floor, but found nothing. Upon entering each of the remaining rooms within the old Victorian he received similar results. Only the signs of shattered bric-a-brac and furnishings betrayed their presence.

Andre continued moving down the stairway towards the main floor.

From the kitchen came the sounds of pots and dishes. As Andre stood in the doorway it was to find the kitchen in shambles, the refrigerator door stood open upon a single hinge with nearly all of its contents spread out upon the kitchen table. There Angie sat unceremoniously shoving food into her mouth and occasionally, missing the mark to smear it all around her face.

"You keep eating like that and you'll kill yourself?" Andre said quietly, but she'd only stared at him with eyes that seem to twinkle with amusement as she continued to eat. Her eyes settled upon a pie nearly three quarters whole and she picked it up to shove it systematically into her mouth. Then something from a white container whose lid she ripped off to send flying against the back kitchen wall. Its contents no longer recognizable, but its current state of evolution had turned it a grotesque hairy blue-green.

"Don't eat that!" He shouted.

'To late,' he told himself as he fought off a wave of nausea.

"Stop that!" He told her angrily then added more softly, "Please."

For a moment she seemed satisfied as she rested sticky fingers upon the table to examine him closely. At the same time Andre realized he wasn't looking into the eyes of his girlfriend.

"If you behave yourself," Andre said taking in a deep breath at the same time struggling with his fears, "I may let you stay in that body a while longer." At that Andre watched as a confident smile spread across her face.

"You have no power over us as we have none over you." Angela's face grinned at him, "In this body you cannot harm us, but we can do much harm." She lifted three of her fingers to her mouth and Andre waited for her to finish licking them when to his horror she instead bit down hard upon them. There was a sickening sound of bones snapping within the quiet of the kitchen.

Andre raced across the kitchen grabbing Angela by the arms, attempting to restrain her from further cannibalizing herself. When she removed her hand, it was minus three fingers which she continued to chew. Blood flowed gruesomely down her chin and from the freshly amputated joints down her palm and arm, which she watched with amusement as she continued to enjoy her grotesque meal. He looked around in panic for a way to stop the bleeding as she continued chewing and crackling sickeningly upon her own bones. Instantly Andre came to the realization it only awaited swallowing before it took a fresh mouthful. At the same time something in her eyes told him it was best to release her.

"Stop this right now!" He shook her gently before releasing her. As expected his words had little impact. Yet he had to say something. "You're right you can't hurt me, but what you fail to realize is that if you kill her there will be no one left here for you to hurt, inhabit or feed upon."

"Not within this place," she said finally swallowing, "but there are other places like this one. We saw them from our prison, and other people walk outside these boarders. Many from which we can feed." She said eyeing the remaining two fingers of her right hand as she moved them towards her mouth."

"Yes," Andre said hastily putting his hand out to recapture her attention, "there are millions of people outside this house but can you reach them? I think not. Irene placed a spell upon this place. Once you've crossed the boundaries of his house, you will be destroyed by that spell." With satisfaction he noticed it slowly dropped the mutilated hand which was bleeding profusely.

"This mind knows nothing of your spell."

"That mind knows nothing of spirits, yet you exist. Her ignorance is the reason you were freed.

As it spoke, Andre had been distractedly watching the pool of blood accumulating on the kitchen table from her hand. It was covering nearly a quarter of the small table.

"If you don't take care of that body it will die. Then you'll find yourself still contained in a prison that's only slightly larger than before.

"Then it makes no difference."

Again he watched it bring the hand up to its mouth.

"Don't be foolish. You can experience everything you once did," and then he stressed, "in that body. Is that worth throwing away?" He could see that it was deliberating upon his words. Even before it reached its conclusion Andre knew he had won, at least the skirmish. That would give him time to look for the diaries and perhaps to remember more of Irene's words about re-containing spirits.

"Yes," she said finally bridging the silence, "we enjoy eating and it has been so very long."

"I will make sure you have as much food as you can eat, as long as you don't cannibalize the body you're currently in."

At that it smiled again, and inwardly Andre cursed himself for revealing that it had a means by which to hold him.

"Agreed," she said cheerfully.

"I have to leave to get you the food that you cannot get for yourselves. While I'm gone," he pointed towards her hand resting upon the table, "you will stop the bleeding from those," Andre pointed towards her hand, "and no more harm to that body!"

Andre stood framed within the closed front doorway of the beautiful Victorian. He looked down at his hands which were shaking with the memory of what was inside the house at his back but Angela was depending upon him. They'd passed together through that very doorway only the day before. Under other circumstances, the recalling of those memories would have been bitter sweet. Now both their memories would forever be scarred with the horrible image of the thing squatting even now within Angie's body. For all he knew it could have been making her chew her own arm off even as he stood there.

With ambivalence to his surroundings Andre moved down the front steps of the property and the concrete walkway. He moved past the manicured lawn, with its roses, lilacs and daffodils. Above him the sun shown from a nearly cloudless sky that threw long shadows across the lawn as he crossed the driveway. But Andre saw none of that as he moved forward on route towards the garage, indifferent. Instead, he wondered what it must feel like to be trapped within ones own body. Forces alien to you, entities that have been dead for years, possibly centuries. Monsters he was powerless against, but there had to be a way to beat them. He thought briefly about calling the police or ambulance, maybe modern medicine could rid her of those demons if he found his own abilities insufficient. Though deep within he realized that would be a fatal error. It would condemn Angie to a lifetime of possession and institutional restraint at best. At worst it would free the demons to kill her since he would have delivered fresh new victims for them to savor.

Inside the garage, and without much thought, Andre took the keys from his pocket and unlocked the door of his Aunts '73 Ford Brougham. It started instantly and as he backed down the driveway, his eye momentarily diverted to the house's front bay window. There he could see Angela's face staring at him with a fixed smile before bringing up the severed hand to wave good-bye. Its meaning had not fallen deafly upon him. He only hoped that it wouldn't call his bluff on the fabrication of the spell, he might then loose Angie forever. Perhaps Irene's attorney Ellerson Wier could provide the some answers.

Andre pulled up before the attorney's address to find a modern three story structure of white marble and glass, totally at odds with its surrounding depression architecture taking up nearly half the block.   Before it was a small plaza containing a low rectangular fountain shooting alternating jets of water into the air and displaying a dark brass plate with shiny gold letters with the moniker Ellerson Wier Law Offices.

"As a matter of fact I do have some of your Aunt's personal effects. I apologize for not getting them to you earlier. I'd planned to bring them over this afternoon."

Ellerson Wier shook his head in self-recrimination. He was a tall slender man, soft spoken, with silver hair, a kind face and sharp piercing hazel eyes. From their brief conversation Andre had learned that Wier had known Irene for almost two decades. No wonder she'd trusted him with her most treasured possession.

Andre watched the elderly man as he rose gracefully from his desk to stride toward the west side of his lavish office. He stopped before one of the two closed doors on the West wall.

"Please excuse me for a moment."

Andre nodded mutely and watched the man leave the room. When he returned he carried a large envelope.

"This belongs to you now." Wier said handing him the sealed envelope.

Andre hastily tore at the paper and a large black leather bound book slid out.

"Is this the only one?" Andre asked still looking at the book.

"Actually no," the old gentleman sounded apologetic but determined, "however Irene was specific about not giving them all to you at once. She specified at least two weeks apart. To tell you the truth I think she probably thought you'd throw them away or something. As you're probably aware, they were important to her."

"Yes, and to me. More important than you can know." Andre rose praying that what he was looking for would be within the pages of that first diary. In any case, he'd have to make do with what he had.

He'd taken several steps towards the door but then turned in afterthought to again face the aged attorney. "If you find anything else, could you give me a call before stopping by? Perhaps in a few days though, I'm still trying to get things in order."

"I understand." Wier said sympathetically.

"Also, is there possibly some place quiet where I can look at it here?" Andre asked. "Some place where I won't be in the way?"

Wier gave him a quizzical look but responded nearly immediately.

"Certainly, you can use the conference room, right this way."

After the door had shut, Andre was sealed in isolation with the last important vestige of his Aunts personality. He shook his head forcing himself to concentrate and remember that Angela needed him. As he read the pages, it was clear that she had been writing for him alone, as if the last ten years that separated them had never happened. Her voice, tone and inflection seemed to leap up at him from every page and again Andre felt nearly overwhelmed by her loss. A half-hour later, he closed the book to reflect.

Andre stood and walked over to the conference room window to gaze out for several minutes. The only thing to be seen had been grass, trees and more trees, the one thing the town had plenty of. Andre momentarily wondered how Wier could afford such a luxurious office with such a small town practice before his mind returned to his more pressing problem. He learned that while it would be possible to force the spirits out of Angela, the danger to her would be severe without their cooperation. Worse, recapturing them would be nearly impossible. He slammed his fist down upon the window's wide ledge were it struck the cool metal base of a small table lamp placed near to a telephone. For several minutes he simply looked down the lampshade, gazing at the unlit bulb before a smile lit his face.

Andre exited he conference room to find the aged attorney hunched over legal papers.

"Mr. Wier, thank you, for dispensing your obligations to my Aunt with efficiency and kindness. I'd like to express my gratitude." Andre said reaching out and shaking the man's hand. "I do have another favor to ask though."

"Certainly Mr. Sanders, if I can."

"Would you continue to hold this with the other volumes in

trust for me as well?" Andre said returning the leather bound volume to the attorney.

"Of course, however, there are some papers that I'll need for you to sign."

"That will be fine. Can we handle it in a few days?"

"I understand."

"Thank you."

They shook hands again briefly.

As Andre left the attorneys office he was a great deal more confident than he'd arrived.

"I brought this for you." Andre carried the box over to the table sitting it down before the image of Angela.

"What is it?" She asked in veiled suspicion before an internal memory registered causing her to smile. "We know. It is pizza!" She tore open the box and it was then that Andre noticed that her right hand no longer bled.

"What the hell have you done?" Andre screamed.

"What you asked of us." She replied mildly, picking up the pizza with her remaining fingers. "It no longer bleeds."

Andre let out a disgusted gasp as he gazed upon the badly blistered hand, in addition to its other problems, but again realized there was nothing he could do about it.

"Was that the best you could do?" He said pointing towards her fingers.

"It was all the time it deserved." She replied between mouthfuls.

"I find your company sickening."

"That is something neither of us can change."

"That may not be true." He said confidently.

At that it stopped momentarily and began chewing more slowly eyeing him cautiously.

"I've discovered a way for you to leave this house, unharmed."

For a moment it stopped chewing and then swallowed hard.

"Why would you wish to help us?" She said giving him her complete attention.

"I already told you why, because I find your company... unpleasant."

"How?"

"We can discuss it later."

"Not later!" She said slamming her injured hand down upon the table. "NOW!"

"All right, fine." Andre said soothingly. "Come in here." He walked back towards the dining room and then into the living area and turned to find her in close pursuit behind him, again her eyes held suspicion.

"We have been inside this place. It avails us nothing."

"Look at this." Andre walked over to the television and turned it on, shortly images began flickering across its screen.

"It is TV, this mind has memories of it."

"I believe that you have the ability to ride the same current that powers this set. It should be able to take you past the protection placed on this house, unharmed and to freedom."

"You lie." She said confidently, and then seemed less sure. "How do we know that you do not lie?"

"Why not read Andrea's memories? You've been doing a good job of it up until now. Perhaps she can better explain it to you but essentially you are nothing more than energy. So like current you can travel through the wires within the walls making it possible for you to escape from this place. The wiring will mask your escape. You'll be free of it, and I'll be free of you."

"What of this body, of the others outside this place; you no longer care for them?"

"She's a friend, and once you leave her she'll be fine. As for the people outside these walls, why should I care about them? I don't even know them." Satisfied she began to laugh.

"How will we proceed?"

"This way," Andre walked over towards the wall were the outlet covering had already been removed, "this is the gateway outside these walls."

Again she eyed him with suspicion before replying.

"We will leave this body, one at a time. If there is deception the remainder will kill this body."

"That's, fair." Andre said forcing a smile.

Several small bursts of energies exited Angela's body, and each time they did she seemed momentarily pained. It had continued that way several more times before finally she looked again into Andre's eyes, and he knew it still wasn't Angela that stared back at him. "I sense nothing from the others. No word that they are free. There is deception."

Andre gazed back at her undisturbed. "Or perhaps they're so happy to be free they've forgotten to look back. Well, you can stay within that bruised body if you want, while the others frolic about happily. I wonder how much they really care about what happens to you."

For a second there was indecision upon her face before another burst of energy escaped. Angela fell onto the floor. When she opened her eyes they were wild, confused and frightened and when she looked at her hand she had begun to scream.

Andre moved towards her to fall to the floor in front of her, grabbing her struggling body and forced her tightly to him. With one arm he grabbed her waist and the other he forced her head down upon his shoulder keeping her injured hand between them and out of her sight. Her agonizing screams tore at his heart. With the absence of her possessors, Andre knew that her pain surfaced, apparently in waves as she thrashed about wildly.

"Everything's gonna be all right. The worst is over now."

"What did," Angie clenched her teeth between tears and sobs, "what did you do with them?"

"I re-trapped them."

"Then you found it?"

"The book, yes I found it."

"But how did you..."

Andre pointed upward before she could finish, toward the overhead light bulb. Angela gazed upward only just becoming aware that it now glowed amber.

"Like I said, I found the book." He said looking upwards at them and smiling. "How you doing up there guys? They can enter it," he said still eyeing the bulb, "but they can't exit it. Kinda like a roach motel.

There really was such a thing as a protection spell. It wouldn't work on something as big as a house, but it works just fine on little things like that squash container, and light bulbs. All I had to do was get them to willingly exit your body. The spell did the rest. It just pulled them in as soon as they exited."

"But, that stuff about traveling through the wires?"

"That was just nonsense." He pulled away slightly, eyeing her with affection. "I knew you wouldn't know any better, in fact I counted on it and I needed them to feel confident, protected."

At that she'd laughed again placing her head against his shoulder. "I feel very grateful, and stupid."

Andre looked back down at her, "Well the important thing is that you're safe now. Everything is alright, unless someone from the outside frees them."

"Or until the bulb breaks."

"Yeah, that would be a problem." He said smiling as he helped her gently to her feet.

"Andre that bulb's awfully small, and there are a lot of them in there. A bulb is inherently fragile, are you sure that thing'll hold?"

"Sure, until I can come up with a better solution." Then his smile faded, but he continued to hold her tightly. "Come on, let's get you to a doctor."

"Like hell! You're gonna come up with that 'better solution' now, before I'll leave this place!" Another pained expression crossed Angela's face and she grabbed Andre for support.

"No, I'm getting you to a doctor, even if I have to carry you."

"It's not that! I can deal with the pain and thanks to you it's no longer life threatening, not anymore.

Andre I'm sorry, I was such a stupid fool. I nearly got you killed. I nearly got us both killed. You should have left me, that's what I was going to do to you."

Angela dropped her face down again upon his shoulder nearly

muffling her words. "When I saw you leaving, driving away, it seemed like justice but you came back."

"None of that matters now. Everything's back right again with the world and I swear that for as long as I live, they'll never escape to harm you or anyone again."

"I know that stupid." Angela said smiling at him and had looked up at the small bulb and at her tormentors of only a few minutes earlier, and her eyes hardened. When she again looked down into Andre's eyes it had seemed a different Angela than the one that had driven down with him, causing him to wonder if it was really her. He pulled away involuntarily knowing that she had seen the fear in his eyes.

"Don't worry, it's me. No they'll never escape again, not with us here cause two guards are better than one."

"No!" Andre shook his head with finality. "I'll never allow you to stay here, not ever again Angela. This was entirely my fault. You should hate me for what's happened to you. I was the one charged to take her place, to look after things. She tried to teach me, to explain to me, all those years ago." Andre hung his head and added more softly, "I let her down, and I let you down. Angela I'm sorry. I'll never put you in danger again."

She pulled away slightly, crying softly, her head also downcast but suddenly chuckled. "Andre I've experienced first hand," she said bring her injuries again into view, "what it means to have them free. I'm not leaving here. I swear from now on I'll be the best guard you've ever seen."

"Best guardian," Andre said correcting her as he hugged her again, "times two."

To Hell in a Hand Basket

Jordan walked over to hand his friend a cup of coffee before returning to the sofa, which sat in the center of his small studio apartment. For a moment he allowed his eyes to become distracted towards the window where large snowflakes were accumulating on the sill. Ten floors up Jordan couldn't see the ground, but judging from the accumulation he was grateful he had no where to go.

"There's no such thing as good, maybe there was once," he said softly returning his attention to his friend Grant. "Now good is just an obsolete, meaningless word that no longer has a basis in reality."

"Ah you think too much. Okay, then there's no such thing as evil." Grant offered as he set his cup down on the small end table beside his chair. "Where there's one, there's the other. The universe maintains its own balance of both positive and negative forces."

Jordan laughed at that, shaking his head as if he pitied his friend's naiveté. "You give new meaning to the term head in the sand." Jordan said amazed. "Don't you watch TV, read the papers? Just stand out on the streets for five or ten minutes. Hell is all around you! I mean, how could you not see the evil that exists, it saturates our world?" Jordan said as he looked down intently into the oblivion of his coffee, holding it between his two palms and moving it back and forth in alternating fashion. "Grant it's sweeping over us all in gigantic suffocating waves and threatens to drown all good and decent people, and there aren't many of us left."

For several minutes the room was uncomfortably silent as Grant watched his old school buddy staring down into his cup, as if conjuring images that reflected a catastrophic future. He'd heard rumors that his friend was poised on the edge of insanity but had never believed them. Jordan had always been too smart, too level headed for that to ever happen. The friend he'd always been

71

envious of. Grant decided finally it was time to see for him self.

It had been years since he'd seen Jordan, the old college buddy he'd known since grade school. Now it was like watching a stranger and a fanatical one at that. Dirty and unshaven with dark circles under his eyes, it seemed to Grant's mind fate had indeed been cruel to take his old friends sanity just as Dr. Jordan Rico had accomplished nearly every college goal he'd set for himself. He hoped it wasn't too late to pull his friend back from insanity's edge.

"This is quite a down size from your place at The Plaza," Grant said abruptly into the vacuous silence, "when did you move?"

"About six months ago." Jordan said blankly. "It fits my needs and more importantly, there are at least some good people here."

"Most places have good people Jordan," Grant said off-handedly. "In fact most people are good and I'll bet there were even a few good people at The Plaza."

"That's not true." Jordan said finally, still nursing his cup. "That place was just a Mecca for evil. Besides you make it sound so easy. As if there were only the two states of good and evil, like it's either black or white."

"I wouldn't think it would be." Grant said evenly. "Nothing is ever just black or white. People are people. They come in all varieties, good to bad flavored and all degrees in between."

"No! Jordan said impatiently reaching for his coffee, which in the absence of a nearby end table sat on the floor at his feet. His irritated shaky gestures sent the fluid spilling around the cup onto gray carpeting. "Don't you see? What I'm talking about here is true evil! Grant not everyone you see is a normal person. Some are so evil they've transformed into bona fide demons encased in human flesh and some are agents for those demons, though they may not know it. In either case they're not always as easy to see as you might think. Because they hide and stalk you from those in between gray areas," he said taking a gulp and putting the cup back down within the spot he'd created on the carpet, "but first they infuse you with fear."

Jordan waited for some hint of understanding from his friend but none came. "You still don't see, do you? Fear is evil, stage one. It paralyzes you to the point that you become too frightened to act and stage two is when you've become so jaded by what you see everyday that you stop recognizing and fighting against it at all."

"Jordan you've been working too hard." Grant said laughing. He'd hoped to lighten his friend's fanatical mood, without luck.

"I haven't been working at all." Jordan offered. "Not for about six months or so."

"I'm sorry to hear that." Grant said uncomfortably, "Cutbacks?"

"No. I resigned. There was nothing else for me to do."

"Resigned?" Grant exhaled whistling slowly. "Well, it must have been a hell of a reason for you to leave that good cushy hospital job of yours."

"Everywhere I went there were minions."

"Minions, what the hell does that mean?"

"Just what I said," Jordan said adding angrily, "and I refuse to be a part of the devil's army. I can't see why people have such a hard time understanding that!"

"Okay, okay, take it easy." Grant offered quickly throwing up his hands to placate his friend. "I understand, just calm down okay?"

"Yeah right," Jordan said sadly slumping down within his chair. "There just aren't any soldiers for good anymore."

"And that's why you moved from The Plaza?" Grant asked into the silence that followed but noticed Jordan now seemed lost, possibly in a sea of fears and phobias.

"I tell you its good that's on the decline!" Jordan shouted abruptly startling Grant before falling momentarily silent again. When he continued it was in a calmer, more reasonable tone. "Actually, I have doubts whether it exists at all any more. I mean, if good did still exist it would be able to recognize evil. Just as I can.

Now take Okrin. He's a preacher at the church down the street. Takes all the good offerings from his parishioners, clothes and whatever that's supposedly destine for the poor. You know what, he sells it at the flea market down in Danielsville to line his own pocket. I've seen him do it plenty of times. Now if he's the best good has to offer, a man of God and such, then that must prove my point."

"Even if that's true, it doesn't mean that good doesn't exist."

"Oh you still don't believe," Jordan settled back into his chair and the timber of his voice seemed to drop several octaves as if he were about to confess something truly ominous. "Okay."

From the straight chair opposite his friend, for the most part Grant had sat silently listening. Now as he watched his friend muse on the point of good and evil, he sat steeped in an internal debate of his own and wondered if he should voice his own thoughts.

He looked back across at Jordan to find him watching his hands intently. Grant had unconsciously sat clinching the arms of his chair. He forced himself to relax and released them in favor of retrieving his coffee cup.

He and Jordan had been good friends and college buddies for a long time but that had been a different Jordan, certainly not the fanatic who now sat before him. He wondered briefly what had happened in the past year since they had seen each other.

"Then take Jonathan for another." Jordan said suddenly. "He's the premier of evil, a demon of the highest rank."

"The kid," Grant asked astonished, "the one you only just introduced me to on the steps when I came in?"

"The same," Jordan said calmly.

There was silence for several seconds as Grant waited for more, but none came.

"Man," Grant moved uncomfortably in his chair, "you're way out there, you know? You in some cult or something or are you just loosing it all on your own?"

"I'm as serious as Hell! He's an archangel of evil. Oh, I know he goes to church on Sundays, sings in the choir and takes food to the elderly but that's all an act, I swear. Like the devil his real abilities lie in misdirection, he's a powerful and dangerous evil."

"You're crazy. You're on the dust, right? Well if you are, then give it up. If not, maybe you should start." Grant said laughing before taking a large gulp from his cup. The coffee was strong, hot and black making him grimace. "Shit! Don't you have any cream and sugar around this place?" He stood and casually walked over to the small island that separated the kitchen from the rest of Jordan's small studio apartment hoping it would effectively end the current topic.

"I'm not crazy Grant."

Grant turned to gaze at his friend who now appeared to be staring blankly before him.

"In fact," Jordan continued, "there are times when I think I'm the only one who's not. I'm the only one who can see things clearly around here." At that Jordan seemed to snap back to himself and looked away uncomfortably, "Always have." He said giving Grant a weary smile. "Remember Blake? Wasn't I the one who told you about him long before the rest of the campus found out he was that man in the ski mask?"

"Okay, you lucked up on that one." Grant said as he opened Jordan's refrigerator to find it nearly empty, save for a few crackers and a package of salami, with only two or three slices remaining. His friend must be nearly starving, judging by his appearance and the refrigerator's contents. He closed the door and returned to his chair with his cup.

"It has nothing to do with luck Grant. It's a gift. I've always had it. It's just that…" Jordan stopped and there was silence.

As Grant looked at his friend he could see the turmoil churning deep within, when Jordan suddenly flung his cup towards the far white wall of the small apartment. It shattered sending ribbons of brown liquid cascading down, startling Grant. "Man you really are crazy!"

"No!" Jordan glared. "I tell you Grant I'm not. I'm the only one who's not." Jordan looked down at his now empty hands and his expression melted into embarrassment. "I'm sorry. Guess I'm a little on edge. I'm trying to be strong, to do what's right but I have a feeling this thing's about to come to a dangerous head."

Jordan got up to walk over to the wall, picking up several of the large fragments of the cup. Its dark liquid already absorbed by the carpet.

"I've always been able to see evil clearly. Why can't everyone else? Ever since I can remember, and I've always tried to fight it. It's what I was taught to do since my earliest memories of Sunday school. But it's easier to be brave when you're a child, with parents to run to. But now I'm an adult with adult fears, and I find myself cowering and backing away when I encounter it. I've got to be stronger. I've got to fight back!"

"Jordan calm down."

Jordan straightened up and approached his friend with two of the jagged cup fragments. "Grant, don't you see? Acceptance of it without fighting makes me the same. It makes me evil!" He said looking at Grant with eyes that pleaded.

"Take it easy." Grant warned. His eyes remaining fixed on the cup shards in Jordan's hand.

"The only thing I haven't figured out," Jordan said continuing as he returned to his chair, "is whether he's trying to fool us or himself."

"You're still talking about that kid, right? Jordan how evil can he be? He can't be more than fourteen, right? You said yourself he sings in the church choir. I just can't picture a devil doing that."

"I never said he was the devil but he is a demon. Grant, I told you, evil is about misdirection, it takes many forms," Jordan said calmly, "and it's ageless."

Grant realized he'd heard enough. He'd found out what he needed to and they were right about Jordan. "Yeah well look," Grant said standing suddenly and walking over to place his coffee cup on the island farthest from his friend, "I've got to go."

Jordan relaxed his head back onto his chair and exhaled loudly and began to stare up at the ceiling blankly. "Well," he said finally, "I guess that's typical."

"What is?"

"I've been putting my ass on the line trying to protect yours and everyone else's around here, but okay think whatever you want.

76

Someday, I'll force the truth."

There was a knock at the door and Jordan rose to answer it, passing his friend who now stood silently at the kitchen island. Jordan opened the door to find a boy on the other side. He looked up at him with large angelic eyes.

For a moment it seemed Jordan had been too startled to speak.

"Jon, good to see you again," Grant said from behind Jordan. He smiled broadly expecting Jordan to back away from the subject now, "we were just talking about you."

"We sure were." Jordan said confidently. "I was just telling my naive friend here that you are the personification of evil. In lamb's wool of course, right Grant?"

Jonathan turned toward Grant smiling, and watched the smile dim on Jordan's friends face.

"I'm the devil's hired gun all right." The boy said laughing. "Grant, you gotta tell me why you hang around with this loon?"

"It passes the time." Grant replied with a dry smile.

Jon laughed. "Right."

"Well, I've got to go." Grant said quickly moving to past Jordan through the door that Jonathan still stood framed in, and as he moved towards it, Jordan couldn't help noticing that Grant had given him a wide birth nearly knocking over his small thriving palm that was nearer to the door.

"Before you go," Jordan said over his shoulder, his eyes still fixed upon the boy, "I'd like for you to witness this." He drew back quickly to hurl his fist into the face of the boy who sailed back into the hallway nearly falling over the banister behind him."

"You are crazy!" Grant angrily grabbed his friend to throw him back into the apartment and onto the floor. "Stop it now or I'll beat your ass my self." He said standing over him between him and the teenager.

Disappointed, Jordan rose to casually walk back over to his chair reseating himself.

When he was satisfied that Jordan would remain seated Grant turned to look down at the boy noticing that blood now flowed freely from his nose. "You okay?"

"Yeah," he said a pained expression on his face that seemed to come as much from hurt feelings as from bruises.

"Listen, this has gone too far." Grant said turning to his friend and pointing threateningly at him, "Man you are crazy!" He went over to the phone on the small kitchen island and began dialing. "I'm calling the cops."

A youthful hand reached around him to depress the switch hook terminating the connection.

"It's no big deal, I'm fine." Jonathan told him before turning back to Jordan. "Mom sent me down to find out if you wanted anything from the store, she's waiting down in the car."

Jordan sat there for only a second his expression unreadable before his face seemed to light. "Yeah," He said suddenly remembering, "would you bring me back some eggs? I think a dozen." He reached into the pocket of his jeans as if nothing had happened.

"Good Lord the man's nuts!" Grant said glancing at the boy uncomfortably who glanced back with mischievous eyes.

"The whole building thinks so." The boy said smiling to reveal bloody teeth. "Me, I just think he takes life a little too seriously."

"Bring me some milk too." Jordan handed the boy five dollars. "You can keep the change."

Jon took the money and began backing up towards the still open doorway, his eyes never leaving Jordan's face. When he'd crossed the threshold he'd simply smiled again, nodded and ran down the hallway.

"I've seen and heard a lot of strange things, but man you really are certifiable. Jordan, you need help. You know that don't you? Now I suggest you get it before you really end up hurting somebody."

Jordan had only smiled back easily at his friend.

"Grant, we haven't seen each other in months. Let's find a more pleasant topic. Who knows, neither of us might be around for too long."

"That's it!" Grant said throwing up his hands in impatience. "I'm outta here, all this talk about good and evil. Man you're the only evil that's walking this neighborhood."

"That's not true."

At that Grant noticed that his friends feelings seemed genuinely hurt.

"The fact is there's no one with a purer heart than mine." Jordan said with a tired smile. "Stay Grant, look I'm sorry." Jordan pleaded.

"I'm not the one you should be apologizing to."

"Talk to me about Chicago, about your new job, about Brenda, anything just stay a little while longer. Please."

Grant looked at the man and noticed that he seemed almost afraid. For a second he'd wavered but then his face had hardened and he'd walked towards the door to exit silently, closing it quietly behind him.

Afterwards Jordan remained there in the quiet of his apartment sitting still to wait, it hadn't taken long. His front door opened silently and apparently of its own accord. Behind it there was only a now dark hallway. As Jordan walked over to close the door a stench rose up to assail his nostrils causing him to back away. It was then that he noticed the thin haze of gray smoke that floated in from the hall.

It was nearly an inch from the floor and several feet in diameter and moved in a regular concentrated pattern right for him. As it approached Jordan backed up until he found himself cornered, his back to his front window.

"You just couldn't leave it alone could you?" Jonathan said from the doorway, an evil gleam in his eyes. "Why Jordan, I was no threat to you?" The boy said as he moved forward through the mist.

"I know that!" Jordan said defiantly, "I was never fooled by you."

"Then why?" The boy asked as he took slow deliberate steps towards the man. "Why risk your life?"

"What kind of a man would I be if I allowed the likes of you to continue to spread your evil? How could I just stand idly by when you threatened innocent lives to blind to really see you for what you are."

"I've spread nothing." He said easily, "It's true that in my existence I've killed often. It's also true that I've been known to spread evil. Hey what can I say, it's my nature. Even so I occasionally get tired and need a break. I came here to take a vacation of sorts, to rest, for a while at least. To perhaps give living a normal life a try, and live as mortals do. Then I ran into you.

I have to admit I was surprised, so few people recognize me now a days. In fact, it's been nearly a hundred years since any one has challenged me."

"I guess most just don't see you as I do." Jordan said, with his back still against the front window as he looked around the apartment for an avenue of escape, and found none. "I was always taught vigilance in the battle against evil, and to recognize it no matter what form it takes."

"It doesn't have to end this way you know. I have a live and let live policy these days." But Jordan had remained silent. "Well," Jonathan said raising his arms slightly in a gesture of futility and letting them fall again back to his sides, "have it your way but let me give you a word of advice, better to choose the window."

The cloud began moving towards him and Jordan realized that his moments within the living spectrum could now be measured in minutes, possibly seconds. As the mist made contact with his favorite palm less than a few feet from him, Jordan watched as the outer layers of its stem were slowly eaten away. It was then that he'd understood Jon's remark. The process was sure to be a slow and painful one. His back already towards the window and his pressure against it so great, he wondered why it hadn't already given way, but he would not consciously push it. That would be suicide and then Jon would win. He could never allow that to happen. When the mist touched his legs Jordan began to scream. Too absorbed with the intense pain of the mist as it ate away at his flesh, Jordan hadn't noticed the boy had disappeared from the apartment.

No longer able to stand upon feet that were being slowly and painfully eaten away, Jordan had slid down reluctantly. Pulled by the forces of gravity and met by the hungry mist that rose slowly to engulf him totally.

"But you were right," a voice said from all around him, "with the exception of you, it's been some time since I've found anyone to challenge me, certainly no one I'd classify as *good*."

The Black Pond Witch

Chapter 1 – Secrets

With head downcast and hands thrust deep into the pant pockets of his suit, Julian Collins strolled down the concrete steps of his hill top mansion. It was a cool San Diego night as he passed the formal gardens to the rear of his tutor styled home, its beauty shrouded by the darkness of night.

He walked leisurely. Only clenched fists concealed within his pockets betrayed agitation as he forced his hands deeper and deeper, until he felt the stitches begin to rip. His wife Liz had given him the suit only that morning for his birthday, and the memory caused him to stop in his tracks and smile. It was an Italian number, dark slate in color and stylish he'd guessed but not his style. It took wearing it the full day for Julian to realize the depths to which he hated it. Yet his performance of gratitude that morning upon its receipt could have been worthy of an Oscar. Still, it was the thought that counted and he knew she'd gone to great lengths picking it out. So he'd worn it.

As for the rest of the family, well only time would tell. His oldest son twenty-five-year-old Philippe had been away in Europe for nearly a year and in the past six months he hadn't heard a word from him. Next to him was his only daughter, Alena who was finishing college finals on the east coast. She at least managed to take time out of her day to call his office that afternoon wishing him a happy birthday. Paul and David, were his two youngest, both of whom he'd successfully managed to dodge that evening. They, no doubt, would have some token of affection for his forty-five years of existence, even if it weren't heart felt. He had been forced to recognize, as of late, just how truly distant he and his children actually were.

Sighing heavily Julian tried dispelling the horrible thoughts concentrating within his mind and threatening to overwhelm him.

Instead he glanced about, forcing his mind to clear and refocus upon the garden. Even by moonlight it was breathtaking with its potent mingling of sweet aromas but to fully appreciate it one had to view it by the light of day. He wondered if he would ever have another chance to do that. Shutting his eyes tightly Julian forced himself to etch the memory upon his mind but then another memory intruded. A garden paradise from decade's past crystallized into focus.

It was a familiar daydream experienced hundreds of times over the decades. A place Julian now remembered only as his lost paradise; a favorite place, so restful, so tranquil. He could clearly recall the aromas of the exotic flora that hung suspended about the place. It mingled heavily under the pure rays of sun shining down upon a myriad of colors but as usual the memory turned bitter, jarring Julian's mind back to the present and forcing his eyes to open with a start.

'Yes,' he thought, it was a paradise lost, 'a paradise I lost.'

Turning away from bitter thoughts, Julian instead decided to concentrate upon his present surroundings and circumstances. It was becoming chilly and across the distance a vapory fog was rolling in to blanket his manicured lawn. He watched it for several seconds before turning back to look sadly towards his house. All the usual lights were on and a few that were unexpected. He smiled sadly shaking his head, but the smile quickly vanished. His family, his home, his business, a twenty-five year investment in the three, a lifetime; was it all for nothing?

Less than a quarter mile away was Rosehill Cliff, a shear drop of fifty feet down a jagged face. There was only a thin cosmetic rail to separate the unfortunate from fate, named after a suicide victim from decades past. Without being consciously aware of his actions, Julian found himself piercing the night fog to head towards it. Often he found himself there. Whenever fate saw fit to hurl obstacles his way that were far beyond his mortal ability to comprehend or control, like the events of that day.

Julian gazed upward at the moon with its host of companion stars, more than he'd ever remembered seeing before. He dropped his head bitterly realizing it was another example of his ability to take the precious for granted. A luxury he could no longer afford.

"Isn't it a bit chilly for a stroll?"

Julian found himself smiling as he leveled his gaze from the stars above but did not turn. It was a voice from his childhood that so often comforted his fears, and though he was now a forty-five-year-old man he still found it strangely comforting in an almost childlike way. He continued smiling as he gazed forward blindly.

"I suppose," Julian said finally and added softly, "but I needed the freedom and a little time to think."

"Perhaps you spend too much time thinking. Go inside Julian, you should be with your family. After all it is your birthday. Go inside and relax."

"There'll be plenty of time for relaxing when I'm dead." Julian said feigning more amusement than he actually felt as he continued staring out over the distance. He couldn't see his companion's face but from the chill at his back Julian knew Marion had not been amused.

Julian turned slightly to give the man a sidelong glance.

"I didn't expect to see you, when did you get back?"

"A few weeks ago," Marion said flatly averting his eyes to also survey the valley.

"Weeks," Julian echoed turning to face the man, his smile melting to reveal wounded feelings, "and you're only now just making it here to see me?" His head dropped imperceptibly as he returned his attention to the cliff and the distance beyond. Grabbing his shoulder Marion spun Julian round to face him and their eyes to lock.

"Julian you seldom see me but that doesn't mean I'm not around, you know that. In fact, I've been around enough to know that something's bothering you and has been for several days now. You've left your office for lunch every day this week only to stroll distractedly about downtown. You do the same here. What's wrong?"

"I wonder how Philippe's doing." Julian replied matter-of-factly looking away. "I haven't heard from him in some time. He didn't even bother to call me today, perhaps he forgot."

Marion sighed heavily releasing his grip on Julian.

"Julian, I truly cannot understand how you managed to raise such a group of ungrateful," he let the remainder of the sentence trail before continuing more diplomatically. "I warned you long ago that you were giving them too much. Too much money, too much freedom, and not enough..."

"Time," Julian added sadly.

"Discipline," Marion corrected.

"Philippe's fine. He had a bit of trouble a few weeks back but it was nothing he couldn't solve by himself."

At that Julian looked sharply at the man.

"You've been following him around? You haven't been interfering have you?"

"No." Marion said softly raising his hands to calm Julian's fears. "Any problem your Philippe gets into he also gets himself out of, on his own. He doesn't know me from Adam, this I swear to you."

"That's the problem isn't it?" Julian said, his face reflecting immense pain. "He should know you, they all should. Don't you think that it's time they met their grandfather?" He said sadly moving past his father until they were several feet apart. Still, he refused to face him.

For several seconds they stood there listening to the lonely whispers of the wind across the valley below. Finally Julian spoke.

"I went home father."

Marion's back stiffened with the realization of his son's words and a single step bridged the distance back to Julian. He grabbed his son and flung him around violently.

"You did what?" Julian's father brought both hands up to his son's arms to shake him. "Julian how could you do such a foolish, reckless thing? I thought you understood after all these years that there is nothing back there for us. This is your home now! What possessed you to do such a truly stupid thing?"

"I didn't have a choice." Julian answered. His face was now mask-like but his voice was hollow and small. "Father, how can I continue to go on with my life knowing I've loaded a gun and pointed it squarely at the heads of my children?"

Julian's shoulders hunched as his head dropped and his father released his grasp. "They may be an ungrateful bunch but I still love them. Why should they be made to pay for my mistakes? Why should you for that matter?"

With that last sentence Julian brought his hands up to his face but was unable to conceal his torment and anguish and began to sob. "Father, there's nothing I can do to change what I've done, but if there's the slightest chance of appeasing him I have to try. I won't let my children, or their children, or future generations pay the price for my stupidity."

"It's a price no one will have to pay. Julian your children will be safe I've promised you that." Marion wrapped his son up in his arms as he'd done so often when he was a child. "You used to have more faith in me." He whispered over his son's shoulder attempting to sound hurt. "When did it vanish?"

"It never did."

"Then there will be no more trips back there, not ever. Do you understand? NOT EVER! Even if the worst happens trust me to deal with the situation. Tell me you understand this Julian!"

When Julian hadn't answered, his father brought his hand up to Julian's face to lift his chin the way he'd always done when Julian was a boy.

"Julian, promise me." Marion added in a voice that was only a whisper. Yet Julian heard fearful urgency in it.

"Of course Father," he said sighing heavily, "there's nothing more to be done now anyway but wait."

Marion shook his head sadly.

"Julian you worry about problems that don't exist and assign yourself blame where there is none. You were never responsible for what happened, not any of it. Besides, it was all over and done with thirty-years ago."

He was right, Julian thought to himself. It was an old argument, decades old, but that would never change the facts.

For a moment Julian's heart felt heavier than at any other time in his life and as he looked into his fathers' eyes he saw the pain reflected there as well.

"When will you let go of it and stop blaming yourself?"

"When you die," Julian whispered finally, breaking free to walk off and disappear into the night.

Chapter 2 - *Truths Revealed*

"Thank you." Julian gazed down holding an ornate antique brass letter opener gingerly between the two forefingers of his hands. He turned it thoughtfully, though secretly he wanted to plunge the dagger like instrument into his own heart. Julian looked up from one son to the other and smiled sadly, unable to generate more enthusiasm. "It's a wonderful gift, very handsome and I can really use it. I'll take it to the office tomorrow and set it prominently on my desk."

"Well don't get all sentimental!" Paul said offended.

"I'm serious Paul I do like it, I really do. It's a wonderful gift and practical, I can always use a letter opener."

"You said that already." Paul said dryly as he watched his father coldly, who only continued staring down steadily at the letter opener. He was clearly unhappy and Paul realized he'd never seen his father so miserable. Angrily, Paul swept the discarded wrappings that lay on the table onto the floor. "Do you think picking that damn thing out was easy for me? Let's face it you're not a normal dad. You know that don't you? It's just not that easy shopping for you!"

Nineteen-year-old, Paul Collins threw up his hands as if in disclaimer. "It's like shopping for a stranger, like I don't even know you. It isn't my fault that I'm a member of this dysfunctional family. Maybe if you hung round a little bit more and acted more like a father I'd of been able to pick out something more suitable."

"I see." Julian said sadly.

"It's not like we spend a lot of time together. And we've never had the chance to do family things other kids got to do, like go on vacations together to Disney World or the Grand Canyon. It's those stupid things that bind a family. You know families a lot poorer than ours spend more time together, and they definitely have more fun. Take Lyle down in the valley, his father took them to Nevada in the spring. Dad his father's a janitor for god's sake, but we had to suffer being the children of the owner of a multi-million dollar company. When was the last time we went anywhere together? I sure as hell don't remember because you're always at work. You know what, I bet Lyle doesn't have a problem shopping for *his* dad, and you've got the gall to lift an eyebrow to my birthday present!"

Paul's tone was harsh. He'd spoken his tirade without gazing at his father, but when he looked again into his eyes he'd seen the hurt. He laughed hoping to lighten the impact of his words.

Julian gazed away to look out into the darkness past the large picture window behind his son. For only an instant he'd seen a familiar face separate from the darkness to reflect an angry scowl. His own father's face had been displayed there momentarily, as if he somehow sensed his son's unhappiness and was angry. Yet in his heart Julian felt Paul's assessment of him was accurate. He'd always spent more time building his business and their home believing there would be time later for them to spend together as a family. He'd been wrong.

Julian felt his eyes misting but was determined to regain composure.

"Paul, it's not the gift that matters to me."

Julian got up and walked over to his son still holding the letter opener gingerly within the palm of his left hand, as if it were a truly precious gift. "Paul, this is important to me because you spent the time to pick it out, even though I didn't deserve it. I would have loved anything you chose. You're right though, I truly have been a miserable father if you didn't know that by now." He said quickly turning his back on both sons to walk over to the window, realizing he was again loosing his composure.

"I have to admit though," he added over his shoulder, "I don't recall your ever expressing interest in such family activities. In fact, one has to hire detectives just to locate you for dinner, let alone Thanksgiving and Christmas holidays." Julian said leaning heavily against the thick frame of the window's sill for support. Outside the forbidding silhouette of hills could be seen on the horizon, reminding him of a distant predator in pursuit. "You always seemed more interested in being elsewhere." Then he added softly. "All you ever had to do was ask, and you never did."

Each time Julian thought his day had reached an all time low, it had gotten worse. Now he was beginning to feel as if everything he ever touched somehow had become ruined and he no longer had time to fix any of it.

"Why? You wouldn't of taken us." Paul came up to stand behind his father, flinging words at his back like knives. "You never had time for us. You were too busy flying here or there," then he added coldly, "to busy building your *empire*."

Sitting quietly and forgotten on the sofa, fifteen-year-old David at first was amused by the proceedings. It had all seemed light-hearted at first. Now as he sat watching his older brother grill their father about his short comings, David thought he saw anguish on his father's face before he turned away. Now as he watched his father's back, David also thought he saw him trembling ever so slightly.

"Are you all right Dad?" David asked softly into the momentary silence.

Julian turned to address his youngest son smiling weakly. "Yes, I'm fine." He brought a shaky hand up to rub his chin distractedly. "It's just birthday blues I suppose."

"Look I'm just saying," Paul continued, "it would have been nice to do things together as a family once and a while. I mean instead of nearly existing as strangers who happen to share the same blood ties and address."

Julian returned his attention to the window. His back again to the room, but it hadn't escaped his youngest son that his father seemed more reflective that night than usual. As Paul spoke David noticed their father occasionally seemed lost in thoughts of his own and no longer appeared to be listening. A strange revelation struck

David. The man who always seemed so strong and invincible now appeared on the verge of collapse, right before his eyes. Yet if his sibling saw it, he gave no indication.

"I wish I'd known you didn't want anything," Paul continued harshly, "hell I'd have given you a Heidi-ho and a happy birthday and of been on my way."

"It seems I'm quite the failure." Julian said softly turning to again face Paul, this time the tears were there for both sons to see. "I wasn't aware of this limitation until now but you've sufficiently driven that point home, thank you."

Paul stood there in shocked silence by the anguish he saw reflected in his father's face. For the first time in his life he didn't know what to say.

In grief Julian turned toward his youngest son.

"Is this also how you feel?"

Paul came forward grabbing his father's arm and shaking him playfully. "Dad look I'm sorry, I really am. I didn't say, I mean, that's not what I meant. This whole thing just got out of hand. I was just trying to say that you should slow down, that's all. Maybe I could of found a more eloquent way of saying it, but hey, it's me remember? Anyway, it's not as if you can't afford it. You just said I should have known the money wasn't important." Paul smiled and this time seemed sincere. "That's sound advice you should also listen to. You've got more money then you'll ever be able to spend, slow down and enjoy it while you're still sort of young." Then he added laughing lightly and more in character. "Let's face it, you can enjoy it with us now, or we can enjoy it without you later. After you've worked yourself to death, that is. I for one would like to enjoy it *with* you."

Uncomfortable with the sudden spotlight David looked away, yet urgently felt the need to rescue his father from Paul's verbal assault. "Paul no, it has nothing to do with the money!" He said finally.

"I agree."

Alena stood in the doorway. She had hoped for a more joyous entrance to surprise and embrace her father on his birthday but caught the tail end of the conversation. The need to chime in and sharply correct her brother was too overwhelming. Seeing her father's anguished face Alena realized her response must have sounded like agreement with Paul. Her timing had been all wrong and despite her ruse of calling him earlier that day she'd noticed her father hadn't seemed the least surprised to see her.

"Daddy, I just want to spend more time with you. It doesn't matter where." She came further into the room carrying a small gift wrapped in shiny purple paper with matching bow that was much too large. "I brought this for you." She extended her small offering noticing her father only looked away. If he'd heard, he gave no indication.

"Well you have to admit, we *can* afford it." Paul said going over to the sofa and sitting down. He stared forward stubbornly, refusing to let go of his argument.

"*You* can't afford anything!" David said snidely. "Look Dad, Alena is only saying it would be nice to just sit around and spend more time together, maybe talk a little more to each other. If we had a TV we could watch it together, as a family."

"Which we can also afford," Paul added.

That snapped their father back.

"Television doesn't bring families together, it tears them apart." Julian began, aware that Paul had thrown up his hands in frustration and was sinking further down into the sofa as Alena softly laughed. He continued unable to stop himself, aware that his voice, words and attitudes mirrored his own father's. "It's a corrupting device. It tears individualism from the minds of the young, and turns both young and old into useless mindless simpletons who can't think for themselves and do you know why? Because they've spent years in front of it being told when they should think, how they should think, and what they should think. Its only purpose is to desensitize, dehumanize, create stereotypes, and elevate one's fears and phobias. My father would never allow one in his home, and it wasn't until I was a grown man with children of my own that I realized his wisdom. Now I totally agree with him."

"I guess it's just as well." Paul said. "What would have been the point anyway having a TV way back then? There couldn't have been anything on. That had to be before satellite *or* cable."

"Well at least we could get together every blue moon and talk to each other." David added sadly. "Maybe talk about interesting events of the day. Some families' talk around the dinner table…"

"I bet that's a TV stereotype!" Paul yelled.

"…we don't even seem to have that." David continued, ignoring his brother. "We always seem to be coming and going at different times, like we're avoiding each other."

"I'd of liked to have gone camping as a kid, maybe told some scary stories around a camp fire." Paul said, his voice sounding whimsical.

"Scary stories…" Julian said amazed.

At that moment the room began to spin painfully, forcing Julian's arms to momentarily grab at thin air for support. He didn't know exactly when Stewart entered the room, but as usual his friend and chauffeur, was there when he needed him most. There for support that was both mental and physical the moment his world began to collapse all around him and as his children formed a uniform front in their expression of his paternal inadequacies. 'Of course they're right,' he thought realizing he had been thinking along those same lines earlier. He didn't know why he made some of the decisions he had, remembering his own father had been wonderful. Lavishing all the time and attention on him he could ever have asked.

As Julian was gently guided back to his chair, he looked at Stewart's sympathetic face. It seemed only at that moment had his children become cognizant of his weakened state to converge upon him. Stewart had no children himself and now to Julian's mind the look on his friend's face suggested that had been a favorable thing.

Julian looked at his chauffeur with a tired smile.

"You spend your life trying to *do* for them, *build* for them and this is what you *get* from them. Aren't you glad you don't have *them*?"

"I'm grateful," David said, "really I am. Bryce is always

telling me how lucky I am to have such a cool father, and I am. I've always known that, even if I haven't always said it. He sees you as a successful rich GQ type that gives us everything. All his father has to give mostly is time. I guess you're right about television."

Julian smiled looking down to conceal wounded feelings. Paul's comments were hurtful, yet they couldn't compare to his youngest born. One who never intentionally went out to hurt anyone and he knew that was why it had.

For a long time Julian sat there silently looking out through the large bay window of their living room, at nothing in particular. Outside the sun had set nearly two hours earlier. Now the only thing visible was the reflection of his living room and the faces within, reflected off the glass and the darkness on the other side. It was several minutes before he returned his attention to his children.

"Well," Julian said softly in a voice reflecting exhaustion, "scary stories. I've never really understood the concept of one enjoying being scared. I've just never really believed it, but in case I'm wrong is it ever to late to tell them?"

"What?" Paul had become uncharacteristically quiet but shot upright all of a sudden. "You mean *you're* going to tell us a story?" He laughed before getting up and going over to sit next to David who he elbowed good-naturedly and returned his attention to his father. "I'll have to tell you old guy, at nineteen, I think it would be fairly difficult to hold my attention let alone scare me."

Julian shook his head realizing that perhaps he'd made a mistake just as his wife Liz came into the room pushing a cart. Upon it was her prized antique white tablecloth, napkins and silverware that had been in her family for generations. Also upon it sat two bottles of Champaign, several glasses, and a large cake, ablaze. He quickly turned away before their eyes met.

"What's going on?" Elizabeth Collins sensed an unusual mood in the room the moment she entered, glancing from one child to the next who only stared back guiltily. She whined as her eyes fell upon the familiar wrappings from Paul's discarded gift where it lay on the floor near the table. "Paul, I told you I wanted you to wait until I came out with the cake. Alena, what are you doing down here? You were supposed to be a surprise. Was I the only one sticking to the game plan here?" Liz scowled momentarily before releasing her disappointment. "Ah well," she said parking the cart and coming up behind her husband to throw her arms around his waist, "it worked on paper. I would have been out sooner but I had a slight accident, but it was worth the wait you'll see." She said smiling proudly and nodding towards her cake.

Liz seldom stepped foot in the kitchen. It was Marie's exclusive domain but that morning she'd unceremoniously ushered their sixty-five year-old cook out determined to do the cake thing alone and from scratch, the first time in their twenty-five year marriage. She was momentarily disappointed noticing her husband had taken her hands tenderly within his own about his waist but had not turned to face her.

"You look better than James Bond in that suit." She said smiling at his back. "Fortunately for you, I have another surprise." She reached under the cart to pull out a wrapped gift.

When Julian turned to face his wife, to his children he seemed more like his old self. He smile was suave, yet almost instantly her own vanished. She glanced over to Stewart who had returned to his favorite position to stand just inside and to the right of the doorway.

"Stewart, what's going on?" This time her voice was edged with concern, but her husband lifted her hands to his lips to kiss them gently.

"The cake is the most beautiful I've ever seen." Julian told her catching her within his arms to gently rocking her. "Butterscotch, isn't it?"

But she hadn't answered continuing to stare at Stewart.

"Is that for me?" He smiled down broadly as he gently pulled the package from her grasp. When Stewart hadn't answered Liz returned her attention to her husband. He'd been fidgeting with the wrappings of her gift, but it has clear he held no real interest in it. She grabbed his face between her palms forcing his attention upon her.

"What's happening? Julian what's wrong? Tell me."

"Everyone keeps asking me that. Can't a guy have a mid-life crisis around here?" He said forcing a smile that didn't go over well. "Liz it's nothing, just those forty-five year old blues. That's all."

"Dad's going to tell us a story!" Alena said laughing far too loudly within the quiet of the room.

Liz jerked her head immediately towards her twenty-three year old daughter who went over to the sofa plopping down onto it and flung her blond hair back before settling comfortably.

"Well," Alena said finally ceasing her fidgeting, "I'm all set. I think I've been waiting all my life for this." She said eager to put as much distance as possible between themselves and the conversation that proved so hurtful to her father. She looked up with a face that brightened to reveal an idea. "I know, we can each tell a story every Friday. That'll give us a week to come up with one. What do you think?" She said in general.

"I don't know," David said slightly embarrassed, "I'm not one for telling stories." He blushed and looked away.

"What do you mean, it was your idea!" Alena said.

"It was not!" David shouted. "And what are *you* gonna do, phone yours in? I thought you were going back in a few days."

"We can talk about it afterwards." Paul said getting up to walk over to where his sister was now sprawled across the sofa. He seated himself on the floor to rest his back against it near her. "I'm set to." He said clearly mocking.

Julian continued to stand there staring intently into his wife's eyes. Just as with his father he now saw concern, even fear there and knew it was for him. There was no way she could know the extent of his problems, yet she'd certainly seemed to empathize to some degree with him. He smiled kissing her cheek before leading her towards the chair on the far side of the room. He'd hoped the distance would break their connection, not wanting to hurt her more than he already had. She'd been so happy when she entered. Now the pain in her face mirrored his.

The room fell quiet as all eyes focused upon him as he made his way back towards the window. Upon passing the cake, still lit, he'd placed the small unopened package upon the cart, taking only a step away before turning to blow out all the candles. As the smoke from forty-five candles rose towards the ceiling he only smiled and seemed to be listening intently to the silence of the house.

"Must be time to change those batteries," he laughed softly before returning towards the window that revealed only darkness.

"Is it a really scary story?" Paul asked, partly to mock and partly to recapture his father's attention.

Julian didn't speak immediately. When he did it was in a voice little more than a whisper.

"When I was a child, I thought that it was." He said and his eyes remained fixed upon the blackness framed beyond the window. "I remember not being able to sleep comfortably for years afterwards."

Finally Julian returned his attention to his small audience of wife, daughter, two sons and chauffeur who still stood in the background, a worried look upon his face. He and Julian stared at each other for several seconds before Alena looked over the sofas back to follow her father's gaze to where Stewart stood uncomfortably.

"Stewart, sit down!" She waived impatiently.

"I should go," Stewart said speaking for the first time, "after all this is family time." He turned to leave.

"You *are* family," Julian said with a smile that instead showed sadness, "please sit." He motioned towards the bench that was near the fireplace and close to where he reseated himself. With uncomfortable steps Stewart moved toward it and sat down.

"Well," Julian said, "I'm tempted to begin with the traditional 'once upon a time,' but I guess I've missed that window haven't I?" He smiled, but it quickly melted away as his face settled into an expressionless mask.

"When I was a small child up until about nine I lived with my father in our ancestral home in the south of France."

"You were born in France?" David said eagerly but his father had not answered, merely looked downward a brief moment before continuing.

"Our home was a chateau built in the fifteenth century," Julian continued, "very old and very elegant, filled with antique treasures which the mind of a nine-year-old could never fully appreciate. Now as a grown man and father, I wish I could go back in time to peruse some of those old and rare volumes upon our family's library shelves, or gaze once again upon some of our ancient tapestries and art works, but I digress.

Yes it was an elegant place, but it was also a dark brooding place that silently bespoke of many mysteries and adventures to the mind of a child. I was always exploring my dark, wondrous world, much to the exasperation of my father who seemed forever trying to keep me on a short lease.

Behind the chateau was a large formal garden. It was both elegant and elaborate. In all my years I don't believe I've ever seen its equal with its manicured hedges, sculptures, fountains, and flora from all over the world. All set in complicated geometry and on differing levels. Our gardener, René Laurier, could coax the most exotic of varieties into bloom and tended the garden lovingly. My father was very proud of it. Behind the garden was a fairly dense forest on the corner of our property.

One afternoon society ladies from one organization or another visited us. They came to view our gardens bringing with them men with large lights and cameras. My father told me not to get under foot but I was an only child and somewhat spoiled. So I was everywhere poking and prodding at things.

I found out something wondrous that day, that behind the formal gardens existed an old cemetery. I'd glimpsed it between a gap in the tall rose bushes that concealed an old rusting iron fence. I'd never seen it before. I looked back towards the chateau and saw the reason. It was behind the west wing which was an unused portion of the estate and hidden from my view. I'd never been allowed to go within that wing. I couldn't even if I'd wanted to because it had been walled off generations before. Lack of maintenance made it a dangerous place by the time I'd come along.

Yet I'd easily have seen that cemetery had I been able to explore it. I realized excitedly that I'd find a way in there somehow and see what other treasures it concealed. It would be my next adventure, after the cemetery.

That day, father and his staff were busy with his guests and my tutor had taken time out to talk with the ladies as well. I'm sure she seldom got such networking opportunities since there couldn't have been that much of a demand for governesses. You see father was from the old school and believe in a mentor's approach to teaching. He didn't think anything worthwhile could ever be learned in a group. When he thought I'd learned enough from one person he'd dismiss them and get another. He oversaw every phase of my education and it was quite structured. I believe he was very proud of me and why not, I was very bright.

Well, she saw me briefly examining the bushes and came over.

"What are you doing?" She asked in that high-pitched nasal voice she had.

I explained that I was just taking a break to examine the foliage. This seemed to pacify her and then she was called back by one of the ladies. Father was nowhere in sight so the exploration continued.

I suffered a few scratches as I poked about those thorny bushes, but as I said the gate was old and rusted and as I was going to find out about the rest of the cemetery, in ruins. I found a large enough gap finally and wiggled through.

I remember thinking to myself, 'This is glorious.' It was over grown from decades of ruin. Trees were everywhere a few times I even stumbled over headstones due to the heavy over growth of foliage. There were actually trees growing over some of the graves breaking the caskets and pushing some upwards. I could look downward into holes and actually see remains. It was a strange feeling for me at first but I'd always been inquisitive, I soon got over it. The sun was full overhead, yet I could barely see it because of the canopy of over grown trees.

It was nearly lunchtime and I was getting hungry so I decided to start back. The cemetery was larger than I'd thought and it would take time to fully explore it. I'd already lost my way, but began to retrace my steps as best I could. I was looking downward for my footprints upon the grass when I heard someone whisper my name. It was a soft, playful voice that seemed to be coming from a graveled path that led into the thickest and most over grown part of the cemetery. I knew I had to have been mistaken. Father always said I had too strong an imagination, so I continued on my way out, but there it was again. I began to follow it. Then I heard another voice, but this one seemed different. It was even softer and whispered as the other had, but there was seriousness to it as much as the place in which I stood. Finally it said, '...death awaits you at the end of that path.'

At that I ran, fortunately it was back the way I'd come.

I was scared to death and I panicked, it was amazing I'd found the correct path out. As I squeezed again through the gap in the iron fence I heard the voices of father's guest and the sun began to stream down again fully upon my face. It was only then that I realized how cold I was and that my hands were clammy and shaking, my heartbeat was strong and fast like a drum. I looked up guiltily when I heard father call my name.

I remember my father in those days as a tall man, the tallest in the world. He was strong and used to bounce me into the air and catch me. Other times he'd pick me up effortlessly to toss me onto my bed at bedtime. His dark green eyes seemed to look right through me whenever I tried to lie. His hair was the darkest of brown.

"Julian, what are you doing?" He asked in a voice that held suspicion.

"I was just wandering about the garden, looking." I lied. "This is the only time René will let me in."

He laughed.

"Do you remember the last time he let you and Laurent in?"

He seemed amused by the recollection and I smiled, but it must have been a shallow one because he clasped my face between his palms.

"You're cold, are you feeling alright?" There was worry in his voice and eyes as he gazed at me.

"Father I'm fine," I whined pulling away. It was then that the leader of his little troupe of guests came over to thank him for allowing them in, and I slipped away. With the increased distance between the cemetery and myself, my nerves began to return.

I rounded the property and found Laurent, the son of René the gardener, working like a slave at tasks his father had assigned him.

"I've found a new place," I told him, "a secret place."

I waited for a reaction but got only a glance.

"I'm sorry," he said with reserved irritation, "I can't play with you now. Some of us have work to do."

How to describe Laurent? Well to start he was three years older than I, about twelve at the time, tall with auburn hair. His eyes were grayish and I always thought they looked somewhat watery, except when he was angry or annoyed, like then.

I was never sure, one can never really be, but I used to suspect that Laurent held a secret dislike for me, because there were times when I could see his patience straining. Perhaps he resented what he thought was my carefree life, while he slaved for his father. Also, I believe he resented being forced to treat me as better than him self. There were times when he was angry with me and I could see him measuring his words to me carefully. Though in retrospect, I realize he treated me better than most siblings treat each other. Whenever he denied me anything he always came round later to make amends for it.

There were no other children on the property, Laurent was the only one. All my friends were to far away and to difficult to see when I really wanted.

"Fine," I said with anger, "go back to your *chores*. I don't need you."

I don't know what he saw in my face, but when he found me again sitting on the main steps, he put his hand on my shoulder and sat down beside me.

"Julian," he said and I shrugged his hand off, "I can't just drop everything and leave as you do. My father will whip me good if I don't have this done before school tomorrow."

I winced at the thought of his going to school. If he resented me what he thought was my carefree life I resented his going to school. All the friends he had there, whom he could see anytime he wished. He had none of the restrictions I had and could come and go off the property as he pleased, after telling his father, to play with them. I was never allowed to. They never wanted to play with me anyway. I think they felt uncomfortable around me. I wouldn't have been the least surprised if their parents hadn't warned them against me. Perhaps even Laurent had. That incident in the garden my father mentioned had been my fault but Laurent got the beating for it by his father. I can't be sure he ever told anyone publicly but I know he blamed me for it, rightfully so.

I guess he saw trouble again when I talked about my secret place, but if Laurent had any faults at all it was his kind heart. Within five or ten minutes he'd found me and promised to meet me in the center of the garden later that evening. In fact, I'd known even before he placed his hand on my shoulder that he'd come around. It was just a matter of manipulating him just right. In that regard, I was an expert, with him and with father. I could work miracles.

"But not until after supper." He said.

I whined because that was much too late for me. I was planning to take him into a cemetery and I didn't want to do it in the dark. But he'd been steadfast and wouldn't leave before that time.

"Well what are you going to tell him?" I asked referring to his father.

"That you told me you were lacking in math and that you asked me to help you study." He said laughing.

"You told him you were helping me study math," I asked in disbelief, "and he believed you?"

It was a joke to be sure. One I wasn't sure my ego would allow me to swallow. I guess I did have a severe one, one that wouldn't give him even the pretense of being my equal, especially in math. Actually, I did believe that I was his intellectual superior and that was reinforced in my mind every time I'd gotten my way as I had then.

"Alright," I said irritated, "I'll back you on that to your father, just as long as mine doesn't hear about it. He'll know it's a lie."

"That's no problem. My father will just think pride forces yours to delude him self."

I scoffed at that and he laughed. I think after a few minutes we were both laughing."

Julian smiled briefly, and looked down as if remembering a pleasant moment but the smile quickly vanished and his eyes seemed to mist. As he continued, the air in the room seemed to be one of profound sadness. He continued refusing to meet the eyes of his wife and children who glanced at each other not knowing how to stop what they'd started.

"The sun started to set as we met in the garden. I'd started to have bad feeling about the whole thing when I saw Laurent approaching. He seemed genuinely enthusiastic and wanted to know what I'd found. He hadn't been like that since before the garden incident so I couldn't let him down.

"Maybe we should do this in the day?" I said rather timidly.

Laurent was clearly irritated by this.

"My free time is limited but I'll let you know!" He said starting to stalk off in anger.

"Wait!" I called after him, and he paused a few feet away. "All right, it's just that it's a little creepy at night, that's all."

"Creepy?" He asked clearly interested now. I guess I should have told him the truth in the first place.

With a finger I beckoned him to follow and he did. By the last rays of the setting sun we both peered through the gap in the fence.

"The cemetery," he said knowingly.

"You knew it was here?" I was amazed.

"Of course," he said and there was no fear in his expression or voice. "I've explored it thoroughly with my friends but don't tell anyone, it's off limits and we'll all get into trouble."

I swore and crossed myself.

"You mean at night?" I asked wondrously.

"Of course at night," He said in a disdainful voice as if I were a much smaller child, "we couldn't risk being seen. So we'd sneak out of bed late at night to explore it. I've been here many times."

"Have you ever heard anything?" I asked cautiously.

At that he'd looked at me with surprise. My face must have said that I heard something.

"What kind of things!" Laurent asked focusing attention upon me.

I looked away. He'd laugh at me if I told him, I just knew it. I had developed bad feelings about the whole thing and no longer wanted to go in, but he'd laugh if I turned away too. Worse, he'd know I was scared and would probably tell all his friends. I guess I'd deliberated on it a bit too long because I glanced at him and saw a look of sympathy.

"Let's go back." He said.

"Fine," I said relieved, "if you're scared."

I'd started walking back up the path and glanced beside me to find him no longer there. I turned in time to see him go through the gap in the fence.

"Stay there," he ordered.

"Where are you going?" I shouted.

"I changed my mind. Just stay there till I get back." He said laughing and disappeared inside.

It was getting late and I was frightened he'd never be able to find his way out in the darkness. I wanted to leave and run back towards the house, but I couldn't leave him in there. It wasn't until afterwards that I realized that's actually what I should have done.

I squeezed through after him and called him several times before he answered. When he did he was right behind me. I screamed and he laughed.

"I'm sorry," he said and I knew his apology was heartfelt, "but I did tell you not to come in here."

I was as mad as hell, probably more for my own cowardice than at him and stomped off into the growing darkness of the cemetery.

"What do you think you're doing? Julian come back, I said I'm sorry. Where are you going?" He said behind me.

"I'm going exploring!" I said disappearing into the heavy

brush. I heard him continuing to shout for me to come back which I ignored him and in no time had lost him in the darkness. He continued calling me but I refused to answer still too angry, my ego too bruised.

"We can't stay in here, we're not prepared." He'd shouted in the distance behind me. "There are holes, deep pockets in the ground that you could fall into in the darkness and hurt yourself. We both could. Julian it would be difficult for anyone to find us in this place, especially if they don't know we're here!"

At first I thought he was just trying to scare me again. Then I realized that he was right. I was acting like a fool.

"Where are you?" He asked and I could hear in his voice that he was becoming alarmed.

"Here," I called and started to move towards his voice.

"No, stay where you are and I'll come to you." He screamed.

It was then that I realized, like an older brother, he was concerned for my safety.

"Don't move." He shouted again.

I couldn't figure out why but something in his voice changed. I heard fear, I just didn't know why. He'd been in there before, he'd said so. It was then that I heard it. From somewhere in the darkness beyond, my name was being called. The voice was soft but it was a masculine adult voice. Telling me to come to him, I took a step before I realized it. My fears seemed to just melt away. I concentrated on the voice, but then there were two voices. The other I recognized, it was Laurent. He was telling me *not* to move, begging me *not* to move. He said he would find me if I just *didn't* move.

I listened to Laurent's voice and stopped. He was moving fast and in that instance I realized he was scared. He'd heard the voice as well, he must have and I realized he was moving swiftly, dangerously in the darkness and only concerned about me. He'd been there many times, he knew the way out. He could have left me, but he didn't. He was rushing about recklessly trying to get to me before..."

Julian looked down, bringing up his hand to massage his weary brow. There was an uncomfortable silence in the room that no one was sure how to breach.

"There were the voices." Julian continued. "The one I recognized as Laurent's, and the one I didn't, but it continued to call to me. I wanted to move but Laurent kept calling frantically for me not to. There was a frightening urgency in his voice. Again it seemed to be more for me then himself, I'm sure he must have heard the voice.

For a few moments there was silence. Then I heard another voice, it wasn't Laurent's voice and it wasn't the voice of earlier. Yet it was familiar, this time it called not for me but for Laurent. Telling him frantically that it needed help, telling him to come at once, telling him to hurry that he was drowning. It certainly appeared so. There were terrible loud gasps. It said that it was dark, that it couldn't see and that it was frightened. I heard Laurent call out that he was coming. At the same time the horrible realization hit me, I'd heard Laurent's scream. It was blood-curdling and then there was silence. The voice I'd heard had been my own, though I'd been silent. I let Laurent rush head on towards it while I'd just stood there like a fool listening. What happened?

The clouds were beginning to part unveiling a full moon high in the night sky and make it somewhat easier for me to see now. For a long time I heard nothing, everything was silent, even the night sounds. It was broken only by my own voice as I called cautiously for Laurent. The voice that answered was not his.

It was the same voice as earlier, but this time it had an amused quality to it. It asked me if I wanted to see Laurent. It said it knew where he was and could take me to him, if I followed his voice. What could I do?

I followed the voice until I saw the moon glistening off a small glassy black pond. I looked at it only briefly as I scanned for Laurent or for a strange man. Then I heard him, Laurent's brief tortured cry. I glanced at the pool in time to see its waters break to reveal a bump in its center and realized it to be Laurent. He was drowning.

My scream had been perfectly timed with Laurent's own just

before it was again cut short by the water. When his head broke the surface again he'd only had time to scream 'NO!' before I stepped into the waters. Again his head rose above the waves and he screamed for me to stay back. It was as if something was pulling him down into those black waters.

There was laughter all around me as I ran panic stricken into the waters. I continued wading forward. The waters now nearly up to my chest and then I heard the sound of something cutting through the air to fly in an arch overhead. It landed with a sickening thud against the headstones in the distance. Then I heard Laurent's moan now from the land behind me. I turned to move towards it but something grabbed me before I could take another step.

It grabbed my chest tightly and pulled me down below the waters, I can still remember its taste, rank and vile as it filled my lungs. The touch of my hands against my restraints told me that my bounds were skeletal-like arms about me. I didn't know why it sought to kill me but it appeared it would succeed. The last thing I remember was wondering if I'd see Laurent on the other side, I knew he'd hit those headstones hard, but instead I awoke.

I turned my head to see flames shooting high into the chimney of my bedroom fireplace. I was in my bed. Near me sat my governess. She seemed pleased when I awoke and quickly left the room. When she reappeared she was followed by the doctor from the village and several of my father's staff. I noticed that two of them were shedding tears as they whispered amongst themselves.

I asked about Laurent and was told he was dead. As I said, that wasn't entirely unexpected though it hurt, I think I cried. As I scanned the faces that were also crying I noticed my father was not amongst them. When I asked where he was everything fell silent. The doctor stood there. I could see him busily handling a gold pocket watch on a slender gold chain which was hanging from his vest. He didn't open it, only turned it nervously between his fingers. Finally he told everyone to leave the room, that I needed my rest, thrusting it back into his vest pocket. There was something they weren't telling me. I started to panic rising off my pillow.   The doctor came over and gave me an injection of something and everything started to fade.

I awoke late the next morning and my room was flooded with the morning's light. Laurent's father was sitting next to my bed. His face was pale and shallow with dark circles under his eyes and I knew he hadn't slept since hearing the news.

"I know you've been through a great deal," the tears were swelling in René Laurier's eyes and his voice was broken and raspy, "but I have to know, there'll be no peace for me until I do. What happened to my Laurent? I have to know."

I didn't know where to start.

"We were exploring the cemetery." I said honestly.

"He would never take you there!" Laurier said angrily. "He knew that place was cursed, and what it might mean for you!"

I didn't understand and the doctor chose that moment to reappear.

"Tell me what happened to him!" Laurier demanded rising from his chair to stand beside my bed. He grabbed my shoulders and began shaking me painfully. "TELL ME!"

The doctor came to my rescue and pried his hands from my shoulders.

I'd begun to cry, I think I asked for my father. I asked why he hadn't come to see me. In my mind I thought he was angry and probably disappointed with me but I needed him desperately. The doctor moved towards his bag and I knew he was about to again plunge me into darkness.

"No please," I begged, "I'll be good. I promise!"

He saw the fear in my eyes and patted my shoulder and told me to sleep now. I wasn't the least bit sleepy but I turned onto my side and pretended. He soon left the room. I was disappointed when Gabrielle our maid came to sit beside my bed. I didn't say anything to her, but laid there with my back to her, and soon I think I did sleep.

When I awoke again it was later that afternoon and I was alone in the room. With shaky legs I got out of bed to cross over to the window overlooking the front of the property.   There were numerous cars parked outside and many people stood about talking. Their facial expressions told me that the conversations were somber, but my father was not amongst them.

I grabbed my robe and cautiously opened my bedroom door a crack to peer through. The corridor was empty. Outside my room I went first to father's bedroom but he wasn't there. I knew I couldn't go anywhere near primary rooms such as the kitchen, dining or living areas. They'd be saturated with people from the cars I'd seen out front. Instead I went outside. I peered around corners, well out of sight of people but couldn't find him. From upstairs I heard Gabrielle call that I wasn't in my room and the search was on for me. I was determined that I wouldn't go back to my room before I'd found father. I needed time to think so I ran to the only place that I thought they wouldn't look for me, it was a small chapel on the property just north of the formal gardens.

As I stepped inside there was the heavy scent of candles burning and of flowers. There were people in some of the pews and the sounds of whispered prayers could be heard. This was unusual. There were never people in our private chapel. My eyes moved to the front of the church were the altar stood. At its base were two closed coffins close together. I moved forward as if in a nightmare. I knew one held the friend who tried so hard to save my life and at the cost of his own, but I was at a loss as to the other. Everything fell silent as I made my way down the center isle and I could feel all eyes upon me. Suddenly the priest from the village church was before me to block my path further. The sounds of brisk footsteps to my rear told that the doctor and others from the house had caught up with me. They surrounded me.

I screamed asking who was in the other casket but my questions were met only with silence. The doctor grabbed me tightly and I realized that I was not going to get any answers unless I composed myself.

"I'm all right." I said calmly and I brushed myself free of them. "I have to see."

I think the doctor must have motioned for them to release me because all the hands dropped at once.

Continuing forward, I remember seeing the colored lights from the stained glass as it fell upon the closed caskets. One casket was considerably smaller than the other and I knew that one must contain Laurent. I stopped before the largest, lifting the lid which opened silently under my exertion."

Julian stopped and began to cry silently.

"Dad," David came over to stand beside his father placing a hand upon his shoulder. Julian looked up and into his son's eyes and for a moment was reminded of himself.

"I'm all right." Julian said with a sad smile. "It all happened so long ago it's strange that it would still affect me in such a way." He sighed heavily as he tried to reassure his son, and waited until the boy reseated himself before continuing.

"It was my father," Julian said, "lying in repose within the silken interiors of a mahogany coffin. He seemed as if asleep, dressed in one of his finest suits, on his finger was the emerald ring he always wore. I placed my hand within the casket and began to shake him gently. I think I called his name a few times softly and when he didn't rouse, I began to scream for him to wake and shook him furiously. They pulled me from the church kicking and screaming.

Laurier had come to me asking what had happened to his son earlier that day. Now I understood how he felt. I clearly remembered up until Laurent's death but of my own father's death I remembered nothing at all.

Back in my bedroom I recall my governess telling me I would someday inherit and be master of the estate and that I had to be brave. She'd also said my father was going to be interned miles away, within the cemetery of Saint Adela. I couldn't understand why they were taking him so far away from me. While she spoke, my eyes traveled towards the doctor who had been standing mutely at her side, an uncomfortable expression upon his face. All while she spoke I'd remained impassive, and for the most part staring into nothingness. When they both stepped out of my line of sight, and supposedly out of my ear shot, I again heard her voice.

"Doctor Basset, I can make allowances for the villagers, they're simple people for the most part, but I don't understand you, an educated man! How can you stand by and allow such a thing to happen? This boy has no one to look after him now or protect his interests except me, and I tell you I won't stand by and allow such a thing as this to happen. Marion de Rousseau was always kind to me and to everyone and I will not let these peasants cremate him. He deserves a proper burial."

"What are you talking about?"

At my voice they'd both turned round. There was venom, even contempt in my voice. "I asked you a question." I said sounding more like my father then I could ever have dreamed and I think they also heard him in my voice.

"It's nothing you need worry about." Doctor Basset said from the corridor.

"If you hurt my father..." I began.

"You're father is in a better place," Father Caston called to me, overhearing our conversation as he ascended the steps at the middle of the hall, "a place where he'll never know pain again." I shook off his words as well, turning my head and refusing to look his way as he approached. When he was within arms length he gently turned me to face him and knelt down putting us at eye level. "Julian," Father Caston said soothingly, "I don't know what you heard but tomorrow your father will be buried within the cemetery at Saint Adela," and then he added as he looked from my governess to the doctor, "on consecrated ground and heaven help anyone who tries to do him differently. Evil cannot reach there."

There was a firmness and conviction to his words but I'd thought it an odd thing to say. I was led back to my room. Again I thought of Laurier who had questions for me only the day before regarding Laurent, perhaps I could provide those answers now, and perhaps he could afford me a few.

Hours later I found Laurier seated in the front pew of the now empty church. He was no longer crying but staring fixedly upon his son's casket.

"He was trying to save me." I said to his back and he'd startled at the sound of my voice. I hadn't meant to disturb him in that fashion it had just blurted out.

"I didn't know there was a cemetery there. I told him about it after father's garden party but he already knew about it and had been there many times, he and his friends. He didn't want to go in that night, he said we weren't prepared but I'd gone in anyway. I didn't want him to think I was scared. He didn't have to follow me in but he did. I think because he was frightened for me."

I stopped and started crying again with the memory. Laurier got up to come over and stand before me. His face looked as I felt as he put his arm around my shoulder to guide me back to the front pew where he'd been sitting.

"I kept going further and further into the darkness, ignoring his calls for me to come back until I'd gotten lost. Then I heard two voices calling to me, Laurent and a strange distant voice.

I think that maybe Laurent heard it to because he really started to call out for me then. There was fear in his voice, and I think it was for me! He told me to stay were I was, that he would find me and so I did. I ignored the voice I didn't know. Then it stopped calling for me and began to call Laurent, in a voice that was my own."

I'd started crying against Laurier's shoulder, his arm still around me.

"I heard Laurent running in the darkness and he seemed to be getting farther from me and then there was silence. When I heard him again there was a scream and I ran towards it."

I was still crying. Laurier was trying to comfort me as best he could, though he himself seemed to be crying again.

"He was in the water," I continued, "and something seemed to be pulling him down. He screamed for me to stay back when he surfaced again, but I ran in anyway to help him. I think I got within a few feet from Laurent before I saw him sailing over head to hit the ground on the other side, and then something inside the water grabbed me."

We both cried softly for a time before Laurier released my shoulder. He got up and walked over to his son's casket raising the lid. I hadn't seen Laurent since his death and I didn't want to.

"He was wrong to have taken you there. He knew the stories of the witch that dwells in that cursed pool of water. Everyone is safe who walks through that place *except* de Rousseau children." He'd begun to cry heavily as he gazed downward at his son. "But he died trying to protect you and us all."

I didn't understand his meaning as I got up and approached the casket and when I looked down, I was unprepared for what I saw. My father's expression had been so serene in appearance, as if he only slept. Laurent's face expressed a battle fought and lost, with a devil. His facial expression was contorted, his mouth agape. Even after so many hours passed there still seemed so much pain expressed there. It almost seemed as if he were about to warn of something. I don't remember hitting the floor but I do remember Laurier gently shaking me. I was still in the church and Laurent's casket was closed. Laurier was apologizing saying he shouldn't have allowed me to see him like that but I knew I had to.

I'd recovered somewhat and understood that Laurent had given his life for me, but I still didn't understand what it all meant; that Laurent had died to save me 'and us all' or what happened to my father.

His face colored slightly at my questions and I knew he was conflicted as to whether I should know or not.

"Your father never wanted you to know," he told me finally, "and in a few years you would have been beyond the influence of that demon. But it seems only right that you know the whole story now."

Laurier glanced sadly at my father's casket before taking in a deep breath and sighing.

"Four hundred years ago your family line was very nearly decimated by his evil, nearly wiped off the face of the Earth. It was said that Alexandre de Rousseau, master of the estate at that time, had an agent who had designs on securing your families property and title for his own. It was also rumored he was well versed in the demonic art of witchcraft. If that were his plan, then he was nearly successful. The de Rousseau line was almost completely decimated until only Alexandre remained alive, after having watched his wife and children die one by one under sad and sometimes horrible circumstances. No one knew how Alexandre came to the conclusion his agent was responsible but no one questioned his logic either.

Before a public gathering upon that very spot within the cemetery where you stood and against the wishes of the church, Alexandre cursed the man ordering he be drowned. It was locally believed to be the best way to kill a witch, the popular way being burning but somehow it was rumored that his evil would disperse with the smoke to possess the crowd. So Alexandre decided that the depraved scoundrel was to be drowned in a pool of consecrated holy water. The local church, while not questioning Alexandre's right to dispense the law as he saw fit, did question where he saw fit to do it. They argued that the grounds would never more be consecrated. It was done nevertheless. Alexandre ordered a large stone be brought to the pool and a length of chain. The witch was secured to it at the throat, hands and feet. Before they dropped the huge stone in, Alexandre cursed that the witch would remain in that place forever guarded by the angelic souls of those he'd wronged meaning his wife and children. He was about to have the man thrown in when the witch added, 'and there I shall remain, except for the 'angelic' soul of a de Rousseau child who shall step within the waters to take my place. Then I shall live again and heaven help the descendants of those who sit in judgment against me this today.'

The man was thrown in and drowned. They say that same night the waters turned from its pristine color to the vileness you see today.

That would have been the end of the story except over the passing years there were other de Rousseau children who heard the witch's call and were nearly enchanted to their deaths. That was why a tall iron fence was erected around the place, to keep the de Rousseau children safe. Again, only de Rousseau children have ever been at risk and they cease to hear him after the age of thirteen or so."

"That still doesn't answer how my father died." I said, and my heart grew cold as the realization hit that I would never see him again, that I was now an orphan.

"I had been out in the garden looking for Laurent when I heard him calling to you. It was then that I realized that you were both within the cemetery. It's my fault that he's dead, I should have run in immediately. Instead I ran back to the Chateau for help.

Your father and I found the spot where he'd seen you standing earlier that day at the break in the fence and we went in. He knew we'd find you both by the pond. We found Laurent lying against a headstone. He only lived long enough to tell us that the witch had pulled you under," at that moment Laurier choked up, his grief spilling out uncontrollably, "then... he... died... in my arms."

Laurier fell silent and despite the fact that he still hadn't told me what I'd needed to hear, I remained respectfully silent as well. After a few minutes he managed to control himself, taking a deep breath before continuing.

"Your father dived in after you. Though I confess, I don't know how he found you in all that inkiness. You floated towards the surface, and I pulled you out. Your father didn't surface for some time, when he did he was expelled from the water, just as you say Laurent had been. He was dead. It seems the demon couldn't do anything with a child who isn't of the de Rousseau bloodline, or with a de Rousseau adult.

If you wish to believe in any of this, then there is a witch at the bottom of that pool. One of considerable power to have lasted for so long a time and one who bears a grudge against a great many people, not just the de Rousseau family."

I sat there considering his words. I must have been deathly still as I sat there staring at the two closed coffins before us because I could feel Laurier turn to stare at me and when I spoke my voice sounded strange, even to my own ears.

"One who knows how to cheat death." I added finally.

Laurier continued looking at me for some time and I knew he read my thoughts.

"They're both gone Julian, you must trust in Gods will and release them. It hurts me too, but don't entertain thoughts that can only cause destruction, maybe even to their immortal souls."

My ears heard his words, but my heart wasn't listening.

Later that night, while everyone else slept I left my bedroom and the safety of the Chateau to return to the chapel. I looked again at my father, one last time. I knew what I had to do, but I didn't know what the result would be. A few minutes later I stood again within that dark cemetery, just outside the influence of those haunted waters.

The voice that spoke was all around me but no longer able to enchant as it had that first time.

"You've returned." It said stating the obvious. "As I knew you would. It must be terrible to know that both your best friend and your father died because of you. After all, you brought them both here, one directly, the other indirectly. It's all so tragic! It's also tragic that both their souls are trapped here with me, to suffer for all eternity."

"That's a lie!" I'd never thought of that and the prospect infuriated me.

I can prove what I say is true, but I have so little energy of my own with which to channel his voice. I know, perhaps a bargain can be struck. If you step within the waters I can allow you to speak with your father and you will know my words to be true.'

I shook my head in disbelief.

"Whoever you are, do you really believe I'm *that* stupid?" I said defiantly.

"No, I can see that you are not. Well, tell me what do you want and we can discuss it."

His voice was light and youthful and even held a friendly carefree tone. It was difficult to remain frightened by such a voice.

"I want my father back, and Laurent."

"I want my freedom, what's your point?"

"Give me the former and I'll give you the latter."

"You drive a hard bargain."

There was silence for a time as if he were considering.

"All right," he said finally, "you have a deal. Step into the waters to consummate our agreement."

"I think not," I told him, "your reputation lacks in honesty and goodwill. Prove good faith by performing *your* part of the bargain first."

"That doesn't particularly sound like a good deal from my perspective."

I turned to walk away, remembering what Laurier said in the church earlier that evening. I was making a deal with the devil, or a near one at least, and I knew I would not be returning. He must have known that as well for it was at that point that I heard him call out after me.

"All right we will do it your way, but only one. The other will come after you've performed your part of the bargain."

"After I've performed *my part,*" I said angrily, "I'll be dead, I won't know whether you've done the rest of it or not!"

"I see your point. Alright then after I've released your father you will at least place your feet within the waters, say to your ankles. As a measure of good faith, then I'll return the boy."

"Then we have a deal!" I said with satisfaction. I'd sold my soul but didn't care. It didn't matter what happened to me as long as I got my father and Laurent back. It had been right about one thing, it was true they were both dead because of me.

Somewhere behind me came the sound of bushes moving and then of footsteps. The instincts of a near ten-year-old caught doing something decidedly wrong often tempt him to run, and so did mine. As I turned to do just that the voice stopped me.

"Ah..." the voice said disapproving of my maneuver. "If you run, I'll drop him where he stands."

At that I turned to see my father standing there in the moonlight, wearing the same suit I'd seen him wearing in the casket. I ignored the voice and ran towards him throwing my arms about his waist, but there wasn't the slightest reaction from him at my hug. After a few seconds I pulled away to gaze up at him through teary eyes. It was then I saw the strange expression on his face, a vacancy in his eyes that only stared forward towards the pool.

"I've done my part. It's time for you to do yours." The voice said.

"This isn't my father," I said starting to cry, "it's only a shell, a puppet you're pulling the strings on."

"Of course little fool!" The voice said angrily and added with impatience, "You didn't expect him to be fully cognizant all at once did you? It will take him some time to again acclimate himself to life, maybe hours possibly days, but that has two positive attributes. One is that despite what you and many people may think, true natural death is only dealt once to a customer. That means your father will be around for a long time. I can't wait until we're face to face and he can thank me on that count. Second, and I suppose I alone will benefit from the latter, he can't interfere again in our dealings this night.

Now, I've held up my end of our bargain. I've done exactly as I promised, will you do the same?"

It certainly seemed as though he had. I could only pray it wasn't a deception, but I'd done the best I knew how. So I placed my feet within the waters a second time and again everything started to go black all around me. For a second time I was surprised to find my eyelids were again fluttering open, to see dark familiar images coming into focus all around me, lit by the glow of a full moon's rays at the apex of my bedroom window. It was still night, and everything was dark and quiet. In the fireplace the logs were nearly extinguished. I was focusing upon this when I realized that somewhere outside my vision there was movement. I called to whoever was there and from the shadow came a familiar form to step through the rays of moon light cast through my window. I could just make out my father's face. I was too moved to speak.

"You're awake, finally." He said softly clearly relieved. "Good. It's time we left this place."

He lifted me out of bed lowering me onto the carpeted floor and still too stunned to say or do anything, he dressed me. It was only a few minutes later that he crept carrying me within his arms down the darkened hall steps. In fact the whole house was cast in shadows. There was something wrong but as usual I didn't know what. As he reached for the front door knob we both heard the sounds of voices, lots of them. Father put me down gently and went over to peer out one side of the glass that was on either side of the double main doors and I could see the headlights of cars shining on the house.

"Come." Was all he'd said as he again picked me up.

There were the sounds of running feet up the stone steps and I also heard the sound of my governess' voice, which caused father to stop as well.

"Wait," she'd said, "listen to me. There is a perfectly reasonable explanation for what has happened here. You must listen to me. You can't do this! You're talking about murder pure and simple and what about Julian, are you going to kill him to?"

"You can't murder someone who's already dead!"

I recognized the voice even if I couldn't see him. It was Doctor Basset.

"Can't you just admit you made a mistake? People don't return from death."

"I agree with you on that point, only I didn't make a mistake. That water witch had something to do with his return. If we don't take care of this situation now, we may all die! You're new to this area you don't have to worry, you're not at risk! But our families have lived here for generations and we know the curse is real.

As for the boy, well he might have died in that water, we'll never know. So why take chances."

"Doctor I'm appalled at you! You are supposed to be an educated man, siding with the superstitions of these ignorant peasants."

I was only a child but even I knew that approach wasn't going to win converts to her side. According to what Laurent had once told me, they never liked her anyway.

At any other time I'd have been scared to death. But after what I'd been through, nothing seemed as scary as loosing my father. Not when I had him back, and while he carried me in his arms.

There was the sound of scuffles and then of breaking glass. father still held me as he returned up the stairs we'd just come down, this time he mounted them three at a time but not before the crowd had entered and seen us.

"Where are we going?" I whispered to him. "To America I think." Was all he had said and he hadn't sounded the least bit afraid so I wasn't either.

I thought I knew everything there was to know about the Chateau, I was wrong. Father pushed one wall panel after another, closing them behind us and before I knew it we were groping our way down a deathly dark corridor.

Father put me down so he could feel his way along in darkness with one hand, as he held mine with the other. I didn't ask were we were for fear of being over heard but there was a strong smell of death and decay. Some parts of it were flooded and as the water rose up to my chest. My fear returned and I immediately froze, refusing to walk any further. All I could think of at that moment was skeletal arms rising up to grab me. Father lifted me again, though he needed his hands to find his way in the darkness. We proceeded forward more slowly.

When we exited, it was from the only structure that existed in that ruined cemetery and its locked door gave easily under father's weight. I was glad to feel the fresh air until I again saw the pool by moonlight.

"Well if it isn't the little betrayer." The formless voice echoed loudly. It was clear its words had been meant for me.

"Take your little liar Marion, and run as far and as fast as you can. I assure you there is no way you will ever out distance me. I will find him. I can't hurt you any longer so my revenge against him will be particularly gruesome, with interest for the time it takes me to catch up with him."

The voice began to echo slurs and obscenities, which boomed across the darkened landscape. I had no doubt that they'd heard it from the Chateau and I wondered if they had nerve to follow us in.

In the days that followed, I was frightened for sometime between the voice and the villagers. It was also sometime before I was able to sleep with any measure of security, but father assured me I was the only de Rousseau child there was. Therefore the witch would never be free to hurt me. As for the villager's well, we out distanced them when we reached America. Still, father and I buried our past and strove to fit in and rid ourselves of French accents and mannerism. We were well established in our American lives before I got up enough nerve to ask him about what happened after I'd gone into the waters.

It turned out that the voice was correct. Father saw and heard everything that was happening around him upon re-awakening but was powerless to act, except with the influence of the witch who was surprisingly strong. But he told me that when he saw me step into the water, he'd found the energy, power or whatever from somewhere deep within to act and dove in after me. It seems the witch underestimated him. Father saved me just as he had the first time, the time that caused him his life but this time he was beyond death's influence.

As time went on I continued with my life and the aging process, but he didn't. On my twentieth birthday I remember going into his study upstairs." Julian pointed overhead and his family's gaze had followed. "The tears had dried on his face but I could still tell he'd cried. I asked him what was wrong. It seemed that time appeared to be standing still for him. Yet everyday upon waking he could see the changes in me, as if some invisible magnet were drawing me towards death. It was becoming too difficult for him to deal with. I understood of course. As a child I couldn't comprehend what the consequences of my actions might be, and when I saw the opportunity to bring him back I jumped at it. It wasn't as if Laurier hadn't warned me. I suppose I was just selfish and held little regard for the consequences to him. The thought of dying before him was actually easier for me. Bringing him back had been selfish. Because of me he was separated from everything he'd ever loved, his home, his friends, his country and soon even I would be gone. As I've grown older I've had to live with the realization that we might have been together in whatever awaits after death, if I'd only had just a little faith and left things alone. Now I've deprived him of ever knowing that peace.

It's been a long time since I've thought about any of this, but a few months ago nightmares that I haven't experienced in decades returned.   This afternoon I was sitting at my desk when Lisa knocked and stuck her head into my office. She said there was a caller on line one. He wouldn't tell her who he was, but said that he was an old friend that I would remember. He also said it was a matter of death and life. She thought he was just a weirdo but said it would break up the monotony. She was still staring at me smiling when I picked up the phone. I think my expression must have been one of shock because her smile dropped immediately.

"It's been a long time." The voice told me. "Thank your God for de Rousseau bastards."

The rest was idle chatter. He kept talking as if we'd been friends for a lifetime and how he marveled at the modern conveniences of life nowadays. He ended the conversation by asking me what we were having for dinner tonight. He said it had been a long time since he'd eaten anything but told me not to worry, he wasn't picky."

At that Julian fell into a silence that Paul was the first to break. He'd been sitting quietly during the entire narration but sat up suddenly.

"Well the ending was kinda lame but otherwise it was a cool story. I don't know how anybody's going to top it Friday." He said trying to dispel the gloom that had settled over the room. "So we should all stay awake tonight waiting for that mysterious knock at the door." There was a gleam in his eyes as he made scary sounds for a few seconds. "Question! What happened to your dear old Dad?" He said slyly.

"He comes around from time to time. Father was thirty-five when he died *and* when he returned. I suppose he'll be thirty-five until the end of time." At that Julian sighed heavily again turning his attention towards the bay window that seemed of such a dark and glossy black. "I guess that brings us to today."

"It does."

The voice came from the doorway, and though Julian recognized its deep familiar timber he'd nevertheless startled. Along with everyone else, he turned to look in that direction to find his near image standing framed there.

Chapter 3 - A father Returns

Julian reseated himself and forced a weak smile. "Father you do pick your moments for entrances."

"Well Dad, it's your birthday but I can't help feeling we got the best present." Paul said laughing. "And who are you?" He walked over to the stranger offering his hand, which the man made no motion to take. "You're Dad's brother, am I right? Well who ever you are I'll give you both an *A* for effort but I'm sorry, I just couldn't see any of it."

"Tell me what happened?" Marion said softly and past Paul as if he didn't exist. "Julian you know I have an interest in only two things," He said moving towards his son with what seemed like exaggerated slowness until he'd stood just to the left of his son's chair. He smiled warmly leaning forward to lightly kiss his son's forehead, "the first is you." As he raised his face again it turned immediately stony, his words equally cold, "The other, to destroy the witch, there is nothing, between those two extremes."

"Father..." Julian's smile faded.

"I haven't forgotten my promise." Marion replied soothingly. "I'll keep my word I swear. Even though my heart might not be in it, but Julian if I'm to protect them you mustn't keep secrets from me."

For a moment, Julian seemed indecisive but seemed to reach a conclusion. "I believe he's been communicating with me for some time, at first it seemed through my dreams or rather nightmares. They started a few months back. Each nearly the same and began with his voice in darkness and from the first syllable I recognize it as his, even after three decades. His is a voice I will never forget until the hour of my death. That disembodied voice of his has echoed across the landscape of my nightmares since that night, but these dreams are different. He always begins jokingly and talking pleasantly enough at first before matter-of-factly turning the conversation to how he will terrorize my family torture my children."

Julian's voice became emotion filled echoing painfully across the room as he stared unseeingly.

"Nothing in life has frightened me more than him and loosing you that night. I would give anything; do anything to appease him if he would only spare them. I told him as much."

"Julian, can't you see? You're being deceived." Marion implored. "It's not possible for that demon to have freed him self. I don't know who is responsible for this farce but I swear to you I will find out," His father said adding softly, "and deal with them." His mind was already processing the names and faces on his property the night they'd fled for their lives and crossing off those names he knew to be no longer alive. When he glanced back into his sons eyes he'd seen a faint smile there and something else, sympathy.

"Father this isn't something you can help me with. I'm the cause of all that's happened. I'm only sorry that so many people are paying the price for my stupidity."

As his father started to speak Julian raised his hand to silence him.

"He demanded three things of me," he continued, "before he would be satisfied. The first was the Chateau. That was why I went back to France. Actually I've been back there several times over the past few months. It was necessary to reacquire title to the property, which had been abandoned for some time. He demanded that it be completely restored. No small task, nor an inexpensive one."

For the first time Julian remembered his wife sitting quietly across the room and rose to approach her. Kneeling before her Julian again took her hands within his own. "Liz, what can I say to you?" He said looking down at her hands enclosed within his own and unable to meet her gaze, "I know I must sound like a lunatic, but I assure you I'm not."

Liz brought his hands up to her face and kissed them. "If you say this thing exists," she said, "then it does. End of discussion on that. We'll deal with it, by whatever means necessary." Then she smiled adding, "I can be a pretty creative problem solver when properly motivated. We are not beaten."

"Oh come on!" Paul said exasperated. "You don't really expect *me* to fall for all this do you?" He laughed turning to wave towards Marion before looking again at his father who only ignored him and didn't notice as Marion silently crept up behind his son to stand at Paul's back. As Paul turned a hand had clamped firmly against his throat.

Everyone could see Paul straining against his assailant. Liz released Julian's hands in panic and rose to rescue her son, but a slight touch from her husband's hand upon her shoulder caused her to halt. A glance towards Stewart similarly rooted him as well.

"My dear Elizabeth," Marion said calmly still holding Paul's throat, "it appears that I may have misjudged you and for that I apologize, but in my grandchildren I have not erred. They are stupid, selfish, heartless creatures not entitled to the air they breathe let alone their miserable lives." Marion lifted the young man off his feet. "Listen to me, all of you. From this moment forward we will operate by a new set of rules. I am not interested in anything any of you three may have to say. Therefore, you will sit and not speak again until I authorize it." At Paul's resistance he'd tightened his grasp until the panic upon the boys face became evident. "You *will* do as I say. Do you understand?" Marion looked at the boy until he'd felt a slight nod and released him flinging him back onto the sofa.

"Father," Julian chastised, "I don't recall you ever using that maneuver when I was growing up."

"It was never required, and I only said I would protect them from the witch. You never asked who would protect them from *me*, or if the experience would be pleasant."

Julian shook his head before returning his attention to his scared wife, who continued to stare at her father-in-law, the near image of her husband. Julian turned Liz gently bringing his hand up to her face to gently stroke her cheek, forcing her attention again upon him.

"Liz, it's taken a great deal of our resources to reacquire the Chateau, and I had to furnish it with antique period pieces from his era. Then there was the garden which also required extensive restoration. It was all, expensive. It has taken a great deal, nearly everything that we've worked so hard for over the past twenty-five years."

Julian placed a protective arm about his wife's shoulder drawing her into an embrace to rock her gently. His head was upon Liz's shoulder but his eyes were upon his oldest son still sprawled upon the sofa and glaring hotly at Marion. Realizing the very real threat of reprisal from Paul, Julian released his wife.

"Paul, listen to me, please. This man is my father, your grandfather. Everything I've told you this night is true and if some thing unfortunate should befall me, your grandfather has promised me to protect you, all of you and only he can. The next few days will undoubtedly be difficult and tonight the hardest of all. I know I can count on father to look after all of you. I hope I can count on you to Paul. Promise me, please."

Paul's eyes flared angrily, and it was a second or two before he could force words from this throat. When he did they were hoarse and broken. "This... is... insane..." Paul replied grimacing, his expression full of pain, "you're... all... insane!"

"So this is what you've spent your life anguishing over," Marion said with disdain, "and trying to protect?"

"Soon," Julian's said ignoring his father's words, "everything I've said will be painfully apparent."

"You said he wanted three things." Liz asked.

"The second thing was financial. He wanted money, whatever was left. Everything and I've given him full disclosure. I had no choice. If I held anything back he would have gone after all of you, including you father. He might not be able to harm you but I do believe him in his promise of being able to make your existence a hell. I haven't transferred anything over to him yet. He didn't seem to be in too much of a rush for it, odd considering I'm almost out of time."

"What..." Liz opened her mouth to say more but her husband only smiled and continued.

"Soon we'll be paupers, with nothing left for our children, except what I would be unable to touch due to our marriage. He'll own everything that I have ever owned. Twenty-five years of working for our children's legacy and soon it will all be gone."

"Honey, they're just possessions," Liz said with a smile that seemed sincere, "not as important to me as you are. If that were all he wanted than I would say fine and consider ourselves lucky but you're holding something back, I know it. Tell me!"

Julian looked into his wife's eyes sadly, and when he responded it was in a shaky broken voice. "That I comply with our bargain," he said turning his head slightly towards his father, "and I agreed."

"You don't really think I will allow you to do such a thing do you?" Marion said.

"Yes, I do. Father, you have no choice. I've drank his potion, spell or whatever it is. It's already done. I only have tonight before my life ends."

"No…" Marion began in disbelief just as Liz sprang to life grabbing her husband's hand to furiously pulling him towards the door.

"Stewart, get the car!" She screamed but her husband's resistance proved too great. "Alena, help me!"

"…Julian I tell you it's just not possible." Marion uttered shaking his head furiously.

Frightened, both Alena and David had stood mutely on the sidelines. Outside the influence of the stranger that bore such an uncanny resemblance to their father, but who proved to be nothing like him. But at her mother's call Alena ran to her side also grabbing her father to pull, with David in close pursuit as Stewart ran for the door to get the car.

"No!" Julian grabbed his struggling wife about the waist rooting her in place. "It's too late." He shouted, his words meant for Stewart who immediately stopped turning to look sadly at his employer. "Liz," he repeated more softly, "it's too late." But his wife continued to struggle. "Liz, please stop. It's too late and what would we tell the people in the emergency room. That a witch has cursed me?"

"No that you were poisoned," she screamed, "Julian please

they'll know what to do!"

"That would open up questions I couldn't even begin to answer and how could they help me? I don't even know what I drank, but whatever is to happen I'm sure it'll be entertaining, for him at least."

Julian released his wife to move towards his father gazing at him sadly.

"It seems I'm to leave you holding the bag. I'm sorry." He grabbed his father hugging him tightly. It's time to say good-bye. I've tried to reconcile myself with that demon as best I could but it's you that I wish I could truly make amends with. I just don't know how, so all I can do is ask for your forgiveness.

It's difficult for me to leave this world and have to impose upon you further but I must. I need to again hear your promise to take care of my family, please. Don't let me die afraid for them."

"I would trade them all if it would save you."

"Father, please!"

"Very well, you have my word. Everything I do will be for their protection, I swear to take care of them as if they were my own. You must not worry. Will he come here tonight?"

"I believe so."

After their parents left the room to talk in private, Alena and David reseated themselves in the living room, locked in uncomfortable silence with the man they now knew as their grandfather. David glanced across at Alena who sat in an arm chair across from him but she'd only stared vacantly at the carpet before her. Sitting on the sofa next to him, Paul only stared at Marion's back in silent hatred. Like his father only moments earlier, Marion now stood before the large bay window to stare out at the darkness beyond, hands clasped together behind his back. After a few moments, David rose leaving his position on the sofa to approach his grandfather. As he stared at Marion's reflection David was again struck by the uncanny resemblance he bore to his own father.

"It will be morning soon." David said softly to his grandfather's back but Marion didn't turn and continued staring forward. "Maybe then Dad can relax and understand that this was all just some kind of nightmare." At that David noticed a smile spread across the face of Marion's reflection.

"Is that what you take away from all this?" Marion asked matter-of-factly turning his head slightly.

"It's what I'm praying for."

"Then your prayers will not be answered. You see the witch does exist. Our only hope lies in his still being imprisoned within those cursed waters." Without warning Marion turned violently upon the boy. "If he isn't then I will destroy him. Nothing will prevent me from tearing him limb from limb. I swear he'll never live long enough to reach my son."

It was only then that the boy saw the slender blade of the knife, possibly seven or eight inches in length, clutched within the mans tightly clenched fist and Marion was approaching him with it poised for action.

"And I have much to repay him for." Marion added.

As he took a step toward the boy both Paul and his sister noticed the knife and reacted, jumping up to intercept their bother and the crazed man. They reached their brother to find the knife instead protruding out of Marion's chest, yet not a drop of blood flowed. The movement that placed it there had been too swift for them to see, slowly Marion raised his hand to grasp and remove the knife.

"No, wait!" David reached out to stop his hand. "You'll bleed to death. Alena help me, Paul get me something to stop the bleeding."

Paul stood there motionless for only an instant before grabbing the tablecloth and sending the cake, glasses and Champaign crashing to the floor.

"Give me that!" Alena snatched the cloth from her brother and moved towards Marion who only stared at the three in amusement. "Help me get him over to the sofa." She ordered.

David moved to one side and his sister to the other as they attempted to lead the injured man forward, but like their father only moments before he hadn't budged. Instead Marion only gazed at

Paul who stood distant from them before pulling the anchored knife free from his chest to toss the still clean blade casually to the floor.

"Are we having fun?" Julian asked from the doorway, his shocked wife at his side.

Marion looked away embarrassed.

"Dad..." David approached his father, his face deathly white.

"Easy." Julian soothed grabbing his son by the shoulder. "See," he said pointing at Marion, "father's fine."

"But the wound..." David looked from his father to grandfather before pulling away and going over to stand within arms length of his grandfather, grabbing the fabric of his shirt and flinging it open. The wound was evident for all to see but no blood flood from it.

"Ouch! Is that going to heal?" Julian said curiously as he also stepped forward to where his youngest son still held his grandfather's shirt.

"Don't be silly Julian, how can it? I'm dead, remember?"

It was then that the boy fainted.

"Well I hope you're proud of yourself." Julian said angrily as he bent down to revive his son who lay sprawled at their feet.

"I was just giving my grandchildren a lesson in the new realities of life."

"And scaring them to death in the process it seems."

"Well a man my age has to take his fun were he can find it, besides they're none the worse for the experience."

A heavy knock sounded at the front door freezing everyone while David, still on the floor, began to rouse.

"I'll get it." Paul said angrily stalking off towards the door. Whatever tricks and craziness was spreading about the house he was determined not to be ensnared in it. At the door he paused only briefly before swinging it wide open.

"Stewart when the hell did you leave?" He asked the man on the other side annoyed but only received a confused smile in reply. "Well what are you knocking for? You live here just like I do." Paul walked away leaving him standing there within the open doorway. "You know we could use a little sanity in here." Paul called out over his shoulder as he reentered the living room but stopped instantly. Less than five feet away Stewart stood leaning over his brother David. They'd lifted him off the floor and carried him over to the sofa were he now sat staring past Paul at the man behind him. Paul turned to glare at Stewart's mirror image.

Chapter 4 - *Resurrections*

"Well, good evening to you all." A familiar looking tall, slender blond man stepped into the room with a lively springy step and bowed deeply from the waist, extending his arm in a gracious gesture. "How wonderful, I can't believe we're finally getting the chance to reacquaint ourselves." He said looking directly at Julian.

"You..." It was the voice that caused Marion to vault into predictable action and Julian and Stewart tackled him to their visitor's amusement.

"Marion, you're looking well." He said watching the momentary violence being played out before him with an occasional chuckle. "Does anyone have the time?" He asked clearly still amused.

"Twin demons," Marion declared struggling against his son and the chauffer. "Julian what is the meaning of this?"

Julian hung his head over his father's in silence. His eyes reflecting deep pain and regret as he and Stewart continued to hold Marion pinned to the floor.

"You have what you've always wanted Lothaire, Chateau de Rousseau." Stewart said quietly, his knee in Marion's back. "Don't be greedy, that's what did you in the last time."

"Is that so?" He responded sarcastically moving over to examine the remnants from the over turned table. "Well, that's certainly not the way I remember it. Then again, I was out of circulation a lot longer than you, wasn't I? So perhaps my memory may be a bit faulty, due to that long isolation." Lothaire added dryly but then smiled. "Was this a coming out party, for me?"

"That was all a long time ago Lothaire, and we were both different people then."

"That at least is true. I've grown a great deal since then, but I am not so quick to forgive or forget, particularly those that imprisoned me for so many centuries."

Liz moved to her husband's side but stood there uncertainly as she watched him struggling to restrain his father. Beside her, holding her arm, was Paul as he attempted to distance his mother from the violence.

David looked on at the scene in indecisive disbelief. He'd finally convinced himself that just as Paul had said, the knife thing had been nothing more than a parlor trick, it had to be. But now he wasn't so sure, realizing he'd never seen his father act violently before. What ever was going on, it was no joke.

Still pinned to the floor Marion had ceased struggling. Sensing this, Julian began releasing his weight from his father.

"Lothaire, the people that did that are all dead!" Stewart told him.

Concentrating his efforts Marion leveraged his left arm nearer to his chest to swiftly raise his upper torso toppling Julian over his back and onto Stewart. He'd gotten completely to his knees before both managed to again subdue him.

"True and their descendants except for..." Lothaire allowed the words to trail as a smile relit his face. "What the hell happened to you?" He asked gazing at Marion and the bloodless wound evident through his open shirt. "Marion you really should be more careful. That will never heal, you know that don't you? You don't really want to spend your eternity trapped in an ugly corpse." He chastised.

"These people are my friends Lothaire, don't think I'll let you hurt them."

"Then you'll stop me?" Lothaire asked clearly amused. "Like you did before? You really never learn do you? Alexandre was also your friend and what did he do for you?"

"That was more your doing than his."

"Oh now you're just being stupid. He buried you alive, remember, and for how long?"

"I know what happened," Stewart said bitterly, "I was there to remember?"

Lothaire turned towards Julian pulling out a pocket watch that seemed vaguely familiar. "I understand that sunrise will be at five-fifty-three, any second now. A brand new day but then I've already warned you haven't I?" He said returning his attention towards Julian. "Those eyes of yours will never see it."

It was then that Stewart released Marion to charge at his twin brother. Without Stewart's support Marion easily toppled Julian to also rise, following Stewart in close pursuit. They both froze in mid-stride when Julian cried out from behind them. At the same time Lothaire also hit the floor.

With his fist Stewart broke a nearby lamp shattering it into jagged pieces, the largest of which he picked up to hold over the unconscious form of his brother. He'd held it there motionless for several seconds before Marion knocked him aside to grab the still unconscious man's throat.

"I swear I'll destroy you, you bastard!" Marion shouted tightening his grip around the still unconscious man's throat.

From his sprawled position on the floor, Stewart watched as Marion attempted to squeeze the life from his twin. A revelation struck him as he'd gazed from his brother to Julian, also unconscious only a few feet away.

"No, Marion stop!" He shouted rising to grab Marion's arms pulling them free from his brother's throat, but Marion only changed adversaries moving instead upon him.

"I knew when I saw you two were twins that you were also twin snakes!"

"Better a snake than a fool!" Stewart shot back angrily. "At least I always know *my* enemies!"

At that Marion clasped his hands together, rearing back and striking Stewart with several blows that sent him sailing backwards. Then he charged at him. Behind them Liz knelt at her husband's side. With a groan Julian's eyes began to open. He turned his head to watch the ensuing violence, an ever so slight smile curling his lips.

Julian's children rose leaving their father's side and were

attempting to break Stewart and Marion apart but their grandfather merely tossed each aside violently, throwing David across the table. He moved for a second attack on Stewart. This time grabbing him violently by the throat, at their feet Lothaire was only just rousing.

"What's going on?" He asked groggily. His eyes opened wide as he looked across to see Julian on the floor staring back at him.

"Stewart, what are you doing?" Lothaire asked seeing the violence and trying to rise but couldn't. "Stewart let him go!" But instead Stewart struck the man several times in succession momentarily stunning him.

"I will," he replied, "as soon as you're out of here. Are you all right?" He asked after managing to get Marion in a choke hold. "Can you get to the door?" He yelled.

"But..." Lothaire was gazing at Elizabeth who held her husband tightly and stared deathly at him.

"Now damn it, go now!"

Marion broke free, flinging Stewart backward but he quickly righted himself. As Marion charged towards Lothaire, Stewart again intercepted striking him three swift blows to again send him sailing backwards.

Passing through the doorway Lothaire caught the blur of his image in a large mirror that hung just inside the main entrance, causing him to slide to a halt. He took several steps backwards to confirm what he'd seen. Upon the realization, he picked up his pace on route towards the door. In a few seconds he was gone.

After he'd left, Stewart remained fixed, ready against an unexpected charge from Marion.

"Do you break all your promises so easily?" Stewart shouted and he saw that Marion understood immediately turning his head to see all of his grandchildren rising painfully except one.

Marion exhaled loudly realizing defeat as his eyes fell upon his motionless grandson but it was clear his heart was not with the boy.

"I *will* find him," Marion whispered murderously referring to Lothaire and glaring at Stewart, "wherever he goes. I'll destroy you both."

"Perhaps," Stewart said easily, "but not tonight. For now I think you have other matters requiring your immediate attention." Stewart said glancing sharply towards the overturned table and backing up slowly. Behind it they both knew that David lay motionless, but Marion's eyes were still fixed upon Stewart. He could see Julian's father calculating which were more important, destroying his enemies or the life of his grandson. His eyes remained on Stewart as he backed up moving away from the door and back into the interior of the room.

Chapter 5 – *Dispossessed*

It had been less than twelve hours since he'd stood upon that very spot at Rosehill Cliff. Instincts forced him there and now two twins stood facing each other, staring eye to eye, one of them shedding tears.

"My god!" Julian raised his hands to look at his now slender fingers, much like the fingers of a fine pianist. The wrists were also slim. He picked up a lock of loose curls that hung onto his chest and examined it shining golden in the rising sun. "What have I done?"

"Julian, don't worry. After all you're still alive. Everything's going to be fine. We'll fix all this, I promise." But if his new twin heard, he gave no indication. Instead Julian sank down onto the grass to weep. It was several minutes before he'd recovered enough to speak again.

"How can you say that?" He sobbed. "How do I know what's going on up there even now? Stewart, he could be killing them, I've got to go back!"

"There's nothing going on up there, I know Lothaire. Right now he's simply reveling in his new found power. Do you really think he did all this just to kill them? For that he wouldn't have needed your body as a disguise would he? Besides, if we go back there now there'd be a line of enemies we can't fight back against. Not just your father."

"Why didn't he just kill me? It would have been preferable to this."

"Not for him. They say that revenge is sweet and there'd have been only a few minutes of pleasure in such a hasty action. No, the possibility of dragging it out would be much more appealing to Lothaire."

"Put me in that damned pool then, that's what he'd threatened. Why would he want to switch bodies with me?"

"Julian, Lothaire suffered for a very long time, it would take a strong soul to survive for the period he did. I doubt seriously if you would have, apparently Lothaire thought so too. So what would killing you get him? The best he could look forward to was briefly torturing and killing you. This way your anguish will last for a very long time, because like your father you're in a body already acquainted with a mortal death. Now you can suffer as much and for as long as he did, at least in his mind.

Besides, you said yourself he wanted everything, a *full accountability,* and remember you also mentioned how odd it was he never asked you to sign anything over. Julian you really should have confided all this to me sooner. We might have been able to better prepare for it. The good news is your father is a formidable enemy. Lothaire would never have been able to relax with Marion at his back if he'd killed you. The bad news is he's formidable for us as well, now Lothaire can sleep easy because Marion is tracking us." At Julian's misery he added, "You were unconscious, there was no way your father could have known it was you."

"You knew."

"I know Lothaire and how he thinks, and still I was slow in realizing his plan."

"Stewart, you've been a good friend. It's difficult to believe that Alexandre was ever stupid enough to believe you'd betray him. When I freed you I'd prayed for nothing more than you keeping your promise to talk to your brother on my behalf. Frankly, from what I'd read about your family I had little reason to hope." Julian reached out grabbing his friend's arm. "Thank you."

"You took quite a risk alright." Stewart said softly. "I confess though, I never really understood why."

"Well you did try to save me."

"What do you mean?"

"I spent years trying to find out who the other voice in the cemetery that day had been. Then I found out Lothaire had a twin. Father had shown me the way into the wing the night we escaped. Years later I returned to finish the exploring I never got the chance to do as a child. Eventually I found both your journals and your tomb."

"Ah, the journals, I'd forgotten about them. I suppose in death we continue to cling to the moral code we embraced in life. I did what any normal person would have, protect the life of a child. Besides, I should be thanking you. You'll never understand what you did for me when you released me from that prison. I was languishing in that place. Trapped between life and death for all time, or so I thought but it had to be." Stewart involuntarily shuddered at the thought.

"But why, I understand what was done to your brother but why were you in that place?"

"I was there by choice. Alexandre was a fool and Lothaire had him wrapped around his little finger. Even after I warned him that his children might fall victim to Lothaire's evil he did nothing. Alexandre saw Lothaire as a trusted friend, almost a saint, but..." Stewart broke off suddenly.

"But..."

"It wasn't completely Alexandre's fault, it was mostly mine. I knew of Lothaire's plans from the beginning, but how could I stop him save killing us both. You see what happens to one happens to the other. It had been that way all our lives, feeling each other's pain and pleasures. We were always told that we were born together and doomed to also die together. If only one were to die, it was prophesied the spirit of the other would fly to inhabit the body of the survivor. I confess, the prospect of death was infinitely preferable than the thought of sharing a body with Lothaire. So you see I was as guilty as he. I knew what was happening but did nothing out of fear. Fear of what would happen to Lothaire and subsequently to me. I didn't act until it was too late. At least Alexandre could legitimately plead disbelief and therefore ignorance.

Alexandre's favored son had been his youngest named Chevalier. He was a bit strong willed at times but otherwise a good boy who would have grown into a fine strong man. I was also fond of him. I don't suppose you ever stumbled across any paintings of his when you were looking for me?" Stewart asked.

"It was so long ago, but I don't think so."

"Well if you had you'd remember. Even after so many centuries, I still remember him clearly. His face and David's were the same. I knew I couldn't let him kill the boy yet if Lothaire's body died his spirit would possess my own. I never liked sharing the same roof with him, I certainly didn't want to share my body. So I made arrangements with Alexandre to handle that eventuality, too late to save Chevalier though. It took Chevalier's death before Alexandre was convinced that the tragedies occurring to his family were not the result of accidents. So we were both imprisoned, separately out of mercy to me. So you see I have much to thank you for and much to make amends for. Though I still don't understand how you were able to secure my release alone."

"You're as much a victim in all this as we are," Julian said looking at his friend sympathetically, "and your blood ties to him mean nothing to me, you know that. Besides, if you feel the need to thank anyone it should be father and the excellent education he gave me. I was able to translate the Latin of your journals easily."

"I'll remember that," Stewart said with a smile, "maybe I'll get the chance to thank him someday, before he cuts my heart out that is."

"I'd say we're even now so I'll understand if you need to walk away from this, especially if you feel and suffer as he does. After all he is your brother."

"How do you figure that?" Stewart said with an easy smile.

"He's your twin."

"Not any longer, *you're* my twin."

At that Julian smiled.

"So you see," Stewart added also smiling, "he's not even a blood relative any longer so I have no further fear of my curse. Best of all he's completely mortal." Stewart said laughing wickedly and startling Julian. "I don't think he realized how much of a shield that was for him. It'll be easy for me to kill him now."

"You want to kill him!"

"Relax Julian, I was only kidding... mostly. Okay only as a last resort." Stewart said raising his hands to calm his new brother's fears.

"You're right of course. I can't leave my family with that monster! I'd die at my own father's hand if I could be sure of killing that bastard first."

"That wouldn't be the most favorable outcome. Anyway, it's best not to think about it for now. Your father will protect them, even from you." Stewart said with a smile. "What bothers me is that now he has your influence and power."

"You mean my business, my home, my children and my wife."

"You mentioned you now control your father's former estate right?" Stewart asked and his brow momentarily furled, "So Lothaire has all the things he's ever wanted, plus." He waived his hand to dismiss the thought. "But he gains nothing from harming your family."

"Doesn't he? Elizabeth, the kids, their all insured!"

"I told you not to worry. He hasn't had time to acclimate himself to his new body yet, let alone this time period. Take yourself for instance. Look at you, you're a long way from being a hundred-percent and so is he. Lothaire will need time to rebuild and he'll never try anything with your father there. More importantly he no longer has his book, I hid that many centuries ago."

"What Book?" Julian asked but then shook his head dismissing the question, "Look at me Stewart, your brother seems to be doing just fine without a book."

"Don't call him that Julian, please." Then Stewart added confidently. "Trust me to make this thing right. I helped imprison him once, I can do it again."

Stewart brought one finger up to gently tap his lips as he considered. "You know," he said after a moment, "I'd love to be there to hear Lothaire explain how I managed to be in your employ. Marion was shocked to find me there but I'm sure my *former* brother will come up with a suitable lie."

"Well?" Julian asked with a tired smile.

"Well what?"

"Was I right in not telling father about you?"

"Oh yes." Stewart laughed. "I didn't think so at first, but that was a perfect call.

It's been a long night, we've got to find somewhere safe to stay, its time to go."

Julian looked back at his home, his eyes again reflecting misery.

"Julian, we only lost this day's skirmish but I promise you we'll win the war."

The Curse of Ravenhurst

Chapter 1 - Halloween

She was running blindly through the night, down deserted streets and darkened alleys screaming. Her heels echoing loudly off the surrounding buildings shattering the quiet but there was no one around to hear those cries. Behind her IT stalked, following slowly. She turned yet another corner, arms flailing wildly as she tried to keep her balance, nearly stumbling several times. Too late did she realize the approaching dead end could also be her own.

Trapped, she continued forward until met by a brick wall and turned her back against it. To the right was a door barred and chained. She ran to it in a desperate attempt to pull it free from its anchors but no use. To the left was only another solid wall of bricks. Just then she saw IT, a dark mass separating from the shadows before her and her screams intensified.

"Where you going *this* time?" I asked Earl laughing and at the same time eagerly trying to see the movie's outcome past his silhouette passing before me.

"None of yo' damn business." Earl replied squeezing past me on the sofa on route towards the kitchen.

"You know were he's going," Perry said with a laugh as he sat comfortably slumped in Sunny Mac's old man's recliner, "to take his chicken-shit-ass in the kitchen to hide under the table," and we both laughed irritating Earl.

Though I'd only been hang'n with the group a few weeks, I'd started showing off, becoming braver with my words, especially where Earl was concerned. I guess it was because of the three, he was the safer, saner and more mentally stable member of the group. Truth be told, he was also the reason I was allowed in the group since neither Sunny Mac nor Perry looked on me favorably. Maybe that was why I always tried so hard to impress them whenever I got the chance. Yet from time to time, I'd forget that at fourteen, almost fifteen, my bones were still pretty damn fragile. I was the youngest of our little crew, and a long way from being either of the other three's equal, particularly Earl's. He was only three years my senior but it might as well have been measured in dog years. Earl had a good two-feet and maybe even a hundred pounds on me. At the same time that occurred to me Earl's fifth or sixth quick exit had also struck me as funny and I wondered what he'd do if he returned in time for the movie's finale.

Earl simply shrugged it off and continued his route towards the kitchen adding over his shoulder, "I'm going to take a leak, if it's any damn business of either of you two asses."

"Whatever man, whatever!" I said, diplomatically returning my attention to the TV program, which had broke for a commercial.

"Maybe you oughta see a doctor," Perry said to Earl's back clearly amused and causing Earl to stop mid-stride. Perry twisted the top on a large beer bottle that he'd been holding and lifted it to his lips. He took several large swallows and I watched the heavy gold chain he always wore move up and down several times before he continued. I couldn't help noticing that when he finally brought the bottle down again its volume had decreased by over two-thirds, "to get that yellow streak removed."

For a few seconds the air was electric with the threat of violence and the glare from Earl's eyes seemed to send rays of rage. I knew Earl well enough to read his expressions. We all did, including Perry and for anxious seconds I knew that Earl was nursing an idea of going over and pounding Perry down. Perry saw it too. I'm sure he did but he just sat there all calm and amused and after a second's hesitation the clash had just seemed to evaporate.

"Man you lucky my Momma taught me better than to beat the

shit outta crazy-ass bastards like you," and he added with malice, "but don't push me too far now, hear?"

His threat seemed real but I could see in the seconds afterwards that his anger was dissipating. Finally, he waived his arm in a dismissive gesture and left the room.

Now if it had been me instead of Perry, I'd have collapsed from the sheer delight of surviving that near death experience, maybe wipe the beads of sweat from my face. At the very least I'd have exhaled loudly with relief but Perry did none of that. He simply laughed softly to himself and took another swallow from his beer, this time finishing it. I couldn't help being impressed.

Earl was right, Perry had always been more than a little crazy, always the character and totally fearless. He was also tall, athletic and as popular as hell, especially with girls. Perry lived on the second floor of the red brick two-flat across the street from mine. You'd say the name Perry to anybody in and around our neighborhood for blocks and they'd know instantly who you were talking about, before you could utter another syllable. He and Sunny were the same age, seventeen. They'd grown up together and were Siamese in nature but I'll tell you that fearless streak in Perry, that was the difference and truth be told that was the reason nobody messed with him. At least that's what I've always believed. If you messed with Perry you'd probably have to kill him to finish it.

"Hell, maybe he's just as board as I am."

Startled I turned to see Sunny Mac had re-entered the room. He stood just outside the doorway of his bedroom, at the far side of the living room and his voice reflected disgust. Now like Earl, Sunny also been doing a disappearing act. Going in and out of the room for the better part of that last hour, but unlike Earl, his reasons were a lot less obvious. Although I had heard him talking in whispered tones a couple of times behind his closed door, so I knew he was on the phone. He'd glanced at his watch in irritation, a curious thing with a thick black band sporting a large faced analog watch. It certainly was unique because I'd never seen it in stores but not stylish by any stretch of the imagination. Now

Sunny was always meticulous in his appearance and I could never figure why he'd drop the ball when it came to that ugly watch.

As usual Sunny's old man was out in the streets somewhere, probably drunk. He stayed that way mostly but the point was that he could have come home at anytime. If he had, we'd have been sitting there, enveloped in a thick haze of stagnant smoke, which alone could have gotten us arrested. It mingled with the smoke from his father's personal stash of cigarettes that we'd swiped. Empty beer bottles and take-out trash lay scattered everywhere. I'll tell you, I was real uncomfortable with the scenario of his busting, in but not Sunny. He knew his old man and always said it didn't matter much if he was there or not, that his father didn't care anymore what he did, not since his mother's death. I guess she'd always been the backbone of their household. Gossip was that with her death, almost five years earlier, everything had started to disintegrate including Sunny's old man. But my guess was that the greatest change had occurred in Sunny.

Yeah, we were drinking his old man's beer, smoking his cigarettes among other things and cracking up over that corny movie that was at least fifty years older than any of us.

"Hey man," Perry said finally to Sunny, "the floor's open for suggestions." Then he added slyly, "Obviously you got some."

"We can go over to my place." I offered. "My Momma's at work. We'll have the place to ourselves till she returns tonight, about one."

"Oh that sounds really entertaining." Perry said. "In fact why don't we take a tour of all the neighborhood slums?"

"Hey Darius ain't it past yo' bedtime?" Sunny asked me irritated and Perry laughed. "Who the hell keeps letting this kid in anyway?"

"Hey man he's not hurting anything. Leave the kid alone." Earl said reentering the room in time to catch the tail end of the conversation.

Wounded, I returned my attention to the TV. The movie had long since finished and the credits were now rolling. I wondered briefly what had become of the woman.

"Look, I'll see you guys later," Earl announced and I could see he was already putting on his Nike jacket, "it's time for me to head on home."

"WHAT! It's still early." Sunny stammered.

"For you maybe, but my old man's gonna fry my ass. I was 'posed to be back an hour ago."

"Hell late is late! You can stick around for another hour or so at least."

"Why?" Earl asked. "What's gonna happen in an hour?"

"Someth'n." Perry said lifting the bottle to his mouth. Clearly he'd been hoping for some residual traces of the liquid but brought it down again in disappointment to let it drop to the floor. He smiled adding, "I can always tell. I bet I know your ass better than your own momma do."

"Somebody better define someth'n pretty damn quick or this ass is outta here. Cause you know what? I'm not the least bit interested in hearing the 'I pay the cost to be the boss' or the 'you better abide by my rules or I'm gonna throw your ass out in the streets' speech my old man's gonna give if I come back too late." But Sonny seemed neither interested nor listening.

"You know," he said finally a broad smile lengthening across his face, "I was thinking we ain't done noth'n interesting in a hell of a long time. We oughta do someth'n to make this Halloween more… special."

"Shit!" Perry laughed. "What are we talking about? You wanta go see some fortune teller or someth'n?"

"Say what?" Sunny asked but then shook his head realizing he wasn't interested in an explanation. "Naw man, I was thinking of something a bit more passive."

Earl looked from Sunny to Perry, clearly confused but his steps back into the center of the living room clearly spoke of interest.

"More passive?" Perry asked waiting for more.

Sunny reached down and retrieved Perry's keys from the nearby coffee table and threw them to him, "I'll tell ya, in the car."

That was how it had started. I've thought about it a lot over the years and to this day I still can't say for certain why we ended up doing what we did, we just did. At the time I thought it was just for fun. Now looking back almost twenty years, I'm not so sure anymore ... but like I said, I was only a kid then, thirteen, fourteen nearly. To tell the truth, I still lean more towards the idea that it was because Sunny knew Earl would nearly piss on himself in fear. That the suggestion was just to see his reaction, but I have to admit the years have certainly softened this position.

It must have been around eleven-thirty or so that night, and we'd gone several blocks with Sunny giving directions to his dumbfounded chauffeur Perry. By the time he'd revealed his plan, we were pulling up before our destination, his idea; taking a tour through the Peaceful Valley Cemetery.

So there we were, the four of us, Sunny Mac, Perry, Earl and myself, Darius Sneed, standing outside the gates of Peaceful Valley that October night. I guess all the trick-or-treaters had long since gone home, if they were ever out in the first place. I sure as hell hadn't heard any that whole day, not in our neighborhood. I guess they knew even if they got something, which was highly unlikely, they would have been to damned scared to eat it, or been robbed or worse for the effort.

The weather was perfect, cool and breezy. There were only the cars that passed every now and then under the dark cloudless sky holding a three-quarter moon. Dry leaves were scraping across nearly empty streets because of the hour, and I thought about the woman in the movie we'd watched earlier.

"You kidding?" Earl said amazed. "Man, you crazy?" He asked finally and seemed earnest in his desire for an answer.

I'd sat there quietly in the car with its door open, watching other lonesome cars that whizzed passed every now and then. Outside, they argued. The fact of the matter was that I was afraid to voice my opinion either way, least they pull me out of the car then and there and leave me stranded. Besides, it did seem appropriate to the season; after all it was still Halloween night.

"Perry, what do you think?" Sunny asked.

"Shi ..." Perry's voice trailed as he considered.

It was difficult to see Perry clearly in the dark but I knew his answer would be affirmative even before he voiced it.

"Why not?" He said finally.

"Both you asses are crazy!" Earl shouted.

"Darius…" Sunny asked.

I startled at that. It was unusual for Sunny to ask my opinion about anything. In fact, as he'd voiced earlier he wasn't ever keen on my tagging along so I knew I was walking on ice, thin ice.

"Whatever." I called back neutrally.

"Little chicken shit…" Sunny began hotly.

"Man, why you always picking on the kid?" Earl said cutting him off in my defense and I cringed at being called a kid, even if I was one. "Anyway, I don't have time for this shit," he added angrily, "I told you that already. Now, are we going back or what?"

For several seconds the three of them stood there in silence, outside the cemetery gates before Sunny finally spoke again.

"There's the sidewalk, hit it." Sunny said evenly, without the slightest hint of anger and even I knew he had some angle. At Earl's hesitation he added, "There's the way back dude, get to step'n." He said smoothly pointing to the direction back. "Have a nice walk, and take junior with you."

"You two better step lively," Perry said amused. "I hear spooks party hard in and around cemeteries at midnight on all Hollows Eve, might even try to pull you in … for a permanent visit."

"Don't tell me, talk to that ass next to you." Earl shouted. "He's the one talk'n bout a visit but if you really believed that you wouldn't be parked right outside one would you?"

"Hey, spooks don't frighten me," Perry said evenly, "but if I see one I'll be the one in a car and I'm sure I'll be able to put more distance between me and it than you will." He said grinning.

"Both you clowns start'n to make me mad," Sunny said finally, "I don't believe either of you are stupid enough to still believe in that shit!"

"I don't!" I offered trying to recover my position somewhat. I figured if I could swing Earl over into coming I might get on Sunny's good side. That might make my position in the group a bit more stable. "Earl, why not hang?" I pleaded. "I mean, even if we got out and walked, by the time we got back home they'd already be there."

"Damn straight," Sunny added, "just your five or ten minute general tour, a quickie."

From my position in the car I could only see Sunny's back which suddenly shot straight.

"Hear that?" Sunny said anxiously. He turned his head and I could now see his profile. He seemed to be straining to hear something. I turned around in my seat looking frantically about the car but saw nothing. Outside Earl was also looking about nervously. When I again turned towards Sunny I could see both he and Perry smiling back at us both.

"That coulda been the sound of us right now, coming out of this place."

Perry laughed and Earl made a disgusted noise before finally consenting.

"Can we just get on with this?" Earl said angrily.

Sunny was the first over the five-foot stone fence, then Perry. I'd jumped up and was about to try to pull myself over as well when Earl's arm pulled me down again restraining me.

"Look Darius," he said as he whirled me around to face him and began talking quickly, "I hang with those two because I can handle them. They can't ever talk me into doing what I really don't wanta. I'm only here cause I know Sunny'll make your life miserable otherwise."

"Hurry up!" Sunny whispered urgently from the other side of the wall.

I thought Earl's sermon was over but it wasn't.

"Don't you know Sunny and Perry are always trying to keep me outta school," he whispered, "they'd like noth'n better for me than to stay at their level forever but not me. I'm just in this school and this neighborhood temporarily. I got priorities and I suggest you get some too."

I'd only been half listening; instead I'd kept my eyes upon the wall wondering what Sunny was thinking about out delay, it must have been loathing I'm sure.

I didn't say anything back to Earl, just jumped to grab the top of the wall and pulled myself over. The sermon was over, as least as far as I was concerned.

It's strange that you can sometimes see clearly the turning points of your life. Even at that young an age I knew that I stood upon a meridian, on one side was Sunny and Perry, the bad asses I'd always wanted to be. On the other side was Earl, the person who for some reason unknown to me had always treated me like the brother he never had.

I'm sure it had only taken me a second to make the decision to follow Sunny. But at the time it had seemed more like an eternity before I reached up to grab the fence and scale it, not nearly as gracefully as the two had. Standing on the other side of the wall beside Sunny and Perry, I felt more like one of the group. I knew Earl had been hurt by my decision to side with them. Unfortunately that thought hadn't bothered me nearly as much as having Sunny and Perry think even less of me than they already did.

Anyway there we were, Sunny Mac, Perry, and me standing there whispering on the grounds of a cemetery for Earl to join us but his head hadn't appeared at the top of the wall. Finally Sunny Mac burst letting out a string of obscenities that started both Perry and me to cracking up.

"What the hell are we laughing at?" Perry whispered to me finally sobering up as Sunny moved closer to the wall to talk with Earl on the other side.

"Maybe it's the thought of those two asses getting the four of us put in jail." I whispered back. All the while Sunny continued to shout like a psycho at Earl.

"Hey man," Perry went over to stand beside Sunny and pulled him around to face him, "what the hell are we doing here anyway? Look around you, everything's even deader here then it was at your place!"

"Yeah, everything supposed to be dead on that side." Earl's said adamantly from the other side of the barrier. "That's why I'm on this side. Hell don't you know its bad luck disturbing the dead at any time? I'm sure as hell not gonna do it on their home turf and at night."

"We're here now," Sunny whispered to him before turning back to address Perry. He jabbed his finger on Perry's right shoulder to underlie violence in each of his words should he be contradicted, "and we're go'n in!"

With a fluid gesture Perry knocked Sunny's hand aside and smiled coldly at him.

"Man I'd advise you not to forget yourself," Perry told him, "or who you're talking to."

Sunny Mac quickly relinquished.

"Okay, okay... chill." He said throwing up his hands to Perry. "If you two piss asses so scared why don't you just jump back over with Earl? Then you three punk asses can hold hands all the way back home!"

With that Sunny took a step further into the cemeteries interior, "Come on Darius."

You know, I wish I could have been standing outside myself looking at the scene at that moment. I bet I must have looked like that black dude in that old Bob Hope movie. Black as night with the only thing clearly visible on me being my eye's wide open like two headlights in the night. I was rigid with fear but what could I say? Sunny never really had any interest in me tagging along with them. Another false move and I'd have been a permanent outcast. What I had there was a tremendous opportunity, so when he walked off, I reluctantly followed though I knew he was just using me.

"Darius," it was Earl's voice calling to me and I ignored it as I kept walking, "wait up!"

Both Sunny and I heard a soft thud and a quick couple of steps and I turned to see both Earl and Perry following silently close behind. Two or three minutes later and the four of us were walking deep within the cemetery's interior passing headstone after headstone. It was a strange feeling, one of stillness and darkness, like the world on the other side of that wall had ceased to exist. I could no longer hear anything from it. Like the deadness of the place swallowed up everything except the sound of the wind and the rustling of the trees. That got old fast.

"Well," Earl said angrily to Sunny from behind us, "now what?"

It wasn't until that moment that I'd noticed the crowbar that Sunny carried parallel to his right arm. It had been concealed between his arm and body. He now made a slight gesture that to my mind suggested he contemplated striking Earl with it, but either that had been my imagination or he'd decided against it.

"This way." He said measurably before walking off.

We weren't out to make a profit, not at first. At least that's what I always believed even after seeing the crowbar but in retrospect, I guess it was pretty unusual that Sunny also happened to pull a flashlight out of his pocket. At the time, I swear I thought the crowbar had just been for protection.

"Will you look at this?" Sunny cried out excitedly and we gathered around the object of his interest. It had been a monument that looked to be bronze. Anyway, that was how it started. It had just been an accident that Sunny had seen the opportunity to make some money for us, right? The next day, we'd all gone with Sunny to fence the stuff we'd *found*. Strangely Sonny had known exactly were to take it. The owner of the salvage yard business had been an older gray haired man who looked as if he should have retired from the business decades earlier. At the time, I had thought it odd that he hadn't seemed the slightest bit surprised when we'd pulled up, and hadn't asked any questions as to how we obtained the monuments. Well, we ended up scoring about two hundred dollars our first night from the stuff we *found* laying about. I noticed that Sunny had waited behind to talk to the man for some time before we were able to pull off. Two hundred dollars wasn't bad, even when split four ways and it didn't seem it didn't seem to hurt anyone. That's how it started. We did it a couple of times, even got some notoriety on the local TV news.

Yeah, we did pretty well that first night and we were soaring high, 'cept for Earl. He continually brooded bringing all of us down with his fire and brimstone speeches.

I finally broke down and asked him why the hell he came along then. What he said surprised me.

"Shit fool, don't you know how dirty that bastard is?" He asked referring to Sunny. "He'd found away to hurt you just to get back at me! You think that ass gives a shit about you? Hell no! Darius they don't even want you round, can't even stand you. You know that. I'm not sure I want you around either cause I don't think your head's screwed on tight, not anymore.

I don't even know why I bother try'n to look out for you, cause some people you just can't help no matter how hard you wanta."

So just like that Earl had as much as said he'd see me thrown out of our group. I knew he spoken the truth about how little they valued my presence there and each day that I'd seen them I'd expected to hear them tell me to take a hike but it never happened. As for Earl, I used to look up to him, but in the weeks leading up to Halloween night things began to change. I never told him so, not in so many words, but inside I'd started to hate him. What a hypocrite! How he could stand there and preach to me I'll never know, not when he was standing right there in that cemetery beside us. Not when the money from the take that night was split four ways. I sure as hell didn't hear him turn it down. Now he was a threat to my standing within the group.

We laid off trying it again for few weeks. When we did it was a different cemetery in another part of town. It was Perry who got nosey and wanted to enter the mausoleums and started prying some of the vaults open. Earl flat out refused to be apart of that.

"Then go." Sunny said softly, not the slightest bit troubled. "I'm sure me and Perry can count on Darius."

It might have been my imagination hearing the added inflection upon my name. Maybe it was just vanity because I wanted him to think highly of me.

"Yeah, right," I chimed in, perhaps a bit too eagerly because I saw Earl's wounded glance and the mischievous smile Sunny Mac shot back at him. It seemed an amusement Perry also shared but Earl wouldn't budge, even when told he'd forfeit his part of whatever we found. Only we never found much worth selling, only rotting corpses.

We expanded our radius. The last time we tried it was at a cemetery called Ravenhurst. It was a small cemetery nearly thirty miles out and on the outskirts of a small town. It looked to be really old with some of its headstones dating back as early as the seventeen hundreds. Again we'd found nice shopping there and again Perry had wanted to view some of the deceased in their native habitats. I laughed and told that ass 'this ain't no museum trip.' That set Earl off.

"Listen," he said, "we made some money, let's just go home."

He was scared as usual but by now I was getting used to the routine and the money. Sunny had been trying to break the lock on the outer mausoleum door and seemed to be ignoring him. I went over to where he was working and crouched down to whisper to him.

"Why do we keep taking him along?" I asked. Brave words considering Earl would probably have stomped me into the ground if he'd heard.

"Cause if he's an accessory he won't talk." Sunny whispered back nearly under his breath before glancing sideways in Earl's direction.

I stood and moved off to stand beside Perry who was the look out. Why we needed one I didn't know, the cemetery didn't have a caretaker but Sunny liked being careful. I was sure that neither Earl nor Perry had heard us.

"I'm just say'n it ain't right." Earl said talking to Perry, loudly. "None of us are gonna live forever. Would you want people doing this to you?"

"When I'm dead Earl, it won't much matter." Perry had replied matter-of-factly.

"Don't any of you believe in God, can't you see this is wrong?"

"You develop a conscious," I shouted, "*after* spending the money!"

Earl's anger flashed fast like lighting, and he reached me and drew back his fist before I could react, fortunately Sunny came between us.

"Man take your crazy-ass back over there before I stomp you into the ground!"

"This is between me and that little weasel over there." Earl said pointing over his shoulder at me, but his voice cracked with fear of Sunny. But that was nothing compared to my fear of him. My heart was thumping fast enough to explode. He'd looked at me threateningly before moving off. I'd made a serious mistake, his glance told me that much. It wasn't over.

In my heart I knew that the only reason Sunny had stopped him from slaughtering me was because it interfered with his agenda for the night. Like I said before, Sunny had never been to keen on my hanging around them, it had mostly been Earl who had gotten me in and it had been Earl who championed me whenever I had ... conflicts. He'd always treated me like the little brother he didn't have. Now I'd betrayed him. I hadn't recognized that fact until I'd seen the anger and disappointment in his eyes as he'd turned away, it had been mixed with hurt. I looked up to Earl before Halloween and before our tomb robberies. I don't know when I completely threw him off the pedestal replacing him with Sunny as hero, who immediately resumed his task at the door. Like that guy in the *Indiana Jones* movie, I chose poorly.

The largest vault on the grounds was named Ravenhurst, the same as the cemetery and finally Sunny had broken its lock. The door opened with an ominous creak. As we stepped within its stone interior, it seemed like stepping into a refrigerator as the cold musty air hit us. Sunny had been eager and was the first to step inside. I have to admit I hung back. There was something in the air, a foreboding. I'd felt it almost immediately. Or maybe I was beginning to mirror Earl's perceptions, possibly out of guilt.

Perry moved past me to follow Sunny inside and switched on his flashlight. The interior was huge. It must have housed about fifty or sixty bodies within, in drawers on three sides of the walls. As the flashlight passed its beam across the area I could see that the middle interior had been set up like a living room with an old style sofa and chairs and dark wood end tables. The whole thing looked like something out of one of those Victorian movies. The tables even had pictures on them. Rich white people, from about a century and a half earlier.

'Used to the finest things in life and death from the looks of it,' I thought to myself still standing unmoving in the doorway. Suddenly I was propelled forward to fall hard face down onto the cement floor, which had been covered by a thin oriental carpet. I turned to see Earl standing where I had stood, his anger still more than apparent.

"Save it for when we get outta here." Sunny replied with only the slightest interest, and again I realized how serious my mistake had been replacing my heroes.

While the others went over and started prying open the drawers I hung back looking at some of the pictures on one of the tables. Call it morbid curiosity. One of them was a woman and she was beautiful. She must have been about twenty, maybe even younger. She seemed to have dark hair worn pinned up just like in the old movies. Her eyes seemed dark from the old picture, so I couldn't tell what color they were for sure. I wondered if she'd died shortly after the picture or if they'd just decided to put that picture there. Maybe it was her favorite or something. Perry called to me and snapped my mind back to the task at hand.

The first one we opened was that of a woman. A small petite skeleton draped in a silken type dress and surrounded by the musk of perhaps a hundred years confinement. I wondered what she'd think if she could see that whatever influence and power she may have had in life had all been reduced to this. I think I was staring at her hair. It was still so neat and proper even after so many decades. Perry cursed beside me, loud with excitement. I followed his gaze downward to her throat and fingers.

"Look at that! Shit, I bet it's real. What do you want to bet that it ain't real?" He said.

"Of course it is, why else would they bury it with her." Sunny Mac said echoing Perry's excitement as he stared over my shoulder, once he got a better look he pushed me roughly aside.

"Who the hell are we gonna sell that to." Earl added worried.

"Man if that things real, it must be worth a fortune! They'll slap our asses in jail as soon as we take it outta here."

"Man, what's the matter with you. These pieces ain't been in circulation for a minimum of a hundred years. Ain't nobody gonna be looking for um." Perry turned his back toward us and walked over to Sunny who had left our side and was furiously prying open the next drawer. "Sunny will you talk to this fool!"

While they were talking, I'd just stood there staring dumbly at the corpse, not even listening anymore to what they were saying. I was trying to figure something out in my head. It was like a tiny voice deep in my mind trying to tell me something. Then it occurred to me that she was the one I'd seen in the picture, the one on the table near the sofa where we'd entered.

"Where the hell are you go'n?" Sunny Mac yelled at my back as I crossed the room. I'd gone back and picked up the picture and came back over to the drawer that held the body of the image in the frame. "Look, it's her." I showed the picture to Earl and to Perry who had returned and was huddled beside him. They'd still been arguing over whether it would be safe to fence the broach when Sunny came over. He'd glared at me for a second before grabbing the picture out of my hand and slamming it down to the carpeted floor.

"Who gives a shit?" He said, crushing it with his foot for effect.

We'd been robbing the dead for weeks now and I'd gone outta my way to emulate my new heroes, I'd never had a problem with it but this time, it all seemed different, maybe because my victim now had a face. She wasn't even alive to care anymore but still she seemed more like a real person to me now.

It felt as if a dream that turned into a nightmare. The only difference was I could clearly see a cliff a head. I knew something bad was going to happen. My feelings were all jumbled and confused, in ways it never had been before. Nothing I felt was making any sense. I felt as if this woman had been good and kind and that she didn't deserve what was happening to her.

"Man ... you know," Sunny seemed all choked up with

emotions of his own, but for different reasons, "all these people are from the same family so what do you wanta bet that they're not all similarly accessorized." He laughed.

I didn't know what he found in the next drawer, but it seemed to please him. I knew that he thought he'd hit the mother lode.

"Come on get busy, rip the rest open!" Sunny commanded as he waved Earl and me towards the other drawers. He could barely contain his excitement; only Perry seemed to surpass him in his fever.

It had never occurred to me up until that moment that Sunny had always been our leader. I guess I just never really thought about it until that night and then I realized that we always seemed to be acting according to some suggestion of his, no matter how wild or dangerous and we never did anything that he wasn't interested in doing. He was the reason we were there and I was beginning to regret it.

Earl and I were still standing over the woman, whose plaque read Sarah Ravenhurst. She had died over a hundred and fifty years earlier and had never seen her eighteenth birthday.

"We shouldn't be doing this, she doesn't deserve it!" I don't know what made me put words to my thoughts because I'd been try'n hard to swallow the impulse. "Earl's right, we've gotta stop, this ain't right. Something terrible's gonna happen if we don't, I can feel it."

Perry had moved over and was opening the next drawer but came back over to stand directly in front of me. For the second time that night, I knew my safety was in jeopardy.

"Between you two chicken asses, I'm getting pretty damn tired. If you want a piece of any of this," he said pointing his finger in my face "then I suggest you get to work with the rest of us."

There was such hostility in his eyes. I knew he was trying hard not to hit me. I'd never seen him that angry before, at least not with any of us. There was greed reflected there too and something else, I believe I saw fear in them. Maybe he was afraid he'd lose the treasures he'd found.

Now I was usually not troubled much by intuition or conscious but something told me that if I didn't go along with him, he was going to cut short our friendship and maybe me along with it. I turned back to the vault that held Sarah Ravenhurst's remains and made to remove the ring from her finger, which had been forgotten in the excitement. Instead I just played with it, I didn't remove it, just twirled it on her skeletal finger a few times. It seemed to satisfy him.

"I want to be far away from this place well before sunrise." Sunny called from where he was squatting in the far corner.

None of us spoke for several minutes. Fear just hung there in the air between us. I stared down into sunken sockets that once held dark blue eyes. I don't know how I knew her eyes were blue, I just knew. The others were in various stages of opening other drawers, even Earl who was bent over a drawer that was beside me, grimacing as he reached within.

"Hey," I shouted and my voice echoed louder that I'd expected, "did you guys notice that all the people we've come across so far have all died within a few months of each other?" I said.

No one replied immediately, Earl's voice finally broke the silence.

"What do you think happened to them?" He said. "You know these people coulda had some kinda disease or something." He straightened up and looked at Sunny, waiting for a response. When none came he dropped what he'd been fingering back into the open drawer and hastily whipped his hands onto his shirtfront.

I don't know if Sunny heard him or not, if so he'd ignored him. But I suspect he was too enthralled in his own activities.

"Shut up Earl, just keep work'n." Perry responded irritably.

I wanted to stop them but I couldn't, and I knew I couldn't be a part of it either.

For what seemed like eternity I'd stood there in indecision. Finally I bolted for the door. Half way to freedom my foot got caught in a hole in the rug that I hadn't noticed. This gave Sunny a chance to grab my arm before I could complete my escape. I felt like a coward and I was. I couldn't stand up to him and realized at that instant that I never had, to any of them. I glanced back towards Earl, hoping he'd support me the way he always had but he just turned away. I guess I deserved that.

"I have to get out of here," I stammered, "I think I'm gonna puke." I tried looking as miserable as I felt, though for other reasons. "You wouldn't want me to leave any evidence laying around do you?"

"I don't give a shit what you do as long as you get those drawers open. Spew inside them for all I care. Just grab the valuables, you can wash them when we get back."

Sunny looked at me as if he'd book no more excuses so I started to turn back and do as I was told but for some reason I didn't, I couldn't, I don't know why. I can only say that something seemed to possess me. "You're all fools!" I was angry, angrier than I'd ever felt before, it seemed to come out of no where. "Someth'n terrible's in here, I can feel it."

"No, what you can feel is this!" I watched Sunny as he drew his arm back to strike me as if in slow motion and I felt fear but it wasn't of him. I easily sidestepped his blow before he could connect and in retaliation I punched him as hard as I could in his stomach. I hadn't expected much beyond it being suicide but the force of the blow sent him back several feet and he hadn't straightened up immediately. The expression on his face told of his pain.

"Take whatever you want," I told them all smoothly, "do whatever you want," then I head my voice drop to a more icy sinister tone, "but do not think you will not pay for it!"

For a few seconds Sunny seemed uncertain as to what to do but he no longer seemed to have the nerve he'd had only seconds before in challenging me. He turned away and told the others to get back to work. I started walking forwards the door with a confidence I'd never felt before. "For all the good it will do you." I said over my shoulder before leaving. I went through the mausoleum doors and welcomed the warmer winds that caressed my face and body. It had been so cold inside. I thought to myself that it had been so many, many years since I'd felt warmth. I took several steps and collapsed into darkness.

Chapter 2 - *Waking with the Dead*

When I awoke it was morning. The sun was just appearing over the trees and buildings in the distance. I lifted my head enough to notice the stillness in the air and that the leaves of the trees were completely motionless. There were no birds flying or chirping, no city sounds penetrated the oppressive quiet of the place, and then I realized I was sprawled across a fresh grassless grave. Appalled, I quickly righted myself and was startled by the sound of soft laughter. It seemed to come from everywhere. I spun round to find a white boy only a few yards behind me. He couldn't have been much older than me. I was lucky it was day, because at night he'd have scared the hell out of me. He was the whitest white boy I'd ever seen, but he must have been mixed with something way back in his bloodline because his hair was thick and black, or I thought maybe it just seemed that way against his pale complexion. He was seated on a headstone and seemed completely at ease with his surroundings.

Everything seemed different in the daylight. Only the isolation and stillness of the place, which had struck me from the night before, had remained constant. I was completely disoriented and the gate was no where in sight. I was about to ask him which way to the exit, but quickly thought differently. Maybe it was the expression on his face. He was smiling, but it was an unnatural, cold mask-like smile, and there was stillness to him as he sat perched on that headstone. For some reason I was reminded of the corpses from the night before. There was just something about him that wasn't right, and it unnerved me nearly making me too scared to turn my back on him, but it was nothing I could rationalize so I watched him. I remembered my brief encounter with Sonny the night before and was confident that I could take him if I had to, and if he had a mind to start something. He was certainly no heavier than I was, but if he attacked when my back was turned he could probably strangle me with that thick gold chain he was wearing round his neck, the parts of which I could see through his partially unzipped jacket.

I continued sizing him up when I noticed him slowly glance down at a thick black band on his wrist that held a large ugly watch. I had hoped he was starting to get bored and would soon leave but he continued to watch me with a gaze that now seemed somehow more intense, almost expectant. He continued to stare at me with a cold vacant smile.

Something changed. I'm not sure if it was real or something just inside my head but the vacuum-like feeling of moments before left me. I felt gentle winds on my face that pushed at my clothes, and I watched it play with his blue windbreaker jacket that held a Nike logo. It was then that I noticed that nothing else about him moved, not his hair, not his pants. Everything else about him was completely immobile, like a wax museum dummy in a vacuum. Only the jacket seemed animated.

I was becoming unraveled and despite the weather I felt cold inside. It was time to go. I'd have to take my chances turning my back on him.

Looking around me, I couldn't remember having walked so far from the mausoleum but I must have because it was nowhere in sight. I was a long way from home and in a completely white neighborhood. I was going to stand out 'like a fly in buttermilk' as my grandma used to say. It was dawning on me that it wouldn't be hard for that white boy to identify me when they found out what was missing. I had an impulse to run but resisted it. My mind was generating irrational thoughts, of beatings and lynching. At least I hoped they were irrational.

Calmly I brushed off my clothes and turned to leave hoping that if I didn't do anything else memorable maybe he'd forget me, when something about him made me turn back to again face him, but he was gone.

I didn't want to stand there trying to figure out what it was. Obviously, my 'friends' had left me and I knew I'd better leave to. Otherwise I'd be left holding the bag and an empty one at that.

In the light of day, I could see that the cemetery was larger then it had appeared last night and I was completely disoriented.

It was some time before I finally saw a familiar landmark within the cemetery, telling me I'd come that way in the darkness the night before. A familiar cluster of hedges and trees within the cemetery's interior, but the effort had done me little good when I saw in the distance the wall of stone we'd scaled the night before. I didn't want to be seen doing that in broad daylight. I'd have to keep searching for a gate. I walked until I found it. It seemed to take forever but the wall finally lead to an open iron gate. I walked bravely through as if I belonged in the place and cautiously looked up the street. It was then that I saw Perry's rusted old pickup parked exactly where I'd last exited it, in front of the cemetery's North middle wall. There were as least two tickets on it and it was in the process of being towed. It was then that it hit me what it was about that white boy that had bothered me. I remembered that he glanced at a watch with a thick black wristband, like the one Sunny always wore. I'd found out later Sunny's had belonged to his father, memorabilia from the sixties or seventies. Then there was the gold chain resembling the one Perry always wore and I think it was the only jewelry he owned. At the time I hadn't taken it all in, but at that moment I also remembered the jacket. It had stood out the most, a deep sky blue with the white Nike emblem, just like Earl's. My knees felt turned to rubber as I watched the tow truck pull away with Perry's car, and I knew that for whatever reason they were still in that mausoleum.

Chapter 3 – *Phantasms*

I hadn't gone back to find out for sure. They were just too damn greedy. I found my way out of that area on foot and walked for miles before I felt there was a gas station I was comfortable enough to go in and use the phone. I called my Ma, collect. She begged and pleaded and eventually got someone to come out and pick me up.

Sitting at home in the kitchen, eating cold luncheon meat from the package at the kitchen table, I was surprised when Momma quietly came up behind me and slapped me upside the back of my head.

"What the hell did I tell you about following behind them damn drug dealing thuggy friends of yours? They left your stupid butt out there didn't they?" She didn't wait for a response before slapping my head again and continuing. "I don't know what the hell's the matter with you, you heard what they said on the news about that area last year, they full of them Nazi's."

She opened her mouth to say more but her anger wouldn't let her and I knew her pressure was going way up. I could see it in her face. I also knew she'd been worried to death about me since my phone call, maybe since she'd gotten off work late last night. I hadn't once even thought about her since leaving Sunny's place.

The next day was Saturday and Momma hadn't said another word about it or to me for that matter for almost that entire day. I stayed inside my room, staring out my window but I never saw what I was looking for.

Sunny Mac lived on the street behind mine but spent most of his time across the street from me at Perry's house. I'd heard that in a few days it would be his eighteenth birthday. Despite his underage status, Sunny had done it all. He'd robbed, assaulted, been caught and had ended up in jail, sometimes in adult jails, all in support his drug habit. He'd even spent unsuccessful days in drug treatment centers, with the aid of the state. The last time had been two months earlier. He'd spent a month locked away that time. When Sunny returned home he'd sworn himself free of his demon for good, though early on almost everyone knew that wasn't true.

As I sat there thinking, I realized that many a times we'd been patsies for his schemes to support that habit. In his defense, Sunny was there when his friends needed him, and he knew enough of the neighborhood locals that they left us alone.

Like Sunny, Perry had grown up on the streets. There was seldom a morning when Perry's yelling down to someone on the streets below from his window didn't awaken me. Didn't matter to him what time of the day it was. His Momma had lost their phone earlier that spring to bills.

His uncle died a few months earlier and he'd inherited his '73 Chevy Impala. It wasn't much, but it did run. We knew how much he loved it, must have been nostalgia or something. Daily either Sunny or Earl would tease him about it. Perry's every free moment was spent catering to it but whenever Sunny wanted to go anywhere Perry seldom hesitated. I think he liked the power he felt it gave him over us. We'd jump in, Sunny on the front passenger side and Earl and me in the back.

Earl lived up the street and despite his pompous words in front of the cemetery; I'd always believed he followed Sunny around like a disciple, as much as I did. Out of our little cluster of four, his family had been the last to move into our neighborhood. I did believe Earl's words about making it out of the 'hood. Earl would go perhaps furthest of us all because he found school so easy. His only downfall had been his need for friends, a need as bad as my own. Maybe that was why he could never be my idol, I just saw too much of myself in him. That and the fact that Earl was pretty straight laced.

His only other sibling was a younger sister. Earl was one of the few kids I knew who had both parents, married and under one roof. He hung out with us a lot but still managed to get to school and bring home A's so his Dad was tolerant. I wondered how he was going to explain staying out all night but as I sat there thinking further about the three of them, I didn't need psychic powers to know that something had gone wrong. They were probably sitting in a jail cell somewhere but there was nothing I could do about it. They were just too damn greedy.

I had been sitting on my bed watching the sunset through my bedroom window when Momma knocked on my door. I'd expected her to come in earlier preaching about how I was getting older and was on a fast track to ending up like one of those street hoodlums. I knew she was still worked up cause we hadn't said two words to each other since the kitchen that morning. When I didn't answer her knock, I'd hoped she'd think I was asleep but instead she opened the door and peeked through.

"You been in here sulking all day. I know its someth'n more than my hitting you." She hesitated and seemed uncomfortable. "I'm sorry about that, I was just so mad but someth'n else's wrong. What have you been do'n?"

I didn't answer right away and she immediately jumped to the worst conclusion.

"You do'n drugs?"

I could hear alarm in her voice and saw her sway a little as she stood by my bed. Grabbing her hand I pulled her down to sit beside me.

"No Ma!" I said trying to sound as offended as I could, but she wouldn't let go of the conversation. Not until I'd defeated her concerns completely.

"Then where'd you go last night?"

I tried to think up a suitable lie, but my mind was a blank. I stared out the window for a few seconds and it was then that I saw him, the white boy from the cemetery standing across the street and staring back at me. I think my whole body must have gone completely rigid. Momma saw my facial expression and also turned to look out the window.

"What's wrong?" She asked frightened.

I looked at her for the briefest instant and when I turned back he was gone. I got up thrusting my head out the window and continued looking for him up and down the street, but he was no where in sight. It wasn't until Momma started to shake me hard that she got my attention again.

"I want you to talk to me." Momma said firmly. "Tell me where you've been and what you've been do'n?" When I hadn't answered she took my hand into hers and placed a small dried gourd in it, enclosing it there. "I have to know Darius, and if you won't tell me then I'll ask the Obayifo."

There had only been a few times that Momma had put me under such close scrutiny that I found myself under that evening and during each of those times I'd found it impossible to put her off, or lie to her in any way but she had never threatened to use the influence of the Obayifo.

You see there has always been a little ritual between us. Whenever Momma felt I was worried about something, scared or was being untruthful she'd always pull out this funny little gourd. On the one side it was painted a bluish-green, and on the other brown. Tiny symbols were scratched onto both sides. Momma had always told me it was a powerful talisman, brought over by our ancestors in chains. It had been in our family just that long. Through the gourd, Momma believed that the spirits of our ancestors could be reached. That it was the gateway for our family's power and wisdom.

As a child, I believed in those stories. I'd been comforted when she'd given it to me to hold. With it I knew somehow that I didn't have to be afraid of the dark. I had ancestors, family, that cared about and who were looking out for me. The last time I saw the gourd I was nine years old and I'd been totally absorbed in all the stories she'd told me. Now, over four years later, I was nearing adulthood and didn't have time for childish games anymore. I tried to pull away, but it was as if I no longer had the strength. It was like my hand had gone numb and a deadening sensation was traveling up my arm.

I can't be sure, but at the same time I felt as if there was some kind of unspoken language passing between us. Most of it I couldn't understand until there was a clear image of the cemetery in my mind.

Why did you go there?

My response could only have been images of money and the things I hoped to buy with it.

That place is cursed. Could you not feel it?

I tried to convey what I felt and then there was a concurrence that I had been touched and communicated to by one of the trapped souls there.

The souls within that place are trapped within their rotting bodies by the demon that now guards them. It feeds their existence and so they cling to it. They cannot know peace until the demon does. Your friends are now counted among those lost troubled souls. If you truly care for them then you will free them but be warned that will call for a sacrifice from you.

From this point until the sun sets on your journey you must travel alone, but if you are successful all those you care about will await you.

The connection was abruptly broken. I didn't understand why until I saw Momma on the floor by the side of my bed, she was gone.

Chapter 4 – *Alone*

I never knew my father, there was only Momma and as far as I knew we had no other relatives. So I was totally alone now, no relatives, and no friends. I didn't know what to do, how to go about burying Momma. In the end the state would have to bury her cause we had no savings of any kind. Only a little bit of money that she saved to pay one month's bills in advance if necessary or to eat with if times got hard.

The next night after she died, I came into our apartment that afternoon and found our greasy landlord standing at our china cabinet putting items in his arms. When our eyes met, I turned away nearly crying. It was too much of a reminder of my own guilt. Afterwards I sat on her bed and cried.

No one had heard from Sunny, Earl or Perry. While I didn't know for sure, the voice in my head had confirmed that they were dead and I was beginning to believe it. To that end I'd just kept tormenting myself. If I'd stood up to Sunny maybe I could have convinced him not to go. Maybe they'd all be alive now. Momma would still be alive.

I'd managed to dodge the child welfare people that day by telling the police and ambulance people that my Dad was on the way home. They didn't bother checking, but I didn't know how long that would work. Somebody was bound to call in on me.

Well I just sat there, in our modest living room, stewing in self-pity. I don't think I'd eaten much in two days and that fact was beginning to make itself known, despite everything.

As I sat there, fingering the gourd Momma put into my hands, I realized it was the only material thing she'd ever cared about. I grabbed it tightly holding it to my chest and got up and went into the kitchen to find something to eat.

Everything was dark as I walked into the kitchen. I switched on the light and was alarmed to find him sitting there at my kitchen table watching me, the white boy from the cemetery. Again like in the cemetery he only smiled at me, but the smile seemed different this time. It seemed sympathetic, but he said nothing.

I tried to act mean, crazy, and full of the courage that I didn't have as I reached for a cleaver from the butchers' block I'd bought Momma on her last birthday. "I don't know who the hell you think you are but you better get your sorry ass outta my kitchen!"

I don't know maybe he saw right through my act, maybe he was better at acting crazy than I was, or maybe he really was crazy, but he didn't move a muscle. He just kept on smiling at me.

I hadn't realized that I'd been holding my breath, but with my last tirade I'd felt the sudden urge to exhale. As the air escaped my lungs so to it seemed had my strength also left my body. It was all I could do to put the cleaver down on the table and drop into the seat opposite him. Besides they do say crazy people can be pretty strong, and who knows how a battle like that would turn out. That's certainly what I'd call a white boy I didn't know sitting at my kitchen table in my 'hood.

"I know the strain on you must be tremendous Darius." The pale youth across from me spoke in a thickly proper southern accent. "You really should try to calm yourself, please." He'd spoken softly, as if we were friends. Yet there was oddness to his voice and speech, exactness to each syllable he spoke that I found grating. "Unfortunately, the stress for you won't end, at least not for a while," then his eyes narrowed, "but I do believe I see an end in sight."

"Man I don't know you, now I said get the hell out of my house!" I jumped out of the chair and took two steps or so towards the door. I didn't know where I expected to get with that, he obviously wasn't going anywhere.

He didn't say anything to that, just sat there patiently before again motioning me back towards the chair I'd only just vacated.

I returned to my seat in a sea of irritation.

"Who the hell are you? What do you want from me?" I could hear the grief in my own voice.

"Darius I am sorry. Where are my manners? I should have introduced myself but I assumed you knew my family intimately." He leaned forward in the chair slightly and I could feel a chill spread across the table. "After all, why else would you and your friends have paid your respects to my family's mausoleum?"

I was too shocked for words but tried not to show it as he continued.

"I had a lengthy conversation with my stepmother, and she informed me that you were different from your friends. It seemed you alone heard and acted upon her pleas, where they ignored her. For that reason Sarah beseeched me to grant you leniency."

"Man, I ain't never met your Momma!" I shouted noticing that he'd again fallen silent as he awaited calm from me before continuing, so I tried to talk more reasonably. "Listen, you're confusing me with somebody else. I don't know you and you sure as hell don't know me," I continued with strained patience "and I don't know your Momma.

Look, it's late now I suggest you leave this neighborhood before it gets any later."

He seemed amused at that and chuckled silently. "I assure you Darius, there is nothing here that can harm me."

"Oh is that what you think?" I said hostilely but he was no longer looking at me. Instead his eyes were roving about the kitchen, taking everything in.

"Then let us talk instead about you and *your* mother then." He said focusing his attention again upon me. "I am sorry about her passing."

"You don't know noth'n about my Momma, so drop it." The whole conversation was straining me but I didn't know how to end it.

Perhaps you should stop fighting me and listen.

169

I was confused for a second, but then figured he'd responded to what I'd obviously spoken aloud. Then I realized that I hadn't actually heard his voice, instead it seemed more like a thought that had appeared in my mind.

"Just say what you came here to say and get out!"

"Very well, arrangements have been made for your mother, Miss Sneed. Her body has been transported to Johnson's Funeral Home here in your neighborhood. On Tuesday at one she will be taken to Saint Martin's where her funeral will take place. Interment will be that same day at three on the grounds of Heaven's Gate Cemetery. There I have procured a vault for her. This arrangement is a temporary affair really, while I have larger accommodations built within Ravenhurst."

He paused and there was an evil, sinister smile with teeth and everything that chilled me to the bone.

"Now that I have been released, I can see that it is long overdue for expansion. Oh yes," he said amused and almost in an after thought, he reached inside Earl's jacket pocket to pull something out. "It seems only appropriate that she wear these." He extended his hand palm up, inside was the ring and broach I'd seen within the Ravenhurst vault. He then added. "Call it a welcome to the family gift. Lets see how long *she* keeps them."

I'd been listening in silence and made no motion towards the jewelry. Instead I turned my head toward the kitchen window. It hurt so badly hearing about a funeral for my Momma. Then I heard his voice cutting through my thoughts, again in my mind. *Don't look so despondent Darius, she hasn't gone anywhere, not really. Very soon I will help you to see that.* I returned my attention to him at that. At first I hadn't known how to respond. My Momma had been gone no time and already my mind was caving in upon itself. Guilt voices I decided as I looked at his still extended hand offering the jewels.

"No thanks." I said dryly, trying to sound convincing despite the fact that my initial anger had long since turned to fear. My Momma was destined for a cardboard box and maybe a common grave until I could do better, someday. Perhaps the jewelry would have helped but still I hadn't reached for them. It seemed that his hand had hung there suspended for an eternity before he finally withdrew it and the jewelry. I returned my attention to the window.

"Darius, make sure you are at Saint Martin's on Monday. It would be a shame if Miss Sneed's only living relative and son was not present at her funeral and I would be … irritated."

I looked back again towards him only to find the chair now empty, and pushed up toward the table as if it had never been occupied.

We had a back door to our apartment. It was in the kitchen, but the door was locked from the inside. Then I realized I was the crazy one.

Sunday afternoon I went outside to sit on the front doorstep of our apartment building. I don't know how long I sat there when I was startled by a long shadow that fell across me. I looked up to see Erik, the neighborhood dealer standing in front of me.

"Hey man, what's up!" He asked slyly. There was a glint in his eyes and it was obvious he had news.

"Noth'n." I replied from the emotional pit I'd dug for myself.

"Then you ain't heard Dartanian, yo other three Musketeers all dead." Then I saw it, an open laugh, "I seen um take Sunny Mac's body outta his apartment last night myself. Can you believe that crazy ass old man of his had been go'n in an out of that place for three or four days before he realized that the smell from his son's room wasn't dead rats." Again Erik laughed.

By mid day I had confirmed it for myself, Sunny, Perry even Earl, all dead. Each one found in bed fully dressed each one dead. Sunny Mac had been the last one to be found.

Until that moment I'd continued to harbor a distant hope that they were just avoiding me because I'd let them down. Though deep inside I knew the truth, I'd been told as much from the voice in my head the night Momma died. But I didn't have time to dwell on my friends for to long though. I spent all that next day trying to find Momma. I'd gone down to the city morgue. They were supposed to keep her there the few days or so it would take to get the paperwork done for her grave but now they told me they couldn't find her. Terrible thoughts kept going through my mind. I'd heard the things they do with bodies of the poor. I nearly cried myself to sleep that night. I'd let her down, again. By then I had relived the events of those last few hours over and over in my mind and no matter how many ways I analyzed it, I was always to blame. I started altering things in my mind where I'd manage to save everybody just to alleviate my pain. It got so bad that at times I wasn't sure what really happened. Of course eventually I would again realize my friends were dead, including the one person in the world that mattered most to me.

Chapter 5 – Haunted

It was Tuesday morning, nearing nine o'clock and I was still in bed. I can't say exactly what it was that had awakened me. It might have been the light streaming through my windows or the street noises from outside. Whatever caused it my eyes had flung opened, focused and immediately I'd felt anger, full blown, because there he was standing over me, arm casually draped over my headboard, gazing down at me intently. He was still in the clothing I'd seen him in that first time we'd met in the cemetery.

"Well, Sleeping Beauty awakens." He said moving away and over to my closet. I watched him open the door and delve inside pushing back racks of my clothes with disdain.

"Man who the hell are you!" I shouted. "What do you want from me? Why won't you just go way and leave me alone?"

He ignored me in favor of holding up a pair of pants that hung from a wire hanger. He scrutinized them briefly before dropping them onto the floor with a turned up nose. Finally he returned his attention to me.

"We have already had this discussion Darius haven't we?" His voice was soft and untroubled, "We have moved well past the time for introductions."

That response wasn't sufficient to motivate movement on my

part and when I hadn't, he seemed genuinely irritated.

"Very well, my name is Edward Ravenhurst! There, are you satisfied?"

I still hadn't moved and then he took a step towards me, and while his face was unreadable I felt foreboding and then genuine terror.

"I told you to be ready." He said advancing slowly towards me. "You have a busy day today." His voice was still soft, but now seemed to possess an icy menace that chilled the room and caused me to pull the covers up. "I said get up Darius, NOW!"

I got up quickly at that and got dressed. There's just something about crazy people that have that affect on me. The only problem was I wasn't sure who the crazy one was. It might have been me. Suppose he was just a figment of my imagination. In any case, real or not, I was as mad as hell. My night had been sleepless joined by nightmares that now seemed to haunt my waking hours.

There was a knock at the door.

"Don't answer it!" He ordered irritably. "She'll go away eventually."

"Just a second." I yelled running for the door, Ravenhurst had not tried to stop me. I heard him call to my back as I reached the door.

"You'd better be at Saint Martin's by ten-thirty Darius." I looked around to see him standing in the doorway to my bedroom before disappearing inside as I opened the front door.

"Good morning." The woman standing in front of me was a tall and stout motherly type who looked at me with extreme sympathy. I recognized her immediately.

"Do you know who I am?" She asked.

"Yes Ma'am, Mrs. Harris."

"I heard about your Momma's death. I'm so sorry. I didn't have a chance to stop by earlier, I've been grieving myself, over Perry." She looked as if she was going to cry for a second or two but then I saw resolve in her eyes. "Well, there's nothing more I can do for my boy. Is there anything I can do for you to help?"

She was still standing in the doorway and I remembered my

manners.

"Would you like to come in and sit down?" I asked.

She consented and I directed her over to the sofa. I sat in a straight chair opposite her.

"I heard that your Momma's funeral was being held at Saint Martin's."

I was shocked and it must have shown because I'm sure she misunderstood.

"I know you're hurting. With the death of my brother only a few months ago, and now my only boy ... well nobody understands the pain you're going through more than I do, but I think we have to stick together, as a family and as a community. My family's gone now, and I hear yours is to. I thought you might need somebody to help you, somebody to talk to. I just don't understand why they left you in this apartment all alone."

"I'm all right," I told her hastily, "and I'm not leaving here."

I think she saw the fight that was looming on that front and decided to let it go for a while.

"I visited your Momma at the church this morning." She said softly. "Who made the arrangements for you?" She paused only briefly and didn't press me when I offered no explanation. "Well, someone did a fine job. I'm sure somewhere your Momma's looking down on you and she's very proud of you."

Somewhere along the line I had let my encounter with Ravenhurst force my mind down dark corridors that spoke of fantastic nightmares, memories that were unreal but Mrs. Harris was rooted in reality, as were her words. I checked myself to keep from crying like a baby.

"I haven't been there yet." I said with a sadness that was now swelling inside of me.

"I was just getting ready to leave."

She looked at my sweatshirt and jeans confused but only for a second.

I wasn't really expecting to go to my Momma's funeral that day but it wouldn't have mattered anyway, it was all I had. I think Mrs. Harris must have understood this because she asked me to go back with her across the street. She said that her son had a nice suit that I could have. The thought of wearing one of Perry's suits gave me a sick feeling but my Momma always taught me to be gracious and to never turn down a gift.

"Thank you. I'd appreciate that. I just have to get something from the bedroom." When I entered I noticed that Edward Ravenhurst had done yet another disappearing act and was nowhere to be found.

As the two of us walked up the steps to the church I was grateful for her company. I hadn't realized how much easier it was having someone to lean on emotionally, someone who understood.

The first thing that struck me on entering the church was the overwhelming fragrance of roses. They were everywhere, draped over the closed casket, and on all sides of it. There were even clusters of them on each row of the pews. My attention was directed toward the casket at the base of the pulpit. It looked to be of a shiny black metallic finish trimmed in gold everywhere. It gave the appearance that it held something truly precious and it did. I was amazed to find that the church was nearly two-thirds full, I'd always thought we were loners, my Momma and me.

As I walked up the center isle I was aware that all the heads had turned and their eyes were now on me but what actually made my knees buckle was not that, but the fact that now I had to say good-bye to Momma. The ceremony had now made everything real, casting it in stone.

They'd reserved the front middle row for the family and Mrs. Harris and another woman guided me there. I was to sit there, all alone. I don't know why, but I grabbed Perry's mother's arm before she could get out of reach.

"Would you sit with me, please?" I think I must have sounded like a lost child, and that's exactly how I felt. I don't know when they'd thrust the program into my hand but I now sat there looking down at the image of my Momma who smiled back up at me. The picture was an old one because she was a lot younger. Strangely there was a young man in the picture with her. They held each other's hands and seemed to be very much in love. I was still reading the program when the service started and the Minister began. It seemed that the young man had died in a street brawl at an early age and had left a pregnant fiancée. There was no shame in that, I wondered if it was true. The man's face did seem to bare a resemblance to my own.

I was aware that Mrs. Harris had placed her free hand upon mine, both of which still clung to her right hand, a gesture from the Minister broke me free from my thoughts. It was time to view the body. The roses had been removed form the top half of the casket and it was now open. With shaky limbs I rose to move forward. I was prepared for the worst but not for what I saw.

She was dressed in a cream colored dress with lace all over it. I'd never seen it before. Her shoulder length hair had always been worn in a bun at the back of her head but now it was in loose curls framing her face, which as always appeared makeup less. She seemed as full of life as she always had. I think the thing that really shocked me was that her eyes were open and fixed skyward. They were as bright as I remembered them and they held an expression that something appeared to be amusing her and her lips were curved slightly. I must have stared at her for some time because Mrs. Harris eventually pulled me back to my seat.

It wasn't until that day that I became aware of Mrs. Harris and the other kind people that existed all around me on my block. They were there when I needed them, strangers to me. Trying to console me, helping me to my feet and understanding when I started crying like a baby, I couldn't help it. I think I said I was sorry because I felt Mrs. Harris' arm come around my shoulders and she said there was nothing to be sorry about and no shame in expressing sorrow over the passing of a loved one. She would never know the extent of my guilt.

I don't remember the rest of the service. When I next remembered anything the church was empty, the casket was closed and Mrs. Harris was still seated beside me. She seemed lost in thoughts of her own but my movement caught her attention and she seemed grateful that I'd come out of whatever state I'd been in for the past half hour. The pastor came into the church from one of the rooms behind the front pulpit. I could tell that he was eager to go and that I was all that stopped him from locking the place up.

He walked up to us and when he spoke he address me.

"Look son, I think it's wonderful that you want your Momma to be buried in the jewelry that she must have loved in life but don't you think that she'd want you to have them. Maybe pass them on to your wife when you marry. Haven't you heard about the grave robbing going on nowadays? It would be a shame if somebody just snatched them off her."

I'd felt as if he'd slapped me in the face at that. I didn't know what he was talking about. Momma didn't own any jewelry, except some cheap costume stuff. Nothing worthy of the dress they'd seen fit to bury her in.

"I know you're hurting now," the Pastor continued, "but you'll regret it if you don't keep them, to remember her by. No point giving them to some no account, hell bound, atheist crooks."

I was still seated but stood with difficulty and moved toward the casket. The pastor stopped me and pressed a key into my palm. He seemed uncomfortable about something and he sat down beside Mrs. Harris. As I fumbled with the lock I could hear the muted conversation between the two but could only make out bits and pieces in the quiet of the church, not enough to make sense out of it.

The lock turned and I lifted the lid. I hadn't noticed it before when I'd first set eyes on her but there they were, the diamond broach on her throat, that I'd first set eyes on in that dark vault of Ravenhurst Cemetery. On her finger was a matching ring, several carets large. Everybody that viewed her body that day must have seen them, there'd be little chance of either remaining with her. But what did it matter they didn't belong to us anyway. Still I didn't like the thought of strangers desecrating her.

I think that was the moment that I felt my sanity returning. I was starting to think that in that cemetery that night I'd gone crazy. That everything that had happened since was a delusional nightmare. I reached out to touch my mother's hand. It was cold, but still soft to the touch. I bent over to kiss her forehead. It was then that I remembered that I still carried the gourd she so cherished in my pocket. I'd placed it in the jacket of the suit that I'd gotten from Mrs. Harris' and from my now dead friend Perry. I pulled it out and looked at it. More important than the jewelry was the gourd. It didn't matter what happened to them but the little gourd meant something to her, and now to us both.

I reached inside the casket and gently took her hand. I'd expected it to be rigid, instead it gave easily to my pressure to bring it from the casket's confines. It bent naturally as I brought it up to me and into the dim light of the church. The ring sparkled brightly and I ignored it as I turned her palm upward to place the gourd in it. I enclosed her fingers around it and held her hands in mine and in that instant something happened. It was like electricity and it passed from her hand to my own. I realized then that family treasures are to be passed on to loved ones. That was what she would have wanted. She'd always believe that the gourd was a talisman that would protect us from evil.

I'd never known Momma's mother, my Grandmother. She'd migrated here to America from Haiti. Momma used to tell me bits and pieces about our family's religion and her own Grandmother, back in the days when slaves were brought to Haiti. Maybe that's why Momma never really embraced the western concept of religion. It made me smile standing there surrounded by the stained glass and images because I knew she'd laugh at the irony. Ending up in a place she never wanted to be. Momma told me often it was her Grandmother's great power that had caused her to have to leave Haiti. Their system of beliefs was wide spread, and there were many that feared her. Fear can make people do strange things, make them see evil influences were there aren't any. Of course most of our family's beliefs and rituals had been lost. Maybe every generation had a few like me. See after I got older, old enough for friends and peer pressure I stopped paying attention to the family stories she'd share with me. It all seemed loony as I got older. I was embarrassed to believe my family had ever participated in them, but something had happened that night when Momma tried to use ancient solutions for a current problem, and

I'd received answers of sorts. I was also remembering some of the things Edward Ravenhurst had said to me.

I removed the gourd from her palm and gently replaced her hand within the casket, returning the gourd to my pocket as I lowered the lid and locked it.

Mrs. Harris and the pastor were still engrossed in conversation but it stopped when they saw me approach.

"Are you done?" The pastor asked me looking at my empty hands.

"Yeah," I told him, "the jewelry can stay were it is. It has no value for me so I don't really care what happens to it. The only thing I do care about is Momma."

I looked back towards the locked casket.

"You know what? I think the jewelry's safer there then anywhere else in the world, cause there's a high price to pay for anyone that tries to take it."

The pastor looked curiously at me at that and then shook his head.

It was mid-afternoon when the three of us stepped back outside into the sunshine. It was a cool November day and the remaining dead leaves on the trees made a restless rustling sound. I watched the pastor lock up the empty church. My Momma's remains its only inhabitant. I felt guilty about leaving her there all alone in the darkness. I started to ask the elderly man if I could stay, but I noticed that he was ill at ease about something as I watched his hands shake trying to get the key into the lock. Mrs. Harris said her goodbyes to him as she grabbed my elbow pulling me along.

As we neared my apartment she asked me if I was going to be all right. I told her that I would. She seemed profoundly sad and I realized we were both going back to empty apartments. She'd been so strong all day but the closer we got to her home the more she seemed to loose her resolve. There were tears forming in her eyes. I took her hand in my own.

"Someone told me recently that your loved ones are never that far away. Today it felt like it was true. I can feel Momma so strongly everywhere I go. That helps me to get through this."

She tried to smile but it was a useless gesture because I could tell that she wasn't comforted much. Still holding her hand I asked her if there was anything I could do for her. She kissed my cheek lightly and said she'd be fine. Then she made an automatic gesture to erase the lipstick marks that must have been left.

"Perry always hated when I did that." She took a deep breath, "At least he's with his uncle now. Neither of them will be lonely." There were tears streaming down her face now. "God willing, we'll all be together someday."

"Sure." I said.

Then she looked at me.

"Where did your Momma go to church?" She asked.

"She didn't." I said. "We were of a different faith than you generally find around here." I said with a smile. Only this time I wasn't embarrassed. She looked at me curiously but I didn't say anything further. She probably now took me for some kind of heathen.

"Well, next Sunday," she said in a strong powerful voice. "I'm coming by and we're going to my church. It may not be what you're used to but you should at least give it a try."

Ah well, I thought, she's trying to offer me a gift of sorts in her own way, how could I refuse.

"Mrs. Harris, you've done so much for me. I couldn't of gotten through today if it weren't for you." The fact was, I was more grateful than I could ever put into words.

"You know you can't stay here alone, don't you? There must be somebody that you can go to."

"No but don't worry, I'll be fine."

I could tell that she wasn't ready to leave. There was a questioning expression still on her face but she seemed to be unsure if she could ask it. I didn't press. I hadn't slept well for the past three nights and even though it was only late afternoon, all I wanted to do was throw myself across my bed.

"I had the chance to talk with Pastor Thompson a short while ago. He said your Momma died Wednesday night and the death certificate said natural causes."

"Yeah, she had a heart attack."

"He said a lawyer in Boston made all the arrangements over the phone. Maybe you've got relatives that you don't even know."

I thought about that for a few moments but rejected it. I knew who was responsible though I didn't know why. I could tell she hadn't said what was really on her mind. I said nothing.

"Well," she said finally. "You take care of yourself and I'll see you tomorrow and I won't let you forget about next Sunday." She turned away from me briefly but then turned back. "I'll let you know as soon as I've made Perry's arrangements."

"Thanks. I'd like to help in any way I can."

She smiled and patted my arm then walked away. I felt as if I was a substitute son, and a poor one I'm sure.

I mounted the steps to my apartment, each one grueling. As I opened the door I noticed that the apartment was dark. All the drapes were closed. Momma would close them each night to prevent people from seeing in and they were the heavy type. They'd cost good money. I remember how mad she'd get each time she came into my room and found them tied in a knot at the bottom so I could catch a breeze. She was also the one who'd open them first thing in the morning, but Momma died during the day and the curtains had been open. I'd never bothered closing them. Then I noticed something else, for a second time I smelled that heavy scent of roses coming from somewhere in the darkness. I fumbled for the light switch and the living room flooded with its yellow light. I was disappointed but not necessarily surprised to see him sitting there on my sofa staring at me.

There were roses all over the place, and as I stepped into the apartment I could see that they filled the dining room and kitchen. I could even see some of them through the partly open door of Momma's bedroom, all from the church I'd guessed.

"Not at all," he said sounding as if he were chastising me for even thinking it, "*I* would never steal from the dead."

I came in all the way, closing the door behind me. "Am I so stupid that I wear my thoughts across my face?"

"Forgive me. It's just that when you've been around for a

while you pick up certain talents."

"Yeah, right." I said sarcastically, dropping into the chair opposite him. "Just tell me what it is you want, why you're hounding me."

"You know the answer to that." He said.

There was silence in the room for a few minutes. I remember thinking it would be better to be rid of him no matter what the cost and for some reason he smiled suddenly.

"Look, if you are a Ravenhurst then I'm sorry that I trespassed."

"You did more than trespass, you violated." As he spoke he continued smiling but his voice was icy.

"Well you could turn me in. I did it and I'll say so but you know I didn't take anything, don't you?"

"Of course. If you had you'd be in a state similar to your *friends*.

"You don't know noth'n about my friends!" I countered.

"Not true." He said. "I know a great deal about them. You should have seen the damage they caused, before I stopped them."

I sat up straight in my chair at that, a gesture that hadn't escaped his notice.

"Yes, they had ripped open most of the drawers by the time I took action. There were bodies all over the floor and not all of them intact. Apparently they'd come across dear old uncle. He believed if he swallowed the jewels before death you really could take it with you, but just between the two of us, I think that was what really killed him. He hadn't realized that grave robbers a hundred years later would only have to open the drawer and his treasure would be on display for anyone to see.

Well after that they started tearing the rest of the bodies apart. It took me quite awhile to reassemble the pieces. That is, after I took care of your friends. That's not the way I normally like spending my early morning hours." He looked at me directly for several seconds until he was sure that the full weight of his words had firmly sunk in before he continued. "Yes, the next time they are involved with a grave robbing, it will be from the other end of the spectrum."

"You're saying you killed all three of them?" I asked in disbelief.

He sat on the sofa, one arm resting casually upon its back. His whole attitude suggested one of extreme relaxation.

"Of course Darius, you were the only one to escape and you wouldn't have if Sarah hadn't warned you and pleaded to me on your behalf. I don't know why she bothered. It was obvious the four of you were just vermin."

"You're a damn liar! They didn't die anywhere near you or that dammed cemetery. They were found at home, in their beds so it's more likely it was from celebrating with bad drugs. Look, I don't know for sure how my friends died but it sure as hell wasn't by the hands of some scrawny-assed white boy! And, if that's your opinion of me, I mean vermin, then why go through all this? All you really had to do was to call the police and be done with it." Then something else occurred to me causing a sharp pain deep in my soul. "I know you're responsible for Momma's funeral arrangements, why?"

It was then that I sensed a change in the air around me. I can't explain it. Everything seemed different suddenly. Ever since I walked into that mausoleum my feelings had been constantly kicking in to feed me information. I don't know why, it's like it had been dormant up until that time.

Ravenhurst looked at me as if we'd been friends all along.

"Darius, I'm sorry. That was a slip of the tongue. My opinion of your friends hasn't changed," he said softly, "but I do realize I misjudged you, you're obviously different. Sarah knew it from the start, maybe that's why she saved you from me long enough for me to cool down and come to my senses."

"Look, I appreciate what you did for Momma. When I'm in a position to pay you back, I will. Until then I'd appreciate your doing another of those disappearing acts of yours."

"You'll never be rid of me Darius."

"Or call the police, there's the phone!"

"I've made you angry, I can't imagine why. First of all, I have all the money I could ever use. Secondly, you'd never be able to compensate me for what you did, even if you had all the money in the world. Lastly, get used to me Darius because you'll never be rid of me. Besides, I'm trying to be patient and explain everything to your satisfaction but I do wish you'd cooperate because my patience has limits."

"Then tell me what the hell you want!" I shouted.

Chapter 6 - Surrender

Ravenhurst exhaled, long and slow. "All right," he added with a cold smile.

His voice smooth and even, as always. Though I sensed he concealed elation. A slight sensation shot through my soul, like a mild electrical charge warning his satisfaction could mean my ruin. Things appeared to be progressing just the way he wanted.

"But first," Ravenhurst said, "are you still carrying the talisman your mother gave you?" .

At first I didn't know what he was talking about but then I remembered the gourd and reached instinctively in my pocket, finding it there.

"Ah, then you do have it." Ravenhurst said with satisfaction settling back comfortably on the sofa. "Darius, remember when I told you your mother would never be far away from you? I meant that Darius. In fact, I can feel her presence all around us now."

This was the only thing he'd said up until that point that I believed unconditionally.

"I can easily feel the presence of those that have departed," he continued, "that is why I'm so protective of the souls that dwell within our mausoleum. Why I protect them so viciously, because they cannot protect themselves.

"Right now I feel the spirit of your mother. It's so very strong Darius. I think that she's concerned. You're walking around casually with something that was very valuable to her. She seems to be indicating that you should take it out of your pocket and return it to the box, the one in her bedroom that she kept it in, on the top shelf of her closet."

I know it was stupid, but on some level I believed him almost immediately. That he was communicating with Momma. Yet some of the things he said didn't quite feel right, and I wasn't about to let on to him that I believed him to any extent. But whether he was or not, he sure as hell wasn't being completely honest. Instead, I was sure that he was twisting things to fit some agenda of his own but he was right though about where Momma normally kept it. There were times that Momma would feel things weren't going exactly right. She'd feel that certain energies weren't aligned properly, angry and troubled souls she'd say. At those times she'd carry it with her constantly until she felt things were right again, then she'd replace it in its box. Her most precious jewel, that wasn't a jewel at all. Now I felt that way. Things just weren't right and somehow I felt my connection to her was the result of my keeping her precious talisman close.

He knew the conclusion I had reached almost as soon as I did, I wasn't parting with it. I could see the resolve in his face to accomplish his ends, whatever they were.

"You can feel her presence too can't you? Maybe as well as I can, but you can't hear her voice as I can. Darius I can change all that. I can make it so you can once again speak with your mother, just as before. And, I can increase your sensitivity allowing you to reach out and speak with your friends, even though you currently exist in a different state from them. There is no reason for you to suffer with guilt, or for you to be separated from your mother." At that point he smiled again, "I have friends and relatives on both sides, so do you. Relatives you haven't even begun to met yet.

For instance, how could you know that your father was dead, that was something even your mother didn't know. She never told you who he was, but do you know why? Because she thought he deserted her when he found out she was pregnant. The truth was, unbeknownst to her he died the very night he was told. Perhaps he was too lost in thought to be careful I suppose. That was all long before you were born but she knows now Darius. Now that her soul is separated from its physical form and they both exist in similar states. She's happy though torn, she misses and wants to be near you. Darius she wants to communicate with you but can't, and that is why I'm here. I realize she had nothing to do with your intrusion into the mausoleum so why should she suffer? I only want to help her and you both.

How do you think I know these things Darius, about your mother and father?"

I just waved my hand briefly in a tired gesture, trying hard not to listen to him. What he was saying was impossible but I wanted to talk to Momma so badly I could hardly think straight anymore, but I knew I couldn't give him that kind of power over me.

"Darius, why are you fighting me? I know you believe me. Do you need further proof? Would you like me to tell you her likes, her dislikes? Darius, I just want to help you both, can't you see that? What could you possibly have to loose? And look at what you might gain. There really are no risks."

Finally he was silent and I tried to keep my mind clear. I didn't know how but he certainly seemed to be able to read my thoughts. Or at least fragments enough to be able to react to what I was going to say even before I knew I was going to say it. Whatever it was he wanted from me, he wanted it badly but I still didn't know what *it* was.

"I'm having a hell of a hard time following you. First you tell me that you know I was one of the 'vermin' that robbed your family's graves. Then you tell me that you are responsible for killing my friends and you would have killed me too if I hadn't left. I think you followed me here at first for that same reason. Then I find out that you've footed the bill for Momma's funeral expenses and you've even taken the jewels that you say you killed my friends over and placed them in the casket with my Momma. Now you tell me that you've had a change of heart and you want to be my best friend. Well I'm sorry, I choose my friends carefully, and I sure as hell don't choose those that have ever planned to kill my ass!"

I noticed that the last comment seemed to make him smile, but whatever he was thinking he chose not to share it with me.

"Darius, I feel badly in regards to the loss of your mother. I can't help but feel partly responsible. It is true that my initial plans for you were potentially lethal. I was in close proximity the night she died. I believe my presence coupled with my malicious thoughts in your regards might have had an adverse affect on your 'religious' artifact, and on your mothers heart that night."

"So now you're saying you caused Momma's death to?"

"Possibly, but even if that's true I assure you it was unintentional."

"I've had to start believing in a lot of things recently, I'm even willing to maybe give you the benefit of the doubt in being psychic and all, but I'm not buying into the idea of psychic murder. The same goes for your claim of killing my friends, I don't buy that either. Is there anything else?" I asked him calmly.

"Just one more thing which may sway you to my line of thought, I had hoped that I wouldn't have to mention it. It's not something I'm proud of and there's nothing worse than carelessness."

For the first time I saw the aloof smile drop from his face, it was replaced by something nearly akin to pain.

"I really am responsible for your mother's condition." Ravenhurst was looking away from me now, staring at some fixed point on the distant wall. "At the time I was trying to kill you but the two of you were connected in some form of ritual which I couldn't discern. It dispersed my energy between yourself, your mother ... and that talisman. I suppose the dispersed energy was insufficient to harm you, the target, but your mother's heart was already weak."

I sat there, still unmoved by his words.

"Well, perhaps this will have an affect. I've gone through a great deal to ensure that she didn't have to undergo any kind of autopsy or embalming and I could see how impressed you were with her lifelike expression."

The image of my mother's face from the funeral only a few hours earlier flashed across my mind.

"That's better." He said with satisfaction. "Let me tell you a little story. It's about a very wealthy and influential Boston family by the name of Ravenhurst.

You know, I believe it was nearly two hundred years ago now. Boston was my family's primary residence, but we also had a plantation in Georgia were I spent my summers."

"Wait, wait... you're saying two-hundred years ago you was spending time vacationing in Boston?" I asked rolling my eyes at him.

"That's right."

At that I'd simply whined softly, shook my head and sank into my chair. Ignoring my actions he continued.

"I'll be honest, the bulk of our fortune at the time stemmed from human trafficking, I'm sure you understand. Please don't look at me like that, I wasn't personally involved. I'd like to be able to add that I wasn't there at the time, but in truth, I was.

Those were really superstitious times and I'm sure I don't have to tell you the kind of things that went on back then between the owned and those who owned. I also shouldn't have to tell you that my parents were far from being saints. I loved them and they me, and I couldn't see any fault with them or the system at the time.

In the summer of 1800's our small town was visited by a band of gypsies. Actually, they passed through each summer and it seemed my parents knew them well, even looked forward to their visits. I suppose it broke up our otherwise boring existence. They had great skill of showmanship, acrobatics, juggling, sword swallowing and seers. They'd petitioned father to stay on his land for the few days and he always agreed. I visited there often, everyday in fact and they were very kind to me. Actually they treated me as if I were one of the family, particularly their leader. He had a daughter that must have been the most beautiful woman my fourteen-year-old eyes had yet to see. I'd often ride out early in the morning and stay long after the sun had set. My father would ride out most evenings to fetch me. Somewhere along the line mother discovered that my father was having ... relations with the girl. It seemed she'd caught them in the forest. She'd confronted father about it on at least one occasion and he'd promised it would never happen again. Mother believed the girl placed some kind of spell on him. Of course mother was more disposed to believing those kinds of things than the true fact, that father was drawn to a younger, more beautiful woman. Well, the last time she caught them unawares she'd crept back into the clearing of the gypsies camp, where she saw a cauldron of soup boiling unattended. She went back to where they were both dressing and tossed the scalding soup on the girl.

I remember hearing her screams all the way back at the plantation from my window. Father grabbed my mother who was kicking, scratching and cursing and flung her onto the horse. I think they narrowly made their escape. The gypsies went into town demanding justice but their pleas fell on deaf ears.

The next day gypsy horses and wagons were gathered on the grass in front of our home and father came out of the house with his rifle. My mother stood behind him in the doorway. The leader stood there stoically but did not speak. Instead an older woman came from one of the wagons to stand in front of him. She turned to whisper something to him. Then I saw the Gypsy's eyes glance up briefly to where I stood peering through my bedroom window. I will always remember his express, one of profound sadness which I assumed was for his lost daughter.

When the old woman turned back towards the house and my father, I noticed she also looked up at me but her expression was cold. She waived her hands muttering something guttural and after a while limped away.

I thought they cursed us in some gypsy language and it seemed they had. The man spoke finally to my father. He said, "Your murderous wife killed my beautiful daughter. You will pay!" Father offered to compensate them for their loss and I was amazed, he would offer to put a price on the girl's life but then I remembered it was what he did every day.

The Gypsy shook his head saying sadly that father would pay a much higher price and then he pointed up to me. He told my father it had been decreed that for the loss of his child, the murderer should also loose a child. I heard my father ask if they were planning to murder an innocent child. The gypsy only shook his head saying that the curse had been cast and that in one weeks time I would be dead, to die every bit as painfully as his beloved daughter had.

At that point my father asked him if he really would do such a thing, and wouldn't that make his pain doubly great. I never knew what he meant by that but the gypsy didn't answered, they just gathered their wagons and horses and departed. As they left I could hear my mother yelling obscenities at them from the doorway.

I came downstairs and out into the main hall to watch their retreating wagons from the doorway behind my parents, until they'd gotten out of sight. Yet my mother's obscenities hadn't stopped with their departure, they'd simply been redirected, now at my father. He said nothing just stood there and took it until she got tired and stalked away. She was coming up the stairs when her eyes fell upon me. Her change in attitude and appearance was always so striking when her conversation changed from my father to me. She knew I'd heard everything. She came up the stairs and put her arms around me and told me not to worry. 'They are just savages.' She'd said, 'Every bit as primitive as our own slaves.'

I used to have a good friend about my age named Thomas. He was one of our slaves. When I was eight or nine we were inseparable. He'd tell me all the slaves' secrets swearing me to secrecy as well. He even told me that his grandmother, who everyone referred to as Momma Yeman, was a witch who could cure or cause any illness. One summer afternoon while she and the slaves were in the fields, we visited her cabin.

I vividly remember my first steps into Momma Yeman's cabin. It was a small single room, cold and stark, and while it was a brilliant day outside, the cabins interior was cast in dark, menacing form-like shadows. Partially due to having only two small windows and because dark fabric hung from them, but it was clear Momma Yeman valued her privacy. The place held eeriness and I felt a sensation of being watched, though I knew we were alone since you could see every square foot of the place nearly at a glance. I'm sure Thomas felt it too because while it had been his idea to bring me there, I could tell he now held serious reservations. He wanted to leave, which I resisted but I moved about uneasily as I examined everything.

With the exception of a small bed, the only other furnishings were two small tables and a barrel. All of which were covered with oddities which overflowed to border the surrounding walls. Jars were filled with strange looking things floating in liquids, and there were animal skins, bones, bowls with powders, stones, shells, gourds and several odd looking little dolls. On the far end of the room was small fireplace. There a black kettle hung suspended from its iron crane. I lifted the lid to find something putrid and dropped it as a vile odor assailed my nostrils. Thomas was insulted when I asked about its contents and that of the jars, wondering if she regularly made meals of those types of things. Thomas told me Momma Yeman was an *obayifo*, a witch with supernatural powers. It seemed that the various items were simply the instruments with which she worked her magic. Of course I thought that was nonsense. My father had told me by then that there were no such things as ghosts or magic, but Thomas insisted otherwise. He told me she could walk ghost like, leaving her body. Move through walls unseen to spy upon her enemies. That she could suck the blood from a body without so much as touching you to increase her strength. That she could capture a departing spirit and force it to do her will, and that she could turn her enemies into zombies.

"Momma Yeman, will be angry with me for being here. I tell you she possesses great power." He warned.

"She's not a witch. If she were many people would probably be dead," I assured him, "there are no such thing as witches, father says so."

"Witches and vampires are powerful and dangerous, but no matter how powerful, they can not fight the masses that would come for them. They survive by remaining in the shadows, unseen and unknown, Master's wrong!" Thomas told me.

"He is not wrong! My father is an educated man," I boasted,

"knowledgeable in the arts and the sciences, and I think he knows more of such matters than slaves."

I knew I'd hurt his feelings at that, I could see it in his eyes. He'd wanted to argue the point but he didn't.

Afterwards, something happened to our friendship, there grew a distance between us. Maybe Thomas began to realize how much of a difference there was in our stations in life. I couldn't understand his resentment because everything was the same as it always had been. Yet he certainly changed over the years. I finally grew tired of his coldness and asked my father to sell Thomas and his mother to the plantation on the other side of town.

That had been months earlier, but I remembered Thomas and his grandmother, Momma Yeman that next day, after the gypsies departure. I came down with a severe headache forcing me to retire to my room. Towards evening I was deep in fever and the following morning every area of my body ached. I quickly weaken as a result of not being able to hold any food or liquids down. The doctor from town visited me several times but was at a loss as to the problem. The only thing he was sure of was that I was dying. He never told me as much but I could see it in his eyes and in fathers. Every hour my pain increased. I was scared.

Mother spent all her time sitting by my bedside. She cried constantly. My father tried to pull her away telling her she wasn't helping matters crying over me but she just pulled away telling him that the situation was his fault.

I begged father to fetch Momma Yeman. I was sure she could help me. I told him she was a witch, Thomas had told me so but he insisted that was just superstitious nonsense made up by ignorant people who didn't know any better. 'Besides,' he'd said, 'if she really is a witch you wouldn't want to ask her for help would you? After all, we sold her daughter and grandson, remember? She might hold a grudge.' Then he laughed. I was sure he was trying to show how absurd the thought was before adding, 'But don't worry, in another day or so you'll be fine.' He was wrong.

By the next day I was passing in and out of delirium. Everything seemed to be a dream but for a single moment of clarity when I thought I was awake, and looked up and into the face of a frightening old Negro woman. She looked at me with such contempt. I think the only thing that kept her from spitting in my face was my father at her back. Her words were difficult for me to follow at times, but she seemed to tell my father that people died because their souls departed their bodies, but with her potion mine never would. Obviously she meant that it would cure my illness, right? She said that the potion would demand certain sacrifices when I was well enough for it. I heard my father ask what kind of sacrifices. She said that would be for me to decide. She lifted my head and poured the contents of the cup she was holding down my throat. It tasted like swill and I started coughing halfway through it. I wanted to die rather than swallow the rest of it, but swallow it I did.

After a few hours I did begin to feel better. My room was dark when I finally awoke and oddly my bedcovers were over my head. I still felt weak but managed to get out of bed. My youngest sister was the first to see me on the steps. She screamed at the sight of me and just seemed to collapse tumbling backward down the stairway to land at the bottom, her neck at an awkward angle.

The servants came running into the room in answer to her scream. They found her at the base of the steps and then looked up at me as I slowly and painfully made my way down, and towards my sister. Two or three went screaming from the house. The old Negro butler I'd known my whole life took a cautious step toward me to ask if I was flesh or spirit. I wasn't sure how to answer. It was a poor joke at best. As I neared him and my sister he dropped her head, which he'd been holding in his arms, to also run from the room. My mother, father and older sister came running in and I could see the shock on their faces as well. I found out later it was because the only son that they'd had was dead or so they thought, and the daughter who'd been alive only a few minutes earlier was now certainly dead.

When father believed me dead, he demanded of the old slave what had happened, she just stood there over me laughing saying that she never said I wouldn't die, just that my spirit would never leave my body.   I was later told that she'd said, "I have cursed the selfish, evil boy and the curse of an Obayifo is a powerful one never to be broken.   You will all suffer for the pains you have given to me and mine."

Momma Yeman had been taken out and hung by father afterwards but not before she had dispersed a protection that would shield her children from the affects of my 'cure'.   It appeared she considered every Negro on that plantation one of her children.   This was also true of the neighboring Johnston Plantation where her daughter and grandson were, so they were also protected.   Even to this day, I can easily tell the descendants of the Ravenhurst and Johnston Plantations, the only people I cannot affect.

Well I was alive but weak, and getting weaker by the hour.   It appeared that they might lose me after all.   My mother came in and placed her arms around me hugging me tightly assuring me that everything would be all right.   I don't know why I did it but I brought both my hands up to her temples.   There was a strange feeling that came over me. Much the same as you sometimes feel just before a lightening storm out in the pasture. I felt stronger and I noticed that instead of her supporting me, I now supported her, and then she collapsed in front of me. I didn't know what was wrong with her, perhaps it was the same ailment that had affected me, but it wasn't. She didn't seem to be in any pain. She slept for several days and eventually died in her sleep.

It didn't take long before this new ailment swept our plantation, curiously only affecting whites. Of course I think that silently both my father and I reached the same conclusions at about the same time because I noticed he began avoiding me.   Eventually he decided to send me away to be educated in Europe. I returned the following summer for a holiday and by that time he had remarried. His wife was the beautiful Sarah.

I understand you were admiring her likeness in the frame on the desk of the mausoleum. She was as charming as she was beautiful and so very kind of heart. She didn't believe in slavery and father ended up freeing his slaves rather than loose her forever. They were working for him now as free men and women. Everyone in town thought father was crazed, and of course it hadn't really helped the economic situations of the slaves any. You see that gave the towns merchants the idea of charging double to freed slaves for everyday items they needed to survive, now that they could afford it.

Before my scheduled trip back to school, Sarah had succumbed to the illness that had claimed the others less than a year before. Father, of course, blamed and never forgave me. I left Georgia never to return. That is until he asked me to, on this deathbed some twenty years later. When I stepped into the room I thought he was going to die right then. I guess he'd expected to see an adult son. Instead he gazed upon the form of the child he remembered.

He lifted his hand to mine, which I took and pulled me down to sit on the side of his bed.

"I know that nothing that's happened in the past is your fault, it's all mine. If I'd only been faithful to your mother then none of this would ever have happened. I guess I wanted revenge against her. Edward, you know that I've always loved you like you were my own son, don't you?"

I asked him what was he trying to say but he hadn't answered and had just continued on some track of his own.

"Instead I've turned you into this monster. A blasphemy against God and he's punishing us both." He said.

There was such distance between us now, too much for me to grieve with him as I might have once. I told him that it was time for him to release all the guilt he'd been feeling over the years. He wasn't responsible for any of it. I think it was what he wanted to hear even if it wasn't true and I was about to release him from it when he asked me to summon the servants, which I did.

I may be a monster, but I'm not a very strong one, at least not when attacked unexpectedly by the three adult men that rushed into the room at the summons of the bell. They pinned me down facing the floor and tied my hands behind my back. A heavily gloved hand quickly shoved rags into my mouth and turned me over to face my father who was now standing over me. His tears had dried up but not his resolve. As I looked up at the three strangers I noticed they had all worn gloves.

"I've watched you carefully over the past few years." He said. "I know what you've been doing and how many lives you've taken. I can't die knowing that I've left you free to kill like some evil angel of death. I know I am the reason you are what you are. This is why I have to stop you while I still can."

Once you realize that death can never claim you it does a great deal to liberate you from fear. There was nothing he could do to me, we both knew it. He motioned to one of the men who brought in a casket.

It was large and I realized that he intended to bury me in it. The prospect of an eternity buried in the ground didn't appeal to me. I tried thrashing around to free myself but by now they had bound me securely with rope. I couldn't move an inch. As two of them lowered me into the casket I continued to kick but heavy padding sewn into the casket muffled the blows. The last thing I heard was one of the men asking for their payment and my father replying that he had already signed the papers. It seemed the plantation and everything on it now belonged to the three of them.

Strange, but I don't recall the trip from Georgia to the Ravenhurst cemetery here in Boston. It must have been my father's wish that I not reside alone within this place. He seemed to have transported nearly my whole family here, only he was missing. People can't survive without food, its energy for them. Yet I could no longer digest food, I have to have energy pure and simple, a bye-product of food I guess. Deprived of it I suppose I hibernated like an animal. I was revived when one of your friends was unfortunate enough to touch me. My body naturally pulled his energy at that point. Apparently he was trying to relate my physical appearance with the date on the vault. The other two ran, but not far or fast enough. I caught them one at a time before they got off the cemetery grounds." Ravenhurst said finally with a cold smile.

I could tell that his tirade was winding up to some terrible conclusion.

"Afterwards, I strolled about the mausoleum realizing that father had surrounded me with those I'd killed. Perhaps he thought they would be the only suitable guards for me but the reverse was actually true, wouldn't you say.

I killed nearly my entire family, I'm sure your ancestor would have been quite proud of me." He said. "I've learned nothing over the past century if not patience but most importantly I've learned when *not* to kill. Take your mother for instance, won't it be a shame tomorrow afternoon when she is consigned to be *buried alive*."

Only God knows what I'd sat there thinking about before his last sentence struck me, and as my eyes shot over to meet his I saw him smile. It was then that I jumped up running over to him. I wanted to kill him for even saying such a thing, and I tried to. I swear I did, picking him up and throwing him to the floor, I only wished I'd had something sharp in my hands but each blow seemed useless. He didn't even seem to feel them. Worse he didn't even feel the need to defend himself, and there were no scars, bruises or anything. I soon got tired and straightened up and he picked himself up from the floor, brushing away imaginary dust from his clothing.

"Well," he said, "if you've got that out of your system we can get back to business."

"You damn liar!" I was amazed at the callousness of a mind that could think up such a story. Eventually I calmed telling myself that it was useless contemplating killing a lunatic. "I know you have a right to be mad but this is sick. Even you should be able to see that." I struggled to push back my anger and keep a clear head with great difficulty. "If my Momma was still alive, then the doctors would of known it."

"Some things never change Darius, and the poor will never be considered important in society. Your mother *is* alive, a fact that's obvious for anyone to see who really cares. But even if you went out right now and shouted it from the rooftops it wouldn't matter. No one would care enough to take action save possibly committing you to an institution. Money on the other hand will always talk loudly. I can have her back and sipping afternoon tea with you tomorrow. If," he hesitated stressing the word, "if you'll help me."

In the last sentence I'd heard an imploring quality in his voice. It all sounded crazy, and maybe I was to. Crazy or not I had to do whatever it took if there was even the slightest chance of saving Momma.

"What do you want me to do?" I asked knowing I'd been beaten.

He smiled, but this time different then before. Now there seemed genuine sympathy in that smile.

Chapter 7 - *For All Time*

I returned Edward Ravenhurst to his drawer in the mausoleum realizing that this time he would never leave it. At the same time I wondered if anyone else would ever stumble across him and notice that his appearance was as if he'd only just died, in spite of the grave marker. In fact he *had* only just died, despite what he believed but he was right about a lot of things. He could have killed Momma that night but had felt the mental link we were engaged in and recognized Momma Yeman voice echoing in our minds even after too many generations had passed. It seemed that I had indeed possessed protections against him, passed down from my father, a descendent of Momma Yeman. But Momma Yeman responded to the Haitian talisman my mother possessed. Perhaps she sensed I was one of her descendants, and perhaps the close proximity of her enemy. I hoped Momma Yeman didn't think I betrayed her, but I had to save Momma. Besides, it did seem Edward Ravenhurst had suffered enough loneliness and isolation, for his part in separating her family.

In the end, she was the only one who could transfer the curse, and I was the only one of all her 'children' who still had a means of reaching her. The potion she'd given out nearly two hundred years earlier, like the curse, was as potent now as it was then. Ravenhurst must have realized when he couldn't kill us both that his moment of liberation was at hand.

In return for my assistance, Ravenhurst had made sure that his resources where turned over to me, it seemed we were no longer poor.

Momma and I spend a lot of time sitting on the terrace of our house in the Bahamas. It's been nearly twenty-years since that night. She's a little grayer but she's happy. She spends a lot of time shopping with Mrs. Harris and has to tell people that I'm her grandson instead of her son, but she doesn't seem to mind that much.

I held out telling Momma for as long as I could, thinking she would hate me when she found out. You see the curse can never be lifted, only transferred. Now I had needs for sustenance other than food but it's like Momma told me when she was recovering in the hospital, after she'd used the stone to force me to tell her everything.

"Now Darius don't you worry, there's a lot of bad people in the world, maybe it's time to go out and find some of them."

Nightmare's Demon

Chapter 1 – Family Ties

Nearly thirty years had passed since Darius surrendered his mortal life to Edward Ravenhurst on that cool autumn day. Ten years since his mother's death, this time there would be no returns for her. With the passing of his dear friend, Mrs. Harris, four years earlier the last anchor to his past life had been severed.

"Darius, let's do it again ... tonight."

It was Evan's voice that broke through Darius' thoughts bringing his mind back to the present as the sixteen-year-old youth came to sit beside him on the bed, his expression one of pleading.

"No." Darius responded softly aware that his voice was little more than a whisper. He'd been unable to muster enough energy to be any more adamant.

For several months he'd been feeling strangely drained and melancholy, soulless. He knew that Evan had been hoping to cheer him up and usually the act alone would accomplish that, though Evan would never really understand the real reason as to why.

Darius had been sitting there wondering how he was ever going to survive even a normal lifetime, let alone the nearly two centuries Ravenhurst had. His thoughts again turned to Evan sitting at his side. How willing he was to experience the extraordinary, never knowing the dangerous game of Russian roulette that he played. Ravenhurst's curse had caused him to exist in a seemingly endless state, pulling energy from others to survive. In the three decades that had past he'd learned a great deal about controlling his powers, if one could call it that. Better, he'd learned to control the constant need to replenish his soul that seemed from moment to moment to disperse, as if mist; leaving him feeling drained, weak, as if the world around him were somehow spinning away, out of his grasp. He often wondered what would happen if he allowed himself to cross that final threshold but his fears prevented that. In parting,

Ravenhurst had made one point clear, that mortal death was now beyond his reach. If that were true, then crossing that threshold might pose a problem far worse than his current one. To be trapped in a hellish void of dark isolation within his own corpse, however well preserved, unable to move or speak for eternity would be a hell far worse than his current one. His only temporary release came from unwitting victims who would satisfy his needs at the cost of their lives. He knew his only permanent release would come when someone appeared merciful enough to take on his burden upon them selves but that was now impossible. With the curse now upon him, Darius was no longer able to use the stone or contact Momma Yeman. He would never be free.

Realizing that there was no point brooding over what could not be changed, Darius instead decided to focus upon his current dilemma, finding a constant source from which to feed. He was now a forty-three year old black man forever trapped in the youthful body of a thirteen-year-old boy. While it took only a few minutes to accomplish the feeding, it was still a challenging task for his strength less body. Recognizing the need for an environment that would bring willing victims to him led Darius to his new home.

Now Darius don't you worry, there's a lot of bad people in the world, maybe it's time to go out and find some of them. His mother's words echoed through his mind. She loved him deeply and had always been a good and kind person but looked the other way on moral issues involving his existence. However, in the months leading up to her death, the realities of what he routinely did to survive began to weigh uneasily upon her until he could see the pain she felt. In the end, she'd gone uneasy to her grave because of him. Perhaps she began to realize that the distinction between good and evil had become blurred for them. She'd made him promise to never stop trying to find a way to put an end to his curse and the killings.

Afterwards he'd stopped his attacks altogether, and in doing so stumbled across a new way to sustain himself, one nearly involuntary for him. That was how he discovered death's dream realm. It had taken time, patience and considerable mental effort on his part before he'd learned to kill only when he wished it. While it was not as fulfilling, it was the only way he could exercise the level of control in the way Ravenhurst must have, a way that didn't always involve death. At the same time, it was more entertaining, and a better way to pass the decades.

It seemed destiny intervened to place him within the cemetery that night and into the grasp of Ravenhurst who carried the two hundred year old curse that could never be broken, only transferred. Ravenhurst insured his cooperation by holding his mother's life as ransom and under a death-like shroud. Darius had been forced to give Ravenhurst what he wanted, release. What other choice had there been? With only a few decades under his belt and possibly an eternity to go Darius sadly realized that he would never be free. It was unlikely destiny would intervene to save him as it had Ravenhurst.

Again he became aware of Evan, sitting still by his side attempting to read his expressions.

"It's not a game," Darius said finally, "and I have to be in the proper frame of mind, otherwise there are ... consequences. I can't just turn it on and off at your whim, and I'm tired."

At that point something in the expression on his face must have softened, which Evan took as a crack in his armor. Mentally Darius couldn't help but smile. There he was, a forty-three year old man whining like a ten-year-old. However this mood quickly turned sour again.

"Would you just go to sleep, please?"

Darius had been sitting on the side of his bed with his elbows on his knees, hands cupping his face when Evan had entered the bedroom that they shared. Though they hadn't known each other long, it seemed that Evan could always easily guess when something was disturbing him.

As he turned his mind to listening to Evan's thoughts Darius realized that Evan considered him aloof and quiet but also a friend. He realized that to Evan, he seemed even more out of sorts than usual, indifferent to everything, even gloomy. Evan thought he knew the reason why, but of course it wasn't what he thought. They were prostitutes for various reasons, societal outcast living dangerously on the edge, victims by choice. 'It's not something that was likely to change.' Evan thought to himself, and Darius realized he was right. Only Evan could never fully appreciate the unique nature of his problem, or the fact that he was more the victimizer than the victim. Evan had stopped hoping for miracles long ago, and Darius reasoned that perhaps he should as well.

"I bet if Gordon asked you would." Evan said abruptly.

"Gordon wouldn't ask." Darius replied in that same soft, passionless voice. They both knew full well that Gordon hated him. He didn't believe Darius deserved to live let alone share an apartment with them. Yet Evan had taken Darius' reply the wrong way.

"I see." Was all Evan said before jumping up to return to his own bed on the other side of the room, and throwing himself across it.

His actions were an exclamation point to his thoughts for Darius, who watched him briefly as he'd lain there on his stomach. A long narrow window at the head of the bed took the place of a missing headboard, and he stared out distractedly through it. From it hung pale green bed sheets in place of curtain panels, which Darius had tied in a knot at the middle to afford the room the occasional breeze.

For a few seconds Darius couldn't read anything from Evan as he'd gazed out onto the streets. Then his mind focused upon kids playing below, the two men working on a car up the street, and other people gathered in clusters here and there talking and taking advantage of the warm spring evening. It was nearing dusk. It was then that Evan began to wonder why it was that he spent so much of his time trying to cheer up others. 'We're prostitutes,' he'd thought to himself, 'not a profession high on anyone's lists, but you are what you are,' as his mother used to tell him whenever he asked her why she did it, sold herself in the streets. Then he remembered being ashamed of her and never feeling comfortable looking other kids in the eye. Yet he also remembered her always managing to put food on the table for the two of them and a roof over their heads. He had only been ten when she died, but he knew even then she had a hard life, and it took its toll on her.

They were painful memories for Evan, and the emotions of those images carried from Evan's mind to Darius'. How well he understood Evan's feelings of taking his mother for granted. Darius remembered how he'd felt when he'd first thought his own mother had died; he'd wanted to die as well.

Darius turned his attentions back to Evan who was remembering the day she'd found herself unable to support them by those means any longer. She'd brought a guy home only to find out he hadn't the slightest interest in her. He waved a hundred dollars under her nose and told her that it had been for Evan. She ranted and raved for a few minutes, but never asked him to leave. She must have known full well that even if she'd done a dozen tricks she'd never make that much. In retrospect Evan could now forgive her everything, even for eventually saying yes to that stranger, but he couldn't forgive himself. Afterwards the guy left the money on the bed and walked out leaving him there crying.

Evan remembered as if it were yesterday. His introduction into the world of prostitution and she did it daily, he'd felt so dirty. His self-esteem was nonexistent even then, yet it had still managed to nose dive. He snatched the money and went out throwing it at his mother as she sat on the edge of the sofa. She was crying too. What had he said to her? Yes, he remembered. 'I'll hate you for as long as I live! Why didn't you just leave me on somebody's doorstep, even if I'd died it would have been better than being your son!' He'd often thought it but had never spoken so harshly to her before. Though he was sure she'd always known that was how he felt.

She had already been crying, huddled on the corner of their worn sofa surrounded by their tattered and torn furnishing, cracked ceiling and yellowing wallpaper. He'd just left her there, in the living room of their small apartment and in a pit of sorrow that he figured she'd dug for herself. Evan now knew that he never really cared how she felt, or the sacrifices she'd made for him. It had always been just about him.

About three that morning he'd heard the shot fired, it had sounded close. He found her in the same spot he'd left her in. The tears on her face had not yet dried, spilled from open eyes red rimmed from crying. He never even knew she owned a gun. His deepest regret was that he would never be able to tell her how sorry he was.

That had been six years ago and Evan had found himself thinking about her often that week. Had she lived, she would have been thirty-seven. 'All my fault,' he thought to himself, 'if only I'd been there for her, shown her a little more kindness. She did so much for me.' He knew that was why he was now so sensitive to the feelings of the other members of his *new* family.

Yet no one ever seemed to care how he felt but then he thought, 'Perhaps that's justice. They just see me as a pest'.

"That's not true."

Evan glanced across angrily at Darius. There were times when he was amused at Darius' ability to read his thoughts, but that wasn't one of them.

"Just leave me alone." Evan said acknowledging that he knew Darius was in his mind and turned to face the wall, his head resting upon a nearly flattened pillow. He shut his eyes tightly, trying to forget about his past and his future, but Darius was far from ready to let go.

Darius stood in shadows as all around him a world began to form, first in shades of gray and gradually blending to colors. Then there was Evan as he walked up the driveway toward a large white wood framed house surrounded by a white picket fence. He hesitated only briefly at the gate before going into the yard, the grass was manicured and yellow daffodils surrounded its boundaries. He bounced up the stairs hoping she was home and twisted the doorknob. Beyond the threshold the room was dark

"Hi Mom, I'm home." Evan called nervously, sensing something was wrong. Yet he couldn't quite put his finger

on what it was. Instead he spun round to see someone standing in the middle of the walkway. Though he was close, it had taken him a few seconds to realize who it was.

Darius stood there before him, both aware of Evan's momentary embarrassment about something.

"Hello Evan."

"Hi yourself," Evan said finally, "I wasn't expecting you. What brings you here?"

"I wanted to say I'm sorry."

Evan laughed nervously, realizing he was no longer interested in the answer. He was beginning to remember something unpleasant and with the memory he sensed things about him beginning to dissolve. He'd shut his eyes tightly, hoping to stop whatever was happening but when he'd opened them again he'd found only the two of them surrounded by velvety darkness.

"It's all gone." There was deep regret in Evan's voice as he spoke. "Why couldn't you just stay away? Everything was perfect."

"It wasn't." Darius walked towards him until they stood staring eye to eye. "It's just a dream, Evan happiness starts in the real world."

Evan pointed to where he thought his imaginary home had stood. "This can't happen for me in your REAL world," but now he stared only into darkness before returning his attention again to Darius, tears forming in his eyes, "and it's what I wanted, so badly I could taste it." Everything had been perfect he thought and now it was just ashes. "So this has to be my real world."

Darius' laugh angered him.

"Don't get mad at me, don't you know where you are?" He asked looking at him as if he were a child incapable of grasping some rudimental lesson. "Here," he lifted his arms to encompass the darkness, "ashes can be made stone, again and again, or in this case wood." He smiled. "Isn't that all you really want? But I don't know why anyone *would want to keep trying to rewrite the past, no matter what you do here it won't change anything, not where it counts because it can't. It's already been written."*

"I didn't ask you to bring me here."   Evan said with a sad, defeated voice and noticed that somehow Darius had been affected by it.   "I was just asking for an adventure, like the last time."   He wanted to cry then.   "But for a while I thought it was real, couldn't you have given me that, at least for a while longer?   At least long enough for me to tell her I was sorry?"

"No."   Darius told him sadly.   "I brought you here because I thought it would make you happy and you seemed so miserable.   Then I realized that I'd made a mistake.   You always get lost in here so easily.   Evan there's nothing here but shadows, generated by your unconscious mind."

"I touched the gate and the doorknob.   They were so real, but so what if they aren't!   What's wrong with that?   If it was a dream, then it was a perfect one.   Other people have worse vices."

Darius laughed again, "How well I know." And realized Evan caught his slightly sinister tone.   He also realized Evan had been right, being there enfolded within Evan's although temporary world had brought him out of his stupor, since he could see the amused glint of his own eyes reflected in Evan's.

"It was a dream."   Darius said mocking him.   "Look around you.   What do you see?"

"Look at what?   There's nothing here to see now and I have you to thank for that!   You've destroyed it all."   Evan said glaring at him.

Darius only shook his head.

"Where are you?"

"I know where I am, I'm not a fool!"   Then he added angrily, "Darius I know it's a dream but it was a happy one, until you interfered."

"You weren't asleep and you're not asleep."

"You said yourself what I saw was just shadows generated by my unconscious mind."

"That's all they were."

"Then I'm asleep."

"That's were it always starts, but that's not where it ends and it's not where you are now." Darius said, "you're very near death Evan. I told you there is a price to be paid for coming here and you pay it ever time you do. I don't know why it is exactly that a person's concentration seems to focus and even strengthened as they approach death, but it does, their minds generate more energy. The closer you are to death, the more real your dream becomes. That's why you could touch what wasn't there. I pull you back and forth across death's boundary every time I bring you here.

It's a risk but you do keep asking for it. You're sinking in quicksand my friend, and here it's best not to tarry for too long. I might loose my grip on you and believe me, I'm your lifeline."

"I don't believe you! If I'm dead or nearly so, how can I be here talking to you? Are you saying you're dead to?"

"Well now, that's a difficult subject for me to explain, and even harder one for you to comprehend. The bottom line is I have a stronger constitution here. It's easy for me to pierce the sleeping minds of others. What can I say, it's a curse." Darius told him with a cold smile. "Once inside, their minds are pretty palpable to my will. I can make them walk this way or that, like puppets twisting in the wind."

"Is that what you were doing to me?" Evan looked at him evenly and Darius could see it was what he thought regardless of anything he might say.

"I've done it to others, but not to you. You've been a good friend to me Evan. As I said, I was only trying to give you something that I thought would please you."

"How could you know of the house I've always dreamed? And you've never even met my mother. How could you know what she looked like?"

"I didn't."

"But you built all this."

"No I only brought you here, you set the stage. Whenever I bring ... guests, I always allow them domination over the world that they create, at first. Ultimately though I step in and assume control but I would never have done that to you. You've had complete control in building this place and in destroying it."

"Then it can be rebuilt!"

"I suppose. If that's how you enjoy killing time." Darius said with a cold laugh. *"Because that's exactly what you'll be doing. Building the prison where you'll spend your eternity. Evan I'm your friend, I could have walked away and left you there within that illusion, you'd never have been able to leave this place without me. As I said, staying here too long is dangerous. The mental bridge back is composed of billions of synapses that are destroyed over time and the energy needed to generate this place destroys them very quickly.*

I can create this vacuous domain anytime I wish, and it's easy enough to draw in sleeping minds. Whether their experience here is pleasant or not depends on the subject, and my mood, but as of late I've rarely brought anyone here." Darius fell silent and could feel Evan was about to question him further but Darius shook his head sorrowfully.

"Awake!" Was the last thing Evan remembered Darius saying.

Chapter 2 - Nightmare

Darius awoke early that next morning leaving the apartment. He had a quota to fill and didn't want to waste time. Though he didn't have to do it, it did pass the time and he had lots of it to pass. It was amazing how many clients there were who had an interest in what they perceive as an inexperienced thirteen-year-old. They usually harbored images of innocence and vulnerability, never guessing that the vast majority of them would never leave alive. To Darius' mind, most didn't deserve to, not by the rules that he had been playing by for the past thirty years. Male or female, young or old, rich or poor, it didn't matter. Only the state of their mind would determine what his response would be. That and how impressed he became by what he saw. The conscious mind could often lie, even to itself, but the subconscious mind usually rang true when he cut deep enough.

Around noon Darius gently closed the door of a high-rise condo on the gold coast side of town. As he stood in the quiet of the hall he'd thought briefly about the man on the other side of the door. He'd gotten what he wanted but paid a greater price than he'd anticipated. The only evidence of that price was an expression of horror etched forever across his face. The memory caused Darius to smile. He hadn't been able to help it and remembered how evil and monstrous Edward Ravenhurst had seemed at first. In retrospect Darius realized he was far more of an angel by comparison, he only killed.

'One has to get their kicks were they can find them,' he thought, 'and lets face it there aren't to many opportunities for a forty-three year old man in a thirteen-year-old package. Physiology aside, I do have needs and this satisfies them, on more levels than one. It was never fair that this should have happened to me.' He thought angrily as he made his way down the corridor and out of the building.

However Darius realized his own existence was probably more exciting than Ravenhurst's. He got to travel through numerous unimaginable worlds and times that never existed, and probably never would. Yet that didn't make them any less thrilling for him, or dangerous for them. Again he thought about the John Doe at his back in his expensive condo spoiling. 'All in all, a good days work.' Darius left the money behind. 'Why not?' He thought. He didn't really need it thanks to Ravenhurst.

As he approached their apartment Darius had seen Gordon sitting on the steps of the two-story brownstone where they lived.

It was late afternoon and the neighborhood was jumping with activity. Gordon's face reflected only mild interest as he came strolling towards him from up the block.

"So you came back, lucky us." His face was as cold as his voice was dry.

Darius walked past him as if he weren't aware that he'd spoken or existed.

"Tony's upstairs," Gordon added, hoping for a reaction, "and he's been looking for you." But the only sound he'd heard was Darius shutting the front door as he passed through it.

Gordon had always been a hard person for Darius to get along with and he'd never tried to figure what had made him that way. There were always some people whose thoughts were more of a challenge for him to read. Gordon had been one of those people. Since entering their little part of the world he'd been too busy drowning in his own apathy to try to delve any further. Now, he smiled to himself realizing that he'd make time and take the effort.

Without his 'gifts' Darius normally would have reasoned that Gordon was of the prejudiced variety, in the extreme. He had a type of Nazi look to him. Yet his very presence there seemed to dispute that, as did his clientele. Soon his mind would provide the answers, perhaps before the night was over. He would enjoy tearing Gordon's mind apart.

"Boy," Tony's Culver's baritone voice with its cruel lecherous tone cut through the apartment. "I done told you, I ain't running no social service agency. You better have something more than this for me the next time I come!"

Darius entered the apartment in time to see Tony exiting their bedroom, slamming the door behind him. When their gazes had locked, Tony had taken several angry steps in his direction.

It had been a long time since Darius had felt anything remotely close to physical pain. In fact, he wasn't sure it was a sensation he was capable of feeling any longer. Yet its memory had lingered, causing him to instinctively reach into his pocket and pull out the thick bundle of bills he'd had concealed there. He threw it onto the table that separated them causing Tony to smile even before his hand reached out to grab the money.

"Well all right! Now, this is more like it." Tony said with a laugh fanning through the bills and Darius realized that his own Hyde-like personality was starting to reassert itself. "Damn boy! What you been doing to earn this?" Again he'd laughed before turning his back upon him. "Yeah, this'll do nicely and it'll even make up Evan's short fall." He headed towards the front door still counting the money and called over his shoulder as he went. "Oh yeah, he'll be out of action for a day or two." At the door Tony stopped and turned to look at Darius again, only half way through his counting. "You know, I knew you'd make a nice addition to our little family." He reached for the doorknob. "Keep up the good work." The door closed gently but Darius had continued to stare at it and after a moment it reopened. The smile on Tony's face had faded. "I'll be back on Monday and I do mean, keep up the good work," now as Tony left Darius turned away.

Externally Darius' expression and mannerism had been serene and undisturbed. Yet for an instant he had felt fear, and had been sure that Tony Culver had been aware of it. A short time later Gordon had come angrily running through the door Tony had just exited.

"What the hell where you thinking?" He screamed waiving his arms. "That ass was waving that wad of money you gave him under my nose in the hall just now. He said if you could turn that kind of money in a weekend, I sure as hell could do it in a week. Do you know what you've done to us? Evan isn't keeping up with his quota as it is. I thought you were supposed to be his friend. Have you seen him yet?"

As usual Darius wasn't listening to Gordon until the mention of Evan's name. That had an impact. He'd left Gordon there shouting at his back to walk into their bedroom where he found Evan curled up on his bed, his face to the wall. He appeared to be asleep. Darius had been about to reach out and shake him when Gordon grabbed his arm jerking him around roughly.

"Leave him alone!"

"What happened?"

Gordon made a gesture for Darius to follow him out of the room. As Darius passed through the bedroom doorway Gordon closed the door gently. When he turned again to face Darius he could see that Gordon's anger was nearly boiling.

"What the hell do you think happened fool, you to damn stupid to figure it out? He beat the crap out of him."

"Tony?"

"Who the hell do you think?" Gordon added hot-tempered. "I already told you he didn't make quota and you've just made things hundreds of times worse for him, and for me."

The bedroom door opened and Evan came out. He'd glanced towards them only momentarily before turning away in embarrassment to hide bruised and swollen features and a split lip. A sorrowful gasp escaped Darius' lips before Evan had completely disappeared limping his way towards the bathroom to escape their gaze.

For a moment there was silence, and when Darius spoke his voice was cold and there was a hardened resolve in his icy glare. Despite this his smile held amusement.

"You know Gordon, there's an entrepreneurial spirit sweeping the country. I think it's time we joined it. What do you think?"

For a moment Gordon looked at him puzzled before the hatred returned to his eyes.

"You can laugh, but I don't see the joke. Evan is in there," Gordon pointed toward the bathroom door, "and he's hurting." He walked away leaving Darius standing in the room alone.

For a moment Darius had just stood there looking at the closed bathroom door before returning to the bedroom. Internally his mind had returned to the old cord of fear that Tony had momentarily generated within him. Now he had two scores to settle with Tony.

Darius had lain there, in the quiet darkness of his bedroom for nearly an hour before his ears alerted to the sound of the doorknob turning, and he'd decided to feign sleep.   There was a slow creaking of the floorboards as Evan carefully tiptoed across the floor on route to his bed. He moved gingerly towards the middle of his bed and Darius had felt painful misery in each of his slight gestures.   Darius realized Evan hadn't heard the earlier conversation that passed between himself and Gordon, but he had been able to tell from their gazes that it concerned him. He'd lain back down on his pillow wondering what would happen first. Either he or Gordon would eventually get tired of fronting for him and always having to chip in on his portion of the money to save him. Or Tony might eventually get wind of it and cut him up into bite sized pieces, throwing him in an alley somewhere.

As Darius had lain there eavesdropping on Evan's thoughts he'd realized that Evan had not been exaggerating. He'd heard about Elaine from various sources, their previous roomy. She had once been a member of their 'family.' She'd gotten fed up with Tony and left only to relocate in a different area of town. Elaine found out that the industry she worked in was a small one. Tony found and shot her, nine times, in the face. Evan reasoned that he'd gotten it bad that day but he'd also been lucky.

Too scared to run, too scared to stay Evan realized that his next run in with Tony would probably also be his last, but perhaps that wouldn't be such a bad thing. If only he hadn't gotten mixed up with him in the first place, but no matter what happened he knew he'd never return to the foster homes he'd run away from. He'd met Tony in a bus depot where he'd been sleeping. Of course now he knew vultures like Tony frequented those types of places in search of fresh meat.

Always willing for conversation, for the first time Evan was grateful that Darius appeared to be asleep as he pulled the covers over his injured face.

Evan found himself in unfamiliar surroundings. It was a strange place, an apartment building with grand designs. Outside, a doorman helped patrons in and out of taxis' that waited at the curb in long lines. He noticed Darius as he walked towards the front door and right in front of the doorman who hadn't bothered opening the door for him. He wondered vaguely if it was because Darius was black, then realized why. He hadn't seen him. Darius had walked right through the closed door, without ever opening it. It was a dream. It had to be.

Usually being aware of that realization was enough to pop Evan out of it, but this time the dream had held. He didn't know where he was but it was just a dream so ... it was time to have some fun, he thought.

Darius had disappeared into the building and he had no way of finding him. He walked into one of the open elevators and found that there were twenty-three floors. He wasn't sure which one to choose when of a sudden one of the buttons lit on its own, the twenty-first floor.

The building was massive, with dozens of apartments on each floor. But as he'd passed the door plaques the apartment number twenty one fourteen had begun to glow, and so Evan cautiously turned the knob.

It was as if the floor had disappeared from beneath him, more, as if the world had also disappeared.

"What are you doing here?" Darius' amazed voice asked from the darkness.

"I don't know, but that's my question. Don't you have any dreams of your own?" Evan asked laughing as Darius separated from the surrounding darkness to shake his head, also amused.

"Well," Darius said, "Why don't we sort this out in daylight, when we're both awake. In the meantime, we should pay our respects to the host of this little party."

"I thought I was the host?" Evan said but Darius had remained silent. "Well, I don't know what you're talking about but I'm game." He said starting to look around at the apartment, which was materializing around him. Like the building, it was lavish in its furnishings with a living room

that had a balcony with a view of the city. "Who lives here anyway?"

"Come on, I'll show you. I think you'll get a kick out this."

Darius walked towards one of the rooms to the rear of the living room. He guessed it to be a bedroom.

As he entered Evan was aware that the environment changed, even before his unconscious senses could completely register it. It became dark, the room somehow seemed much larger than it should have been, and the air cold and damp. The little bit of light there was seemed to come from torches hung in brackets high along dark stonewalls.

"Where the hell are we?" Evan asked confused.

"An old Vincent Price movie, I think." Darius said laughing. "I can't remember the title or the plot, but I do remember it had a dungeon, with a torture device that I believe was called 'seven steps to heaven.' But none of that is really important. It doesn't matter what I remember about the movie, only what he remembers, and he must have seen it a long time ago."

"What are you talking about?"

Darius gave Evan a wide sinister grin. "This is what makes this place so much fun."

Darius grabbed Evan's arm guiding him through darkened corridors. They'd continued to walk until Evan heard a long terrible scream and immediately stopped, tensing up in his tracks.

"What was that?"

"I'm going to show you, come on."

The more steps they took, the louder the screams became.

"I don't think I like this dream anymore." Evan yelled over the screaming. "I think I'll go now." He said imploringly.

"No you don't." Darius laughed. "I told you, you can't

go anywhere unless I take you."

The screams continued, distracting Evan momentarily and Darius again started to pull him forward until a fresh scream had compelled him to yank away.

"As I recall," Evan began, "you didn't bring me here. I got here on my own and I'm game for trying to leave the same way."

"I don't know how you did it but I doubt you know how to get back yourself. I strongly suggest you stay until it's finished."

"Until what's finished?" Evan asked aware that they now stood before a massive wooden door with a heavy iron handle.

"Open the door." Darius said pushing Evan toward it as the screams renewed.

"First tell me what's in there?" Evan shouted.

"Something you're really gonna enjoy."

When Evan hadn't moved Darius added. "You know Evan, you're a warm hearted person, and you're also a coward. I never realized that until now. This is just a dream, what are you scared of."

But Evan had remained steadfast.

"All right, stay here." Darius said, impatiently. "This shouldn't take too long. I'll come back for you."

Evan heard the disappointment in Darius' voice and reached out to pull the handle on the door, he was surprised when it had glided open easily. Inside the room was dark except for a single spotlight from above that shown down on what seemed like a casket. Darius motioned for him to come closer to it, and as Evan did so Darius lifted the lid to find Tony Culver inside.

The casket was constructed of metal with shackles inside restraining Tony's neck, wrists and ankles, all of which were raw from his exertions. Over him were seven partitions fitted to his form which created compartments, six of which were overflowing with rats. They were not ordinary by any definition but huge, hump backed rats capable of devouring the largest alley cat. Strangely they also possessed huge fangs that they used to tear at Tony's clothing, skin, and in places even exposed bone, and Evan could hear the scraping of them as they did so. Blood was everywhere except for Tony's face, it had been the only compartment yet to be breached.

Tony had been lying there, as if unconscious and Evan wondered if such a thing were even possible in a dream but then reminded himself that this image of Tony wasn't real. It was then that he'd noticed one of the monstrous rodents beginning to penetrate the last barrier. It thrust its head through the small opening, wiggling furiously until it was completely in. Evan turned away in horror as the thing crawled over to begin chewing at the side of Tony's throat, he continued to repeat to himself that none of it was real. The sound of Tony's renewed screams forced his attention back in time to see the rodent as it climbed the side of his face towards his left eye.

The image that resembled Tony looked to Darius, who had been standing there smiling and pleaded for help before finally focusing on Evan. As the rodent tore at his right eye Tony's words had become unintelligible and Evan had turned away again in disgust, unable to look as the rat feasted closing his eyes tightly against the nightmare.

"This has to stop, it has to." He continued repeating it over and over but the screams had continued. Finally he'd brought his hands up to his ears to block the sounds and felt Darius as he attempted to pull them back down again.

"Let me help you." He said amused and the screams stopped.

Evan had been facing Darius, his back to the casket and the image of Tony that lay there.

"Turn around." Darius prodded him gently.

At first Evan had refused but eventually turned expecting the terrible image of Tony to have dissipated but it *remained.*

"He's dead." Darius said matter-of-factly, with no trace of sympathy reflected in his voice or expression as he gazed downward at the corpse in the box. The rats were gone. "What time is it?"

For a moment Evan had only stood there before the question sank in, when it did he'd thought it an odd one. His eyes were still fixed upon the dead man's face with its one remaining eye that stared wide into vacant space. Everywhere blood continued to flow freely from lacerations too numerous to count. The largest was a gaping whole near the center of the dead man's chest, revealing a heart, half eaten.

Darius struck Evan good-naturedly.

"Pick up his wrist and look at his watch." He commanded.

Again Evan hesitated before complying, it was covered in blood, which he'd had to wipe away. The expensive Rolex on the dead mans nearly skinless wrist read 3:45 AM.

"It's amazing how many people there is whose greatest fear in life are either rats or insects." Darius laughed. "Ah well," he said finally, "time to go, nothing else to see or do here." He said walking off to disappear within the darkness.

"Darius, wait. You're not leaving me here alone."

"Why not! As you said, you got here on your own." He said sarcastically, but a moment later he was again standing at Evan's side. "All right, but the next time you will be on your own."

Again, "Awake!" was the last word he'd remembered Darius saying.

Darius had been standing in the doorway of their bedroom watching Evan. He could tell that he was about to wake even before he'd made any physical gestures to that affect, he'd seemed more or less to be in a dreamless state now. His eyes had seemed to pop open all of a sudden and he'd glanced Darius' way, as if aware that he was being observed.

"Well, good morning." Darius called over.

Evan hadn't replied immediately, instead he sat up and gazed at his watch. It was a simple enough gesture, yet Darius could hear Evan's mind trying to work its way through why it somehow felt significant. He was also trying to capture fragments of his dream, but like smoke it had nearly dissipated upon his waking and was already well beyond his minds ability to grasp. Whatever it had been about, Evan knew it had not been pleasant and that he wasn't eager to return to it.

Darius realized that his own mood was uncharacteristically cheerful that morning. Both Evan and Gordon had also seemed to notice and both glanced at each other when they thought him unaware.

"I think I liked him better when he wasn't talking." Gordon said finally, rolling his coffee cup between his palms as he nodded towards were Darius stood at the kitchen sink. As usual he was speaking to Evan as if Darius hadn't been there, typical for him.

"Now why is that?" Darius asked turning to face him. "Especially when I come bringing such glad tidings."

"I suppose I should ask what the hell you're talking about," Gordon said with a mild smile, "the problem is, I don't really give a shit." With that he'd stood and walked out of the kitchen.

"Hum," Darius continued to watch the doorway that Gordon had just exited through, "you know, that guy could use a personality adjustment," he said pondering the thought for several moments, "but how to go about it, I mean from a psychological perspective?" He'd asked the question almost to himself than laughed remembering Evan. "But playing with peoples minds can be tricky business, and the chances of a successful outcome are usually pretty damn slim." Darius looked at Evan who only gazed back in confusion.

"Tell me," he said sitting down at the table and leaned forward as if to reveal some secret confidence, causing Evan to also leaned forward, "do you think he's scared of rats?" Darius whispered.

Without knowing the reason why, Evan nearly jumped from the table throwing his seat backward in the process to quickly leave the kitchen.

Concealed within his sanctuary, Evan brought his forehead to touch the cool surface of the mirror over the basin. He closed his eyes trying to force himself to relax, noting that his head felt as if it would explode, and his heart pounded fiercely. He gazed down at hands that were cold and clammy. "What's wrong with you?" Evan asked his reflection softly. "Did you get hit in the head too hard yesterday?" But memories of Tony's assault the day before only served to trigger a wave of nausea, forcing Evan to grab the basin tightly for support. He struggled to remember something on the edge of his consciousness, but the effort only served to concentrate his headache. When his hands stopped trembling Evan splashed cold water on his face. He wanted to hide there forever but knew that was impossible. He had a day to get started, and a quota to fill.

Evan exited the bathroom to find Darius still seated at the kitchen table, his own overturned chair had been righted.

"So, what are your glad tidings? Or don't I rate hearing the information." Evan said in a voice that was humorless.

"Oh, I nearly forgot," Darius said easily, "Tony's dead."

Chapter 3 – *Celebration*

"This is great!" Gordon was nearly bouncing with excitement. "Don't you get it Evan? Not having that parasite breathing down our necks is the best thing that could ever have happened."

It was midday as the three of them had stood in the modest living room of their small apartment. Evan had spent most of the morning pacing uncomfortably back and forth in front of the window since hearing of the news, stopping only occasionally to gaze out deep in thought.

"How can you say that?" Evan asked clearly agitated. "When Davis finds out we'll be thrown out on the streets."

"Evan, you're such an ass! If he cared about what we were doing he wouldn't have let us stay here in the first place. I'll tell you what he does care about and that's his money. As long as we keep paying the rent on time he won't bother about us, and who the hell says he even has to know Tony's dead anyway." Darius had been sitting quietly on the sofa exhibiting only mild interest in the conversation up until that point.

"I tell you it doesn't matter one way or the other." Gordon said irritably.

"Gordon, it does! His lease was with Tony not us, we're not even supposed to be here. He can throw us out if he wants to, I'm not saying he'll do that but he could. I mean, I don't think he will, but it's something to think about. Maybe he'll only raise the rent. He knows it'll be difficult for us to find any place else. He has us by the short hairs."

"The two of you really like making problems where they don't exist." He said waiving an arm to include the silent Darius in his comment. "If anything, we should be celebrating. Okay listen, we won't bring it up to Davis. We'll pay the rent on time and there won't be any problems, you'll see. The good news is we won't loose our earnings anymore. We'll have more than enough to keep on going just the way we have, even buy some stuff for ourselves." Gordon looked from Evan to Darius both of whom said nothing, but it was clear Darius had no problem with his proposal. Evan however seemed troubled.

"What's *your* problem? Have you looked in a mirror lately? Did you forget that it was Tony who rearranged your face like that?"

"I haven't forgotten anything! I was just wondering what happened to him. How did he die?"

"Who the hell gives a shit!" Gordon shouted angrily. "As long as he did, that's all I care about."

"He was kinda young Gordon, he only just made what ... twenty-five?" Evan looked down, lost in his own musings and continued, almost to himself. "He seemed in good health, athletic and everything." Evan's face twisted into a frown. "I wonder what killed him."

"What are you suggesting?" Darius asked, his voice low and serious.

"I'm not suggesting anything. I was just curious, that's all." Evan said turning away from them to gaze out the window unseeingly. "What happened to one could easily happen to another." He whispered.

"You're both nuts." Gordon said throwing up his hands, and left the room.

There was silence between the remaining two for several minutes. Quietly Darius rose from his place on the sofa and went over to stand beside Evan.

"Now there's just the two of us." Darius continued in the same low voice. "What's bothering you?"

Evan turned slowly to look at him, his face mirroring uneasiness.

"Nothing. I guess Gordon's right. I'm just nuts."

"They say that the insane are the last people to know it, or something like that. So you're probably safe on that score. You know, it's been a few days since you and Tony had your little tête-à-tête, I'd have thought that your face would have started to heal by now but your eyes, the dark circles under them are still so pronounced. Not flattering on any kind of skin, least of all yours." Darius said with a smile. "Having nightmares?"

"Is it that obvious?"

"Afraid so. Your problem is you're a bleeding heart for everything that happens around you. Even if Tony was the best person in the world, which he wasn't, why tear yourself apart about his death? Why care?" Then Darius' eyes narrowed and seemed to lock Evan's gaze. "You were on the endangered species list with him and you know it."

At that Evan turned away with difficulty.

"I'm not some kinda alien from another planet that can just turn his feelings off and on like that." He said snapping his fingers. "I've never been able to. I feel even for my worst enemy if something tragic happens to them. I can't help it."

"It goes back to your mother, yes I know." Darius said mockingly.

Evan looked up at him shocked.

"There's nothing safe from you is there?" He said angered.

"You're the one who told me about her."

"That's a lie, I've never told anyone. Not Gordon, not you, not Tony, NO ONE!"

"Calm down." Darius said with an easy smile.

"They're not just dreams are they? Of course I knew that there were times when you seemed kinda insightful but it's even more than that isn't it?" Evan felt weak in the knees as a thought occurred to him. He found himself fighting the increasing pull of gravity, which threatened to pull him towards the floor. Darius had continued to just look at him, a frozen smile on his face. "You killed Tony!"

"You know, you're right." Darius said, "What happened to one COULD happen to another, easily and it's a lesson worth remembering."

They both turned as Gordon stuck his head into the room.

"Listen, if you two clowns think things have changed around here or that you're going to get away with not holding up your end you're both sadly mistaken. I suggest you two start the prowl. NOW!" He said.

"Well," Darius said after he'd left, "it looks like I'm going to have a busy night."

"Don't kill yourself trying to make quota, Gordon's all talk." Evan said reassuringly.

"Not to worry," Darius said, "it's not my self I intend to kill." He said a sadistic smile crossing his face.

It was about two in the morning when Evan climbed the steps to their building. He was still short his quota for that week. He hoped Gordon would understand his difficulties with his face still less than perfect but he knew Darius wouldn't give him grief. Entering their dark and quiet apartment Evan wondered if either was home. In the bedroom he found Darius in his bed but Gordon's bedroom was empty.

He thought about the first time he'd met Gordon and how resistant he'd been to him staying there. 'Well' he thought, 'as the most senior member maybe he thinks he's earned a leadership role. He's certainly making a late night of it.'

"Yes," Darius said into the silence startling Evan, "but he can't stay awake *all* night can he?"

"What's that supposed to mean?"

"You know what it means."

"So you admit it. We were responsible."

"You weren't responsible for anything." Darius said sighing heavily and for a moment there was silence. "Evan for a long time now I've punished those that have tried to hurt me, but never those I care about. However, I've outgrown childish concepts of good and evil, of heaven and hell. I don't believe in either anymore. For me there's only here and now, and I have no intention of ever letting anyone hurt or walk over me, ever again. That includes Gordon."

"But he hasn't done anything to you!" Evan said pleadingly.

"He annoys me, that's enough!" He said softly. "His very presence now irritates me."

"No, this is stupid." Evan shook his head fiercely to dispel the thought. "It was just a coincidence. Darius it's impossible to kill someone by entering their dreams."

"You keep thinking that tonight. Tomorrow as you stand over Gordon's lifeless body we'll see if you still cling to that belief." Darius said cruelly. "He's got to sleep sometime in the next few hours and when he does I'll be waiting for him, it won't matter physically where he is."

"How can you think like this Darius?" Evan asked shocked. "We're family!"

"HE'S NOT MY FAMILY!" Darius shouted into the darkness. "And neither are you." There was quiet for a time before he spoke again and when he did there was sadness in his voice. "The only family I ever had died years ago."

"I'm sorry you feel that way." Evan said and Darius knew there was sincerity in his voice. He'd hurt him with that last outburst. "But I still see you both as my family, and I won't let you hurt him."

"There's nothing you can do to stop me. I'm surprise you haven't figured that out by now. Don't annoy me Evan because that would be dangerous. I don't want to hurt you too."

"That's true for me too," Evan said sadly, "but I'll fight you, anyway I can."

"Well, I guess there's nothing more to be said then, pleasant dreams."

With that he turned over and went to sleep just as Evan heard the front door open, it appeared that Gordon was home and calling it a night.

Evan lay in his bed trying to sleep, an impossible task given the circumstances. His conversation with Darius was still echoing in his mind and worry eating at his heart. Yet he knew that with Darius already asleep it was only a matter of time for Gordon, and he was as defenseless against Darius as Tony had been. He also believed that to the best of his knowledge, Tony had never done or said anything against Darius, yet he had killed him horribly. So what fate awaited Gordon? Evan turned over and tried again for sleep, he had to. Sleep was his only hope to stop Darius, but still he couldn't. His state of mind was unconsciously fighting it off. He got out of bed and approached Gordon's bedroom door knocking softly.

"Yeah, what do you want?" Gordon's voice was irritable.

Evan poked his head in despite not having been invited.

"I just wanted to see if you were all right." Evan said testing the waters and causing Gordon to look at him strangely.

"Well you know same old same old." He said finally. "But I am pretty tired, some of us actually work for a living so if you don't mind..." He let the rest of the sentence trail. Evan knew there would be no explaining the fears he had for his friend's safety. Not that night.

"So I guess a card game or something is out of the question?" Evan said.

"Afraid so." Gordon said with a laugh.

"Well, good night then." Evan closed the door behind him. 'Guess there's only one way to protect you now.' He told himself after a brief second of wondering why he'd even want to.

"Evan," Gordon called softly from the other side of the closed door causing Evan to open it again, "is something wrong?"

He'd looked miserable for a second pondering whether to tell Gordon everything or not, but only shook his head and smiled weakly closing the door again.

Evan looked around at his surroundings. He was in an old abandoned warehouse. Parts of the ceiling had caved in to reveal a starry nighttime sky above, and everywhere he walked there was the crunching sound from glass and debris underfoot. Where was Darius? Remembering his purpose Evan realized that a better question was where was Gordon, and why was he there? Briefly Evan worried that he might have missed them both and was walking through some nightmare of his own when from somewhere there was a familiar scream. He ran towards it, it was Gordon.

He entered a small room with two support beams that were within arms lengths of each other. Gordon was tied at the wrists between them. In front of him a strange man stood with a blooded knife in hand, he was cutting off layers of Gordon's face, showing it to him and then tossing them onto the floor in favor of a fresh piece. Gordon was begging, pleading for the man to stop.

"Daddy please!" He'd said between his screams. "I won't do it again, I swear." But the man had just tossed down another piece of flesh and was cutting again. From Evan's perspective he could see that the boy hadn't many undamaged areas on his face left. As he moved forward he saw Darius laughing silently in the background. Both Gordon and Darius noticed him simultaneously, look of pleading on Gordon's face and one of anger on Darius'.

Evan expected Darius to intercept him as he stepped

forward to aid Gordon, instead the man had, blooded knife in hand as Gordon screamed.

"This is a dream!" Evan shouted to him. "Gordon get up, there's nothing wrong with your face." But Gordon only looked at him as if he hadn't heard, in fearful pain and shock as the specter of his father approached them. "Gordon you're not tied, get up!" Still Gordon hadn't responded and Evan realized he had to act spectacularly if he wanted his friend to understand and to survive.

The man had raised his knife towards Evan's face, about to plunge it downward when Evan grabbed the arm that held it and wrenched it free from its socket. With the other hand he grabbed the man's shirtfront to toss him across the room and into oblivion. The arm he'd held darkened and vanished completely. As Evan looked down into Gordon's face it was to find it still bloodied and mutilated.

"Gordon, this is just a dream!" He said impatiently. "You have to free yourself if you want to live. I can't do it for you. Gordon, fight, if you don't Darius will kill you." With the mentioning of his name Evan remembered Darius at his back and turned to face him leaving Gordon tied there.

"I told you I wouldn't let you hurt him. We'll both fight you if we have to, but Darius don't make us."

Darius looked at him angrily.

"Then you side with him?" He asked and there was hurt reflected in his eyes. Seconds later he vanished.

"My face," Gordon cried hysterically, "my face!"

Evan turned to find his friend still bound and looking down at the pieces of flesh from his face, which was lying in lumps at his feet.

"Oh please," Evan said impatiently, "Gordon will you get a grip! I told you this is only a dream." But Gordon wasn't listening and Evan remembered what Darius had told him earlier. 'What was built could be rebuilt.'

Evan brought his hands up to his friends face,

concentrating upon it, as he did so the pieces of flesh at his feet vanished. When he dropped his hands and had stood back, a look of satisfaction crossed his face. He'd raised his hand again to reveal a mirror.

Gordon stared at himself for sometime gazing at his restored features before he spoke. "It's a dream?" He asked still touching his face and as the realization had hit him, he'd begun to fade and was quickly gone.

That morning Gordon awoke with a tired, irritable demeanor and dark circles under his eyes that nearly matched Evan's own still recuperating features. He went into the kitchen to find Evan sitting there.

"I'm only going to say this once so listen carefully." Evan said and Gordon had only looked at him surprised by his uncharacteristic candor. "The next time I tell you that it's only a dream, listen to me. Don't make me have to say it over and over again, because I can't protect us both and baby-sit you at the same time. Your nightmare yesterday was just a dream, but dreams can kill. I'm sure Tony would testify to that if he could. Gordon, Darius can enter dreams to kill those he hates."

"You've been sniffing the happy dust?" He asked with a tired smile.

"I said listen! Don't think he's going to let yesterday's failure stop him from trying again. Not now that he knows your weakness is your vanity." Evan said angrily.

At that last part Gordon's mouth had dropped open but no words came out.

"Was that man really supposed to be your father?" Evan asked. "Why would you believe him capable of such a thing?"

"You were really there, in my dreams yesterday?" Gordon said starting to shake. "No that's impossible."

"I thought so to at first, but I'm a much quicker study than you."

"But why would he want to hurt me?"

"Because you have the annoying habit of acting like an ass, I personally don't think that's an offense punishable by death. But then again, I wouldn't have killed Tony for driving home his point about increasing my earnings. Darius sees things differently though and I think we're both on his shit list now. Just in case the situation is salvageable, don't annoy him anymore! Worse comes to worse, I think I may at least have touched upon some advantage last night. I think he's always believed that he had exclusive control of that world and in the past maybe he has. But the advantage is certainly his since I don't know how to fine-tune things yet. That's something I hope I won't have to learn."

"You mean the arm."

"Sort of, being able to fight back I mean. The only problem is, I don't think I'll ever be able to fight him on his level. He easily finds other peoples fears and uses those fears to kill them. But I'm not really sure he's scared of anything. Until last night he hadn't considered me a threat and I'm sure he never dreamed I'd fight back," at that Evan had smiled, "especially on your behalf. If I can do that, than maybe I can do more."

"This is great, now I'll never sleep easy again, unless..." Gordon let the words trail.

"No." Evan pounded his fist on the table for emphasis. "I didn't let him hurt you and I won't let you hurt him. I told you, this thing might be salvageable."

"Salvageable my ass, he tried to kill me!"

"Keep your voice down!" Evan whispered. "Besides he probably already knows your plans."

"How could he?"

"Gordon use your head! He can enter your dreams at night, what makes you think he can't read your thoughts by day? If I thought you were going to be stupid I'd never of warned you, and certainly I would never have stuck my neck out for you." He sighed heavily and for the first time Gordon realized how tired Evan also seemed.

"Gordon, I have a feeling that trying not to sleep tonight will work against you. It's not something that you can avoid and when you do you want to be in the right mindset. Just remember that it's only a dream and don't panic under any circumstances."

There was a firmness of conviction in Evan's voice which soothed Gordon's fears somewhat, but then he'd looked up as if something had only just occurred to him.

"You have this ability to?" He said.

"Not originally, it's just something that developed. I guess it's the result of Darius' entering my dreams so often and then confiding in me afterwards. Eventually I learned how to follow him in. He told me of his plans for you yesterday after you left. That's what I wanted to tell you last night, before you went to sleep but then I realized that wouldn't have helped."

"No, I guess not. I'd have just thought you were crazy."

"Yeah."

At that point Darius came into the kitchen and sat down opposite them as both Evan and Gordon sat there staring stiffly. Then an easy smile crossed his face.

"Are we enemies?" Evan asked finally into the surrounding silence.

"Not at all," Darius said smiling back at him, "it's hard to retain anger at someone who's spent so much time trying to lift me out of my despondency. I know why you did what you did." He said kindly.

"As for you," Darius looked at Gordon, "it's not over between us yet." Again he smiled at Gordon who returned only an expression of hatred. "If only looks could kill."

Gordon got up threateningly and Evan rose to check him.

"Sit down damn it!" Evan glared at Gordon as if he'd jump across the table at him if he didn't, reluctantly Gordon obeyed.

"Darius laughed softly, "Gordon he saved you, that's twice now. You were about to make things so much worse for yourself. Oh yeah, and you'd better get over that vanity complex of yours." He added before sliding a newspaper across the table that he'd carried into the room. It struck Evan's untouched coffee cup sending its contents spilling onto it.

"Turn to the obituaries." Darius said flatly.

There were two names circled in red. Evan scanned them briefly and looked up at Darius sadly. "Are these your doing?" He asked.

"One was my case worker, the other a foster parent, but to answer your question, of course not. Evan I never kill. It's their weaknesses and phobia's that ultimately kill them. I do however exercise a great deal of control over their minds." Then he turned to coldly stare at Gordon. "A fact that's true at all times, not just at night. In case you're still pondering a daylight assault."

Darius brought his hand up to his chin and seemed to muse. "Including Tony that makes six Evan and I have you to thank for it all. After all it was you who renewed my interest in dreams, and freed me from my psychological prison." With that Darius stood and laughed as he left the kitchen.

"My god!" Evan said dropping his head down hard onto the table.

"Don't listen to that bastard you had nothing to do with their deaths. He's just trying to get to you. Don't you see? He's fishing for *your* weaknesses, planting seeds during the day that he'll use against you tonight. Use your own advice to me of just a few minutes ago. Don't go to sleep tonight afraid or depressed."

"Gordon I don't want to be his enemy, I don't think I can beat him. On the other hand, I won't be able to live with myself if I don't do something. How can I live knowing that each and every night he might be entering the dreams of a different person to murder, people who may only have casually angered him that day. How would I know that he wasn't killing *you* as we both slept? Last night, he didn't even try to hurt me but when he does..."

There was a sad resolution to Evan's tormented thoughts as he rose from the table. "Will you check on me in the morning? If I don't wake then you know I failed. In that case I suggest you put as much distance between the two of you as you can. He's already told me that won't work, but I guess it can't hurt either. Gordon, try to manage your fears. I think that's his only real weapon and it's as strong as you allow it to be."

"Why don't we both just leave this place to that black devil,"

Gordon began, but Evan just shook his head, "you said yourself that it can't hurt."

"I told you, I can't just walk away from this." As Gordon opened his mouth to say more Evan again shook his head to silence him. "Gordon I'm tired and I don't want to talk about this anymore. I have to get to work."

Evan rose from the table but stood there for a moment in uncertainty. He'd been hoping for a positive response to his question from Gordon should he fail in his efforts that night. But as he watched him now Evan realized Gordon's mind was preoccupied battling his own fears, his own nightmares. Of course he'd understood. It hadn't been that long ago when all they'd had to worry about was getting back home in one piece, and occasional beatings, certainly not the realm of nightmares and demons that they now faced. That was always left to the movies and television, now it had become their world.

Realizing there was nothing left to do now but wait for the inevitable. Evan silently left the apartment to begin his day.

It was two in the morning when Evan again mounted their apartment building steps, the battle of getting through the day finished. Now he mentally prepared for the far worse battle that awaited him. He'd spent much of the day dangerously distracted. Trying to fish out his own fears and phobias, but he'd found the task to be an open field with too many to focus on.

Inside their apartment he had quietly turned the knob on Gordon's bedroom to find him absent. He clearly understood the reason why. Despite Evan's warnings Gordon was obviously trying to remain awake for as long as possible. Oddly, Evan was more tired then he'd ever been in his life and could resist sleep no longer. He walked into the bedroom that he shared with Darius and turned on the light. His bed was also empty.

Evan allowed himself to drop hard upon his bed, his eyes falling towards Darius' empty one. It was then that his eyes had focused upon the old worn trunk that was pushed beneath it. Darius had been half carrying, half dragging that trunk the first time Tony had introduced them, and Evan realized he'd never seen its contents.

He allowed his feet to drop back down onto the floor. Getting up, he walked to the opposite bed and kneeled down to look underneath. Evan hesitated only briefly before pulling the trunk out. It wasn't something he wanted to do. It was something he had to. If he was to fight Darius he'd need all the information about him he could find.

It was an old trunk. With spring locks, only one of which apparently still worked forcing Evan to lift the remaining side to peer in. He shook the trunks contents for a better view. As he'd held it upwards a small stone and several handwritten pages escaped falling from the trunk onto the floor near his feet. The pages appeared to have been torn from a journal belonging to an Edward Ravenhurst. The last entry had been dated thirty years earlier.

Chapter 4 – Home

Evan couldn't remember having gone to sleep but apparently he had for they had been there for some time. Now they just stood there facing each other and finally Darius spoke.

"You're getting good at this." He said.

"I have you to thank for that of course. Who is she?" Evan asked with mild interest as the woman they had been silently following made her way through her dream. It had been strange but pleasant enough up until that point and she was about to get into her car only a few feet from them.

"Does it matter?" Darius answered but Evan had continued to stare at him expectantly.

"A former teacher, gave me nothing but grief. Now I think I'll give her some." Darius said with a laugh.

"I finally figured it out, why you love this place. It allows you to rule, to be the demon of other people's dreams. Can't you ever do anything good for someone?"

"I don't know, we started out that way didn't we?"

"True." Evan replied. "We did have some good times."

"Yeah." Darius said.

"Couldn't we again, for old time's sake. I promise I won't ask again."

There was a pleading quality in Evan's voice and Darius had responded to it. Evan turned to see that the house from his past dream had reappeared. Complete with fence and daffodils. He wanted to race up the steps but resisted.

"You're home now Evan," Darius said kindly, "this time to stay."

"What does that mean?" He asked cautiously.

"You've been in here too long my friend. You've crossed over, you should never have followed me. If this is your heaven, then welcome to it."

"Yes," Evan said with a heavy sigh, "it is." There were tears about to form in his eyes that hardened when he'd again looked at Darius. "What will you do, when you return to the waking world?"

"The same as I always do. Punish those that deserve it. Now there's no one there to challenge me and I think I'll restart with Gordon." He said with a laugh. "Not to worry, perhaps he has some place equivalent to go to afterwards. Or perhaps he'll be like Tony, forever trapped within that coffin of rats. That happens sometimes you know when the emotions are that great." Darius said placing his hand gently upon the fence.

"How can you be so cruel? What happened to turn you this way?"

"It's not important anymore."

"Maybe you should be leaving now." Evan told him tired of listening to his ranting.

"Perhaps."

"I suppose, now that I'm gone, when you leave this time we'll never meet again. Don't you have a little time, to meet my mother and see my dream house? The one I never had?

It won't be any fun not having anyone to show it off to." He said with a sad smile.

"I'd love to see it, for old time's sake."

Evan started up the walkway with Darius following close behind. As both walked through the doorway it slammed loudly behind them.

Darius had realized immediately that there was something familiar about the area in which he now stood and then he'd realized what it was, it was his apartment from three decades earlier.

"Boy where you been?"

Darius turned to find his mother standing in a doorway on the other side of the room. Behind her he knew was the kitchen where she was cooking and he could smell all the familiar aromas.

"Momma?" Darius' eyes began to tear as he approached her.

"I said where you been?" She asked glaring at him. "Boy I sware you bout to worry me to death."

Darius looked confused for a few minutes. "I was... I mean..."

"I told you about staying out all night with those druggy friends of yours. Boy they go'n get you in serious trouble one of these days."

Evan had been standing behind Darius' but had slowly begun to back away until eventually he was indistinguishable from the back wall.

At the door they'd just entered there came a knock.

"I'll get it."

Darius ran for the door to find Earl standing on the other side.

"Hey man were the hell you been?" He asked Darius irritably.

Darius glanced over his shoulder towards his mother at his back silencing Earl.

"Earl?" Darius' mother called from further inside.

"Boy don't stand out there in the hall. Come on in. Dinner's almost ready, you hungry?"

"No Ma'am."

When she disappeared back into the kitchen Earl whispered something about going over to Sunny Mac's house.

"Naw man," Darius smiled, his eyes still on the kitchen doorway, "I just gonna hang here for a while."

Evan also smiled. It seemed everyone had weaknesses, even Darius. His ironically had been a burning desire to return home again and to the life that had been torn from him by the mysterious Ravenhurst.

On the last page of Ravenhurst's journal had been Darius' hand written plea for someone to rescue him, just as he had rescued Ravenhurst. He'd feared long ago he was loosing in his battle to retain his humanity. The stone that mattered so much to Darius and his mother had become useless for him. But destiny or fate had intervened yet again. For when Evan had picked up the stone he'd been linked to distant ancestors and a heritage he'd never been aware of. It seemed that he and Darius were distant relatives and with the help of their mutual ancestor Momma Yeman, Evan had willingly passed the curse that Darius carried onto himself before sleeping that night, freeing Darius forever.

His had been the force that had pulled Darius there that night.

Evan marveled at the power of the mind that had created such a curse and allowed it to traverse from Ravenhurst to Darius and then to himself. Within that world Evan realized that it had powerfully altered Ravenhurst and Darius, both mentally and physically, causing them to remain nearly immortal and turning them into monstrous killers. Yet in all the time they'd prowled the earth looking for release, neither had realized that it also seemed to have limits within that realm. Perhaps if he returned to the waking world he might also be ensnared by its influence. That was why he knew he could not allow Darius to return and it was why he could not, but that didn't mean he couldn't make it as comfortable as possible. They would both remain there, forever if they had to. After over two-centuries the curse would end with him, everything has to die out eventually.

Darius was home again and had disappeared into their kitchen with his mother and Evan realized that it was time for him to leave. Somewhere distant, his dream house waited to be rebuilt, and within someone also awaited his return. Evan turned to disappear into the darkness.

After a fitful sleep Gordon had awakened that next morning tired from a fresh nightmare, but it hadn't been as bad as the one the night before. The nightmare that Evan said Darius caused. The thought of Evan caused Gordon to jump from his bed and run towards his friend's bedroom. He had to make sure Evan was all right.

Inside the room was quiet. The curtains that were normally tied had been released to leave the area darkened and solemn. Gordon approached Evan's bed to find him lying upon his stomach, his head resting upon his folded arms. With nervous hands Gordon reached out to shake him several times without getting a response. He turned him over to find Evan's eyes open slightly, a faint smile touched his lips but he was dead, it seemed he died in his sleep.

Gordon let out an anguished cry as he whirled round to where Darius was also still in his bed grabbing him by the throat, he would kill the bastard with his bare hands and had struck him several times before releasing him and gasping. His eyes were closed, but a similar expression was upon his face. Darius was also dead.

240

Until Sunset

"SOMEONE HELP ME!" Devin's screams were becoming hysterical as his breathing became more labored. He was finding it increasingly difficult to keep his balance with his blurred vision, and the pain in his left side underscored the direness of his predicament as he continued forward, aware that his run was rapidly turning into a stagger.

His mind raced as he past abandoned and decayed factories that, like his vision, were also just a blur. His movements now were mostly instincts as he ran blindly through the night, behind him a crazed murderer pursued. He'd awoken confused and alone on the floor inside a bloody bathroom but appeared to be uninjured. Where had all that blood come from? But when he stood it was to find he was not alone; inside the tub were the remains of his lovely Alicia, dismembered.

In going through Alicia's doorway Devin realized he'd allowed his ego to master his common sense.

Why didn't I just find help? Why did I have to try to be her hero? If I fall, if he catches me, I'll never see home again!

"SOMEBODY... PLEASE!" Devin's unanswered cries continued to reverberate into the night. His mind was now gripped by terror as he navigated his way down the labyrinth of empty streets in the factory district of Westgate.

It had been uncomfortably warm that June afternoon when Devin started his journey. Now he felt only fear and a cold that chilled him to the bone, and his fatigue was becoming nearly overwhelming with each new step but how could that be? While he'd never run track at school, Devin had been confident he could out distance the old man at his back within a few blocks, but that hadn't happened. But no matter what he had to find help, it was his only hope.

Devin forced himself to try to think rationally, but only the events that brought him to his circumstances crystallized within his mind.

He sat at his desk daydreaming while watching Alicia Stokes from the corner of his eyes in the first period English class they shared. To her left, a row of windows took up nearly the entire width of the east wall of the class, bathing Devin's golden goddess in sunlight. She sat there, chin propped upon her right fist at her desk. She seemed deep in thought as she stared forward and to fourteen-year-old Devin her focus seemed intent, laser-like, as she stared at Mr. Klein, the English teacher who was lecturing. She was only one row ahead and one desk to the left of where he sat, yet she seemed ethereal, certainly as if she belonged in places other than their mundane world, but she was in his world. Why couldn't he speak to her? Why was he behaving as though she were some type of otherworldly goddess?

Fortunately he still had his daydreams to fall back on, in which the two of them would walk hand-in-hand under a brilliant blue sky dotted only sparsely with billowy clouds. They would stroll casually through the park or sometimes by the lake, arm-in-arm, and suddenly he would pull her close. Devin smiled. At that moment the sound of Klein's voice cut through his fantasy. Immediately he felt a rush of embarrassment for allowing such a physical facial gesture to betray his thoughts. Quickly he looked away. Klein had asked some question and Devin knew he'd been fortunate it had not been directed towards him. He tried to take in his surrounding peers, allowing only his eyes the freedom of movement and was relieved no one appeared to notice him. Only then could he feel himself begin to relax and let out a slow measured sigh.

The school year's almost over and I still haven't talked to her, times running out! Next year we'll be in the new, larger school. We may never be in the same classes again at the end of this term. I've got to talk to her now. Grow some balls Devin!

Again Devin allowed his mind to wander. On the farthest reaches of his consciousness garbled words, Devin had no real interest in, occasionally penetrated his consciousness. Sure finals were approaching fast but there was still time. It was Alicia that mattered. He hung his head in self-loathing and again regretted the gesture hoping no one noticed his inner turmoil but again it seemed they hadn't. He tried to focus on the teacher's lecture, but after only a few minutes his mind and gaze returned to Alicia.

There are just too many people around her, and all the time! And what about rejection, there's a very real possibility for that, and on a very public scale. I'll never live that down.

The bell rang marking the end of class to everyone's relief except Devin. For him it only made his day worse. Alicia was only in two of his six classes. His only other chance would be in geometry. There she sat in the back of the class and him in the middle. English and geometry, his earliest classes of the day were his only chances and geometry hardly a chance at all.

Devin startled at the bell sounding the end of second period geometry. The classroom had two exit doors, one at the front of the class' west wall and another at the rear. He quickly turned his head towards the back of the class in time to see the flash of her pastel top as she skirted through the open rear doorway. Another lost opportunity. Further hopes for the day were already dashed. Devin moved through the remainder of his classes zombie-like, with every concept, theory or statement passing right through him. His attention far too diverted for concentration.

To hell with it! He thought to himself finally. *Might as well cut myself a break and skip the last class today.*

It was the beginning of June, only two more weeks of class before summer break. Most of the teachers were already beginning to coast through classes. Devin stood outside his locker shoving his books violently inside and causing kids around him to stare. At that point he realized why he failed each day. Fear! He hated the spot light; in fact he was scared to death of it. This thought froze him as he came to the realization that he couldn't will himself to move until the stares had vanished. When most of his peers had either gone to their next class or left for the day, Devin tiptoed quietly down the corridor towards the buildings front exit, realizing that classes had already begun. Instructors could be heard as he passed open doorways, and jealous eyes occasionally diverted in his direction as he passed the classrooms. He forced himself to ignore mounting uneasiness and continued forward.

At the end of the hall he raced down the steps to the first floor and freedom. Pushing the double doors harder then he'd meant and causing the empty corridor to reverberate loudly. He resisted the impulse to run, forcing himself to remain calm as he stepped out into the glaring sunlight.

Devin my man, I guess it just wasn't meant to be. He thought sadly as he turned onto the sidewalk to head northward towards home. It was then that his mind registered something familiar, what was it? A pastel shape in the distance forced his head to turn. It was no mistake, there was his Alicia walking alone briskly up Westgate Boulevard.

Fool, this is your chance, go after her! But he couldn't force his legs to move and only stood there watching her get smaller in the distance until she'd turned and was out of sight.

He wondered where she was going. Not home, for there were no residences that he was aware of in that area. He'd believed it to be industrial.

Back at home, Devin spent most of that night staring at his bedroom ceiling and making plans for what he would say to Alicia after fifth period the next day, if he was lucky enough to catch her at around the same time.

Tomorrow, everything will be different. I'll definitely talk to her tomorrow even if it's the last thing I do! Anyway, it won't hurt cutting music one more day.

The next day, eternity rose and set with each of Devin's

classes. During fifth period his friend Connor, who was seated next to him, caught his attention and whispered if he was prepared for the music theory test in their next class.

"What test?" Devin mouthed back silently.

"You know the test!" Connor whispered quietly. But his words had not escaped the teacher who shot him an angry glance, which only silenced Connor momentarily. He continued again when she turned to write on the board and shot a quick glance her way before continuing, leaning forward to whisper. "You know the test that makes up a third of your grade! What's your problem? You're usually on top of this kind of stuff!" At that point the teacher returned her attention to the class again.

Devin waved the question off not wishing to risk further attention.

After the bell had rang Connor again caught up with Devin in the hall.

"I skipped sixth period yesterday." Devin confessed as they walked towards their locker.

"Why? What happened yesterday?" There was a smirk on Connor's face mirroring an accusation.

"Noth'n! I just took a break, okay."

"Hey man, in the long run, it won't even matter. Pass or fail don't make a damn bit of difference in this crazy-ass world. I wouldn't worry about it."

"I know you wouldn't!" Devin teased. "Hey, I'm cutting out after fifth period today too so don't say anything."

"No problem, but what the hell's go'n on? Come on man, you can tell me!"

"I told you its nothing, just stuff to do that's all. Hey, if it works out I'll tell you about it tomorrow."

"Okay fine, whatever." Connor said throwing up his hands as if to demonstrate indifference. He turned his back on his friend to walk away but turned back again, "But you better tell me tomorrow!" He said laughing as he strolled backward down the hall.

Devin laughed, waving his friend off.

Outside it was another beautiful day as Devin stood at the front door of the school. Upon leaving the house that morning he'd considered that to be a good sign. Now as he stood there searching in vain for Alicia, his hopes began to fade. Her long beautiful strides had quickly placed her out of his reach yesterday. Despite being determined that wouldn't happen again that day, perhaps he'd failed. She was no where in sight.

Maybe it was just a fluke yesterday? He thought.

As he stood outside at the top of the school stairs considering his next move, someone quickly brushed past him to race down the stairs. By the time he recognized her, Alicia had turned onto the walkway and was quickly leaving the school grounds. Devin stood there momentarily stunned but recovered almost immediately to race after her.

She turned to glance nervously behind her at the approach of his rapid footsteps, but her face relaxed when she saw him. She said nothing but continued walking in that same brisk pace.

Devin stopped running and slowed to match her speed when he'd caught up with her. For a few seconds neither spoke as he sought to control his breathing.

"Alicia," he stammered still winded, "hi, remember me, Devin, in your first period English class?"

Devin noticed her face was blank and immediately felt deflated.

"Oh, Devin, right! You sit behind me in English."

Devin nodded mutely, but his face lit when he realized she was aware of his existence. At the same time he also realized all his practice speeches of the night before had vanished reducing him to a brainless mime.

"So," she said into the growing silence, "you done for the day?"

"Well..." was all he could offer, before a constriction developed deep in his throat.

"Funny, I've never noticed you leaving after fifth before." She said, still racing like a prized thoroughbred. Alicia had never allowed Devin the luxury of completely catching his breath. She seemed to sense this slowing her pace.

"Well," Devin repeated struggling with his next words, not wanting to come across like a complete fool, which is exactly how he felt, "I do have a sixth period class, but I had to leave." He'd been looking at his feet instead of her but shot her a quick sideways glance in time to see that she'd expected more of an explanation, which he wasn't sure he could give.

"When I saw you pass me on the steps," he said finally, "I just thought I'd say hi!"

Devin winced in spite of himself. With all the forethought and practice he'd put into his conversation with her for that day, ultimately he'd failed miserably.

She seemed to sense his discomfort.

"Hey," Alicia said waiting until he'd again looked at her, "I'm glad you did. I never get a chance to talk to anyone during class, too busy running from one class to the other."

She was trying to put him at ease, Devin felt this immediately and began to relax and smiled in spite of himself.

"So," she said as they continued at a more leisurely pace, "where you on your way to?"

Devin's smile vanished as he considered the best response, finally settling upon the truth.

"Well, no where I guess."

Alicia looked puzzled at that. "I thought you said you had somewhere to go?"

"I did." He said pausing to gain momentum, "I had to catch up with you." He said finally. "I've wanted to talk to you since this school year began but the timing just never seemed right. Then yesterday I saw that you left after fifth period so here I am."

"You mean you cut class, just to talk to me."

"It was a no brainer." He said smiling nervously but the nervousness vanished when he saw the broad smile that appeared across her face.

"Wow!"

She was on the verge of saying more when the smile

vanished and she came to a stop.

"Well," Alicia said sadly, "I'm home. Maybe we can talk again tomorrow, okay?"

"Sure," he said quickly, "of course."

"Then I see you in English tomorrow?"

"Say, when do you eat lunch?"

"Fourth period."

"Me too, but I never see you."

"I don't eat lunch, I mean not generally. I go to the library instead and do my homework."

"Everyday?"

"Yeah."

"That's dedication. Well…" Devin had been about to say more when Alicia cut him off curtly.

"Look Devin. I really have to go. I'll talk to you tomorrow."

"Okay," he'd said deflated, "but where do you live?" It was a personal question. He knew he had no right to ask at that stage, but he hadn't been able to help himself.

"Around the corner, there's a small brick building sandwiched between two factories." She said and Devin could see it was her turn to be embarrassed.

"Can't I walk you to your door?" He asked with uncertainty.

She seemed uneasy at the request and Devin wondered if she thought he was some kind of nut.

"Well," she said finally, "yeah, sure. I guess it'll be fine. My Dad's really strict. If he knew I brought someone home… well, things would be hard for me but it's early and he'll still be at work."

There was considerable uneasiness in her face but after taking a deep breath she smiled beautifully, tilting her head forward in the direction of her house. When they reached the corner a small unassuming brick two story came into view. Five steps lead up to a narrow porch, only a few feet wider than the front door. At its base they stopped.

"Well, this is where I live." She repeated.

"Can we meet for lunch tomorrow?" Devin asked doggedly but it seemed as if her attention was elsewhere.

Devin allowed his eyes to follow her gaze. He realized she was staring up at the porch and at a small window in their front door where white panels hung making it difficult to see inside. They seemed to move slightly.

When he returned his attention to Alicia he noticed she seemed apprehensive.

"Alicia what's wrong?" He hadn't given the curtains movement much thought until he'd remembered that she'd said that the house was supposed to be empty.

"Do you think someone broke in?" But she hadn't answered, only continued to stare at the small window. "Look," Devin continued, "I can't let you go in there alone! I'll go inside first and check to make sure it's all right. Once I've checked the locks, windows and doors you can go in. Don't worry I'm sure it's nothing."

Devin walked up two or three steps before Alicia caught his arm grabbing his hand firmly, and pulling him back down the steps. Her facial expression now seemed panicky but her words were just the opposite.

"Devin," she took a deep breath, "it's nothing. It's just my Dad that's all. He must be back early."

"Are you in trouble?"

"Don't worry about it." She said waiving her hand to make light of it. "I'll meet you in the lunch room tomorrow, okay?"

"Sure." Devin beamed back at her realizing that he'd achieved a victory that was nearly ten months in the making. "That'll be great."

She raced past him up the stairs in an instant and was nearly inside as Devin asked again if she wanted him to inspect the house but she'd waived him off, quietly closing the door behind her.

Devin just stood there for several seconds, at the base of Alicia's steps realizing again that he'd achieved his hearts desire and smiled in spite of himself, not caring who saw him this time. Now, he would have something interesting to tell Connor tomorrow. It was at that point that everything started to feel surreal.

He was still at the base of the steps when Devin heard Alicia scream. For a second she appeared in her doorway before being pulled back inside by someone out of sight within. Then there had been another scream. Instincts forced Devin to move cautiously up the steps and towards Alicia's doorway. There he found it slightly ajar but the slender crack had not afforded him much of a vantage of the houses' interior. Devin slowly pushed the door open to quietly peer within. Inside everything seemed still and quiet, but he had not imagined that scream. Pushing the door further, Devin slowly entered.

Upon entering the foyer everything appeared quiet and Devin continued forward until he stood in the doorway of the dining area. Then the faint sounds of incoherent babble could be heard. Tip-toeing quietly in the direction of the sounds, Devin was aware that the volume continued to increase, until he could make out words that were nonsense. From his vantage point Devin could only see along a single wall where pots and pans hung but knew that was the source for the voice. Somewhere close, just out of his sight, someone was talking in the kitchen. As the conversation continued Devin realized it was one-sided with only a single male voice speaking in fractured, broken sentences.

Devin moved quietly toward the doorway, until he could take in the full interior of the kitchen. In the middle of the room, between overturned condiments, table and chairs, Alicia lay on the floor. Standing over her was a crazed, gray haired old man with stooped rounded shoulders. He wore jeans and a tee-shirt, revealing a muscular torso through the thin fabric, a sharp contrast to the man's wrinkled and withered face. Devin knew immediately Alicia was dead, although her eyes remained open, there was a horrible unseeing quality to them. Blood was splattered over a wide area of the kitchen, the table, overturned chairs and nearby wall. It also dripped freely from the knife still clutched tightly within the man's fist.

He continued to stand there, in the kitchen surrounded by chaos babbling about Alicia being a whore like her mother and of betrayals. The one-sided dialogue seemed paternal in nature. Oddly, his tone was casual, almost relaxed. As if he'd done nothing out of the ordinary. Only the surroundings, particularly the knife in his hands contradicted this. Devin sensed the man was probably Alicia's father.

Knowing he should flee before being discovered, Devin had instead continued to stand there too terrified to move. He wasn't sure what eventually betrayed his presence. Perhaps some instinct of Stokes revealed the intrusion and in an instant he was on Devin grabbing his arm and bringing the knife down to strike. But Devin's own instincts forced a kick altering the knife's path somewhat and forcing Stokes to weaken his grip enough for Devin's to stumble backwards towards the wall. He hadn't been aware of grabbing one of the pots until he'd swung his fist at the man and heard the thud of the metal against his skull causing Stokes to fall backwards and the knife to fly across the floor. Devin ran for the doorway. He didn't remember anything else until awaking in the bathroom, but the pain in his head told him he hadn't made it out. As he ran, Devin now understood that the knife had found a target but it hadn't been a fatal blow.

With that memory Devin realized that as he slowly bled away his life's blood, his body was betraying him and his movements becoming more sluggish. He looked down at his shirt and pants finding them badly stained. Much of the blood he'd thought had been Alicia's had probably been his own.

A near stumble quickly snapped Devin back to the present. He was running for his life.

Again Devin wondered why he had followed her, his dream girl, right into death. The girl that he'd never even spoken to until that afternoon, the girl that he thought would make his life finally begin, if only he could find the right words to say to her.

The memory had been like a flash in his mind but life wouldn't begin; it would probably end if he couldn't find help somewhere. Behind him the madman continued to stalk. A turn of his head told Devin the old man followed at a slow, almost leisurely pace. He would soon overtake him.

Devin found himself only a short distance from the new school being built. It wasn't set to open until the fall, but the lights were on inside. He made his way towards it, his legs now feeling like lead. He wondered why the old man pursued him but made little attempt to overtake him.

Devin had gotten to the first step and looked up to see everything change. There were voices all around him now. People he couldn't quite see, only vague shadows. He suspected that he was losing consciousness, still he moved from one shadow to the next pleading for help but non came. Devin looked to the top of the steps to see a black girl gazing down directly at him. Her expression showed little interest and no sympathy with his plight. Where was the old man? In panic Devin looked around seeing the old man was nearly on him and screamed.

The first strike was like lightening, so fast that Devin wasn't sure he felt any pain from it, but the blade came down several more times; and the pain did come. Devin's eyes were open and yet the world was becoming pale shades of gray. From the distance came the sound of sirens and shouts, and of what sounded like gun fire but Devin's body was now too heavy to move.

Then there was darkness.

It was always so strange, every year or two faces and places would change, but my life would remain the same, boring. I pondered the mundaneness of my existence as I made my way toward the exit doors of Bell High, where I'd just started my freshman year that day, being swept forward towards the exit in a tide of bodies equally desperate to shake off academic restraints.

My mom worked for a hotel chain, they'd promote her and move us every year or two to a different hotel in their chain. I guess she was just moving up the career ladder. Though I did wish for a bit more stability and that she'd think a little more about how each move affected me. It was so scary for me each time. Let's face it, it's not easy for a black girl to fit in and make friends in an all white school. And if you're skinny, tall and awkward looking with a dark complexion and generous features you're really at a loss. Adding insult to injury isn't my dark complexion or generous features, but my brown hair. Why wasn't it black? I guess to others I must have looked like some freak of nature. Still, I'd never considered myself ugly and I think that was because of my Dad.

I was always close to Daddy and he'd always called me his beautiful princess, but when he and Momma went their separate ways I didn't fit into his picture anymore. I guess it was at that point I'd been forced to reevaluate everything he'd ever told me, including being beautiful. Afterwards I use to think that I'd inherited the worst physical attributes of them both. I'd look in the mirror and never liked what I saw. I'm still not saying that I saw myself as ugly. Let's just say that I had a tendency to judge myself by how others treated me.

Growing up Daddy especially never liked it when I'd talk to my shadows or invisible friends as Momma used to call them. He always thought I existed too much in my fantasy world and for years I'd managed to ignore the shadows and drown them out of my mind. After a few months they had started to fade altogether or maybe they just left me alone. They seem to have a desperate need for interaction with the physical world, which they could no longer be apart of.

As for Momma, well, I often had the impression that she was ashamed of me. I don't know why I felt that way because it wasn't a result of anything she'd ever said or done. It was just a feeling. Maybe it was because she was so beautiful and the fact that she never let me meet her friends or coworkers.

After their split I didn't see a need any longer to please Daddy by not talking to the shadows, especially since we seldom saw each other anymore. As I got older, I learned to hide the fact that I might be looking at or listening to shadows, and I'd only talk to them when no one else was around and even then only if I felt like it.

We moved, mom and me, from New York to Los Angeles where my best friend's name was Claudia. Well, to be perfectly honest, she was my best friend but I wasn't necessarily hers. Claudia had dozens of best friends. She sure didn't need me, but she let me hang around her and that meant a lot. As I said, I was an odd-looking tall, skinny, wisp of a girl. Always at risk from a fashion perspective and every day was a bad hair day. Worse, I was usually the only Black face in the crowd at school. Claudia was one of those kids that seemed to have everything the world dictated as right from birth; tall, slim, blond and intelligent. To top it off she still had two parents, both of which came from wealthy families. I ask you, where's the justice in life? Claudia was a magnet for all the popular kids at Washington High and she always acted so mature. She really set the trends there too. Even the teachers treated her better, with more respect.

I'll never forget my first day of school. The homeroom teacher had me stand up so that he could introduce me to the class. There was a silence for a few minutes before one of the boys in the back yelled, "Hey wait a minute," then he went through his book bag searching for something and added, "I think I've got a bone in here somewhere."

Everybody started to laugh, everybody that is except Claudia. I even caught sight of the teacher bringing his hand up to his mouth to conceal a smile. I just wanted to die. But then Claudia said in a loud commanding voice that I shouldn't pay attention to that Neanderthal, or his low class friends that found that kind of humor funny. That sobered everyone up fast. Afterwards he'd apologized and said it was just a joke, that he hadn't meant anything. Well, I was touched somebody had come to my rescue and at lunch Claudia called across the crowded lunchroom to me to sit at her table. She even made the others make room for me across from her.

She asked me all kinds of questions that first day and her interest in me seemed to influence the other kids. I can't explain it; they just seemed to give me more respect afterwards, more than I would have ordinarily gotten I'm sure.

Claudia was about the smartest kid at that school. I think I was the only one that gave her any competition; which she seemed to thrive on. Maybe that was what had earned her respect.

At the end of that first day I took a deep breath as I stepped back outside into the warm sunshine. The first day's nightmare was finally over. All the rest would be a breeze.

I like to stare skywards as much as possible as I walk. No matter the weather. It just seems to do something for my spirit, watching the bird's effortless glide. It helps me temporarily forget my problems but eventually I must again return my attention to terrestrial matters. It's always then that I get into trouble and true to form as I gazed downwards, to avoid the embarrassing event of tumbling down the steps and landing on my face; I caught sight of what I had fought so desperately to avoid. It was just out of the left corner of my eye, a teenage boy came running down the walkway towards me. He moved from person to person screaming for help. I'd seen him from a distance as I'd exited the main door of the school. I could immediately tell by the staggered pace of his run that something was wrong. He'd been injured. As he drew nearer I could see him grab his side, which was bleeding, as was his head. He'd been screaming that someone was trying to kill him. Going from person to person frantically pleading for help but no one met his eye, everyone just kept passing him until our eyes locked and he started towards me.

As he'd approached I noticed he was younger than me, maybe by two years or so. I'd stopped near the entrance of the doorway aware that the other kids had begun spilling around me, some of them complaining as they went. As our distance shrank I saw he was terrified and tears flowed from his eyes as he nervously glanced around him, all the while continuing to beg for help. Suddenly, we both caught sight of his pursuer. He was a tall lean man, maybe sixty or so. The kids he passed were indifferent to him as well, despite the bloodied knife in his hand.

At the sight of him the boy started to scream, again pleading for help. He fell at the bottom of the steps and seemed unable to go farther. It only took the man a few seconds to reach us. I watched the boy as he brought his arms up to protect his face as the man began his attack raising the knife to strike him over and over until blood was everywhere. The boy's screams had been brief but seemed to echo continuously across the crowded schoolyard. I walked through them both, indifferent, down the steps and towards home. He had been just another shadow.

That's what I call souls and things that no one else ever seem able to see and they're always so obvious.

I've always had a hard time making friends and was usually happy if I was able to make just one. In my heart I'd always believed the shadows were somehow to blame.

As I walked, from behind me, someone kept pace to whisper into my right ear. I turned to see a handsome boy with brown eyes and hair. The only blemish marring his looks was a single red blemish under his right eye. Another shadow, I thought to myself, the only thing that had given him away was the other kids who passed through him.

He also asked me for help that first day but I turned my back on him as well, walking away and not looking back. I didn't stop until I got home. I later pieced together that the second shadow had been that of Zachary Holmes, a sixteen-year-old whose body had been found dead a few miles from the school. Killed by a single shot to the head several months earlier, they'd never found his killer. There were other shadows on the premises of the school but none ever noticed or tried to communicate with me. They just seemed lost in worlds of their own. Often I'd come into a class and see chairs occupied by non-tangibles that didn't notice or perhaps didn't care if a physical came to sit in that same space, neither did I.

I wasn't bothered by not helping Zachary or the other nameless boy. If I'd spent my time trying to live the expired lives of shadows, trying to solve their problems, I wouldn't have any time left for myself. There were just too many of them. My general rule was talk to them, if I feel compelled to, but nothing more.

I was there at Washington for about eight months. Two weeks before I was scheduled to leave Los Angeles and Washington High, I'd told my lunchroom comrades that I was moving to Utah. I wasn't expecting a party or anything like that but I at least expected a fair-thee-well from somebody. Nobody cared, not even Claudia. That was the toughest lunch I ever had to get through. I wanted to cry.

My new school was Roosevelt and my first day there wasn't nearly as traumatic as the first day at Washington had been. There were no introductions, no spotlights of attention and especially no insults. No one tried to befriend, I ate my lunches alone and spent my extra time studying. It wasn't that bad I was used to it. For the two years that I was at Roosevelt, I was nearly invisible. If I'd dropped off the face of the earth, people would have said "Tiana who?"

My home life wasn't nearly as exciting as my school life. Momma spent most of her time at work. When she wasn't there she was out socializing. She'd get home just in time to grab the pillow and the next day it would start all over again. The only times we'd talk was when she was barking orders to me. Like clean the house, mow the backyard. Or, there's money on the kitchen table go to the store and buy what's on the list. If there were any shadows at Roosevelt High, I never noticed. On the other hand there was a kindly old man who'd sit on a tree stump on the other side of our fence in the neighbor's yard. He'd tell me stories about his life and his children and how ungrateful they were. He was a shadow, still in *his* house long after he'd died of an aneurysm and long after his children had sold the place.

It's amazing how little time it had taken me to get used to that place. After only a few days I'd gotten my routine down to the point where I could do it blindfolded. Two years there and I still hadn't made any friends, but I did have acquaintances.

It was the beginning of October when we moved again. Momma had been transferred to supervise the first major hotel being built within the rapidly growing community of Webster's Plains. I arrived at my new school, Andrew Jackson High, just a few weeks before their Halloween Party and the other kids had begun pairing off for it. I really loathed those things. You just go there and stand around for a few hours.

By the end of the first week we were completely settled in. I'd been enrolled and more importantly, I'd found my niche. Two of my fellow homeroom students had introduced themselves and invited me to eat lunch with them. I was happy for the introduction, until I found out that the lunch table I was sitting at was called Misfit Central.

I was torn between isolation and being lumped with social miscreants. I chose poorly and decided eating alone after that. It didn't take long before they realized I was avoiding them. I tried to convince myself that I liked it that way, being alone I mean.

I spent my time after that trying to locate the shadows I'd ignored, but they were becoming fewer, either that or I was loosing the ability to sense them because I didn't find any.

After about three weeks I realized that my life was nearly useless. Days mirrored the previous days and weeks mirrored past weeks. I decided it was time to do something spontaneous. I took a new route home after school.

There's a park that borders our neighborhood on the west called Abley Park, named after J. John Abley, whoever he was. It had the most beautiful flower arrangements I'd ever seen, and so manicured. Each day I tried to explore a different part of the park but there was one area that was less maintained than the rest. It was all overgrown and abandoned. The flowers there were left to grow wild. I don't know why, but I was completely at home in that part of the park, no one ever seemed to visit it.

At school one afternoon I accidentally ran into one of the stars of Jackson High, the class president Alexis Welks. I'd managed to blend into the background until that point. It was then that I realized that there was strength in numbers. Why hadn't I joined Misfit Central? She picked on me every opportunity. At the end of that day I went home crying. I'd never felt so isolated and depressed. I took what was by then my normal route home, by way of the park.

I'd been sitting in my usual spot. Looking at the fall leaves that had changed color to drop to the ground before me, they melded beautifully with the overgrown flowers. It was like being encircled in beauty. I closed my eyes, breathed in the different fragrances and let my mind wonder. It had been a terrible day, but still I didn't look forward to going home, to an evening of loneliness. So I continued to sit there, well past the time I'd normally have left.

When I opened my eyes again, the sun was perhaps only ten or fifteen minutes from setting. I watched it dip towards the horizon in colors of yellow and gold. As I stared at it I heard the sound of a sigh and turned my head startled to see a boy sitting next to me, close. I wondered embarrassed how long he'd been there. His hand rested on the bench very near to my own and I moved mine instinctively.

I don't know why, but I was annoyed and grabbed my book bag to leave knowing I'd never again return to that spot. My personal sanctuary had been violated.

"Please don't go!" There was a pleading quality in his voice. "I didn't mean to disturb you. Really I didn't? It's just that..." his voice trailed into silence for a few seconds, "it's very beautiful here, don't you think?"

I simply nodded agreement and rose to go.

"This is my favorite spot. I often come here to sit and think." He said.

I suspected that was a lie, I'd been to that spot every day after school for the past two weeks and had never seen anyone else. I turned to look at him then. He was probably about my age, fair with chestnut hair. His eyes were of a light brown and he was handsome, a fact that immediately made me nervous. My tongue was in a knot, now I had to leave.

I took only a step before I realized I was restrained; he'd grabbed my hand and held it firmly.

"What's your name?" He asked, the expression on his face said it was something he had to know.

"Tiana," I said falling silent again.

"Tell me you'll return Tiana, please." He nearly pleaded.

Well I'd seen the movie *Carrie,* and read the book. I looked around at the bushes and trees for the rest of the kids. I knew they were concealed somewhere laughing and watching the show. He seemed to sense my discomfort.

"What's wrong Tiana, are you expecting someone?"

"No!" I said flatly. "I know this is some kind of joke, I just don't understand why everyone has to be so cruel to me."

I felt like a fool knowing I was about to cry, but I couldn't help it. I would have run away but I couldn't, he still held my hand. The warmth of his hand mingled with my own and I hoped that my palms weren't sweating. Finally I asked him if he would please let me go.

"Not unless you promise not to run away." He said but when I'd said nothing he released my hand anyway. I looked down and he was no longer there.

I left the park thinking it was some kind of sick joke. I suspected the next day at school would be the worst of my entire life. He was probably leading up to taking me to the Halloween party and I wondered at what point they were planning to drop the pig's blood. What kind of a moron did they take me for anyway? But that next day had been like every other since I'd been at Jackson. I was completely ignored, even by my nemesis Alexis. I'd begun to wonder if it had been a joke after all. If not, I'd behaved like a complete fool. No other boy had shown even the slightest interest in me since I'd been born, let alone a good-looking one. Yet if I went back I'd look desperate. The truth of the matter was that when it came to love or just plain dealing with boys, I was a moron. Then I remembered how he'd looked at me and how he'd spoken, as if he were so lonely. But that was ridiculous, how could an attractive boy be lonely?

By the end of that day, I'd spent several hours trying to decide whether I'd return there or not. I finally convinced myself that I wouldn't let him chase me away from my favorite spot. Though deep in my heart I knew I was just hoping to see him again.

I sat on the bench for nearly an hour and hadn't even seen a breeze's movement across the tall grass, but that had been what I'd always liked about the spot; it had been so tranquil. He must have thought I was loony and went in search of greener pastures, of which there must have been many. The sun was beginning to set, soon it would be getting dark and I knew it was time to leave.

I closed my eyes and didn't try to stop the lonely tear that traveled down my cheek. I startled at the touch of a warm finger wiping it away.

"What's wrong Tiana, why are you crying?" His voice sounded as if he really cared.

"I don't know, just silly I guess." I couldn't tell him that I was afraid I'd missed my opportunity, that I'd never had a boyfriend or been in love and that at fifteen, I felt that I'd die a spinster."

"Well, if it's any consolation, I felt like crying myself." He said softly, "I thought you'd also abandoned me. You never did promise to return."

"I thought you were part of some joke everyone was playing on me." I told him sadly. "You must know I'm not very popular."

"I don't believe that." He said taking my hand. "I don't believe that at all."

"You must not be from around here." I said. "So, what part

of the galaxy *are* you from." I tried to smile but knew it didn't come off well. "I know why I'm lonely, but why are you?" I said.

"I'm not lonely," he said, and I felt immediately humiliated for even implying a handsome boy could be, "not when you're here." He added smiling at my obvious embarrassment.

"As I said, I do love this place but... it's so strange, no matter where I go I always end up here. I seem to have lost my way."

"Where do you live?" I asked him.

"There," he said point to the horizon were the sun was about to terminate its existence, "just the other side of sunset." He said smiling broadly.

I smiled myself and looked over at it and when I'd looked back he was gone. I hadn't even had the chance to ask his name.

That next afternoon I again awaited him. He'd spent so little time there that I determined to have a line of questions to ask, starting with his name.

"Jason." He said, that following afternoon.

"Jason," I repeated nearly under my breath, "the name suits you, Jason what?"

"Averson, my family has a large farm a mile or two down the road." He pointed in the direction of the setting sun.

"I haven't been here for very long Jason, but I do know there are no farms anywhere around this area. Why are you lying to me?" I'd started to believe in him and he'd lied, blatantly, as if he wanted me to catch it.

Jason Averson stood.

"I've never lied to anyone and I have no reason to lie now. Just because you've never seen it doesn't mean it doesn't exist. You seem to have a low opinion of me Tiana, so I won't trouble you again."

"Wait," I called to his back and he stopped, "I'm sorry. I wasn't trying to insult you. You're right. I've never been there, but if you say it exists then fine. It's just that I thought that

Webster's Plains was at least eight miles in each direction with no farms included," I laughed and added, "but if you say so."

"Webster's Plains," Jason muttered in confusion, "well, I live in Averson it's a small rural town of about a hundred. It's named after my great-grandfather Andrew Averson, the founder. I don't believe I've ever heard of a Webster's Plains around here."

Now it was my turn to be confused.

"I have to go now." He added finally.

"Will you be back tomorrow?" I asked anxiously.

"Yes." He said with a smile and walked away.

The next day, I sat in history class at school daydreaming of Jason. I couldn't wait until the bell rung and I was sprung from my prison. Mr. Ellerson, the history teacher was passing out the test we'd taken earlier that week. It had been long and boring. The complaints started as soon as he'd placed them on the desks. Next to me, Joanna of Misfit Central nudged me asking what I'd gotten. I hadn't even bothered turning the paper over, I really didn't care one way or the other but to pacify her I looked.

"A plus," I told her.

"What?" She asked amazed. "You got an A?" She'd spread the word around the class, it seemed I had the only one. I really couldn't see what the big deal was. There were certainly more important things for me to worry about. Like if I would see Jason that afternoon.

"Joanna," I turned recapturing her attention, "have you ever heard of a small town called Averson?" I asked.

Some of the kids on the other side of me had heard and started to laugh. I couldn't figure what the joke was. It was a simple enough question.

"Averson was the former name of Webster's Plains. Everybody around here knows that, but as you're a new comer," she paused and I guessed that she was about to give me the low down. "It was named after the farmer who founded it in the first part of the nineteenth century." She said and was about to say more but the other kids in the class had started to converse loudly amongst themselves.

"Settle down people." Ellerson called from the head of the class, quieting them.

"Why do you ask?" Joanna whispered.

"I met an Averson in Abley Park. He'd said he was from a town by that same name and that it was named after his great-grand-father."

"He was just lying to you, the last Averson in these parts died over ten years ago."

Mr. Ellerson noticed us whispering and had walked towards us. I was certain he'd heard some of the conversation; definitely the last part and I noticed that he was giving me a strange look.

"Are you serious?" He asked finally and I noticed every eye in the class was upon me.

"Yes, is there a problem?" I asked, realizing how much I hated spotlights.

"Tiana," he said looking uncomfortable, "if you're trying to tell me that you've seen Jason Averson then I have to tell you, I don't believe in ghosts and I'd advise you not to either. You've been the victim of some kind of joke."

If it had been a joke then it seemed no one found it funny because no one was laughing or taking credit for it.

"What I saw was no ghost." I said angrily. "Besides, he's comes to that park every afternoon at the same time, like clockwork for the past week. I don't believe ghosts have ever been considered that reliable." I'd started to raising my voice and getting angry.

"Are you going to see him this afternoon?" Joanna asked, amused shock playing across her face.

"I don't believe that's any concern of yours!" I shot back.

I was publicly rude and ashamed of myself at the same time. I'd started to apologize when Mr. Ellerson interrupted me.

"Let's get back to work shall we." He said starting to move away. "Those tests scores were appalling."

He'd begun his review of the test information, but it hadn't stopped wandering eyes from staring at me from time to time. As if I'd grown another head suddenly. I spent the rest of the period trying to decide if I'd seen another shadow. Was I getting to a point where I couldn't differentiate between the living and shadows? Maybe that was why I no longer found them. Yet the hand that had held mine had been warm and firm. No, Jason Averson was no shadow, he was as real as I was and it was all I could do not to shout it out.

The bell rang signaling the end of class. I rose to leave with everyone else but was called back by Mr. Ellerson. I thought to myself great, now I'll get chewed out for my rudeness.

"Tiana, I'm going to take what you've said today at face value and assume you're not lying and that you've met someone... possibly Jason Averson. You know you wouldn't be the first in that claim. Now, if I do that then I think you should be armed with enough information to make some intelligent decisions."

I still didn't know what he was talking about but I'd remained quiet and he continued.

"Jason Averson lived about a hundred and fifty years ago. It's generally believed that he died at about fifteen or sixteen. Supposedly he was killed by a jealous suitor for the hand of his fiancée, Lizbeth Fairell."

I must have looked surprised at that point because he answered my questions before I'd even asked it.

"They married young back then. Lizbeth was I believe about the same age. However her other suitor, by the name of Samuel Goethe, was a much older man. Rumored is he was well into his sixties but he was also a rich man and because of that he had the blessings of the girl's family. The problem was Fairell's heart, it seemed, belonged to Jason whom she planned to marry.

Their marriage though never materialized, because Jason simply disappeared. It was pretty well known that Goethe was sometimes a violent, dangerous man. Many believed Jason simply ran scared, afraid of the pending marriage and of Goethe.

The Averson family however believed it was foul play, but they could never prove it. Though they were descendants of the founding family, they weren't as powerful as they once had been or as powerful as Goethe, the man they accused. So charges against him were eventually dropped.

Goethe and Fairell eventually married. It was said that she didn't have much to say in the matter. It wasn't until after Goethe died that she accused him of Jason Averson's murder. She'd claimed to be an eyewitness, even took the authorities to where she said the body was buried but no one ever found it. Either Goethe didn't trust her silence and moved it, or she was lying. No one knew which for sure. Even before Fairell's death there were sighting of Jason Averson in the park were you say you met him, but he never appeared for Fairell. Over the decades numerous young ladies have laid claims to having seen him. They've generally described him as a handsome young man with brown hair. He always says just about the same things basically, which is the only thing that gives the stories credibility. That he can't find his way home and sometimes that he's lonely. They always seemed to happen in the margin of a few days before Halloween, which it was believed by some to be the period of time in which Jason was murdered. Around the time they were having their Pumpkin Ball. They've never seen him again after that time. Of course there weren't many that have actually gone back to look for him after finding out he's a ghost, and his history, but even those that did never found him.

Like I said, I don't believe in ghosts but I thought you should know the history, just in case."

Ellerson picked up a stack of papers from his desk throwing them into his brief case as if to mutely state the conversation's end.

I didn't know what to say. I think I had just started to walk out zombie like but a thought occurred to me, "Where was the Averson farm?" I asked.

"The last of the Averson family, Victoria Averson, sold the property to the city about fifty years ago and the village hall was built on it. She died at the age of ninety-three about eleven years ago. As far as anyone knows she was the last of their family line."

"And Lizbeth Fairell, what happened to her?"

"She died childless. They buried her in the old cemetery just outside the city limits. I think they buried her under her maiden name of Fairell."

I left without saying another word, only dimly aware that some of the kids from the class where hanging around just outside the door. Probably listening to what Mr. Ellerson had told me.

I didn't go to the rest of my classes that day. Instead I went directly to the park, and to our special spot. I had a lot to think about. I had actually started to fall for him. What if what Mr. Ellerson said was true, then I had been talking to a ghost, a walking dead person, a non-tangible, a shadow! But how could that be? I was better versed in shadows than most. I certainly knew the difference between someone of flesh and blood and that of a shadow. Didn't I? If Jason had been one I'd have seen it right away, right? Sure, it explained why he occasionally disappeared on me, but it wasn't the answer I wanted to hear. Yes, I knew the difference between a warm-blooded, living, breathing individual and a shadow, and Jason was the real thing, he had to be. I would no longer allow myself to even think in terms of the alternative.

It had started to get cold as I walked through the park toward the spot that I so loved. I headed towards the bench and as soon as I got within a few feet of it the weather changed and somehow got milder. Waiting until sunset that evening had been the longest period of my life.

"Tiana, I'm glad you've came." Jason told me.

I had been deep in my thoughts and his voice startled me.

"Did you think I wouldn't?" I asked him.

"I wasn't sure. Sometimes I meet new people here and they always seem to stop visiting after a few days."

"Why are you still here?" I blurted out. I'd been trying to deny it in my mind, but as I sat there and waited I realized that tomorrow afternoon was the Halloween party. If what they'd said was true then I would never see Jason again anyway after that night. In that instance, I threw away the values I'd clung to, which had made up the breath and scope of my existence. I'd always believed that for shadows, their time had past. I'd convinced myself they no longer felt anything and even if they did, it didn't matter any longer. It was how I felt that mattered, my life that came first. Life was too short to spend straightening out the lives of individuals who no longer had lives.

"I don't understand what you mean." Jason looked away uncomfortably.

It was then that I realized two things. The first was that Jason was indeed a shadow, but unlike any of the others I'd experienced up until that time. He had seemed as real as I was. I also realized that he was stuck in a looping time period, which seemed an attribute common to shadows. Perhaps in his case, it was the world that he'd known and loved the most. I had a feeling that if I pressed the matter he was going to do another disappearing number on me again, this time for good.

"I just wanted to know how I could help you." I added.

At that Jason looked back at me, and this time he smiled.

"Your presence here is enough."

"No it's not, I want to do more." I realized I wasn't lying. My old concepts and values regarding shadows were destroyed and in ruins all around me. "Just tell me what you need me to do."

"There's really nothing that can be done. I just have to be patient and wait for my Lizbeth to come. She and I will be married tomorrow at the Pumpkin Ball. It'll be a grand party but it seems to be taking her longer today."

He'd been looking off into the sunset and his eyes held a far off, dreamy quality. As for me, there was a lump in my throat that I was having difficulty swallowing.

"When did you see her last?" I asked him.

"Yesterday, in the meadow, we talked about the wedding

and our future." Jason smiled and in that smile I saw how very much he loved her. "I don't know how, I've lived here all my life, but I seem to have gotten lost. I can always find this place though and we have a standing engagement to meet here everyday, so I know she'll come."

"I bet she just got sidetracked. You know with the wedding and everything. Why don't we just go and find her."

"But the sun has nearly set." He said.

"Is that a problem?" I asked him.

"Well," he paused slightly, "she has to be home before sunset. Her parents are most strict on that point and I don't dare go there because… well… they don't think I'm good enough for her. In truth, I don't think so either."

Jason stopped casting his eyes downward and for a moment I saw pain reflected across his face but it seemed to melt away, to be replaced with a firm conviction.

"But I do love her," he continued, "and I'll do anything for her, and she loves me. That has to count for something. They want her to marry Sam Goethe, but it's only because he's rich. Their as much as selling her to him!" Jason shouted angrily, but then his voice softened. "She's refused though. My mother gave Lizbeth her wedding dress and to me she gave this," he reached into the pocket of his overalls, "her wedding ring. My mother wanted her to have it."

It was beautiful, a simple setting with a fairly large solitaire stone.

"It's very beautiful." I said.

Jason put the ring back into his pocket and looked at me nervously. I've tried several times to leave this spot to find her, every time I've had difficulty. I just seem to get confused, things look different, strange, and so I return here. I have to admit, I am starting to worry. What could be taking her so long?"

"You obviously haven't been looking in the right place."

"But I can't leave here. I told you. Besides, we have a standing engagement at this very spot, the same time each day until just before sunset. If I leave now I might miss her." He said and I noticed how really concerned he appeared about that.

"Don't worry. I don't think you will because I believe I know where you can find her."

His back stiffened at that, I really seemed to get his attention.

"Where, where is she?" Jason seemed almost giddy and my own heart seemed to be beating nearly as fast in my chest as I struggled with what to tell him.

"Do you know where the old cemetery is?" I asked him.

"Old cemetery, there's only the one and its west of here." He said shaking his head. "But why would she be there?"

I could see his belief in me was waning, but I thought it best to get him off that spot in the park. Even if it was painful for him, he had to move on.

"You're not answering my question. Why would she be in a cemetery?" He seemed to be growing impatient and I could see the worry in his face.

"Well it's the last place Sam Goethe would expect to find her. He has been something of a pest you know."

Jason stood silently considering for several seconds. I couldn't determine how he was going to react to my lie. For a few anxious moments I thought he was going to question me on how I knew either, but he'd just looked at me. Then the smile on his face became tremendous. He got up laughing to grasps my hands within his own. Again I was surprised how firm and warm they felt.

"Yes, that's it. It must be. He's been following her everywhere, and he threatens me constantly," Jason smiled embarrassed and looked away, "to the point where I've started having nightmares about him. It was only yesterday that I waited here for Lizbeth on this very spot. I dreamed that Sam followed her here and surprised me. I remember dreaming that he came at me with a pitchfork. I thought I was done for, but when I came to I was here and there was no one else around but me, I was alone. I guess I'd just fallen asleep while I waited for her."

"The sun will be setting soon." I reminded him.

"That's right I'd better be leaving. I only have until sunset, besides she never liked being out a lone in the darkness."

He'd taken a step but then turned to look back at me.

"Tiana, you've done so much for me, I'd hate to ask another favor but will you stay here just in case I miss her, just until sunset?"

"Of course," I said smiling, "until sunset."

Jason had only gotten a few feet away from me before he vanished and I realized that I'd probably never see him again. It seemed that my whole life had changed. I'd never be able to treat a shadow in the same trivial way again.

I rose to leave but remembered the promise I'd made to him. It was still about another two or three minutes until sunset. I thought I owed him that long at least, after all I did promise.

Stretching out my legs and folding my arms about my chest I settled back to relax. I couldn't help feeling a little sad at the thought that Jason was probably gone from my life forever but it had to be. I closed my eyes to rest them for a few moments when a gentle kiss brushed my cheek startling me.

Jason Averson had returned. He smiled at me with genuine affection and I was glad to see him again.

"You never told me your full name Tiana." He said gently chiding me.

"Barrett." I said. "Tiana Barrett."

He extended his hand to take mine and I offered it.

"Well, Miss Tiana Barrett, may I introduce to you my fiancée Lizbeth Fairell." Jason turned his head and I became aware of a blond girl standing only a few feet away. She was pretty, perhaps my age with a kind face. He extended his free hand to her and she moved towards it.

She also extended her hand to me. As I watched the small delicate fingers enclose around my own; I saw the ring that had been placed there and was overwhelmed with happiness for Jason, and for them both.

"I hope the two of you will be very happy." I said still looking at the ring and I think I cried when they embraced and I realized they'd been waiting for each other over a hundred fifty years.

Maybe the way I treated shadows reflected my outlook on life in general and just maybe that was why others treated me that way. Sitting there seeing how much love still existed between two individuals that no longer lived reminded me of how alive I still was.

In my heart I knew my life was forever changed. All my tomorrows would be richer. I had much to make up for.

Before they left, she took my hand again thanking me.

"We have to go now," she told me "it's almost sunset."

After they'd vanished, the sun had begun to disappear below the horizon and I was surprised at how cold the spot had quickly become. Perhaps it had been his love that had kept it warm all those years in the weeks just before Halloween, but I was only cold on the outside. Inside I was as warm as that autumn day had been where he'd spent his time waiting for his love.

"Joanna," Tiana called out diplomatically to the girl she'd been so rude to the last time she'd seen her in class. It was Monday morning and she was headed towards the front steps of the school, presumably on her way towards first period classes. She stopped and turned at the sound of her name and Tiana walked briskly towards her.

"Hi Joanna," Tiana offered nervously, hoping she'd accept her apology. "About the other day, I'm really sorry. I didn't mean to be so..."

"Oh, you mean about that Averson's ghost thing?" She waived her hand dismissing the thought of further apology. "Tiana," she said irritated, "forget about that, tell me what happened!" She grabbed Tiana's arm pulling her towards the schools front steps and down to sit beside her. "You have to tell me, please, I've been thinking about it non-stop ever since!"

"You were right." Tiana offered and immediately saw shock reflect across Joanna's face.

"Are you for real?" She said astonished. "You're saying you really saw a ghost?"

"Actually Joanna that's not that unusual, I see them pretty often."

Joanna laughed. She seemed to be looking at nothing in particular but then refocused her attention on Tiana.

"You're kidding right?"

Tiana only shook her head.

"Tiana, you have to take me with you when you go to see him again. You just have to…"

"Joanna I can take you there, but you won't see anything."

At that point Tiana explained everything to Joanna. Like Tiana, Joanna seemed both pleased and saddened by the outcome.

"Well, it seems everything worked out for the best."

"Then you believe me?"

"Of course, I've always believed in ghosts. There just has to be more than this," Joanna waived her arm to encompass her surroundings, "and why would you make something like that up?"

"Joanna I feel so terrible."

"Why?"

"I told you, I see ghosts all the time but I've never tried to help them, not usually."

"You helped Averson."

"That's only because I didn't know he was a ghost, not until I'd already gotten too involved. But this whole thing has opened my eyes and changed my views of everything. I realize what happened to them could happen to anyone, even me. And who would be there to help?"

"Yeah well, that is a pretty grim thought alright. Particularly when you consider there probably aren't that many people with your talent to begin with. You see them all the time?" Joanna looked around her seeing nothing unusual before looking again to Tiana. "Do you see ghosts now?"

Tiana looked around as well and realized the disappointment must have reflected in her face when Joanna's face quickly reflected disappointment as well.

"No nothing now. Joanna I've spent my life trying to block them out. This may be some kind of punishment for that, but at one of my former schools I did see something that I've never forgotten.

It was almost three years ago now and I was in LA at Washington High. School was over and I was leaving on my way home when from the top of the school steps I saw a boy running, no staggering from up the street, a man was following him slowly. He was about my age and he was hurt, pretty badly I guess from the way he held his side. Joanna he was screaming for help going from person to person but no one heard him, except me I guess and I did nothing.

Joanna I watched until the man caught up with him and killed him, on the very base of the steps where I'd stood." At that Tiana dropped her head in shame.

"You saw all that?"

"Yeah...."

"Tiana there was nothing you could have done. Especially there in front of a crowd of kids that couldn't see what you saw. Everyone would have thought you were nuts and remember, this was all over and done with long before you came along."

"Joanna you don't understand, I saw it happen. Worse he saw me and pleaded with me for help and he knew I saw him."

"But what *could* you have done?"

"I don't know but I should have at least tried."

"Well that was three years ago and we're a very long way from LA. Who knows maybe he's dissipated by now."

"Dissipated, that doesn't make me feel any better."

Joanna's face settled into resolution,

"You're right, we should do something!"

"We?"

"Sure."

"You'll help me?"

"Are you kidding? I've always been interested in this stuff. That's why I asked the question the other day, but I could tell you thought I was crazy." Joanna laughed embarrassed at the thought. "I guess the whole class did."

"No, I thought that's what all of you thought about me."

"No way, I never thought that! Tiana, I want to be a parapsychologist and this will be a great experience for me, and now I've got my own personal psychic to work with."

"Well, I don't know about being a psychic or anything."

"Well you can see beyond our limited five senses can't you? You can see that which we can't or won't see?"

"Yeah, but…"

"Well, that's good enough for me, it's a good start."

"How are we even going to find out who he was? We have nothing to go on!"

"Relax," Joanna said reassuringly, "you're being way too premature focusing there. First we have to get to LA remember? Then we'll just have to do a bit of research." She said confidently. "Say, can you write the account down for me? You know the time of day, the type of clothes they wore, everything. Be as detailed as possible about the environment, just put in anything you can remember. I know it was a while ago but do your best, then I'll begin the research maybe we can find something on the Internet."

"Sure, that's not a problem. I can have it for you by tomorrow, but there's not a lot more I can tell you beyond what I've already said."

"Well think about it, maybe something new will occur to you that you've forgotten. You never know. Tiana, this whole thing could be big! Come to think of it, I've got relatives in California. Of course that'll take time to set up, if it's even possible because I've never even met them." Joanna stood abruptly resettling her book bag on her shoulder. "Okay, we better get to class before we're late, we can touch base on this tomorrow, okay?"

"Okay." Tiana responded timidly. She didn't know why but something unsettled her and perhaps Joanna had misread her hesitation.

"Well I mean, if you don't want to…"

"It's not that," Tiana said quickly, "it's just that this is the first time I've had to deal with a ghost where I actually saw his violent end. I mean, I know Jason was killed, but I didn't actually see it so it was totally different for me. It's a little scary this time."

"Oh," that seemed to reassure Joanna, "I can get with that. It's like a real life scary ghost story movie, huh!" She laughed, waved goodbye and proceeded up the school steps. "See you in class later and don't forget to write down everything tonight."

Tiana stood and briefly watched Joanna's retreating form disappear through the doors of the school. If Joanna harbored any fears they were buried far too deeply for Tiana to see. In fact, she seemed pretty geared up for the prospect, somehow Tiana found her own discomfort easing, but only slightly.

Well, at least we're not both cowards.

After school Tiana took her usual path home walking through the park. She was not surprised to find the spot where she'd last seen Jason and Lizbeth now seem lonely, cold and uninviting. Approaching home she slowed, passing the stump were the old man usually sat. The one who always told the same stories and laughed at all his own jokes, but now that spot was also empty. Either he'd left or Tiana could no longer see him.

Perhaps the abilities that she'd so taken for granted had now deserted her. Once she'd decided that she needed it most to make amends for her years of cold indifference to those energies that live on that other side of the mirror. Tiana wondered what she would have to do to make things right again? Or could anything she did now ever make things right?

As usual Tiana stepped into an empty house knowing her mother wouldn't be home for several hours. She went to the bedroom and sat down at her desk, switching on a small lamp. Taking out paper and pen she began writing down her account of what she'd seen almost three years earlier, but nothing new came to mind. In fact, at the time Tiana had forced herself not to pay much attention. She tried intently to block it all out and now she couldn't force her mind to surrender any additional information. She couldn't clearly remember anything beyond the violent act, not the surroundings, his clothes, or anything.

Frustrated Tiana pushed back her chair and went over to the bed to throw her self across it. Perhaps a few minutes of meditation would help. Something might come if she could just clear her mind and relax.

She found herself moving about a colorless gray soundless world filled with people, but no one noticed or even glanced her way. A normal day she thought, with the exception of the grayness of everything. Yet the place was somehow familiar, she definitely recognized it from somewhere. Then she remembered, but that just wasn't possible. She was thousands of miles away now. Then she saw a figure moving towards her and heard a faint cry. She turned her head to see the boy again, staggering forward, frantically trying to get help from anyone. *This is a dream*, she thought, *it has to be*, but regardless this time she would help him.

Tiana ran towards the boy attempting to quickly close the distance between them, and he immediately saw her. She grabbed him pulling him upright propelling him forward, away from the man who pursued him, pursued them both now because Tiana realized she would do everything possible to save him. She cried out for help, but her own responses were like that of the boy, no one heard. Tiana knew they needed to move quickly past the school but she couldn't, the boy pulled right and Tiana found they were quickly moving towards the same steps where she'd watched him die on her first day there. It was about to happen all over again, and this time she would be a part of it! When she looked behind them Tiana found the man now dangerously close, he'd be on them in no time. One way or another it would soon be over. She needed a weapon but there was nothing she could use. The boy was slowing down, becoming a hindrance to her and she quickly thought about abandoning him but couldn't. He needed her and she was determined to help him, this time.

Tiana knew exactly the moment and position where the boy would fall, and it happened as it had that first time she'd seen him. Reluctantly she released him letting him fall to the ground. Her only choice now was in trying to fight the man off, at least long enough for the boy to get away. It was suicide, but what other choice was there? She made a quick turn to tackle the man, but the boy grabbed her leg rooting her in place.

His eyes were pleading, and he was scared but something about him had changed.

"Run away!" His voice pleaded.

"No! I won't let him kill you, I have to help you."

"You have," he screamed, *"run!"*

Tiana realized he was trying to save her, but she wouldn't just run away and leave him. She broke free from his grip to charge at the man.

It was like falling through a corridor that was deep and dark, cold and foreign. She hadn't run into anything tangible, instead it was like passing through a portal. In darkness she fell, unable to stop her descent for what seemed like an eternity. Finally a pin hole of light appeared beneath her that grew in diameter and by the time she could make anything of it she had already passed through it. Tiana fell hard onto the surface of her bed and the impact seemed to rock it for several seconds. She sat upright forcing her mind to clear. *Was it just a dream? Did I want it so bad that I dreamed it? Or did I really connect with him?*

Realizing it was probably a dream Tiana felt swept away by anguish and regret. Was it possible that one day was the only opportunity she was ever to have to help that boy, whoever he was? If that were true then there would be no second chances for her and with that she'd lain back down upon her bed curling up into a fetal position to cry uncontrollable. To be locked into a pattern of fear, pain and death forever she thought, all because she was too self absorbed to help. Tiana began to cry loudly into her knees, to miserable to even reach for her covers to combat the chill that enveloped the room.

"I guess it's true, there really are no second chances." She said sobbing into the darkness. At that same moment she realized the room should not have been dark, that she'd fallen asleep on the bed with the lamp on, Tiana startled to the touch of a warm hand upon her shoulder, and lifted her head expecting to see her mother; instead it had been the boy from her dream and her first day at school. She wasn't customarily afraid of ghosts, experience had removed that emotion long ago, but lately her world had felt alien. She'd found herself too shocked to move or speak.

"Thank you, for showing me the way out. I'm glad you're alright."

For a few seconds all Tiana could do was blink as she tried to verify the accuracy of her own eyes and when the boy didn't disappear she relaxed into a smile. "Then it was real!" Tiana said still crying but this time laughing as well.

"I didn't really expect to be saved and then I saw you, but once I'd reached you I realized that all I was doing was putting you in danger too. I'm sorry."

Tiana brought up her arms to warm herself in the room that was quickly becoming unbearably cold. "I'm the one who should be sorry."

"Why? You didn't do anything."

"Yeah, that's why."

"I don't get it."

"Well, it doesn't matter now," she said realizing that her teeth were beginning to chatter, "it's over." The chill in the room was making it difficult for Tiana to concentrate and she thought she understood the reason for it with him being a ghost, yet like Jason his touch upon her shoulder had seemed warm. Despite that, the room was now becoming frigid to the point where she continued massaging her forearms to keep the blood circulating as she shivered. "It's so cold in here." She said lightly, not wanting to appear accusatory. "But how did you get here?"

"I followed you, through the opening."

She'd been staring into the face of the ghost boy, about to ask his name when she saw the change in his expression that quickly returned to the horror-like mask he wore when she'd first seen him. His gaze seemed to be focused on the darkest part of the bedroom.

"Yeah, me too," the voice said from the darkness.

Frightened, Tiana turned at the sound of the third voice as a deep harsh laugh bellowed from the darkness.

www.ingramcontent.com/pod-product-compliance
Lightning Source LLC
Chambersburg PA
CBHW070812180626
46818CB00001B/223